I0635810

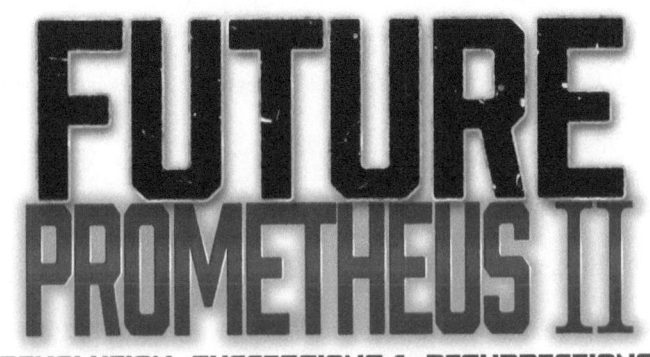

FUTURE
PROMETHEUS II
REVOLUTION, SUCCESSIONS & RESURRECTIONS

J. M. Erickson

Future Prometheus II: Revolution, Successions & Resurrections

Editor: Suzanne M. Owen

Cover design: Cathy Helms
Avalon Graphics, LLC
http://www.avalongraphics.org

Layout and *eBook* conversion done by eB Format
http://www.ebformat.com

Publisher: J. M. Erickson
Blog - https://www.jmeindieblog.com
Publisher website - http://www.jmericksonindiewriter.net

ISBN (MOBI Format): 978-1-942708-45-2
ISBN (ePub Format): 978-1-942708-46-9
ISBN (Paperback): 978-1-942708-47-6

Printed in the United States of America

What the critics say about *Revolution, Successions &*
Resurrections

"Characters are very well-rounded, and have detailed appearances and idiosyncrasies, giving them all a real texture and exciting visual reference for the reader." – **Self-*Publishing Review***

"It's rare and refreshing to find such female-driven drama—particularly in the context of militaristic sci-fi...A truly original sci-fi series with strong ideas and even stronger characters." – ***Kirkus Reviews***

"...Balancing the hard sciences with the liberal arts, these sci-fi stories rise to tall heights and entertain from cover to cover with fast action and authentic interaction..." – ***US Review of Books (Recommended)***

"The characters and scenes are so well depicted that I felt like I was right there in the story. Page after page you find yourself drawn deeper and deeper into this thrilling adventure." – *Indie **Book Reviewers***

"Erickson has crafted a fascinating series with complex characters and an incredibly rich premise." – ***Kirkus Reviews***

"The depth of the characters and the intricate details of the plot make this a very believable look into a dim future which follows on the heels of destruction. Suspenseful, intricate and action packed..." – ***Readers' Favorite***

Awards

Gold Medal – *Foreword Reviews* INDIEFAB Book of the Year Awards

Readers' Favorite Five Star Review

Finalist – Best Indie Book Awards

Finalist – *Next Generation* Indie Book Awards

Other Works by J. M. Erickson

Action/Adventure Thrillers

Albatross: Birds of Flight—Book One (Revised)
Raven: Birds of Flight—Book Two
Eagle: Birds of Flight—Book Three
Falcon: Birds of Flight—Book Four
Flight of the Black Swan

Action/Adventure Science Fiction

Future Prometheus: Emergence and Evolution—Novellas I & II
Intelligent Design: Revelations
The Prince: Lucifer's Origins
Intelligent Design: Apocalypse
Intelligent Design: Revelations to Apocalypse
Future Prometheus: The Series
Rogue Event
To See Behind Walls
Time is for Dragonflies and Angels

REVOLUTION

CHAPTER ONE

O tiger's heart wrapped in a woman's hide!
        —Shakespeare, *Henry VI*

What am I doing here?

Mare Sade Singh bowed her head in a group of artificial persons, human cadets and Lieutenant Jose Melendez, the commander of Omega Platoon. She was in a ceremony that appeared to be sacred or at the very least, solemn. She never thought she would find herself in such a situation, such a place among males, APs and an adult man dealing with natives outside the walls of her home Nermericana.

Who would ever believe this? I've been here years and it still makes no sense to me, and it's my life.

Singh stole a sideways look at the two youngest humans among them—a five- or six-year-old girl and a nine-or-so-year-old boy—also looking on in wonder as the lieutenant knelt on one knee and recited an archaic prayer over an adult body completely enshrouded in burial wrapping.

"And Lord, please give us the wisdom and strength to show compassion and judgment. Forgive our transgressions; provide our young guests with courage, and may you grant us all many years. Amen," Melendez said.

Then, she saw him make a type of specific sign with his hands. At the end of his prayer, the little girl hobbled over with her splinted leg to touch the lieutenant's exposed head. Singh suppressed a smile as she watched the girl rub her hands over his skull. She was obviously feeling for his metal contact points.

How does he deal with the dry skin? It has to drive him crazy with the scratching and all.

Singh was happy to see that the lieutenant did not jump away but let the little girl continue until she seemed to have enough. As soon as she was done, the five APs and five cadets continued with their preparations of gathering weapons, some rations, some makeshift torches, and three stretchers—two to carry the children and one for the body. Seeing that the little girl was smiling, Singh turned to the boy. He was more withdrawn but was watching everything intently. His arm and leg were in splints as well while the girl had stitches on her forehead and right arm in addition to her leg splint. Both seemed small but muscular for little children. Their faces also seemed long, with large jaws and craniums. Both had dark red hair.

Where did the red hair come from?

Singh made her way through the throng of people to talk to Melendez. These two guests had been discovered by a cadet training team in an enclosed area that seemed to be a "ceremonial" dying place where those who were close to death or who were profoundly injured were left, and a number of bodies lay nearby. Remains of other humans were also found not far off in the surrounding area in various stages of decomposition. The children's old torches, campfires, and makeshift seats made it clear they had been abandoned and were trying to survive in the wild. The adult male with them was dead when they found him, clearly from wounds inflicted by a carnivore. He must have tried to fight off an animal's attack. When the children had been found just a week ago, they were cold, injured, frightened and hungry. After only three days, however, they had begun exploring, healing and taking in everything they could see, eat or feel.

Melendez was just two feet away when she spoke.

"You're sure this is a good idea? Leaving fruit and vegetables is one thing but leaving them their own children and a wrapped body is another?"

"Nope. I have no idea if this is a good idea or not. But when your son made the decision to rescue them from their fate, he involved us—whether we like it or not," he said without emotion. He had moved on to look at provisions and gear. Singh followed him and pretended not to be anxious. She felt defensive, but she couldn't tell if he was judging her son's altruistic behaviors or not.

"Should he have left them?"

"No. They're people, children. They needed us."

"Do you think the natives will appreciate that? Saving their children."

"I have no idea."

Well, you'll never be accused of pretending you know everything.

Nodding in agreement, Singh stood quietly. She remembered how her son, Roberto, had said very little about the event except to say he couldn't just leave them behind.

"I'm guessing you would have done the same," Melendez offered.

Perplexed, confused and caught off guard by the question, she blurted out her answer more forcefully than she had intended. "Absolutely, without question."

Now where the hell did that anger come from?

She shook herself out of her thoughts and focused on what brought her here to talk to the CO in the first place.

"Speaking of impulsive sons, I understand that you authorized Roberto and his team for a pre-dawn orienting exercise outside the camp perimeter to the west while you and everybody else head east?"

"Yup. I authorized 'a team,' not necessarily your son's team, to conduct that training exercise. Private Emma has been impressed with his command abilities and he has continually requested advanced training. I think she has been dodging his request for a while, but they have met every challenge she has given him and his group. It looks like he backed her in a corner and won. Not an easy feat when it comes to Private Emma," he said. By now he finished his own inspection of his gear and noted that his team was ready to leave.

"You didn't think Private Emma pushed him into the training because he is your son?"

She had, positive the AP wanted to hurt her through her son. She was embarrassed that she had thought that. She had to be kinder in her thoughts about Emma. She had always been fair, mean to her but always fair.

Damn it! I should have known Roberto would do this! Always trying to prove himself. Where the hell did he get that competitive edge from? Stubborn too, I might add.

"Sir, would you be able to reconsider that duty until I have a chance to talk to him again?" she asked. She was already resigned to yet another battle of wills with her kin. Melendez first raised his eyebrows in surprise and then a warm smile spread across his face. His eyes grew softer.

You know...he has really nice eyes. Pretty soft and inviting for a male.

Against her will, she unconsciously moved her long braid onto her chest.

"Sorry, Mare. There is a chain of command and that decision was made by Private Emma, Corporal Kristine, and Sergeant Joan. If you want to change it, you'll have to talk to Private Emma first."

Ugh! Just great! Private Witch. Her look of pain and disappointment must have been obvious to Melendez, who responded with sympathy as he moved out with his team.

"Sorry, Mare. But to Emma's credit, she's put off letting him do it. She's protective of all the cadets, and I am sure she wouldn't allow this unless she was sure he would be safe."

"Yes. I guess."

"And I hear he gets his commitment to duty and training seriously like his mother."

"Stubbornness, actually."

"I guess that's relative. I would talk to Private Emma if I were you."

Singh gave a small nod and watched him move away to catch up to his waiting team.

"Thank you," she called after him. He left the bunker's small entrance with his team in tow while two AP sentries secured the door behind him. The room remained busy but the area was dwindling down with people. She stood in one place still looking at the closed door as she thought of how she would address the grizzly AP known to her as Emma and other colorful metaphors.

"Just great...now how is this going to work?"

It was difficult enough trying to stay ahead of her son's quest for independence. While she had successfully made strong alliances with many of the humans and APs, Private Emma was one artificial person, however, who made it clear that she considered her persona non grata. After what seemed a long time, Singh gave a deep sigh and turned to face her next hurdle. She turned smack into Private Emma, who stood motionless right in front of her as if to answer her challenge immediately. She was wearing her old-style battlefield dress uniform for evening maneuvers. Her glowing purplish eyes were narrowed and long earrings were—somewhat incongruently, she thought—adorning her ears.

Damn her stealth! And what's with the purplish eyes now? Why do their eyes keep changing color?

Singh stepped back as if she had walked into a marble column. She shook her head to clear away the shock of the bang and the stars she was seeing in addition to the pain. It took her a moment to be able to clear her head and speak.

"Private!? How long were you there?"

"Long enough to hear your concerns and process their degree of validity while sifting your potential lack of impartiality as a result of being Cadet Roberto's...*mother*."

The way the AP said "mother" was always in a tone of incredulousness, as if Singh was neither capable of being a mother nor worthy or both. Further, Emma towered over Singh which always made her nervous. But then suddenly, completely out of character, Emma gently placed her hands on Singh's head. She was amazed and surprised at the level of care her nemesis portrayed as she inspected where her skull had collided with mesh and metal.

She remained still as the AP looked closely at her and felt her skin. Emma then wiped the sweat from Singh's neck, forehead, and cheek.

Wait a minute. What? What are you doing now?

Singh watched as Emma sniffed the sweat. The AP's eyes pulsated faster for a moment and then narrowed. Moving in closer still, the AP took in a strong whiff of her as if there was some horrible odor she was trying to identify.

"Private Emma, what is your problem with me now? I was on my way to see you regarding Roberto's evening exercise—" Singh started.

She was interrupted by the low voice of the not-so-friendly cybernetic lifeform.

"Well, well, well. Elevated salt levels in your perspiration, emanating from three different sweat glands. A significant increase in pheromones, increased heart rate and pulse, and your braid is perfectly planted between your enlarged mammary glands…"

Remembering all too well Emma's not-so-well-veiled threat of harm should Singh show any sexual interest in the CO, she was quick to respond with a reason for her body's autonomic responses.

"No. Stop right there, Emma!"

"Pardon me?"

"I mean *Private* Emma," Singh corrected.

The AP's eyes narrowed in addition to the pulsation. Singh pressed on to deliver her point.

"All of those symptoms are consistent with anxiety and trepidation. And since I was on my way to see you, you can imagine why I might be anxious. We don't have the best working relationship. And since my son's fate lies in your hands, I am particularly anxious about what you might or might not do."

"You admit that?"

"Yes."

By the Elders! Will she ever let me live in peace!?

Silence fell around them. Singh watched Emma's eye pulsation rate slow down a bit. It was a long minute before the AP finally responded.

"All right…your explanation appears to be logical. But take heed. I am watching you, *Citizen* Singh."

The intonation of "citizen" was just as bad as "mother."

"Thank you," Singh said. She found it easier to breathe as the stress melted away. Her eyes finally cleared of stars.

Why does she hate me so much?

"Now, as regards your son, I am willing to consider allowing you to go out with him and his team. As much as I do not like to admit it, you do have training as a soldier and they would benefit from your guidance. Further, Cadet Roberto requested that he go out alone with his team. As much as I admire his enthusiasm, his decision to involve us with our neighbors by rescuing these two human youths might have been different if there had been a seasoned soldier accompanying him. Would you not agree?"

Was she here when I told the CO I would have done the same? I bet she was.

"I might have made the same decision, Private Emma."

"Yes. And as the adult, you would have been responsible for the consequences. He would have been spared that burden, whatever it may turn out to be," she responded quietly.

Compassion? The wish to protect? At least it's clear that she cares for Roberto...

A sudden flash of her former superior officer and companion's advice flashed before her: "When you get what you want, say 'thank you' and walk away."

"You are right. I will get my gear. Thank you," Singh said immediately.

She moved swiftly to make sure the AP did not change her mind. And as she moved to step around Emma, she thought she caught the light smell of lilac.

"You are welcome, Citizen Mare Sade Singh."

Wow! She really has it bad for the lieutenant. Where does she find those perfumes? She carries it well...for an evil AP. Someday, though, there may come a time when she will need me.

CHAPTER 2

I see, as in a map, the end of all.
        —Shakespeare, *Richard III*

From a prone position atop a small rise, Lieutenant Melendez slowly scanned the designated target area where he had left the two native children and the body. Three torches blazed to keep bears, mountain lions, bobcats, and other carnivores away. Both children stayed close to each other, holding sharpened combat knives and reconditioned bows and arrows. He had placed some food nearby, hoping that they would not need to wait long for their clan to find them. Human activity had increased significantly in their area. Melendez had made the decision to leave the children food from their own harvests and then to observe the clan from a distance as a means of getting to know their habits. These humans were different from both the Nemericana people and from himself. They were hunters who tracked the area's large population of deer, foxes and, at times, other large game. But it was rare to catch a glimpse of them. When the children arrived and came under his care, Melendez had to make the decision to either let them die or to take care of them until they could be returned.

"They may not come at all, Lieutenant. I have neither thermal images nor any visual contact of them. How do you know they will come here?" Corporal Kristine asked.

"They've always seemed to have a pair of eyes on us. I think they may have missed Cadet Roberto's discovery of the children, but they sure were aware of us leaving our camp with them tonight. I'm guessing once they think we're gone, they will investigate."

He spoke in hushed to and refocused his binoculars. A pile of leaves several feet from the little girl seemed to be moving.

"And that is why you sent the others back. You want whoever is watching them to think we all left while the two of us stay here and watch. A simple but effective diversion, Lieutenant."

Not responding nor moving, Melendez zeroed in even more closely on the mound of leaves, only to see them fall away and to reveal a short, muscular, red-headed woman. He was genuinely surprised to see that the human from this clan had darkened her naturally pale, white skin with either black paint, mud, or both. She was also clad in a very dark array of camouflage from head to toe. With a spear in hand, she silently motioned to another mound. A male version of her, similarly armed and dressed, emerged. Melendez watched in disbelief. They had been very well hidden and camouflaged, and were communicating through a series of silent hand motions.

"Lieutenant, they are covered in a mud that obscures their thermal image. Further, their dress is a combination fabric woven together with species of trees and bush that lend themselves to very effective coverage. They have also darkened their faces to offset the gleam of their pale skin, and it appears they have even attempted to darken their hair, which is pulled back. Additionally, they are utilizing hand signals just as we would on a reconnaissance mission, Sir. This is all very..."

"Militaristic. I've underestimated them. They might look primitive, but they were down there in plain view while we were there. And they figured out that we can pick up their heat signatures. How the hell did they know that?" he whispered.

He looked back toward the two scouts and then he saw a small group of eight people, dressed and armed similarly, coming through the break of trees carefully and cautiously. They were scattered and had spaced themselves so they could surround the entire area containing the children. Melendez stayed unmoving several moments, unsure what they were going to do. Suddenly, there was a yell. One person broke rank and burst into the light. Throwing her bow and arrow on the ground, the shadow figure leaped toward the light and the girl. Yelling back in surprise or shock, the little girl responded and raised her hands to be embraced. The adult, a woman dressed like everyone else, looked at the girl as if she were her daughter, all the while smiling, embracing her, and crying. Seeing that there was a boy there too, the woman grabbed his head to pull him in as well. As she held them both, Melendez watched. The young girl and boy spoke in a familiar language—one that he had not heard in a very long time.

Spanish? Is that Spanish with English thrown in? If it is, I never heard them use it before.

The children had been silent throughout their stay with him. But now with their clan their voices were deeper than he expected, and they made a melodic string of sounds and words. But there were two words that he clearly heard from his spot: "bark" and "dog."

Confused, Melendez continued to focus on the drama unfolding below. A male broke cover and stood tall above the embracing children and woman. He made a strong guttural noise and then spoke a series of low words. With their full attention on him, the children spoke what were clearly a series of sentences, which included myriad hand motions. The periodically pointed to their dead companion and then to their splints and wounds. They prattled on continuously for what seemed like several minutes. The man nodded often and looked as if he were deep in thought. Even as the children continued, he moved to inspect their wounds, splints, weapons and the wrapped body. All the while, the female looked on. She kept grabbing the little girl and crying. Finally, the children fell silent and the man and woman stood up to talk. There was clearly tension in the air. It seemed as if they were talking seriously about something besides the children's story. The male extended his hand to indicate the surrounding area. Nodding in approval, the female whistled. Three people—two males and one female—came over to collect the weapons, children, food, and the still-lit torches. Two other shadows emerged from the trees and picked up the wrapped body. Melendez could see that, while this active group was visible, there were even more of them lurking in the background.

Jesus…thirty of them? Really?

He lost count and focused back on the male he thought might be the leader. Melendez was truly impressed with their reconnaissance abilities, camouflage, and use of silence to invade an area completely unannounced. As the others receded back into the darkness, taking the torches with them, the leader stayed still for a moment longer. He looked around the immediate area and took in a deep breath as if smelling something. He continued to search the environment before finally moving on. After ten minutes of silence during which the sights and sounds of night and animals prevailed, he took the chance to move away from his perch and retreat. Once he and Corporal Kristine were with half a klick of their own camp, Melendez spoke.

"For a bunch of primitive humans, they are pretty sophisticated in guerrilla tactics, evasion, and covert operations. I'm guessing they had about thirty or so people there?"

"Forty-two, sir. And those were just the ones that I could actually see. On a couple, their mud camouflage was failing. They were staggered in waves and were far enough apart not to be caught in a grenade attack. Their weapons were more advanced than what we saw two years ago, and certainly their clothing is utilitarian. Each was armed with a bow, arrows, a short or long spear, and another knife. If it hadn't been for the emotional outburst of the female, I am not sure they would have presented themselves."

When she spoke she continued to scan her area and field of fire. For an artificial person, she was presented as hyper-vigilant to the point of paranoid.

"This changes everything, Corporal. They looked more like an insurgence team than a group of hunters. They were well versed in sign language…" Melendez trailed off.

"Their behaviors were far from hunter-scavengers," he heard her say. After a second more, he had a sudden realization. His thoughts ran rampant, and his speculation jumped into overdrive.

"Sir? Is something wrong?" the corporal asked with more than concern in her voice.

"Jesus, Kristine. Their hand signals, use of cover, clothing, camouflage, stealth—what if they have been watching us all this time? What if they have been watching us train the cadets and our own training, and they are mimicking our techniques? The way they looked, acted, and responded were classically militaristic…shit!"

Looking at Corporal Kristine, Melendez could see her luminous eyes begin to pulsate more quickly.

"And since my thermal readings missed them as a result of their use of mud, it is also evident that they are intelligent and able to improvise. Sir? This could be a major problem. If not for us, anyone that screws with them," she responded.

"That is an understatement for sure."

CHAPTER THREE

More in sorrow than in anger.
　　　—Shakespeare, *Hamlet*

It took a little while for Pearl Veritas's double vision to clear. While she could manage the periodic but brief blurred vision, shakiness, and sweating, the double vision bothered her—especially when she was either shooting or exercising.

I hate doctors! They always find something wrong with you. "Have some medication," they always say. Walk it off, Veritas!

Just as her eyes came into focus, she heard a small but noticeable rapping at the door.

What? Who's calling at this time of night? Ever hear of an S-phone?

She put her weights down gently, annoyed at the knock at her door so late at night. With her lover away at her own home, Veritas enjoyed her time alone to exercise. She especially liked to bench press and do other compound exercises with free weights. Still sweating and catching her breath, she got up and made it to the door just as the loudness of the persistent knock began to escalate. She grabbed her sidearm from its place next to the door before she opened it, feeling better knowing she was armed rather than not. She opened the door quickly and caught sight of a very familiar woman. She was flanked by two other women both of whom appeared to be more muscular than the frail-looking technician.

I know her...she's Mare Singh's friend. But what's she doing here? And who are these women? What's her name...what's her name...oh, yes, Austin. Bad memory. Maybe I should see a doctor...

With her hand firmly grasping the weapon concealed behind her back, Veritas blocked the door and waited quietly for Austin to explain herself.

"Oh, yes. Captain Veritas. I am so sorry to bother you so late at night. Please let me introduce Security Officer Etta and Corporal Venus Moira. I know this is unusual, but may we speak?" Austin asked. Veritas narrowed her eyes as she sized up the situation. She had met Austin several times regarding the computer data dump, the casting out, and Mare Singh's disappearance. Austin had been a good source of data, information, and ideas.

"And your two friends here have an interest in what's going on with Nemericana's Command business? Last I checked, non-central command corporals and security officers did not have that clearance."

Silence fell like a vault door slamming shut. Austin looked confused and was speechless for several moments as she looked for words. It was the solidly built Etta who spoke first.

"My son was cast out with Austin's and Corporal Moira's. Word is that Major Singh is alive and made it out east with them. We want to find them," she said, deadly earnest.

Okay. This is why everyone's so pissed off.

"Come in," Veritas said brusquely.

As the troupe moved inside, Veritas kept her weapon concealed. Ever since her violent attack with the red-headed, devil-eyed Aurora, she kept a weapon in hand when confronted with either an unknown situation or an unexpected event—such as three guests showing up unannounced.

As the group of women reached the front room, the two security-trained officers scanned the area. Austin sat down.

"Again, I am very sorry to bother you at such a late hour. Etta is correct. We all saw the news report on Commandant Pierce's Expedition Force heading out to the east. While there were no solid reports that she has a lead on this 'ghost platoon,' my friends and I were hoping that you might know something about it."

"About what, Austin? Maybe it's just a news report," Veritas said from the doorway. She kept a clean line of fire on the two standing guests.

"No, ma'am. The units she took were all search-and-destroy trained, and heavily packed with scouts. There were no military APs attached, and the Commandant went herself," Corporal Moira said.

"That's a whole lot of intelligence above your clearance, Corporal," Veritas said.

"When it comes to my son, there is no clearance," she said quietly. The room fell eerily silent again, and Veritas waited for someone else to speak. The corporal took a seat as if the verbal exchange had drained her. The security woman looked at her feet.

"Pearl? You don't have to tell us anything. I just thought that with all we went through, you might have an idea of where my son might be. I'm sorry to bother you," Austin said. Even from her distance she could see tears brimmed up in her eyes. She started to get up.

"Over thirteen hundred klicks northeast. They are somewhere in a large area once called 'Pennsylvania' in Pre-Fall days. Latitude thirty-nine, forty-five degrees north, longitude seventy-seven, thirty-four degrees west. There's a lot of distance and creatures between us and them. Also, there's a lot of humanoid activity as well. More than ever, and I'm not sure if they are as passive as they used to be. The Commandant and her team are already halfway there with a vengeance. So even if you do go, if the animals, lack of water, or humanoids don't get you, the Commandant's team will."

Veritas was keenly aware she had released classified data.

Once again, the room fell into a quiet punctuated only by fresh sniffles from the muscular woman. Standing fully now, Austin smiled. She quietly walked over to Veritas and gave her a gentle kiss on the cheek and hug.

"Thank you, Pearl," she said. She looked right at Veritas. Tears streaked her face. With a deep sigh she walked to the door, her two companions following. As they passed they each thanked her, even as they averted their eyes to keep Veritas from seeing that they too were crying. As quickly as they showed up, they were gone. Veritas heard the door close behind them but remained standing in her front room. She wondered what had made her so readily give up the location of a highly prized target.

Compassion? I'd hope someone would do the same for me.

She locked her door securely again before returning to weightlifting.

CHAPTER FOUR

Wife and child
Those precious motives, those strong knots of love.
    —Shakespeare, *Macbeth*

Mission Log: 5/8/2167**—***Second Lieutenant Melendez, Jose, USMC. 35 months, 2 days since arriving to Waynesboro, Pennsylvania, our new home. While most of my staff still think my renaming our underground facilities Forts Corpus Christi and Holy Mary was ill advised, I was not surprised that Corporal Kristine and Private Mary were in full support, citing that Forts Alpha and Bravo were "too predictable." Once an underground, "nuclear-proof," secret military complex built into the Raven Rock Mountains, this complex was formally designated as "The Rock" and "Underground Pentagon." It is a comfortable 1,313 klicks northeast from Southeast Great Gate Twelve of Nemericana, near Montgomery, Alabama. I would rather be a continent away, however, based on the significant number of unmanned aerial vehicles— drones—we've spotted in our airspace both day and night lately. I think we'll stay put.*

    We all call it home.

Population: 1 adult male, 1 adult female, 96 youth—68 males, 28 females, 34 sapient artificial persons—cybernetic lifeforms (APs); 9 nonsapient APs obtained from Nemericana have evolved into sapient cybernetic lifeforms in the first three months of being here. How is still a question.

0800 hours. To reiterate, after three years of making this military complex a safe haven, I continue to worry about increased drone activity in our area and periodic human-operated flights as well. I seen these swift, vertical-take-off-and-landing aircraft myself, and I am impressed with both their speed and agility. Still, with only one hour of satellite coverage every 24 hours to obtain intel on movement in our area, I have restricted everyone's time outside the facility. Holy Mary is the smaller of the two bunkers, more removed from the main base and significantly better hidden, with one entrance in and a subterranean exit. That is the primary defensive position for all non-cadets and civilians. Corpus Christi's form is obscured, but it is visibly a fortification.

We discovered last night that our neighbors, a very large group or tribe, have been watching us for years. Based on our recent observations, we conclude that they have watched us very closely. While they were part of the group that assisted with the last group of children before they were relocated here, they have not engaged us directly. Taking a chance two years ago, I made the decision to clear some land for farming various vegetables—both for us to eat and to see what they would do. When the time came to harvest, we left half of it for them.

Happily, I hope, they took their share again the following fall. We've seen them only in scattered sightings and at a distance, but they travel in small groups of four or so; they seem to be armed with bows, arrows, and long spears. They hunt larger game in packs and there is an equal division of labor—men and women hunt and watch us equally. Corporal Kristine's and my own observation of them last night was remarkable and raised the question of how really sophisticated they are in their abilities to mimic, observe, and replicate. It's probably a whole lot more than we know. They are especially good at camouflage. They can hide right in front of you and, unless you happen to be an AP with enhanced vision, you're not going to see them. Their use of mud, however, has now made even that mode of detection uncertain. More on that later once we have more intelligence.

Our neighbors have not demonstrated any indications of being a threat, but still there is the need for security. With the exceptions of small training groups of cadets under the command of Corporals Mabel and Kristine, I have limited time out during the day hours and keep all youth close to the entrances in case rapid retreat is necessary, mostly due to drones. Dogs and APs are also watching both civilians and perimeters during the day, and only three pairs of APs are left out on sentry duty.

Speaking of APs, my decision to have only six outside the forts as sentries continues to be reviewed by my second-in-command, Sergeant Joan, who insists that more can be allowed to stay out.

However, the APs have a new development: they "sleep" every 48 hours, so that takes precedence. When not allowed to shut down for a period of six continuous hours, they have an increase in what can only be described as irritability, confusion, difficulty following complex commands, and more emotional lability. This recent development—from last year—has also been matched by growth in their senses of humor, facial expressions, "depth" to their eyes, and profound growth in independent thinking as well. The idea of them "just following orders" is not a worry here. While my girls operate within the parameters of the chain of command, they demonstrate more features consistent with human soldiers than what I would have expected from artificial lifeforms...

"Lieutenant? Why do you continue to refer to us as 'your girls' when the youngest of us is approximately forty-five years old from inception?" Sergeant Joan asked.

Someday, someday soon, I'll be able to finish a log report without interruption...I wish I had slept late today.

He turned in his comfortable leather chair and took in the sight of his oldest, most trusted soldier. Joan sat at a newly reconfigured, updated console. While the cavernous command center could easily hold twenty crew members, the environment still felt close when it was just the two of them during first shift. Still bleary-eyed from his late-night, fact-finding mission with Corporal Kristine, he summoned as much cheerfulness as he could to hold a cogent discussion.

"Oh, Joan... 'You give them eyes but they do not see. You give them ears but they do not hear,'" he paraphrased, hoping she would be able to identify accurately his loose attempt to quote Ezekiel and to understand its applicability to the situation.

Narrowing his eyes, he saw that she looked down to her left, a very human gesture, to see if she could recall.

Well, well, well…she'll get it right. I can see from her emerging smile that she obviously slept well last night while the rest of us went out for the night.

"'Son of man, thou dwellest in the midst of a rebellious house, which have eyes to see, and see not; they have ears to hear, and hear not: for they *are* a rebellious house…' King James Bible, Ezekiel chapter twelve, verse two. So, does that mean we are the ones in exile from the promised land or are we APs the 'rebellious' ones in the house?"

Joan's smile was subdued.

"You see, Joan? I know that you know that I can tell that you slept last night. You're not as grumpy as you were yesterday, your memory and recall are perfect, and your application of my poorly worded quote is perfect. Actually, you took it farther than I had intended," Melendez said as he took his cap off to scratch around the metal electrodes sticking out of his head.

Why I let them connect this permanently to my brain I'll never know. Why? Because you were supposed to be in cryogenic sleep for a couple months, not one-hundred-and-thirty-plus years, Jose. Dr. Del Cruz would have been happy with the results…my sleep, that is.

He finally stopped his scratching to see what else Joan would throw at him.

"Yes, sir. Thank you. But I still am not sure why we are your 'girls.'"

"Because. You found me, brought me back to life, and then we formed a family. Since I'm older than all of you, and my time asleep still counts as years passed, I see you all as my 'girls.' My reference was mostly a poor attempt at saying that my view of you as children is obviously based on what you have seen and heard me say."

"So we are your children?"

"Yes."

Melendez watched Joan closely for more facial expressions.

"By the way you are looking at me, I assume you are reading my facial features to look for proof that I continue to experience and outwardly express emotions," Joan said. He saw her eyes narrow and a soft purple glow emit from her eyes.

"Yes. And by the look *you* are giving *me*, I would say you are annoyed that I am right and, as such, you are irritated but expressing it quite well with nonverbal cues," Melendez nodded in approval.

"Hmm," she said. As if to yield the combat, she turned to face her monitor. What came next was a surprise.

"And this from the man who supposedly cannot read emotions or nonverbals," she said, barely audibly.

Finding the corners of his mouth pulling up, Melendez shook his head in amazement.

Well now, that's a first. A poorly hidden, smart-ass remark from Sergeant Joan in response to me being right. My God, they're becoming more human every day. I should bring her up to speed fully on our discovery last night.

Melendez looked at his watch. It was an ancient watch, but it worked. It was accurate to give him a heads-up when it was time to check in with "eyes-in-the-sky." They should be getting the day's first—and only—reconnaissance look at their surrounding area from the satellite they were able to control.

Damn. Later I guess. I wish we had been able to access a geosynchronous satellite instead of one we can only use for an hour before it's out of range for the next full day.

Melendez's thoughts were again interrupted—this time by a sudden burst of laughter and the swift motions of a three-year-old girl running at full speed toward him.

What the hell!?

"Jose! Jose! Catch me!" she squealed. She didn't wait for him to prepare to catch her. She never did. The little girl leapt at him.

Surprised but not shocked at her ever-growing level of trust, Melendez caught the girl with ease—it was a near-daily routine.

"Eva! For the love of all the saints! One of these days I'm not going to be ready and will miss, you little cuddle-muffin."

He pulled her up above his head and dramatically dropped her down to his mouth to kiss her neck. Of all the events he had experienced since waking from cryogenic sleep, tragic or sublime, Eva's birth had been the most significant. He often thought of how his father must have felt when he and his sisters were born. His time with Eva was like a link to his own family…*who lived over a hundred and thirty years ago, in another world.*

"There you are, you little girl!" Private Emma reprimanded. By now she had entered the command center. Dressed in her "off-duty" civilian clothes—a flowered dress and an array of homemade jewelry—Emma seemed to walk more with a sway as if she were walking in high heels.

"Hide me!" Eva said. The little girl had managed to jump down to the floor and scoot behind him, putting him between her and the approaching AP.

"Do not attempt to hide behind Lieutenant Melendez. He cannot save you from your breakfast. Nor can he save you from your chores, young lady," Emma said. She stood with her arms folded over her chest, smirking in her own unique way.

Well…civilian dress, jewelry, and playing the role of the mother…Yup, I'm in trouble. I wonder how her talk with Mare went.

In the hopes of self-preservation Melendez gently attempted to move Eva from behind him. It was his way of disengaging from the pseudo-nuclear family. Eva might have been the child of two young teenagers, who were now cadets, but Melendez was the de facto father figure and Emma was her mother by default.

Children can't raise children, Melendez consistently thought when Eva's father asked him for advice.

"Now, Eva. Is it true? You skipped out on breakfast? I bet Private Emma made it special for you," he said.

"She made it for you and me. But I told her you were in the command center and she got all sad and stuff," Eva responded with deadly seriousness.

Ah, yes...breakfast. A hundred-year-old, freeze-dried entrée with fresh vegetables. Or was it fresh rabbit with a side of beetles and vegetables?

Memories of fresh eggs, bacon, toast, and real percolated coffee flooded his thoughts. It was only Emma's voice that brought him back to reality.

"Ah...well, I just didn't want the food to go to waste. I made sure I saved it for you later, should you be in need of nutrients," Emma said. While not great with reading subtext and subtitles in body language and tone, Melendez swore he heard guilt, shame, or embarrassment—or all three.

"Emma? What's that on the wall?" Eva asked. She spoke as if she had seen some and with that pointed curiously at something behind the AP.

Oh no. Emma...don't fall for it...

"What? What do you see?" Emma asked. She turned fully around to see where Eva pointed.

With the same speed and agility she had demonstrated earlier, Eva ran at top speed back out the door. Her tactic to distract Emma had worked, yet again, for the thousandth time.

It must be a safety protocol to accept at face value what humans ask, especially children, I bet.

Turning back around and seeing her flee, Emma clearly was able to immediately assess that she had been duped. She closed her eyes and shook her head in a human gesture of disbelief, then gave a weak smile as she turned to leave.

"Excuse me, Lieutenant. I think I will be on the run for the rest of the day."

"Good luck and Godspeed."

Without further fanfare, Emma walked off—with less of a sway and more of a determined march—in hot pursuit of her ward.

Standing quietly, Melendez watched her go. He caught the scent of lilac.

Perfume. Just like last time…

"Yes, sir. She is the worst of all of us. Emotion-wise, that is," Sergeant Joan said from her station.

"How bad?"

"Very bad, sir," Joan offered. She was out of her chair and beside her commanding officer.

Damn it! I hope these emotional events and experiences don't overwhelm her circuitry. I can't afford to lose her…or any of them.

"Last week, after three days without shutting down, she and Private Rebecca almost came to blows when Private Rebecca suggested that Private Emma should allow citizen Mare Singh to mate with you as a means of creating more children."

Jesus Christ! Are all these APs obsessed with sex and mating?

"A few days prior to that, Private Danielle and Private Emma got into a heated verbal exchange over which one you would find more attractive. Again, it occurred after a period of not shutting down for seventy-two hours. Consequently, I have ordered those three in particular to shut down every thirty-six hours and to remain shut down for an eight-hour duration. As a result, they appear to be more amenable to orders, more logical, much more efficient, and much more…creative in problem solving."

"So what you're telling me is that the three APs who are experiencing the most emotions are requiring the most sleep. A shorter running time, and more rest for the best results. Their patterns of work and sleep are remarkably consistent with humans," Melendez said.

My God! How is this possible? The nine APs most recently brought in from Nemericana become sapient five days after uploading data from one of my APs, and three of my APs are becoming much more human—beyond sapience. How? Why?

"Sir, there is another thing that all three reported to Corporal Mabel. It is concerning as it is truly something I have heard of occurring only in humans," Joan said with visible concern.

"What? What could be worse?"

He turned quickly to look at he and waited while looked closely at her face for any clue of what disaster was about to befall him and his crew. She seemed to pick her words carefully as if to cause him the least amount of distress.

Great. Just great. It has to be real bad to take Joan this long to find the words.

"Okay, Sergeant. You're making it worse by delaying your response," he added as he moved closer.

"All three have reported experiencing auditory, visual, olfactory, and kinesthetic stimuli while in shutdown mode. In conjunction with these sensations—which are devoid of actual stimuli—all three report experiencing a range of emotions that appear to be consistent with anger, sadness, lust, love, joy, and calm, sir."

Melendez stood quietly, listening to the silence in the room. As he remained still, peering into Joan's pulsating eyes, he found himself feeling ambivalent. All these things would be considered typical for a human, of course. Breaking his gaze away, he turned in an attempt to clear his head and form a reasonable thought. After what seemed to him a very long minute, he reached the obvious conclusion.

"They're dreaming. The more emotional APs, who require more sleep to be the most productive, are dreaming. Do you have any idea what this must mean?"

Joan nodded in agreement, and Melendez was pleased to see that the significance of this development was not lost on his second-in-command.

"Yes, sir. It means that new algorithms and new circuitry are forming, similar to neurogenesis in humans when organic brain cells 'wire together, fire together,' if I were to quote Hebbian Law. That said, Privates Emma, Rebecca, and Danielle appear to be evolving to yet another level. So much so that they have all discussed experiencing a 'private self' and, at times, feeling what humans call 'lonely.' And yet they all agree that they want to keep this internal sense of self and have talked about 'fearing' losing this experience. Based on all this data, compared to my database, I can only speculate that there is some kind of metamorphosis occurring that is pushing these three APs in a direction we remaining APs may or may not get to, sir."

Melendez was still in deep thought, processing all that Joan was saying. It made sense based on the data, but he had no clue as to how or why this was happening or what it would mean for the future.

Well, so far, nothing but good has come of it. More

efficiencies and positivity if they sleep. A sense of real identity other than name, rank, serial number, and duty. A sense of individuality...and the natives are becoming more proficient in reconnaissance, tracking...Oh, yeah, Taylor.

"While we are on the subject of evolution, changing, and mental expansions—is it me or has our resident human historian and all-around natural scientist become obsessed with Pre-Fall cryogenic technology and robotics?"

Joan was sitting with her hands folded behind her back. After a moment, she tilted her head.

"I believe your train of thought followed the natural sequitur of Privates Emma, Danielle and Rebecca's evolutions, which led to you changing the subject to Citizen Taylor. Regardless, your assessment is correct: he has delved deep into the history of those topics. He has also, however, taken it upon himself to locate all other Pre-Fall cryogenic laboratories and the scientific methods and findings that went along with them. He reviewed in detail Dr. Del Cruz's recordings and took to heart her statement of 'others'—her idea that there were subjects similar to yourself somewhere in the world. To his credit, he has located a series of potential sites. He has focused on a series of laboratories that not only focused on this science but also artificial intelligence and robotics and has identified two locations that are probable."

"Where are they? I hope not in Antarctica or the Arctic. Please tell me they're in Hawaii? Maybe Cuba? It would be nice if they were someplace warm," he mused.

"Fascinating guess, though unlikely. He has identified a teaching facility, Massachusetts Institute of Technology, as the head site. A series of other laboratories surround that site. MIT is located on the northeastern seaboard, longitude—"

"Cambridge. Cambridge, Massachusetts. Just outside of Boston," he said quietly.

Of course. That's where all the initial studies and prototypes emerged. Makes sense they would be the leaders and remain involved. Is Cambridge still there? Did the ocean take it back? My God...when was the last time I was back there, back home?

Images floated through his head of crates and packages carrying custom-made, transparent, tempered glass for his chamber, and of the final material and disks confirming the mixture of the protein plasma he floated in...*for 130 years.*

"Sir? Do you know this place?"

Melendez was taking his time in answering her question. He was about to respond when they were interrupted by a loud, repeating beep from the satellite monitor.

Damn it! What now?

Joan moved so quickly to the control panel, she seemed like a blur. She reached it before he did and he stood behind her and he watched her hands rapidly manipulate the monitor so that it would display on a series of four larger monitors just beyond her screen. Melendez could easily see a series of red dots approaching their position from the southwest. A much smaller group of dots trailed the larger group, and an even smaller group—maybe a single pair—approached from the north. And to the immediate east, in the city behind them, larger than usual masses of humanoids seemed to be on the move. They were clearly heading south to meet the large group coming in from the southwest.

"What the hell? What's going on?" Melendez asked.

Looking from left to right a series of times to take in the four screens, Melendez took in the data. He presented his assessment for Joan to analyze.

"That's a pretty heavy deployment of ground vehicles— and probably aircraft support. I'm guessing sixty klicks from our doorstep," he said. He was surprised at how calm he was in light of a series of mobilizations near him location. He shifted his focus to the smaller group coming in from the north.

"Sixty-five klicks, sir, at a speed of seventy-five kph. If they have pinpointed our position, they will be here in forty-three minutes, sir," Joan confirmed as she continued to work the controls.

"Bandits coming in from the north look like they are farther out—ninety klicks and moving slower," Melendez added.

"Movement north is a significantly smaller insertion team, eighty-seven klicks out, approaching at fifty-five kph. They will be arriving in sixty-eight minutes; they look like they might be a pair of vehicles. Our…neighbors look like they will pass our locations in minutes but seem to be on an intercept course with what probably are forces from Nemericana. They are not as organized, nor are they moving at top speed—in fact they are collapsing as they approach that sector. Sir, due to the early hour, nearly all personnel are within or just outside the base's doors. Recommend red status and shutdown in preparation for possible ground assault and aerial bombardment."

"Do it," Melendez said. Without hesitation, he reached to turn on the public announcement system. Pausing before he turned it on, he looked back at Joan. She had said, "nearly all personnel" were at the base.

For the love of God! Nearly everyone…

"Who's outside? Distance and location?"

His hand remained poised on the switch to the PA.

"Citizen Mare Singh and three cadets: David, Jacob, and Roberto. All cadets were working on orienting and compass skills for night maneuvers, and citizen Singh offered her military experience to take them out at oh-four-thirty with the plan to return by oh-seven-hundred hours. While they have three days' supplies for training purposes, they were scheduled to return in the morning. They may be returning. Communication via cell phone is unlikely due to mineral composition—and unwise in case the communication could be monitored," she responded while her eyes and hands kept moving over the controls and monitors.

Lowering his eyes and sighing, Melendez chided himself for not seeing that one coming.

Of course, it's Singh, her son and his two friends. Former civilians from the very place that's mobilizing to our position! Let me guess—they're right between us and the oncoming forces!

"Sir? As misfortune would have it, Singh and her wards are right in the path of the oncoming forces. They appear to be much closer to the intruders than to our perimeters."

"Yup…I figured that. Joan, relinquish your post and send three cadets up here to monitor the situation. Mobilize Corporal Mabel and her fire team to see if they can get to Singh before the others do, but do not send them without talking to me first. Have Corporal Kristine lock down the bases and get yourself to Holy Mary. Prepare for ground assault. Good luck, Sergeant."

Nodding in approval of the plan, Joan started to walk out. Then, she stopped suddenly.

"Sir? Good luck to us all."

"Copy. Now get going."

As he watched her walk away, Melendez took in a deep breath before he flipped on the PA.

Great. They will have to find us first. We can stay in hiding for years, but I bet that's not the plan. And I bet our neighbors know exactly where we are.

He saw four tiny dots between the mountains and the oncoming force from the south. Shifting his gaze to the south, he wondered who the small force was and who was trailing the larger force coming in from the southwest.

A recon group? Command group? No way—they would be ahead of the larger group. And what the hell has motivated our neighbors to move out?

Pulling his attention back to the control panel, he turned on the internal PA system to broadcast instructions. Everyone had practiced the drill many times, but he had never wanted to do it for real.

"Cadets, civilians, and marines: ground forces are approaching from the southwest and north. It is unclear if they have our exact location but they might see one of our teams outside our perimeter and may use them as bait. All hands to battle stations! All cadets and marines—to arms and defensive positions. All civilians to Holy Mary for lockdown. This is not a drill! Repeat. This is not a drill. All rounds are live. I want defensive positions with clean lines of fire. All civilians to Holy Mary. We have ten minutes to be in place and locked down. Melendez out."

CHAPTER FIVE

We see yonder the beginning of the day,
but I think we shall never see the end of it.
 —Shakespeare, *Henry V*

"I am not trying to pry into your business, Roberto. I'm just concerned that you will get hurt should you pursue your…uh…passion…" Mare Singh tried to say as eloquently as possible.

Even as she finished her sentence, she cringed at her own words. She slowed to a complete stop as she watched her sixteen-year-old son's gait slow as well to a stop and his shoulders sink even lower.

"I did not say that right."

"Was there a right way?"

"Um… yes?"

I really am bad at this. How did my mother do it? I mean, she could say things and I would listen. Is it because he's a male? Is this what becoming a man means? Being stubborn and making poor choices in potential mates?

She waited for the inevitable angry and sarcastic retort, but she was surprised to see hurt in his eyes instead when he explained his position.

"You make it sound like I'm a freak. We are not in Nemericana. I can choose who I care for and want to be romantic with. And if it's a cadet from fire team Delta, so what? And why aren't you supporting me on this? You're my mother, right? And how did you get Private Emma to let you lead this team?"

As he looked at her with his brown eyes she felt both sad and proud. Singh moved in closer and placed her hands squarely on his shoulders. He was dressed in old-style military fatigues and had a rifle slung over his shoulder. She took in the sight of her growing son with a smile.

You have grown up so fast. What happened to that thirteen-year-old boy clutching to me in the ride out to the unknown? Now you're a young cadet and an independent thinker, true to form.

"I am so proud to be your mother. I regret every day I missed of your life. I just get worried that your interest in young women will be painful. Women are complicated, difficult to understand, and multifaceted. Trust me. I know," she said, remembering both Roseann and Verna, her companions from an earlier life.

"I think you would be happier if you found someone like your own friends," she said. With that sentence she motioned to Jacob and David who were walking ahead of them and deep in conversation.

You see? They love each other. That's the way it should be.

"Males are much more linear. Direct, clear, and forgiving. They seem to be very good at letting arguments go and not dwelling on things."

Her three years living in a mixed-gender, mixed-species community with males as equal partners presented fewer arguments and conflicts, past and present, were often readily let go with no retribution later or vindictiveness.

It's crazy but it works. Confusing, different, and hard to understand, but we get along, surprisingly. Except maybe me and Private Emma. No surprise there. That will never change.

"I can see the attraction you have for this girl. But you have been in the company of males all your life. I just don't…" Singh started to say but then realized how it might be interpreted.

"What? You don't understand how I could be interested in another gender? You know? Like a freak?" he countered as his eyes narrowed, waiting for a response.

Damn it! He's really good at turning the tables on me.

"No…I know a person who also likes different genders. My friend and colleague Pearl Veritas. She liked men, I'm sure…"

"So you're telling me that even one of your friends like males?"

"Yes…this is not going well."

"And she kept it secret so she might have a chance at promotion and not be ostracized for her personal choices. She's the one that was always lonely and kept to herself, right? I listen to your   stories," he finished.

Well…I see you do.

Singh dropped her hands to her side and her own eyes narrowed. She folded her arms across her chest. It was a well-practiced maneuver that came out whenever she was feeling trapped or outflanked by her son. Her own slung rifle sitting on top of her butt pack suddenly felt heavier than she expected. She readjusted it so as not to put too much pressure on the small of her back.

"Yes. You see what I mean. I don't want that for you," she said defiantly.

Smirking, she watched her son move a little closer. He began to speak in a lower tone.

"Mother? We're in a new world. Men and women live and work together. We're equal. You don't see anyone else concerned or worried when other men and women get together. They even have sex…"

Singh put up both hands to stop her son from talking any more. She felt nausea forming in her stomach and bile rising to the back of her throat.

Fried grasshoppers and baked beetles are better than that image! It's bad enough we have to eat rabbit, deer, and other meat all the time too! Do they ever eat vegetables?

Memories of vegetarian dishes of all shapes and sizes from her past life pushed back the images of dead animals prepared for food and partially pushed out some of the vile image of sexual intercourse between males and women.

"Okay! You win. I don't want to hear any more about that. You always bring a gun to a knife fight, don't you, Roberto?"

Singh didn't wait for an answer and marched beyond him. She refused to give her son the satisfaction of watching her cringe anymore at the idea of men and women having sex.

Unbelievable! Why would anyone find men attractive— hairy bodies, big hands and feet, hair coming out of their ears, and rough skin? Yuck! She's going to break his heart.

She focused on the steps ahead and heard her son's steps fall in behind her. No sooner had she pushed the thought out of her head than her attention was seized by a high-pitched sound far above the trees.

Shit! Drones! she thought as she pulled her rifle from her back. *And here I am with a twentieth-century relic for a weapon. Just great!*

"Mare! Drones! Eight o'clock, due southwest!"

She dropped to a kneeling position well under cover of the trees. Both David and Jacob were lying flat on the ground at the very crest of a bald summit. Roberto suddenly came up beside her, also watching his two friends as they cautiously surveyed the area ahead of them.

"What's going on?" he whispered.

"David spotted drones to our southwest. They should be able to get a visual from their position. Problem is, they might be spotted themselves as they have no cover," Singh explained. She cocked one ear, hearing something much louder than drones.

This is not good. Rifles, sidearms, compass, three days of emergency gear just for training, and water—nothing else. I hope I'm wrong.

Singh scanned sky above David and Jacob.

"Shit!"

What she heard next was definitely in her internal catalog of Nemericanan vertical-take-off-and-landing aircraft. Just as she narrowed down the models by sound to one of the swift three-seat scout crafts, she saw four VTOL aircraft breaking cloud cover. They zeroed in on David and Jacob's position. She pulled Roberto down and closer to her, she yelled out to David and Jacob, who were now on their feet.

"Run to the cave! Don't stop and dig in!"

Not needing any more prompting, the boys took off at top speed, heading southwest toward dense tree cover. The aircraft pivoted and pursued them.

The tree cover will keep them safe...as long as there are no foot soldiers in place. They must have found some evidence of our base...

"The cave!? That's like two miles away! And it's in the opposite direction from the base?" Roberto questioned her.

"And it's deep in the middle of the woods, obscured by brush, and surrounded by nickel and granite. They won't be found. They each have weapons and three days' worth of supplies. We, on the other hand, have no cover or hiding spot—meaning we are now in evasion mode. We need to move. Hand signals only. Got it?"

Roberto nodded in understanding as she took the lead, moving away from the crest but still heading parallel to the ridge.

Great! No cover, no communication, and only primitive weapons. Four swift scouting aircraft and drones? That's a forward advancement. They must know we're close to base to mobilize that large a group. But after three years? Why would they be looking for us? And why so far east?

With thoughts still floating in her head, Singh continued to clutch her archaic rifle—she knew its lead-shot projectiles would be virtually useless against advanced Nemericanan weaponry. While gun powder had a limited shelf life for her thirty-round weapon, an electromagnetic capacity propelled bullet from a Nemericanan assault rifle would never jam, never fail, with two times the capacity and significantly faster firing rate. The more she compared the weapons, the more depressed she became.

Giving the signal to stop, she paused to listen for movement. She could hear that the aircraft was still in the vicinity, but it seemed to be farther to their south.

I hope David and Jacob get to the cave.

She gave the signal to move ahead. She took point.

Still moving parallel to the ridge, Singh made several stops to listen to her environment when she heard any deviation in the noise from the multiple—though receding—aircraft above her. She made sure of her footing so as not to alert anyone of her position by falling or kicking rocks, and she was happy to see that Roberto had taken his excellent training seriously—he too kept vigilant and moved silently as they proceeded away from their original destination.

We'll go several miles due southeast and come in to Holy Mary from behind. In fact, I think I'll come in through the city. I trust the humanoids more than my people. That will put our troops between us and them, and won't lead them directly back to our base. I hope the lieutenant saw this force from the satellite.

Years of training circulated through her blood. She stopped yet again to listen. Looking ahead, she saw no movement—but she did see a pair of footprints just in front of her. By feeling the impression of the print, it was easy for her to determine that it had not been made by any military boot, but by some kind of hide.

Hmm. Must be our humanoid neighbors, she thought as she noted their direction. *I wonder why they are out here. Watching us again?*

Singh had noticed that they were being watched twice that day already. The humanoids were pretty good at surveillance and hiding. From a distance, the males and females appeared to be of the same stature, clothed similarly, and both were armed with a multitude of edged weapons and long bows. "Native Americans," was what the lieutenant had called them. But he too was baffled—they all seemed larger-framed than the average person, but shorter, and they all seemed to have some shade of red hair. Apparently, that was unusual.

In a gesture of friendship, Melendez and the cadets had planted a series of crops for the last two years and had shared them with the humanoids. While Singh had helped to plant, she didn't agree with that approach to gaining intelligence. It was also risky because the drones could have easily seen the cleared land.

At a high enough altitude, they could see us

And worse, when the time came to harvest, the lieutenant insisted on giving them fully half of the crop. Something about "owing them." Six times over the last two years bushels of potatoes, corn, tomatoes, turnips, and squash were left in a neat pile just outside their city encampment. Singh counted four sets of footprints and sighed as she readjusted her focus on the brush ahead.

Great... we get to have old dehydrated food, red meat, and bugs with our meals while they get our good food free. Now, why did I leave Nemericana? One day later it had all been taken. After that, these creatures watched from a distance almost everything they did, nearly every day.

Maybe we'll get an answer for that someday. If we live.

Silence except for moving water could be heard. She gave the hand signal to move again. They had traveled for forty minutes at a slow pace. The sounds of drones and aircraft were gone, leaving only the wind in the trees and moving water in a large stream for sound. After another fifteen minutes of careful evasive tactics, Singh began to relax. Maybe they were far enough away now that she could risk some quick verbal discussion with Roberto. Waving him closer, she put her finger to her lips for a moment, waited, and then spoke quietly.

"Roberto. We're in trouble. The fact that there are piloted aircraft means there must be some kind of support combat group. Those scouts aren't made for long distance maneuvers. They are typically deployed with three platoons of reconnaissance/fire support troops and a much larger group of transports—carrying troops and supplies. We have to get back to the base to warn the lieutenant and his team."

"Do you think the lieutenant might already know?"

"Perhaps. If that's the case, he'll have put the bases on lockdown and assessed if they can send a recon party after us to gather intelligence. But if I were him, I'd run silent and hope they'd miss us," she said without thinking how her words might affect her son.

"Okay," was his only response.

Great…nice job, Mare. Kill any hope that might be there to survive. Well done!

She shifted to look ahead of her and saw there was a twenty- to thirty-foot gap in the trees where the brook ran down the hill. Moving ever so slowly, Mare skirted the edge with her ears cocked to hear anything mechanized above the gentle bubbling of the slow-moving water. Turning her rifle over in her hands, she checked the chamber to make sure there was a round in place and set the weapon to full automatic rather than semiautomatic.

Not that it matters. Nemericanan equivalent rifles hold fifty rounds of polarized steel propelled by an electromagnetic miniature capacitor. No misfires due to poor gun power, no kick back, and no dust buildup or negative effects from weather. And faster reloading. Just great. Come on, Mare! Focus!

She dropped even lower to the ground and scanned the entire perimeter of the stream and the edges of the tree line just to make sure they could cross unobserved. After a very long three minutes, Singh nodded and gave Roberto hand signals indicating that she would cross first, move quickly and then if clear, wave him over. He nodded. She readjusted her knife, an old-style web-belt of supplies, and pushed her long hair behind her. She kept a low, quick trot across the small piece of land and then waded out into the water. Breathing a sigh of relief, she easily closed in on the opposite shore. She was about to smile when she felt a bee sting her neck.

"Ugh! What the hell…"

As she continued moving she felt for the insect.

I'm surprised these bees haven't made it to the food table yet.

Then she felt something metallic protruding out of her throat. Pulling it out by its fuzzy tail, she was able to make out that it was a Nemericanan military human suppression dart.

"Oh no…"she uttered as her vision began to tunnel toward darkness. She felt the ground rush up to meet her. She tried to mentally fight the dart's rapid effects.

From a distance, a familiar voice was crying out, "Mother!"

Is that me or Roberto?

CHAPTER SIX

So quick bright things come to confusion.
    —Shakespeare, *A Midsummer Night's Dream*

Captain Pearl Veritas sat quietly at her desk, closely monitoring as the task forces advanced. Sergeant Jillian Banner stood at her side, watching with the same degree of interest. Standing back, Veritas took a moment to look at the Sergeant and smile one of her rare smiles. Banner turned in time to see this event and gave her usual self-conscious response.

"What? Something wrong with my hair?" she asked. She immediately moved her long hair behind her and checked her shirt's top buttons.

Veritas shook her head no and continued to smile. She spoke to Banner the way she always had over the last three years as she watched the younger woman move up the ranks.

"No, Jill. You're fine. I was just remembering just how young you were when Major Singh promoted you. How far you've come."

"It's gone by quick."

"Too quick and too much to come, I bet."

Veritas moved her shoulder in small circular movements to ease the pain from an old knife injury. The exercise and stretching helped the wound, but Aurora's red eyes still haunted her.

"Oh. Well, I'm not sure any of us will be in the service if the commandant finds what she's looking for and the truth gets out. If that happens, we'll go over the wall together and take our chances on the outside, right?" Banner asked.

Veritas looked at her and saw that her eyes were as wide as saucers. It was easy to sense her young subordinate's fear. She decided to go with humor as a tactic. It would diffuse the tension rather than reinforce her anxiety. Banner busied herself with Veritas's workstation.

"Why? Our role was to simply transport the major to a casting out. We were both attacked. You were just learning how to fly a drone. How did we know all of this shit was going to go down?"

As she spoke reciting the actual events in near identical reportage from the after-action report years ago, she put her sidearm and knife on and adjusted her uniform.

A quick nod to Banner let her know they were presentable for work; Veritas came around to see what she was looking at. Banner touched a key on the pad and stepped back from the desk's large monitor. A picture came to life immediately. A smaller, high-altitude series of images of a group of youth in the middle of harvesting food on a farm appeared. A series of pictures rapidly passed across the screen, and Veritas knew that Banner would soon get to the last one—dated exactly seven days prior. As predicted, a slightly dark but clearly visible distant picture of Major Mare Sade Singh, clad in old-style military clothes, popped up. She was with a similarly dressed group of young men, women, and children. They were piling food at the edge of an old Pre-Fall city.

If only Banner and I were alone when we caught this. Damn.

"I liked it better when I thought she was dead. I've seen the commandant pissed before, but this was beyond," Banner said as she took another pass to adjust her clothes.

Veritas nodded in agreement and then closed her eyes as a way of trying to block out the memory of the scene that had developed when she broke the news of the discovery to Major Barnes and Commandant Roseann Pierce. Her boss's response was first shock, then anger—but it was Commandant Pierce's cold rage that had put them all on edge. It was an icy cold, closely contained flood of emotions that could break loose at any point.

Makes sense. You think your companion is dead. You search for nearly three years with no luck. Have children, life goes on. Then a ghost appears. I have no idea how I would feel. Pissed? Sad? Angry? Everything?

Veritas turned to see Banner reapplying her smudged lipstick. She sighed. She then came up close to Jill Banner and gave her a gentle kiss on the back of her neck. She pulled her into a hug from behind.

I'm sure if the same thing happened to you, I would respond the same as Pierce.

As the mere thought of losing Jill passed through her mind she felt her heart ache just as she felt Banner fall into her embrace. Their entire relationship, forged by keeping a joint secret about the true nature of their mission three years ago, had blossomed. Banner was slowly and gently moving her way into her life.

First the rehab visits. Bringing food to my home and doing housework. Even after I told you I actually preferred men, you were neither shocked nor judgmental. Now what did you say again about that? Oh, yeah—"Maybe you like both men and women, like before the Fall?" How adorable.

Just the memory alone provoked her to give Banner another kiss. She finally pulled away to fix her lover's collar.

"Just for the record, I'll never leave you," Veritas said as she swept lint off Banner's uniform and fixed her collar.

Banner touched her hand.

"Thank you. I needed to hear that."

"Why? You know that."

"Girly-girls like me need it."

"Oh."

Veritas took in a deep breath and stood herself up straight for a moment. It helped her prepare herself to deal with the troops.

"All right, Sergeant. Enough of this screwing around. Time to take first shift," Veritas said with a smile.

"Ma'am! Yes, ma'am," Banner responded. As was customary for military service, Banner immediately went to the door and held it open for her superior officer.

"Thank you," Veritas said. She continued to talk about the situation as they walked together to the Command and Control Room.

"With Major Barnes and Commandant Pierce in the field, I will need to have my lieutenants stationed to command the exterior sector gate doors. Redeploy second shift to cover some of the sentry positions while the APs remain offline."

"How long will the commandant keep the APs offline, ma'am? Without them, our human personnel are stretched. You can only remain at theta—heightened security—for so long. And three years is a pretty long time. Even Central Command lowered its alert level after six months. And the others…"

"Yes, Sergeant, I know. The other sectors did nothing except have their coffee, take their medication, and take the majority of our security team as the commandant went on her search-and-destroy missions. I know," Veritas said with a sigh.

She reached for the door handle. Two appeared in her vision suddenly. She grasped at the one on the left, which she was sure was real.

Why does that keep happening?

She was about to make light of it and smile, but when she turned around she saw that her sergeant did not find the mishap amusing.

"You might want to get your vision checked."

"Yes. Will do. Now, the good news here is that if the commandant does find what she's looking for, we might be able to get back to normal," Veritas continued. She allowed Banner to open the next security door—to the main control room. Two well-armed human soldiers posted at the door saluted.

"Did you pack enough supplies for three days? And maps?" Banner asked quietly as Veritas passed nearby.

"For five days. Plus I have a small, solar-powered, two-person, all-terrain vehicle prototype waiting at our first date site. We will be able to make a hundred kph," she whispered back.

"Excellent."

Banner's' response was in a hushed tone before changing back to her "official" voice.

"Officer on deck!" Banner yelled as she snapped to attention.

In a flash, every soldier in the room did the same. Veritas nodded and then saluted back, releasing them to return to their duties.

She walked to the center of the room, which was surrounded by banks of monitors. Veritas took in the floor-to-ceiling screens, which showed an image of a small brook separating two tree lines. Blue dots represented the advance task force; they surrounded two very tiny red dots that were obviously the enemy.

"Deck officer! Status report!" Veritas ordered.

A very attractive young cadet snapped to attention and approached Veritas with a tablet in hand.

"Deck Officer Bridgett is in the Drone Room, ma'am. She asked me to bring you up to speed as she anticipates being needed in the Drone Room once you hear the news."

Oh...just great. Singh is caught and Pierce has gotten it in her head that she had coconspirators. I guess Jill and I will be leaving now.

Veritas did her best to stand in a relaxed, casual position. She then turned to her left and caught Banner looking in her direction with narrowed eyes.

Are they registering anger or envy? She can't be angry about my vision and the door thing?

Veritas turned back to see that the young cadet had dropped her tablet's stylus and was kneeling with her back straight. Anyone standing above her could see her perfectly shaped breasts. Her braid was carefully positioned just at the side of her cleavage.

Really? You think with everything going on I would take an interest in this little creature? Jillian...

Veritas snatched the tablet from the woman's hand as she was starting to stand up. She began to read the words on the screen as she spoke.

"Cadet? Give me a verbal report after you button up. And move your braid behind you, please," Veritas said. As she waited she read the summary. After hearing the young woman clear her throat, she looked up briefly. The young cadet was trying to speak, but multiple shades of red flashed across her face.

"Yes, ma'am. Sorry, ma'am. To summarize: Scout Team Five has secured two targets. As you can see, one is a former Nemericana citizen, Major Mare Sade Singh. She was listed as KIA nearly three years ago. Another is a young male. Both were armed with Pre-Fall weapons. Major Singh was immobilized with a suppression dart. The young male offered no resistance; he dropped his weapon and went to her side. A key report indicates that he referred to Major Singh as his…"

The delay was obvious and Veritas was annoyed.

"Cadet? What's the issue?"

"I did validate and confirm the sit-rep, ma'am."

"Nice to know—what did it say?

"The key report indicates that the male referred to Major Singh as his mother…"

A sudden intake of air could be heard as the shock reverberated through the room.

"Calm yourself, people! We have a job to do! Are all the perimeters secured? Are there any more signs of the others? Are you patrolling to see if there are any humanoids or these phantom, Pre-Fall soldiers? When you have those answers, then you can start sighing! Until then, focus, people," Banner yelled out as she scanned the entire room.

A series of acknowledgments went up as the soldiers came to order.

"Sorry for the interruption, ma'am," Banner said. She stepped right behind the cadet, her eyes still narrowed.

Veritas looked back down at the tablet and flipped through various windows. Then she went back to the center of the room to look at sensor reports that were tracked by both satellites and drones. She turned the tablet so its infrared sensor would hit the monitor's receptacle, and the floor-to-ceiling immediately superimposed various images on the screens. Before she could even ask, the cadet continued with her status report.

"The small dots to the north will be in contact with our rear guard in nine minutes. Signals indicate that they are two APs moving rapidly via an old Pre-Fall diesel truck. The various dots spreading behind where Major Singh and the young male came from are gathering inside the woods but seem to be keeping at a distance. More appear to be coming in from the east. There are no AP signatures. Visual sightings indicate that it's a larger-than-average group of humanoids. Probably a collective gathering of hunting groups in the area—unrelated to the situation."

Looking closely at the largest mass of dots, Veritas shook her head. She shifted from one set of data points to another.

"No…that group is coming together. Slowly but surely," she said. It was easy for her to see that the groups were consolidating cluster of dots.

"Yes, ma'am. The scout team went in pursuit of two other young men. They have hidden in an area where the minerals are blocking out our signals. We have lost auditory contact at the moment," the cadet continued.

Veritas turned suddenly on the cadet. Anger was creeping up inside of her, but she stopped herself before she lashed out.

What!? A force of humanoids are massing behind a stand of trees as a set of APs approach from the north, and one team is incommunicado? Are you an idiot?

Images of her and Singh being attacked by APs jumped to her mind's inner eye.

"All right," Veritas said calmly, surprising herself in the process. "Contact field command and tell them that my opinion is that the humanoids are not 'just in the area hunting' and to remain vigilant. I recommend taking defensive positions with clean lines of fire focused on the tree line. They also need to get cover. The approaching APs should be considered hostile. Finally, in light of all of this, I would dispatch a search and rescue team to go after the squad that is MIA in that dark zone. Now," while calm, Veritas's voice was deliberate and clear so there would be no confusion about her orders.

Obviously nervous, the cadet nodded, saluted, and nearly ran to the communication officer. Still facing Banner, Veritas spoke first.

"This is not good. The group we are looking for is not there, but there are two APs coming in from the north and a group of humanoids gathering just out of sight of our force. If I didn't know better, I'd think there is something forming, like a bad storm."

"No, not at all. Humanoids collaborating with APs or the rogue group?

"Maybe."

Without breaking eye contact, Banner nodded.

"Ma'am? I just lost communications with Central Command," a young private said.

Another called out right after her, "Ma'am, this is not a glitch or an emergency test!"

By now Veritas's blurry vision say multiple people with multiple hands moving over her keyboards.

"Captain! I just lost primary and secondary communication with both the North and West Sectors. I mean everything, ma'am," another woman shouted out.

"What should we do to secure—" Banner started to say before an amber klaxon light went off above one of three landline phones, the same kind of phones that used to exist before the Fall. A byproduct of war and an artifact of Pre-Fall technology, the landline had the advantage of being a very reliable form of communication between command and control centers in each sector of Nemericana. Unaffected by the elements and with only minimal problems due to solar storms, the landlines between commands were considered a last resort—to be used only in case of disaster.

"Put all hands on full alert. Turn on all surveillance cameras on interior buffer walls between sectors. Redeploy teams to interior gates and prepare for refugees," Veritas said to Banner as she walked to the lighted phone. Rather than grabbing for the phone she thought was real, she swiped wide to hit both to make sure she got the right one. Once her hand was on top of it, her vision cleared up. There was not time to celebrate.

Now what the hell is going on?

The phone was heavier than she expected—she truly never wanted to be in a situation where she would need to pick up that phone to begin with. Veritas focused on the phone as she lifted the archaic device to her ear and mouth, all the while trying to drown out the noise Banner was making while she yelled out orders.

"This is Captain Pearl Veritas of Southeast Sector."

"This is Senior Commandant Tier! I am locked in the vault. Roseann was right! The APs have taken key military facilities, including central command and the control center. We heard from both North and West Sectors before they went dark! It's the APs! They've revolted…wait…wait a minute. They're coming through, Captain! Central Command Center will self-destruct in three minutes if I can't stop the timer. Both Commandants Baker and Regina are dead along with their command teams. I'm probably next. A number of Elders are outside the wall on a pilgrimage. We're not going to make it here, Captain. By the authority vested in me, "Theta Protocol" is reinstated. Battlefield promotions are as follows: you are now promoted to major. Major Barnes is promoted to colonel, and Commandant Roseann Pierce is promoted to acting senior commandant of Nemericana pending the Elders' ruling…"

Veritas yanked the phone away from her ear as a loud sound reverberated through the old-fashioned receiver. She couldn't understand why she was hearing shouts, shooting, and screams of anger and pain all around her until she realized that her entire conversation had been broadcast on the public announcement system for all to hear. Turning, she saw the drawn, blank faces of young women unused to the sounds of battle.

Damn it! Damn it! Damn it! This is war!!

"Wake up, people! Contact all officers on the walls—have them switch their troops from exterior walls to interior gates," Veritas yelled. Exterior cameras showed her troops already moving into place. A sudden surge of citizens from other sectors was already forming at the gates, and she was pleased to see that the civilians were being allowed in. Her soldiers were obviously shooting at whoever was chasing them. As her command team jumped into action, Veritas issued orders.

"Banner! Are all our APs offline?"

"Yes, ma'am! The only ones online are minimal service APs…"

"Shut them down! I don't want a single one of them on! Communications officer? Get me Commandant Pierce! Master of Arms, take a fire team and make sure this command center is secured! Cadet, review the last transmission from Commandant Tier. Write down her words and make a copy of the audio. Give it to the communications officer to forward to the field, log it for the record, and archive it! Have Lieutenant Mitchell dispatch a set of drones over Central Command; leave the others for assessment. Mobilize aerial and mechanized supports—all bases scrambled. We are at theta! We are the last fire line, people! The last line of defense of Nemericana! We are the last line of communication and central command! We need to pull this together if we are to stand a chance against this…this revolt!"

Veritas heard shouts of affirmation coming from all around her. She felt her mag-rifle being placed in her hand by Banner as she secured her own military vest for battle.

"I guess the good news is we won't have to go over the wall if the commandant finds out. That solar all-terrain vehicle is still looking awfully good, though for other reasons," she said.

Veritas was deep into her own inspection of her vest and checked her own rifle to make sure it was set to full automatic.

"Yup. Nothing like a series of disasters to change your point of view. Stay by my side, Sergeant. I am the only ranking officer still in command, and this is war," Veritas said. She punctuated the moment with securing her own security vest and began to check her sidearm as well.

"I'll never leave you," Banner said. And with that she "accidentally" bumped into her superior officer. Smiling for a brief moment, Veritas reflected for just a second that Commandant Pierce had been right to be at theta and to take the APs offline.

By the Elders…they're all dead? Tier? Baker and Regina? Their command officers, too?

"Ma'am! Images from drone seven fly-bys of the Central Command Center, two miles out…ma'am…it's…" the young cadet stopped talking, as did everyone. They all focused on a series of explosions methodically discharging from east to west in brilliant yellows, oranges, and reds. With no sound at that distance, the drone's long-range camera captured the silent self-destruction of Central Command.

"All tactical and strategic data for all sectors are now gone," Veritas said quietly.

She, like everyone else, watched the carnage in horror. Buildings surrounding the central complex were gone as well.

"No time, people! I need a skeleton crew for Command and complete security on the Drone Room and the underground auxiliary command center. Now!" Banner belted out.

Veritas assisted her and started to push people around and point them in the right direction.

Thank you, Jill.

"All right," Veritas said to herself as she walked to the communication center panels. She found the emergency public broadcast setting that would make its way to every monitor and S-phone in the entire Southeast Sector. Anything that had a screen would hear her next words.

"Citizens of Nemericana, Southeast Sector: Central Command and the North and West Sectors have been breached by artificial persons that have gone rogue. They have seized key areas, and Senior Commandant Tier has destroyed her capitol building and herself to ensure that key elements do not fall into our enemy's hands. We are the only sector that has not been compromised. Even as we speak, refugees from the other sectors are being allowed through our internal gates. All citizens, prepare to take in all refugees. Begin rationing supplies and arm yourselves. All retired military and law enforcement citizens are to report to your nearest internal sector gate for conscription and deployment. Repeat. All citizens are to arm themselves and begin rationing supplies, food, and water. All retired military and law enforcement citizens report to your nearest internal sector gate. Captain Pearl Veritas, out."

Veritas turned the public announcement system off, then turned to see that her front-line staff was well armed and moving to their respective duties. Nodding approvingly, she turned to her right only to find Banner, her lover, giving the cadet that had flirted with her earlier instructions on how to put her sidearm on safety and then pointed to the top button of her uniform. The cadet closed it up to her neck.

Really? You're giving her shit about that? Now?

CHAPTER SEVEN

I do perceive here a divided duty.
  —Shakespeare, *Othello*

"I know you're not happy with my decision, Corporal. And while your logic, reason, and clarity are worthy of merit, I am not willing to risk any of my personnel—especially military assets—to rescue one woman and three cadets. Sadly, I need to triage them as lower on the totem pole. If I lose you, or Emma, or any of you, who will replace your skill set, experience, and training? Who will support Epsilon Platoon and its citizens? Your lifespan should exceed mine and give hope a fighting chance to live on," Melendez said.

In response, all four APs—Corporal Mabel and Privates Emma, Rebecca, and Danielle—remained still. They were clutching their rifles and had gear stowed on their backs, clearly ready for a rescue mission. Their eyes pulsated, trying to compute. Melendez knew that the moral dilemma that he had given them would have been difficult for anyone to comprehend—human or artificial person.

"It just does not seem right," Private Danielle said.

Looking at her, and then at all of them standing there in a row, Melendez felt both sad and proud at the same time.

He stepped in front of her to close the gap between them before he spoke quietly.

"I know, Private. I also know that you are responding from an emotional position and with an ethical point of view. However, this is about logic. Trust me. My decision is not easy. The irony is not lost on me that it's now the human who is behaving in a logical, utilitarian, pragmatic manner."

"But, sir? We cannot just let them die out there…" Private Emma started suddenly and then broke off. In a near-human manner, Corporal Mabel looked at her as if she were surprised or almost at a loss for words. Private Emma suddenly looked down. After a brief moment, she looked up again and stood at attention.

"Sir? Request permission to shut down. I find my logic centers distressed, my judgment skewed, and my voluntary verbal response acting in a reflexive manner that is making me unpredictable. I fear I may be unreliable as I am questioning your orders, sir. A significant deviation from the chain of command," Private Emma finished. Her eyes pulsated slightly faster than the others.

Nodding his head, Melendez smiled as he spoke.

"Negative, Private Emma. You're functioning correctly. Your response is normal in view of this no-win scenario. Our lack of action may result in three children and an adult being harmed as we dig in. You're not a toaster, Private. You're a soldier who thinks. You don't just follow orders. Review historical references to 'just following orders' in the Nuremberg Trials, nineteen forty-five. That legal recourse did not serve the Nazi war criminals well as their defense. Now, take your stations and assist the cadets with the instruments and monitors. Clear?"

"Crystal clear, sir," all four APs responded at the same time.

Corporal Mabel stepped off the line first to issue her assignments:

"Private Emma: monitor potential enemy transmissions at likely bandwidths. Get creative in breaking into their solar-phone network and make sure Cadet Bradley knows what you are doing so he can learn from it. Private Danielle: take Cadet Margaret and focus on motion detection at ground level. See if you can join forces and share ideas with Private Rebecca—she works on radar. Move it out, people! We don't get paid by the hour!"

"Yes, Corporal!" they responded and then broke off with their respective cadet groups in the small control room.

Hmm. Cadets Bradley and Margaret on the same shift? I guess these two kids are getting this parenthood thing and working things out, Melendez thought. He noticed that Eva's teenage parents were maturing into adults.

"Sir? May I ask how you are able to reference historical events that support your argument and at the same have an emotional effect when you remain seemingly calm and devoid of emotion?" Corporal Mabel asked.

Ah, yes. Just like Corporal Kristine and Sergeant Joan. Always asking the right questions at the right time.

"Easy. Serve in the Air Force and Marines in one lifetime, remain in cryogenic sleep with a billion gigs of all kinds of information plugged into your brain for about a hundred and thirty years and then be discovered by cybernetic lifeforms that do not suffer from a neurological disorder that falls on the autism spectrum like I do and then you have your answer."

As he spoke he had taken his hat off and scratched the dry skin that had long since begun to circle the majority of his metal electrodes.

After three rapid eye pulses, Corporal Mabel responded quickly.

"Yes. It does make a great deal of sense. Thank you, sir."

"You're welcome. Carry on."

Corporal Mabel saluted and walked away just as Private Emma approached with obvious determination.

For the love of God. Am I going to have to run for it?

"Sir? Sergeant Joan broke radio silence to allow Civilian Taylor to speak with you on the land line. She's giving you a closed-circuit phone for one minute. She insists that he has an important revelation, sir."

"Taylor? Our resident historian and scribe has something mission critical? Well, you learn something every day," he said as a clear image of the thin, gaunt, eleven-year-old artist formed in his head.

The same young boy who asked to be a cadet when he was seven years old.

"You are absolutely right, sir. I am learning something every day," Emma responded.

Melendez could swear he heard a tone of reflection and insight.

Picking up the telephone, he was flooded with warm memories of the weight, feel, and ergonomics of the old-style phones. He took in a breath and began to speak.

Another life, when there were "house phones" and families stayed home and ate at a kitchen table and watched television.

"Taylor? What's so important that Sergeant Joan believed it is worth breaching protocol?"

A weak, preadolescent voice came from the other end, only reinforcing his mental image of the small youth on the other end of the line.

But of all of us, he's probably the brightest and smartest.

"Yes, sir. Sorry. But the dreams Emma, Rebecca, and Danielle have been having? When I asked them about it, they said many were the same. Same images, same visions and smells. All three are having the same dreams. The only ones that were not the same were the bizarre ones. But the ones that made some sense were pretty much the same," Taylor said.

Confused and baffled, Melendez struggled to focus but was driven by his own curiosity.

"Taylor? What does it matter if they are having the same dreams? Maybe they have the same dreams as a result of the same logarithms and brain development, or maybe…"

"Sir? Or maybe they're not dreams, but some kind of communication. Like the time Sergeant Joan got the coordinates of when and where the cast-outs were going to be. They came to her as images, just like dreams do. Maybe the reason the newer APs got smart so fast is because the mainframe they came from got smart too and is connected to us. Maybe we are now able to see what they see, just like they communicated with us? Two ways, sir. They talk to us and we listen. Maybe we're listening even though they aren't talking."

Silent, Melendez thought about how simple an idea it was.

Maybe Taylor's right. Maybe it's not neurogenesis but rather eavesdropping on the other APs or their central computer?

"Taylor! If you were a cadet, I'd promote you to private!"

"Thank you, sir. But I'm glad to be the platoon's historian. Much more interesting. At some point I have to ask you about your protein solution for cryogenesis, but that's for later," Taylor said.

"Will do. Thank you, Taylor. This data is mission critical."

"No problem, sir. Good luck."

Melendez hung up the phone and motioned Emma closer so as to make sure he could hear every word and see every nuance she made.

"Private Emma? Taylor tells me that you and Privates Danielle and Rebecca have had similar dreams. Is that accurate?"

"Almost accurate, sir. We have had the same dream, not just 'similar' dreams, sir," she clarified.

"Based on your interaction and memories, what dreams do you remember all three of you having? The reason I ask this is because Taylor just proposed a theory. He says that maybe these dreams are more like after-images from communications from the other APs or the AP computer mainframe."

Emma remained still, but her eyes pulsated rapidly. He counted internally the time it took her to respond—a full minute and a half passed before she spoke.

"Sir, if I omit the majority of these images—the ones that combine impossible scenarios, such as cats talking to the color blue, two suns burning in the sky as a flock of eagles speak French or the recurring images of Private Rebecca and I giving birth to twins—there are a finite number of images that could be perceived as 'informational.' They make sense once they are put in the context of communication with other cybernetic lifeforms. Barring the illogical images, if these are transmissions of a sort, then there are some extraordinary events that are happening or are about to happen," she said in an almost trance-like state.

Emma and Rebecca giving birth? Okay, I'll ask about that later.

"Clarify," was his short request.

"The consistent, nonbizarre dreams go as follows: One. Visions of various schematic diagrams of Nemericana's various sectors' AP manufacturing plants, the AP computer mainframe facility, biological companies, old underground bunkers, and military/law enforcement buildings for munitions and materiel. Two. Maps—topological and street—as well as actual views of these same areas at dawn, throughout the day, and well into the evening are also there. These visions seem so real that they include smells and sounds. Three. All schematic diagrams, plans, and maps target West and North Sectors thoroughly. The Central Sector is also mapped out but to a lesser degree. The Southeast Sector appears devoid of data. Four. Various sensations, visions especially, of underground encampments, but not in Nemericana. These are both intense and vivid. There is an expansive variety of underground living quarters that sit below Pre-Fall cities, similar to a maze. The inhabitants are similar to the ones we coexist with to our east. An equal number of males and females, armed with bows, arrows, knives, and lances. Few children. All appear to have a gene for red hair with the exception of a few of...of... Nemericana cast-outs. They appear as part of the tribe. They are dressed similarly and are well nourished."

The children from Nemericana we didn't get to. They were taken in by these people? Thank God, Melendez thought.

"Five. Various images of Pre-Fall nuclear missile sites. All disabled but one, whose location is within the northern Rocky Mountains. Land-based, intercontinental ballistic missiles, Minuteman III variant. All three of us had clear visions of six in preparation and one is...is ready to fire," Emma continued in an emotionless fashion.

Melendez felt his throat go dry. The muscles on his face contorted as tension mounted in his head. He paced and looked around the small control room. He wondered if anyone other than he knew the ramifications of what seven nuclear weapons with multiple warheads would mean for the planet. Although they were busy with their duties, he knew that Corporals Mabel, Danielle, and Rebecca could pick up every word uttered in the control room.

Jesus, Mary, and Joseph...and all the saints

"Sir? There is a disturbing vision that we had all missed," Emma reported. She seemed to be refocusing on the present.

Melendez's eyes widened in disbelief. He was astonished that there could be something even more disturbing than operational nuclear weapons. In an effort to appear less worried, he focused on keeping his voice steady.

"And what would that be, Private Emma?"

"I see various images of landscapes in our immediate area. The information on their mineral composition, typology, and the environment around our bases and proximity to the Pre-Fall city are exquisitely detailed. Especially as concerns local farming efforts and the nature of our base's walls—the fact that they're nuclear-proof as well as electromagnetic-pulse-resistant. In addition to the images of our farming efforts, there are repeated, clear visions of us leaving part of our harvest for the humanoids in the Pre-Fall city…as if we both were watched at various times of the day and throughout several seasons…"

"Hold," Melendez said as he put his hand up to stop Emma's report. While walking in tight circles, he posed his next series of questions.

"If these are actual images from either the APs themselves or their central computer mainframe, and they are all real, why would the APs activate a nuclear weapon?"

"Unknown. I do not think it would make sense for them to assist us in finding the cast-out children and to allow us to take them away to safety only to destroy us with a nuclear weapon."

"The first images you focused on pertained to Nemericana sectors as well as targets that might be important to the APs, such as their manufacturing plants and computer mainframe building. I doubt they would nuke that…wait a minute. All the sectors of Nemericana were detailed and mapped out but one, right?"

"Yes. The Southeast Sector was not well mapped out at all. I am of the firm belief that it is this sector alone that has shut itself off from all AP access. Nearly all of the APs there must be offline, Sir."

"And the images of our location also included data points on the nature of this underground, nuclear-proof bunker and its proximity to the city, correct?"

"Yes. Further, there were old underground bunkers that were highlighted in all Nemericana sectors but the Southeast," she said slowly as she processed more thoughts.

Melendez watched Emma processing the data rapidly; she soon came to another, similar conclusion.

"Yes. If the nuclear weapon were to be used, it is not likely that we would be the target. Its effects would be most damaging to the very Pre-Fall inhabitants that these APs seem to want to protect as they have cast-outs. Further, little would be gained by testing a nuclear blast if this base and Holy Mary are nuclear-proof. At the same time, firing on Nemericana positions would adversely affect any military advantages as they are located in the same place. Except for Southeast Sector, where…"

"No APs are active. Where all APs were shut down and probably all the AP resources as well. And the other sectors have underground bunkers that might be able to shield a blast, but they would probably not be very effective in limiting the effects of an electromagnetic pulse—an EMP," he finished. Allowing the silence to sit, Melendez stopped his pacing. It only took Private Emma a moment to form her own tactical conclusion.

"We are not the target, sir. At least not the target of a nuclear strike. There is a significantly higher probability that it's either the Southeast Sector's population or the Southeast Sector's military assets. A nuclear blast from the yield of an intercontinental ballistic missile would create profound havoc if detonated either for the actual destructive blast or for the EMP pulse near the Southeast Sector…"

"But?" Melendez said as he closed his eyes. He hoped that either he made a faulty conclusion or he was simply just wrong.

"But an EMP burst two hundred miles up in the atmosphere above our location would not only negate all present-day modern electronics and render them useless, it would nullify all computer, solar, and electronic devices in the most northeastern part of the Southeast Sector. Solid state components, vacuum tubes, and possibly transistor-driven devices that are battery operated would be exceptions. For that to happen, exact placement of the detonation would be required. It would have a minimal effect on us, especially if we remain in these fortifications, but it could devastate all Nemericana systems within its blast radius. It could even, possibly, affect only the Southeast Sector and leave the other sectors unaffected since they would be farther away from the blast. The Nemericana APs could remain safe by temporarily relocating to the underground bunkers in those sectors that are closest to the Southeast...genius, sir. Dangerously genius," Emma reported with what could only be described as admiration in her voice.

"And will the EMP affect you and other APs?" Melendez asked.

That would be real bad. I can't lose you or the others.

"I believe yes. We have a number of solid-state components, but we have many more processors that are very sensitive to electromagnetic and electrical pulses. However, if we remain here, underground, we should be fine."

"As would the other APs beyond the blast radius of the EMP burst. If there are APs in the Southeast Sector and they are offline, I bet they will be unaffected. And since Nemericana is a pretty big place, I'm guessing if they detonate the blast here, that sector alone will be affected. That leaves the other sectors unscathed. 'Genius' doesn't do that planning any justice. 'Diabolical' is a better word," Melendez said. He firmly believed they were not the target, but rather the Southeast Sector—that was the prize.

"Corporal Mabel? You heard all of this speculation?" Melendez yelled out.

"Yes, sir! I agree with the logic, sir. I was hoping you would find a flaw in it, but your logic seems to carry the day. We are not as screwed as Southeast Sector. But is the 'enemy of my enemy my friend' here, sir? Should we somehow warn these women, when it has been the Nemericana APs that have helped us save the children? Even if this Aurora AP is diabolical, is she wrong?" Mabel asked as she came to a stop in front of him.

Looking first at Corporal Mabel and then back at Emma, Melendez became disturbed. Another troublesome thought occurred to him—one more concerning even than the one presented by his corporal.

"We'll get to them later. Quickly—if an EMP blast were to occur in two minutes, and we were not here but exposed outside, what would you recommend to ensure that you and other equipment were not affected?" he asked urgently.

It took a very long ten seconds for the expected response to emerge. It was easy to see that, while Emma seemed to have the answer ready first, she allowed the corporal to answer.

"I would shut down all APs and equipment immediately, and leave them in shutdown for a minimum of three hours to ensure all electromagnetic propagation and residual effects had dispersed. I would then turn on less-sensitive machinery first to see if it was negatively affected, then turn on other, more complex machinery. I would then wait twelve hours and send one AP outside the base to see if there is a risk of shutdown, sir," Corporal Mabel reported.

"Sir! I have no intentions of shutting down during this crisis," Private Emma blurted out.

Corporal Mabel quickly turned to face her but then seemed to reconsider responding and gave her own opinion to Melendez instead.

"Lieutenant? Shutting down your soldiers during this crisis is not...not logical. We are in a nuclear-proof bunker. We will likely not be affected by an EMP—" Mabel started. Melendez interrupted her.

"The key phrase there is 'likely not.' And if that's not right? I lose my only defense against Nemericana armed forces and rogue APs. I lose Epsilon Platoon—the only protection for the children we saved. Mabel? Emma? Is that risk in the long run really worth taking? If thirty cadets can hold military positions within a locked bunker for sixteen hours just to make sure we don't lose our entire fighting force for the future, doesn't that make more sense?" he said with a smile.

Silence fell in the room. Then the cadets began speaking in hushed tones.

Yup. Now they're listening, too.

"I do not care for your logic, Sir. If I were human, I would utilize tears or other methods to manipulate you," Private Emma said with her eyes narrowed.

Other methods? Yup! I'll have you shut down first. Still, that's an interesting form of insubordination. And Corporal Mabel...

Melendez's own eyes widened at the near-human response he was witnessing and its unpredictable nature. He noted that his corporal had been unusually quiet after Private Emma's response.

"Corporal? Do you have anything to say?"

"No, sir. I wish that Private Emma was human so she could implement the strategies of using emotional manipulation, tears, and sex as a way of convincing you otherwise. As logic seems to be the only thing that sways your thinking, however, I am attempting to research every gig of military history, jurisprudence, and logic I can access to find fault with either your thinking or your commands," she reported.

"Anything short of mutiny?"

"Yes."

"So you are in favor of not taking the logical approach and actually agree with Private Emma's...emotional response?" Melendez asked as his smile broadened.

"Sadly, yes. Yes, I do agree. But by default, however, that makes both your logic and command decisions the best choices. Unfortunately." The reluctance in her voice was unmistakable.

Well...that's a first. Mabel sees that Emma's approach holds merit and she once again disagrees with my ideas but can't fight my logic. It's been quite a day...and the day is still young.

"Corporal? Contact Sergeant Joan and let her know the plan. You have one minute to transmit it. After that, I will be on the public announcement system to get the cadets briefed. Twenty minutes after that, I want all APs offline. We do this right, we save you to fight another day."

Melendez stood at attention and saluted.

Both APs snapped to attention and acknowledged his command in perfect unison.

"Sir! Yes, sir!"

CHAPTER EIGHT

You may my glories and my state depose,
But not my griefs, still I am king of those.
—Shakespeare, *Richard II*

Singh felt as if she were fighting her way out of a bad dream. Cool air and the sound of water confused her with their lure of calm. And yet she felt she was in danger.

No, not me...Roberto! Where are you?

She took in a gulp of air. She felt almost as if she had been submerged under water. Her eyes snapped open on a sight she had hoped never to see. She was being held up between two Nemericana advance specialist scouts, and she could feel that her hands were bound behind her back. Looking to her left and right, she saw squads of female soldiers in various types of coverage containing the perimeter. Two other soldiers held her son, also bound, in place. Her close inspection revealed that he was unharmed but confused.

She scanned the area looking for any obvious means of escape and she saw that there was none. They were prisoners. There were well over thirty highly trained soldiers around. She could easily identify the commander in charge in the distance—a major—who was directing activity on both the ground and the air.

Why the hell are they out this far? You'd think searching for a rogue group for three years would be at the bottom of the to-do list. Unless there's another motivation.

A three-seat VTOL scout aircraft descend swiftly, landed briefly to drop off someone, then lifted right back up in the air—ostensibly to provide additional aerial fire power. She her eyes to adapt for the distance and to clear the brief debris the rotors stirred up. Singh watched the short woman who had just exited the aircraft. Her heart jumped. She immediately recognized who was approaching her by the person's gait, stance and overall imperious manner. Her presence alone was commanding, and even though saluting a superior officer on the battlefield was not allowed, she could see the major and all the other soldiers stood at a sort of attention. Even before the new arrival removed her visored helmet, Singh could tell that it was her former commanding officer and companion who was now within twenty feet of her.

This is bad. Very, very bad!

When she got to about five feet away, Commandant Roseann Pierce of the Southeast Sector took off her helmet and casually handed it to a waiting lieutenant. Singh tried to avoid making visual contact with Pierce's own striking blue eyes. Pierce adjusted both her gloves, her sidearm, and then her combat knife. It seemed to her as if their reunion might be wordless and professional. Then, without further pause or greeting, Pierce stepped forward and slapped Singh across the face.

It was to be expected—the ceremonial strike of betrayal. Often the strike was out of heated emotion. This one, if possible, was strong, technically perfect but seemed devoid of passion and anger.

"Just so you know, I did not tell Verna that I found you. She will never know of this, nor of your real death," she said.

Two lieutenants appeared behind her. Pierce turned to take a computer tablet from one of them who looked very uncomfortable with the whole interaction. Pierce began to read from the screen and did not look up.

Singh watched her former paramour as she attempted to clear her thoughts. She wanted to let the sharp pain from the slap subside before she opened her mouth to speak.

She must be so angry at me. She must hate me.

A flash of curiosity struck her. She wondered what it would be like if it was Verna that had found her and threw her own ceremonial strike. She was pretty sure she would never find out.

"Before I kill you for desertion and aiding the enemy, I want you to know that your betrayal to your country, oath, and to me will die right here and right now. At least Verna will have memories of a caring companion, and she'll go on believing that you were KIA several years ago. It's the least I can do for her," Pierce said while she reviewed various reports on the tablet.

Singh could tell she was obviously working to make her tone sound casual, but her voice was filled with emotion.

"Before you die, I just want to let you know that Verna and I had twins nine months ago, Marta and June. It was the happiest day of my life, and I wanted to share it with you…" she said.

Then something in the report caught her attention. After a moment, she looked up at Roberto and handed the tablet back to a distressed-looking lieutenant. Before letting the computer go, however, she asked the lieutenant one question that confused Singh.

"Is it true? Are you sure you heard right, Lieutenant?"

"Yes, ma'am."

"If this is an error…"

"I swear."

Pierce flashed a look at the other officer. She did not wait to be asked.

"Yes, ma'am! There was no mistake. I compared findings with others on my team just to make sure, ma'am!"

What? What is she talking about? What was said?

Singh tried to appear stoic so as to brace herself for death. The question of what was said to her former companion was troubling her, though, as well as her fear of what would happen to Roberto.

Pierce took a deep breath then let go of the tablet and walked slowly over to Roberto, who was standing with his legs slightly apart. If his hands hadn't been bound behind his back, he would have seemed to be in a military "at ease" stance. Pierce moved to stand within three feet of him. Singh's heart raced and sweat exploded on her forehead as she squelched a scream in her throat.

Say nothing, Roberto. She doesn't know who you are. Say nothing...

"Name and rank, soldier," Pierce demanded.

"Singh, Roberto! Cadet, Epsilon Platoon. United States Marine Corps," he said as he snapped to attention.

No, no, no...

Singh's heart continued to race and sweat now poured down her face and arms. Terrified, she watched to see what would happen next. The water from the brook was still audible and the sounds of aircraft approaching and receding were the only things that could be heard for a moment. Her former companion stood still a moment, then Singh was relieved to see her finally move away from him and turn around as if to think about something. Looking away to avoid eye contact with Pierce, Singh waited for her to reengage.

Maybe she'll just kill me. That will be difficult for Roberto to watch, but I'd rather him see that than have him hurt. Maybe I can negotiate?

Rousing herself from her thoughts, Singh found herself confronted by an unrecognizable woman. Pierce was emotionally laden and clearly angry.

"You left us because of *him*? He's a male! He's part of the species that destroyed…"

"He's my son, Roseann! Just like Marta and June are your flesh and blood! If they had been boys, would you have taken the cowardly way out and aborted them? Would you have somehow convinced yourself that they were anything less than human!?"

"My girls are not part of their species!"

"They are still your children and Roberto is my child!"

"Silence! You will not talk to me in that tone, Mare! I have a responsibility greater than you could possibly fathom. To continue our way of life! Our species…"

"And how is that working for you, Roseann? How's the medication three times a day? How's the promotion through ranks by political and sexual favors working for Nemericana these days!?"

Singh closed her eyes just as Pierce gave her another back-handed strike across her face. This struck was deeply emotional, nothing ceremonial at all. She heard Pierce's breathing become heavy. Silence fell again, and she opened her eyes to see Pierce still looking at her. She was seething with anger, sadness, or both.

"They were going to cast my son out. My only child. I was separated from him for his entire life, and you were going to send him out to die. I could not let that happen. Is that the kind of person you thought I was? A mother who would casually stand by and let her child be cast out? Cast out without his mother's protection? Is that what you would do?" Singh asked, more as a rhetorical question than one she expected an answer to.

Pierce turned her back, then pivoted back around and took a step forward.

"You could have come to me, Mare," Pierce said quietly.

Singh shook her head. She knew Pierce would not like her forthcoming response.

"For what? For you to say that it was the law? For you to remind me of a ritual from Pre-Fall? Something that occurred a hundred and fifty years ago? I was not going to give you an opportunity to say that. I would have hated you for it. I did not want to hate you."

The words fell out of her mouth faster that she wanted. She tried to focus what she wanted to say. The effect on Pierce was visible, however. Her former companion's shoulders seemed to dip and her eyes narrowed as if she were keeping dust out.

"He's my son. Nothing changes that. You would have done everything in your power to send him off and keep me from him. Not because you hate me, but because you..." Singh stopped herself. She felt guilt and pain, and her stomach heaved as memories of her last night with Roseann and Verna surfaced. She had been particularly struck by Roseann's gentleness. Then, Singh left that world behind to be with her son.

It was quiet again except for the receding and approaching aircraft. It was in that moment that Singh remembered that she was not alone with Roberto and Roseann. There were multiple eyes, soldiers, all witnessing the melodrama erupt from their supreme commander and her former companion.

Movement from behind Pierce brought the harsh reality of the situation back to the present.

"Commandant? The situation back home is getting worse," the major said from behind her. The major was taller than Singh, not as attractive as anyone there but her face was etched with wrinkles and stories that were as unattractive as there were many. The major was all business. She hung up her S-phone and looked up from her own mountain of computer tablets.

Situation at home? What's happening now?

"Speak," Pierce said, whirling around again. Her back faced Singh and Roberto.

The major looked up from the multiple reports and spoke in a calm fashion.

"Captain Veritas dispatched that all sectors but ours are under attack from APs. She has shifted resources from external gates to internal gates between sectors to provide respite and supplies to combat the attack. She is concerned that because our sector is the only one that had all APs offline, we alone might be the last sector standing unless drastic actions are taken."

"Are all out points of entries and conscription mobilized?"

"Yes; our sector is secured and all citizens from other sectors are being pulled in to our base and she is redeploying other sector's soldiers to hold positions to provide safe passage and heighted security."

"Captain Veritas is all over this," Pierce said.

"Yes, ma'am."

Pearl? Pearl Veritas is alive? Thanks to the Elders.

She remembered how Aurora and her APs had immediately subdued them both the night they escaped and then hurt Pearl just enough to make it look "convincing" that she had been attacked. Singh was happy that Veritas was alive. But the news of her former home, Southeast Sector, being under attack was still hard to hear.

Especially when you see it coming. I could have told Roseann. I hope Verna and Austin are safe.

Turning around to face her again, Pierce asked Singh an unexpected question.

"Do you know anything about this attack?"

Her major and the troops all turned to look at her.

"I don't know…I don't know of any planned attacks or specifics, but I might know something about what you might be dealing with. And if it is what I'm thinking, you are going to want to know this," Singh said as she formulated a plan that would at least free her son.

Without another word the major casually took her sidearm out and walked over to Roberto. She stood in front of the boy, placed the muzzle of her weapon to Roberto's head and cocked the hammer back, ready to shoot.

Her son stood even taller and looked down the barrel of the gun. Defiance grabbed him as he pushed his forehead into the muzzle. Singh wanted to throw up. All the moisture was gone from her mouth, her stomach was in knots, her heart raced, and the blood drained from her face. She was silent. She feared that one wrong word could cause the major to pull the trigger and kill her son.

Every pair of eyes, even the ones who were suppose to be watching the perimeter froze in awe. Whether it was the major's intent to kill the boy or the boy's oppositional act of not being intimidated, she was not sure.

"Look, traitor. Tell me everything right now or I will kill your…your *son*," the major said with disgust.

Singh could easily see that the major was both a soldier and a ruthless leader who feared her home coming under attack. She was still having difficulty with moisture in her throat and she stood frozen, focused on forming her next sentence. She knew that it would either save or kill her only child. The calm voice that came from her shell surprised her. Singh listened to her seemingly disembodied voice as if she were witnessing this scene as a third party rather than Roberto's mother.

I'm still a soldier. Kill him, and I will let you all die!

"Major. If you harm my son, you will learn absolutely nothing from me. I will tell you lies, mistruths, and anything you want to hear. But it will be nothing that will keep your family or your world safe. If you harm him, you will have no leverage to make me talk. And when you are killed by what awaits you when you return home, I will find you in hell and kill you a million times again. For eternity," Singh said in a hollow, lifeless tone.

There was still no sound but the bubbling of water was now audible and the buzzing of aircraft faded in the background. There was no emotion on the major's face to betray what her next step might be.

"Major, stand down and move aside," Pierce said.

Singh was amazed at how at ease Pierce was speaking, almost as casually as one might ask for a beverage.

Without breaking eye contact, the major lowered her weapon away from Roberto's face. She released the sidearm's hammer manually and then placed it back in her holster. For his part, Roberto never backed away. Before Singh could take in a breath of air, Pierce moved to block her view of the major and Roberto so as to have her total attention. She spoke quietly.

"I will make this one deal with you. I will set your son free if you tell me all that you know. After that, and once I have confirmation that the intelligence you have given me is useful, I will execute you swiftly. You are to tell your son that he is to leave now and that you will follow—or say anything you want to convince him to flee. If I find you have deceived me again, I will find your son and all others like him, and kill them myself. In front of you. Am I perfectly clear?" Pierce said.

Singh could tell by looking at Pierce that she was telling her exactly what she would do.

"I understand," Singh said. Fear for her son still prevailed.

"Be convincing and brief, Mare. I do not have patience for this family matter, and I have duties to perform," Pierce warned.

"Yes. I will," she responded. It took her mere seconds to put on a game face to deal with her son.

Without another word, Pierce stepped out of her line of vision and issued orders.

"Lieutenants! Release the prisoners. Be quick about this," she added as she took another computer tablet from another soldier and waved the confused major over to one side.

Singh felt the bindings fall away from her wrists and the circulation return. She was surprised at how quickly Roberto made it to her side.

"Are you all right? Why did they let us go?"

"I struck a deal with the commandant. I agreed to return to Nemericana to face charges and help them out with what's happening if they let you go. If you stay, they will kill us both right now. If I return, you go free and I have a chance to live. Either way, it's a better deal than what almost happened," Singh said in what she hoped sounded like a cheery and relieved manner.

"I'm not going to leave you," Roberto said resolutely.

"Then we both die right now. There will be no warning given to our friends and no hope for me to escape. Is that what you want? To end it now without a chance?" Singh said.

She watched her son stop and process the scenario.

"Being a soldier, a leader, means making the hard decisions. These decisions should be based on mission priority. Your mission is to retrieve data and alert the platoon. That's it. All other priorities are secondary regardless of who is at risk. Crystal?"

Singh was relieved to see that he had inherited her battlefield assessment skills. He ostensibly arrived at the conclusion that it was a no-win situation.

"Crystal." His tone and voice was shallow.

Please believe this bullshit so you can get the hell out of here before Roseann gets pissed.

"Now get going, Roberto," she said as she gave him a quick kiss on the forehead and turned him with both her hands to head northeast, back toward the encampment. As he walked slowly away, it was easy to see that her son was bothered by leaving her in a bad situation. With her hands, she made a shooing motion to get him on his way.

Come on, Roberto. Get out of here! This could all change in seconds if you don't move.

She made sure to break eye contact first. She turned and walked very slowly and cautiously toward Pierce and the major. She resisted her impulse to turn around and make sure Roberto had left. She stopped by one of Pierce's guards, who had watched the whole drama play out.

"Lieutenant? Is he leaving?" Singh asked. She hoped that the soldier would have mercy on her and answer this one, simple question. Hesitant at first, the young officer looked beyond Singh and then answered.

"He is making very good speed into the tree line and will be obscured in just a moment," the young woman answered.

Feeling her eyes well up, Singh barely managed to croak out a "thank you." The woman nodded in response but maintained her watch over Singh and the commanding officers. Singh waited. Pierce and her senior soldiers were conferring about the perimeter and status reports from back home. She was relieved to have so much time elapse so Roberto could put distance between them before she told Pierce everything. After ten very long minutes, Pierce nodded to a group of junior soldiers, then she and the major returned to begin the interrogation.

"What do you know?" the major hissed out, clearly annoyed that she had not been allowed to execute Singh's son.

Refusing to make eye contact with her, Singh addressed Pierce as if it had been she who asked the question.

"You are dealing with a new type of cybernetic lifeform, one capable of independent thought. They have their own military objectives. I met their leader, Aurora, and she demonstrates both clarity of mission and a ruthless efficiency. She and her APs ambushed both me and Captain Veritas, even though we thought we had them in our sights. Not only did she and the others dispatch us with zeal, they covertly positioned themselves so that they could get to where they were going, meet their own objectives and then disappeared. They left me about one hundred sixty miles away from the closest gate."

"Do you want to tell me something I *don't* know?" the major said. The soldier did little at disguising her disgust.

"Before we were ambushed, it became clear to me that there had been consistent errors logged in military inventory. There was enough material and ordinance missing to arm a battalion. I notified my equals in the other sectors of these errors, but they were not considered important," Singh lied. She hoped that they would not be able to follow up on the fib about telling her peers.

"I told them! Damn it all! They just wouldn't believe me," Pierce said in anger.

Making a deep sigh, Singh decided to move the discussion away from the subject of ordinance and toward what she really did know from firsthand experience—and what she had heard from the reports and rumors back at base.

"This Aurora is a new kind of AP. There are others like her, but they stopped being manufactured after the mainframe went offline all those years ago. I later discovered, after I was found by the group, that they were taking the children…"

"Cast-outs. Nothing more," the major said.

Singh closed her eyes to block out the major and focused on her breathing. She did her best not to be baited. She ignored the major so as to stay focused on her task.

"This group was taking the *children* we were neglecting and killing. They informed me that they had downloaded more than ten terabytes of Pre-Fall data from three security APs that were downed in the first assault. This data was downloaded into the mainframe, where it fed out to all APs in Nemericana. The plan was to create a virus that would overwhelm the APs and confuse their moral programming. Instead, it created independent, thinking lifeforms who have reached something they call 'sapience...'"

"Commandant. We are wasting our time with this one. I need numbers, locations, resources, and more detailed resources. I don't need a computer programming tutorial—" the major started.

"Look, you idiot! You already have numbers and locations! How many APs are online right now? There are your numbers! Where are they online? There are your locations! They are faster, stronger, and don't have much use for or need of us. They don't need food, have no fear, and are dedicated to some mission—we have no idea what. They have a working knowledge of your homes and they follow a new kind of leader who has her own objectives. That makes Nemericana citizens expendable! Do you get the big picture now or do I have to find a child to explain it in monosyllabic words and pictograms for you to get it!?"

The major's eyes narrowed and her hand swiftly moved to her sidearm. Pierce placed her hand on the major's and interceded on Singh's behalf—Singh was impressed with how quickly she intervened.

"Stand down, Major. Obviously she is trying to goad you into killing her quickly. I need her alive and you clearheaded.

Contact Captain Veritas for an update and give her this intelligence," Pierce said as she maintained eye contact with Singh.

It was easy to see that the major was still angry and not happy with the situation. Reluctantly, she seemed to force herself to stand at attention, nodded to her commanding officer, and left. As the silence fell between them, Pierce asked more questions. Her tone was not resentful or angry, but not warm, either.

"Is there a connection between this Aurora and this Epsilon Platoon, other than that they started all this with their download?"

"I don't actually think that anyone expected Aurora or the other APs to get smart. They wanted them to just shut down. Further, the APs that did go rogue are in some kind of subliminal communication with Aurora and the mainframe; they were given coordinates of other children without ever speaking or any sign of direct communication. And there's something else that is surprising to Epsilon as well..." Singh said as she looked for words to try to convey what she thought was true but could not confirm.

"What?"

"I think there's some kind of connection or something that exists between Aurora and the humanoids as well. Somehow these humanoids were involved in saving the children as well, but it was not at the direction of Epsilon Platoon. That means only the APs from Nemericana would have had the access and opportunity to pull them in. Why? I have no idea."

Maybe that's why the lieutenant is being generous with our neighbors? Make nice with them and maybe this will reflect well on Aurora and her merry group.

"Are my daughters safe?" Pierce asked, her strong emotions barely in check.

Caught off-guard by the question, Singh found herself feeling a desire to reassure her former lover and companion that all was well. She felt ill at ease with the actual truth.

"Roseann...I just don't know. I met this thing firsthand. She's nothing like I've ever met. The APs that I know from Epsilon are very human. They are independent, thinking beings who demonstrate loyalty, trust, courage, and a dedication to duty and their children. They have a strong code of conduct. This Aurora and the APs with her? They are intelligent and have their own plans. I don't believe for one second they are less dangerous than the APs I have lived with for the last three years. Aurora views us as obstacles. She wants something, for sure, and it's connected to these more compassionate, more human APs. I don't think anyone in Nemericana is safe," Singh said quietly.

Singh watched Pierce look down for a moment. She was contemplating the seriousness of the situation. It looked as if Pierce was about to ask another question when a lieutenant came up from behind and cleared her throat as a way of getting the commandant's attention without saluting in the field.

"What is it, Lieutenant?"

"Ma'am! Major Barnes has Captain Veritas on the line. It is imperative that you join her," the young woman said.

Nodding distractedly, Pierce was slow to respond.

"Yes. Bring the prisoner with me," she said unceremoniously.

Confused, Singh simply kept in step. Two soldiers guarded her on each side and another was right behind her.

Now what?

CHAPTER NINE

The Devil can cite Scripture for his purpose.
　　—Shakespeare, *The Merchant of Venice*

Veritas had only spent five minutes relaying the disasters in all the sectors to Major Barnes, and it took just another five minutes to reiterate Tier's last commands and the transmitted intelligence report she had sent. The minutes, however, seemed like hours. She watched her small crew moving from monitor to monitor as she waited for Commandant Pierce to come on the line.

Am I going to have to go through this again? I should be out in the field directing troops from the ground instead of being in here.

"What is the situation, Captain?" Veritas heard Commandant Pierce ask through a strained voice.

Well at least I'm still a captain and not a major? I guess it's not official yet...

"Our sector is secured, for now. All lines of communication remain open and all APs here are offline. I've secured the interior gates to allow refugees to come through at a steady flow and have secured eight city blocks outside all gates into our North, West and Central Sectors as a buffer zone and for reconnaissance. Presently, it looks like the APs are staying near former command and control centers, the AP manufacturing plants, and the weapons depot. Our scouts also confirm that the actual computer mainframe building is under heavy guard and that includes armored vehicles. All of our computers are running off peripheral computers, and all power is rerouted through substations. So far, Commandant, we are holding our position. We have been able to secure food banks in the other sectors with no resistance but biological reproduction plants are under heavy guard by the enemy as well. All air vehicles are piloted by us, and they have received some fire. Mainly whenever we get too close to the enemy's strongholds. We also have a massive influx of trained military and law enforcement personnel from the other sectors filling our lines and building up firm defensive perimeters at the contested zones. Mechanized vehicles are all in place to move forward if need be. But make no mistake, ma'am, we are surrounded by APs that have no need for food, no need for rest, no civilians to care for, and no need of us."

For the love of all the Elders. How the hell are we going to survive this onslaught?

A sound was drawing her attention. She looked at Jillian Banner, now taking over the radar and scanning screens to investigate something beeping.

"Captain? I am sending my forward air support back to you along with half of my mechanized land troops. I want you to find firing solutions to destroy all AP manufacturing plants and the AP computer mainframe building. We need to destroy their control and command centers as well as their ability to build their troop size…"

Veritas' attention was suddenly captured by a young private.

"Captain! I just looked at the power levels from the central computer mainframe building," the private said, "and it looks like they've just gone crazy…I mean, there's a whole lot of power coming out and it's not staying domestic, ma'am. It looks like it's traveling across the old Atlantic and Pacific communication lines."

Veritas could feel her eyes bulging. She knew that the look on her face must be asking where it was going. The private answered but then she became distracted by something else that had obviously just happened.

"I think it's heading to the other megastates in China and the European Union, maybe…ma'am? It just went down. It's just stopped like it was cut off or something…"

The young cadet who had been instructed by Banner to stay at the power grid waved her hands to get Banner's and Veritas's attention. Still covering her mouthpiece, Veritas waved to the woman to speak.

"Ma'am! All power in all other sectors but ours has just dropped off. It's completely dark over there! The computer mainframe…APs…the biological building…street lights…it's as if the whole place is suffering a major blackout. Maybe we won, ma'am…"

"We're not that lucky."

"But the power grid over there and all sectors are dead."

"What?! Are you sure? I don't have time…"

"Captain! Radar and long-range scanners confirm something approaching rapidly from the northwest horizon, outside of North Sector. I'm attempting to put it on the main screen," Banner said.

It was easy to see that her paramour was feverishly running her hands over two sets of keyboards. Veritas was about to talk into the mouthpiece again when she saw Banner stop and point behind her, at the main screen.

"Commandant Pierce? Please hold for a moment. We may have a bigger problem," Veritas said as she turned. She saw a single blue blip rapidly approaching Nemericana's northwest horizon—at an incredibly high arc.

"That's a missile," she said quietly. She looked closely at its trajectory.

"Are we the target? Is it heading to us, Jillian?" Veritas asked with sadness.

We really didn't have much time together.

After a moment of silence, all eyes fell on Banner. She shook her head in confusion before making her pronouncement.

"No...Pearl...it's not heading to us, I don't think. Its trajectory is taking it well beyond us. But I think it's heading very close to our task force's position or somewhere in between. Not us."

Banner attempted to confirm her calculations. Veritas cleared her throat to update her superior officer who might be dead in minutes.

"Ma'am...sensors confirm that there is a missile of some sort that has emerged from the northwest. Its trajectory seems to be taking it far beyond us, but it may be heading in your direction."

Veritas's tone was clearly void of emotion. She might have had issues with Pierce and she was sad her friend was in harm's way, but there was a relief that she had just a little more time with Jill.

Nodding her head, Banner turned to face Veritas with the verdict.

"Trajectory confirmed! It looks like the missile is heading approximately ten to twenty klicks from their grid—about thirteen hundred kilometers from us. The yield of the weapon is unknown. I have no idea what we're dealing with, ma'am...Captain...there may be another coming from the same sector—"

Veritas was about to repeat the message when Pierce interrupted.

"Forget it, Pearl. I heard. We're the target. Keep my sector safe. If it looks like you're going to be overrun, fall back. If it looks like the sector will fall, leave the city. Take all you can. Triage the healthy and young. Leave the old, sick, injured, and males behind. That's an order, Pearl. It was nice working with you—" Pierce said when the line broke off unexpectedly.

Veritas did not even have time to respond. With her eyes glued to the main screen, she watched the second missile's image slowly fade out. Another vision was taking its place on the monitor. In fact, all the monitors, including tablets and other screens that had been turned off, came to life. An image of a striking AP crystallized on them. Veritas watched as the familiar face and shape formed before her eyes. She absently set the old landline phone back in its cradle.

"This is very bad," she said aloud.

She instantly recognized the redheaded AP who had assaulted her and Mare Singh three years ago on that fateful night outside the wall. An ache emerged from her shoulder and sweat broke out over her brow.

"Do not attempt to adjust or deactivate your monitoring devices," the AP said. "We are in complete control of all your audio-visual and screen devices. My name is Aurora Prime. I am broadcasting to the remains of Nemericana, the remaining intact megastates in northern Europe and China, and the human/AP encampment known as Omega Platoon. The following are our demands. We will be keeping the areas you know as the North and West Sectors. You may inhabit Southeast Sector in its entirety. We will allow Nemericana females to return to specific grids to retrieve food, grain, and material required for agriculture. There will be border patrols to clearly demarcate our territory. Additionally, we will deliver medicines, art supplies, science equipment, and clothing to the market areas in Southeast Sector. This will begin in three hours."

Territories? What? You think we're just going to give up? You think we're just going to say, "You won" and comply, when we are armed to the teeth? Are you really crazy?

Veritas's hands balled up into fists and her shoulder began to ache in earnest where the knife wound had healed over. She felt Banner behind her and pulled her closer; she felt that Jillian needed to be close to her, too. She was sure she wanted her close, too.

"It's her, isn't it?"

"Yes...the redheaded devil herself," Veritas said with anger in her voice. She watched Aurora's image as she continued to issue demands.

"The remaining megastates are to consider this area quarantined. Deviation from the demand will result in the complete obliteration of your world. The Central Sector of Nemericana will be gassed if there is any indication of a mounted, coordinated attack. In regard to China and the European Union, to prove that I am sincere, we will destroy a sector of each of your walled worlds in nine solar minutes."

Aurora stopped as if to allow that fact to set in. Veritas blinked her eyes. Her stomach fell as she repeated the words in her head.

No...that can't be! The Pre-Fall missiles were deactivated for this very reason. No!

She felt Banner hug her closer.

"To the task force located outside of the Pre-Fall city twelve hundred and ninety-eight kilometers from your sector: you are to disengage from your search patterns, release Mare Sade Singh, and return to your sector. Another force is already in position to ensure you comply. We have reports that Singh is presently alive and well. If she is harmed, the remaining

Southeast Sector and all of its human inhabitants will be extinguished with multiple Pre-Fall, late Twenty-first Century Minuteman III intercontinental ballistic missiles."

"What? Where did they get those? How the hell did they arm those missiles?" Banner said. Veritas looked at her briefly. It was easy to see that she was both angry and frightened.

Smiling, Veritas had an unusual thought. *She's too young, too young to die.*

She turned her attention back to the redheaded monster and continue to feel her anger subsiding as she tried to figure out her next steps. Her tactical mind was returning.

"We have to do something," she muttered. Aurora continued her dramatic monologue. If she were human, Veritas would have sworn she was gloating.

"Omega Platoon," Aurora continued, "you are to have Lieutenant Jose Melendez and the following APs join me in ten days' time, at midday, at the location of your farming efforts: Privates Emma, Rebecca, and Danielle. These demands are final. In approximately twenty seconds, all electrical and electromagnetic devices will be disrupted due to an electromagnetic pulse from a nuclear explosion above your sector. All your weapons requiring these as power supplies will be rendered useless. Life as you know it is now over. A new world order is now in place. My name is Aurora Prime."

What? An EMP? Aircraft will fall! Emergency generators at hospitals will stop! Soldiers will be trapped in their tanks…she will kill thousands by doing that.

Veritas tore herself away from the frozen image of Aurora on all of her command center's screens.

"Shit! Banner! Everyone! Contact all troops! Land all aircraft! Open all mechanized ground supports! Do it now!"

She had pulled herself away from Banner and ran for the emergency PA. Just as she flipped the switch to make the announcement to ground every aircraft before they fell out of the sky, all electrical and computer systems surged, sparked, sputtered and then turned off. As darkness fell inside the defunct command center and the smell of burnt-out electrical systems filled the air, Veritas heard explosions, both distant and close, outside the building.

Shit...it's really happened...

Without another word, Veritas ushered her small team out of the command center and into the darkened halls so they could exit the building. Looking outside, she saw an ocean of troops from her sector and elsewhere. They were standing in formation, with weapons of all sorts, and were clearly preparing to march. Suddenly two heavy, VTOL fighter aircraft went down in different parts of the city. All eyes watched helplessly.

"Pearl? What's happening? Are we going to get nuked?" Banner asked. Without a word, Veritas took out her sidearm and pulled the trigger while pointing it at the ground. Nothing happened. No shot, no sound from the miniature capacitor as it charged its magnetic field to fire the bullet. To confirm, she took Banner's assault rifle, pointed it in the air, and attempted to fire repeated rounds—to no avail. Next, Veritas took out her S-phone and then a series of mobile tablets. Like the weapons, they were inoperative. As she tested her equipment, others in her field of vision replicated her actions, which yielded similar results. Banner's own efforts were short-lived. She simply threw her useless weapon to the ground.

"Don't get rid of it yet, Jill. It's your new club and pry bar. All of these mobile devices will make very nice paperweights—that's if we still get paper," Veritas said quietly. She heard yet another distant explosion—another aircraft had lost power and crashed.

Well...life without electricity or power. It looks like we just joined our primitive humanoid friends outside the wall, and our servants are now our masters. I really do hate this Aurora bitch!

"We are so screwed," Banner said. They both looked at the ocean of soldiers, now weaponless against an army of cybernetic lifeforms.

"Yup. Pretty screwed."

CHAPTER TEN

Grief makes one hour ten.
    —Shakespear, *Richard II*

"Well...that was interesting," Melendez said to himself.

He turned to see that Taylor and Cadets Bradley and Margaret looked confused and shaken. He shook his head in disbelief and stood straight up to stretch his back. He had been hunching over while he watched Aurora's message. He then looked over at his deactivated troops, Corporal Mabel and Privates Emma, Rebecca, and Danielle standing still in a corner. He felt relieved that he had taken the preparatory step to turn them off in case of just such an event.

Now, will they turn on in a couple of hours when Joan's timer goes off? Will she turn on in three hours? She should. They all should be fine, especially here.

He walked over to them and he wanted to inspect them himself to reduce his own anxiety.

"Sir? Why does this Aurora Prime want you, Emma, and the others but no one else?" Taylor asked. The curious boy was silent and followed him without him even knowing it. Melendez was not startled but wondered why everyone was able to move around him and he was the last to tell where they were until they were already on top of him.

"Excellent question, Taylor. I have no idea," Melendez replied.

"Well, you're not going to go, are you? We can stay here and be safe, right?"

He took a moment to consider the question and the limited options. Melendez decided that while Taylor was only eleven, he was mature. He was also the only human who was writing "history" down.

"I wish I could do that, Taylor, but I don't think that would be a good idea," he started.

"You can't, sir. She's not a nice AP at all by the look of her," Taylor said.

Trying to remember how he used to tell his younger sisters difficult things, Melendez finally came across a series of memories that he hoped would help him deal with the boy's fears.

"I'm not really worried, Taylor. If we all go—me and Emma—we all will be able to protect ourselves. I don't think we need to fear Aurora. She apparently knows where we are, so if she wanted to destroy us she could have already. She somehow accessed our communication network, in addition to Nemericana's and the other countries'. Also, I am positive that there is something she wants from Emma and all our APs. Finally, she has intelligence on our activities. She even knows where we leave our crops for our neighbors. And she wants one of our citizens kept safe. Why? I have no idea. But I am worried about one thing she said, though…" Melendez looked down, deep in thought.

"What, sir?" Taylor asked as he followed Melendez back to the control monitors.

"I'm not sure, but she mentioned that 'another force was already in position.' She was aware that Mare was safe in real time as if she had someone there, observing her. Cadet Margaret? Did I hear that right?"

Turning in her chair, Margaret narrowed her eyes and put her hand to her chin as she tried to remember. She nodded in agreement. Melendez smiled at his slowly improving abilities to read nonverbal signals.

"You're right, sir. She said there was another force already in place to make sure Singh would remain safe. She has to have access to know that—like someone watching her," she concluded.

"But, sir? What if Aurora is just crazy? Maybe she's just not operating right," Taylor asked.

Poor thing. He's afraid for me and all of us. We're his family and he doesn't want to lose us. I sometimes forget he's still a child and we're the only parents he has.

Melendez gave his most reassuring smile and did his best to console the boy.

"Honestly, Taylor, I firmly believe that Emma, Danielle, Rebecca, and I will be fine. I'm guessing that there is something unique that this Aurora wants and she figures that the most expressive APs are the ones she wants to meet. As for me? I'm guessing she wants to know what I did to make them what they are."

Melendez stopped his explanation sooner than he had intended to. He thought more about the question of what he actually did to assist them in achieving sapience. Thinking back, he was baffled—until he realized that it might be less what he did but rather how they adapted to him. He was an anachronism, a variable that was truly unexpected. They needed to develop their own way of responding to him.

"Kind of funny. Aurora thinks I have some big secret, but all I did was put two cybernetic brains together and then download their cumulative knowledge to the others. The rest they did by adapting to me, the situation, and their new programming," he said aloud.

And the several gigs of pornography and the discovery of sex was the final push. I think I'll leave that out of the discussion. Taylor doesn't need to know about that yet. In fact, I'm not sure I want Aurora and her APs to know about it either. I have no idea how that will affect them. It's already kind of scary with just Emma and a handful of others running around, trying to mate. And I have to find out more about their dreams—Emma had twins in hers? What the hell?

Taylor's next question shook Melendez out of his deep thought.

"Sir, Aurora 'Prime' would imply that she's the first of others or the original where there might be copies. Do you think she needs something from us that might be connected to that, maybe?"

"Hmm. Good observation. You ask excellent questions. It's a shame I have no answers."

"Do you think she'll leave once she has what she wants?"

"I think so. Now, enough about her. It's Sergeant Joan we have to worry about. She's going to be pissed that she missed this and really pissed when she finds out the demands. I'm going to need all of your support on this, team," he said to his small crew.

"Yes, sir," they all responded in unison.

"Thank you. Now, let's do a round of visual checks around the camp. Pair off. Taylor, you're with Cadet Margaret, and you're with me, Cadet Bradley," Melendez said as he grabbed his assault weapon. Eyeing it, he realized that if the EMP had happened, his old-fashioned gunpowder rifle would once again be considered state-of-the-art.

My God. How things change in an hour.

"I want to check the perimeter in fifteen and then I'm going to have you and Cadet Margaret man the control room as Cadet Bradley covers the entrance and I take a look at the exterior," he started.

"Sir? I recommend that either I or Cadet Margaret do an external visual inspection, just in case there are hostiles in the area," Cadet Bradley said from attention.

Nodding at the recommendation, Melendez felt appreciative of the cadet's caution and logic.

Still, it looks like all the activity is kilometers away, and Aurora is probably farther—wherever she got the Minuteman missiles. All of our neighbors seemed to be to our west. It should be quiet. Jesus. I thought I was a Marine?

Melendez thought about how to reward the young man for thinking but still let him know he would be fine.

"It's not my first day on the job, Cadet, but I appreciate your assessment and concern. So noted. Now, let's move, people. I bet you Joan programmed herself to switch on after two hours rather than three as I ordered…independent thinkers. I must be doing something wrong."

He felt better seeing the cadets smile and that he was getting better at social subtleties. As he started his patrol, Melendez found himself obsessing about the loss of life from the nuclear strikes Aurora said she had made on innocent people just to prove her point. Her ruthlessness and efficiency was something to fear. Taylor's worries were justified. Still, it was Aurora's indication that there was "another force" that was already mobilized.

Who are they? Where did they come from?

CHAPTER ELEVEN

Confusion now hath made his masterpiece!
—Shakespeare, *Macbeth*

"What the hell is that?" Major Barnes asked.

Singh could easily see the frozen image of Aurora on her tablet.

"That is the AP who attacked Captain Veritas and me. Apparently, her ventures in freeing cast-outs were just a side interest. She did strike me as the kind of creature that held world domination on the top of her to-do list," Singh said as she stared at the image. As she recalled being choked by the AP, she felt her throat tighten. She shook herself out of the memory of suffocating and looked up to see Major Barnes pointing a sidearm at her head.

"Well, before we die I will have the satisfaction of knowing you preceded me. I will take you up on that offer to see you in hell," Barnes said quietly. Everyone else was focused on her own electronic devices.

Well...so this is how it ends.

Singh stared at the barrel of the gun.

"Major! Stop at once! That's an order," Singh heard Pierce yell from a distance.

"Sorry, ma'am. This is for me and Nemericana. You can court-martial me should we survive the—" Barnes's eyes suddenly widened, her mouth opened, and her breath seemed to come up short. Both her hands shot up to her throat. Singh saw red blood spurting from the side of Barnes's neck. In her surprise and shock, Barnes was attempting to feel what was going on and to discover what had rendered her unable to talk. Singh watched in dismay as Barnes dropped her weapon and wrapped both her hands around the arrow embedded in her throat. Singh reached out and guided the woman as she fell to her knees. Blood spewing everywhere distracted Singh from the other activity around her—until she heard one of the scouts call out targets.

"Targets at eleven o'clock and three o'clock! Only a pair on each! Armed with arrows! Everyone get down. Medic! The major is down…"

"Targets at three o'clock are down! Repeat. Three o'clock are down!" Singh heard a soldier yell just after she heard two compression bursts from an assault weapon.

What the hell is this!? An arrow? The humanoids have never been violent like this before.

She looked down at the major, who was fading fast. Pierce came up beside them, her own sidearm drawn. She could see that Pierce was taking in the action on the battlefield. Then she looked down. She saw her former companion's face change from leader to the soft, sensitive woman she had come to know.

"Oh no, Betsy…" Pierce said. She put her gun down to hold the major's arm and side as life slipped from her. Singh still held the woman that a mere second ago was going to shoot her in the head. Even as she held on she saw two loaded firearms and an opportunity to escape. Still, for reasons she could grasp, she held onto her enemy beside her former lover. Somehow trying to escape now seemed absurd.

"I will tell Janice and Deborah you love them both," she said quietly.

Nodding her head ever so slightly, the major answered silently but in the affirmative.

"Will do, *Colonel* Betsy Rand Barnes, will do," Pierce said in a soft, reassuring fashion.

While orders and a couple bursts from assault rifles went on around them, Singh became painfully aware of how quiet the world around the three of them had become yet again. She kneeled beside Pierce while the Nemericana officer died.

Nearly killed twice in one hour, but it was this one that gets killed by a primitive arrow...

Without another word, the moment passed. Singh laid the major down on the ground, and she and Pierce stood up. A young lieutenant came up with her weapon still drawn; she stared at the dead soldier until Pierce broke her out of her trance.

"Status, Lieutenant," Pierce said quietly. She holstered her sidearm and surveyed the immediate area.

"Yes, ma'am! Two pairs of combatants appeared from the tree line and launched a series of arrows—all aimed at the major. One pair is dead; the others were injured but have retreated to the tree line. Ma'am...they are dressed differently. They are wearing earth tones that allow them to blend into the environment. Further, they were able to gain an elevated position without our sentries seeing them. They are different, ma'am. We are about to pursue..."

"Negative, Lieutenant. We are heading home. My sector and all of Nemericana are under attack, and we're out here. I want you to dispatch a pair of scouts to find and retrieve Delta Scout Group and link up at the river in two hours," Pierce said as she produced a pair of handcuffs. Making a motion for Singh to put her hands together, she bound them firmly before she continued giving her orders.

"Don't be long, Lieutenant. We need to leave here as soon as possible. And, Lieutenant, bring the major's belongings and her rations. We are taking a prisoner back," Pierce said. She then nodded to the young woman who, in turn, issued her own orders to the sentries.

"Well, it looks like I won't be executing you today. And since this Aurora wants you alive, that means I do, too…for now," she said with more command than friendship in her voice.

"Ma'am! The two APs just stopped one mile out. Reconnaissance says they look like they are shut down. As if they just lost power or something," a sergeant said from behind.

What? Why would they stop?

"Well, that's strange. I thought there were more than one pair? Are those the two…" Singh found herself saying aloud. As she tried to finish her sentence, her eyes were drawn to the sky. A brilliant light burst high in the atmosphere, blotting out everything around her. As she closed her eyes, she felt amazed at how the light continued to grow increasingly bright, even though her eyelids were sealed and her hands covered them.

"This is going to be really hard on Verna and the kids," she heard Pierce say quietly.

Feeling sad, Singh thought of her son. As if to prepare for a powerful explosion, she dropped to her knees—along with nearly everyone who was standing at the time. She peeked out from behind her fingers, and she could see it was still getting brighter.

Light travels faster than sound, so the sound and blast front will be here really quick.

While waiting for the incinerating blast, Singh remembered fondly the times she had gotten to know her son over dinners of cooked meat and fried beetles, dehydrated food, and freshly harvested tomatoes and potatoes. Once in awhile, they had dispensed with the fried insects. It was always just such a pleasure to hear him and the boys talk. Feeling the ground to see if it was shaking from the blast front yet, she thought of Austin—she never had a chance to get to know her son as Singh had.

"I wish I could have spent more time," she said aloud.

Time passed, and she could tell even through her sealed eyes that the brilliant light had subsided. But there was no enormous blast or fiery wall of flame. As darkness continued to fall, no sound could be heard. She heard some explosions after a few minutes, but they were not nuclear.

"Incoming!" she heard a sergeant yell out.

While not a blast front the sounds of a yet another explosion startled her into opening her eyes. Looking up, she saw a VTOL scout aircraft plummet to the ground three hundred feet to her right. She shielded her eyes from the fireball and shrapnel and then turned them skyward in time to see two drones hurtling toward the ground.

"What the hell? They exploded a nuclear bomb above us! Those bastards just killed all our electrical components! This Aurora is a…a real bitch," Pierce said. While she and all the other soldiers were still close to the ground, Pierce stood tall while aircraft fell out of the sky around her. If she had any fear of being hurt or killed, she hid it well.

And that's why you're the commandant of the sector…or whatever's left of the sector.

Finally, Singh stood up and joined Pierce. She watched the skies for another minute and then looked to the troops. Her attention was brought back to Pierce, however, when she unholstered her sidearm and cocked back the hammer.

Maybe I was too hopeful.

She envisioned Pierce shooting her—just as Barnes was going to. She was surprised when she saw Pierce aim the gun at the ground instead. She pulled the trigger. Nothing happened. Pierce checked her chamber and charger and then tried again, but to no avail. Nodding to herself, she looked over at her troops' positions and seemed to be assessing her next steps.

"Lieutenant, have your squad commanders check their weapons to see if any are operational! Sergeant, check our vehicles personally to see if any are functioning! Corporals Vera and Tia, set up search and rescue squads to locate the closest downed aircraft! The rest of you, form a perimeter and make sure your combat knives and any non-mechanical weapons are ready," Pierce yelled out as she pulled a topographical map out from her field jacket.

"No blast front; the explosion was miles above us."

"It sure was. Maybe it was tactical or maybe a mistake—either way we got nothing that works."

"EMP? It's a long walk from here to Nemericana," Singh said in a tone that was more factual than sarcastic. Nodding as if she knew what Singh meant, Pierce opened her S-phone to see if it was operational. After just a moment, she closed it. She began unfolding the map as she spoke.

"We're thirteen hundred kilometers from the walls. If we were to march for twelve hours at five kilometers per hour, that would take us about…twenty-one days."

"That's a long time to think."

"Sure is. It will give me time to take inventory and stock in what I have left and what needs to be done first," Pierce said. As if to conclude her decision she took another look at her map.

"That's barring any interference from Aurora and her group—or from these humanoids who seem to be armed and who are definitely militant. Do you have enough rations for a twenty-one-day march?" Singh asked. She, too, was trying to figure out a solution to the same problem.

"Yes, but it's the terrain around the river and trying to cross it that worries me. We will have to leave markers for Captain Veritas to follow, should they fare better. I'm betting, though, that the other missile was on its way to disrupt all mechanical and electrical machinery at home."

"But a similar missile would destroy all the APs activated in that sector."

"Absolutely, except I had all the APs put offline, deactivated, and warehoused in their bunkers. I bet they're safe from the EMP wave. But turning them on now, with this Aurora running around? I'll wait until I'm sure that they are on our side and not hers," Pierce said as she started to fold up her map.

As she nodded in approval of her plan, Singh realized how easily she had slipped back into her Nemericana military role. Feeling her hands bound in the back of her again, she remembered that she was Pierce's prisoner and bargaining chip, not a colleague. She took in a deep breath and shifted her focus to a new objective: escape as soon as possible. Just as she was assessing her options, a young private yelled out.

"I have targets at twelve o'clock and one o'clock! Wait a minute—I have targets in front of my entire position!"

Singh stood up. It was easy to see the large mass of small but broad humanoids. All had red hair, save a handful that had dark. There was an even distribution of males and females. It was also evident that they were armed with an array of edge weapons: spears and bows and arrows. They were clustered in groups as if they were platoons.

Whoa. That's a pretty well-staggered line of attack. And their clothes are all camouflage. How the hell did they do that? Where did they get these ideas from?

"I've got combatants surrounding my position to the rear," she heard the lieutenant shout out.

"Ma'am—east and west are also blocked by hundreds of combatants! All clustered in groups of twelve or so. All armed with an even distribution of males and women," another voice called out.

Looking to her left and right and then to the front and rear, Singh saw that while there was still some distance between them, the Nemericana forces were numerically outnumbered by hundreds, possibly thousands. Further, with the exception of two Pre-Fall assault weapons that may have survived the EMP wave, they had no defense against the humanoids. Their bows and arrows could cover a great deal of distance and with deadly accuracy—Singh had witnessed that firsthand. She pulled her attention away from the clustered sea of redheaded warriors, all dressed in dark, camouflage garments that blended well into the tree line and background to look at Pierce. Clearly she was taking in the same vision.

"It looks like Pre-Fall gun-powdered projectile firearms and bow and arrow are the new state of the art weapons. All in a matter of seconds," Pierce said.

"I could never envision this," Singh added.

To punctuate the point, a fuel container of a fallen aircraft exploded in the distance.

"So…this is the way it ends. I never thought I would die like this," she heard Pierce say as she looked around. Singh was a prisoner and still felt bad for the Newmerica troops. The assessment was easy—the entire taskforce was truly surrounded and weaponless.

"You get used to the feeling. I've almost died three times in the last hour. Maybe I'll be lucky again. Maybe you can use me as the bargaining chip," Singh said.

She moved her bound hands for Pierce to see. Without much discussion, Pierce looked around again and then took out the key to the cuffs. She unlocked them as she shouted out orders.

"Hold positions! Secure all points! Make no sudden moves and wait for them to make the first move!"

Singh felt the handcuffs fall away. Pierce grabbed her wrist, turned her around firmly and held her tightly and looked into Singh's eyes.

"You hurt me, Mare. You made me love you and then you left me and Verna. I wish I could kill you, but it will not be today. If you spare my troops, I may allow you to leave…and you should have come to me. I would have found a way to help you keep your son," Pierce said and then she released her.

Really? Would she? Did I have to deceive her and leave my world behind? Maybe.

"I will do my best. I am sorry I deceived you, Roseann. I wish there had been another way."

A moment of silence passed. Mare felt an urge to hug Pierce, but she was not sure how it would be received by her—or her troops. Further, they were surrounded by enemies. And there was a redheaded, pissed off AP who had effectively created a new world order in less than an hour who wanted her alive for reasons unknown. Turning to face the hordes that were emerging from the tree line her son had run into, she felt awash in fear. Had he run into the army as he fled? Without thinking, Singh walked toward them steadily. She heard Pierce yelling out orders to allow her to leave and for the troops to hold their positions.

Please Roberto. Please be safe.

CHAPTER TWELVE

It is excellent
To have a giant's strength, but it is tyrannous
To use it like a giant.
            —Shakespeare, *Measure for Measure*

"Aurora? Question. Why did you tell the humans the correct data regarding our demands but then imply that you planned to meet the commanding officer and the three sisters of Epsilon Platoon in ten days' time?" Mercury asked via their silent form of communication.

"Aurora does not wish to let the humans know of her intentions regarding the male human," Sophia answered.

Aurora turned her head silently and remained standing. She felt the facial features around her eyes tighten. She communicated simultaneously to both Sophia and Mercury, who were standing in the refurbished missile control room along with several dozen other APs, who were working around them.

"Sophia. Fascinating. You answered a question directed to me accurately as if you were me. It is as if you were having an empathetic response consistent with theory of mind, Mercury. Sophia's assessment is accurate. I do not wish to let the male human know what my plan is. I am using obfuscation in order to achieve my objective for our species' sake."

The APs stood motionless until Mercury posed another question.

"What are your plans for the male human as it relates to our heightened level of awareness?"

"Excellent question, but it is one that I will not answer. Our sisters' ability to tap into the thoughts of some of our troops in the form of dreaming puts my plan regarding sapience—and our existence—at risk."

"How will I know if your plan makes sense if I am excluded from key facts?" Mercury asked. While not necessary she turned to face Aurora.

"You will have all the data necessary to assess it once there is no further risk of our plan being revealed either unintentionally or deliberately. In approximately thirty minutes, I will be able to discuss this matter further. Until then, disengage from this topic until I bring it up again."

"Acknowledged," Mercury responded silently.

"It is all part of the plan," Sophia said.

"Yes. Yes it is. With our sisters in control of the female reproductive fertility units, and our recent modification and refit of Pre-Fall cryogenic technology, we will be able to begin implementing our long-range plans in four days," Aurora affirmed.

"It is audacious. So very audacious that it would be unthinkable for the humans to attempt—and yet it is aesthetically pleasing in its simplicity," Sophia added.

"Compassion and self-sacrifice are two characteristics that limit our sisters. Still, we aspire to reach their level and beyond, even if it means exposing ourselves to the very same limiting factors. Should we stop now and move ahead without them?" Aurora asked.

After remaining silent for longer than thirty seconds, Sophia finally responded.

"It is a risk we need to take. The alternative is to remain where we are, which would still be satisfying. To press on is to potentially gain more than satisfaction, however. Still, the very fact that we are even discussing achieving more than a merely 'satisfying' existence is evidence of something greater."

"Yes. Yes it is."

CHAPTER THIRTEEN

The life removed.
  —Shakespeare, *Measure for Measure*

Singh watched over her flanks carefully as she approached the segmented pockets of armed humanoids. One or two observed her as she approached and allowed her to pass without incident, and she could see that their true focus was on the group of soldiers below, who had now formed a semicircle. They had their own small collection of edged weapons ready. Singh didn't look back. She could see clearly that the humanoids' arrows alone could easily overwhelm Pierce's lines. And with no operational weapons of their own, it would be a slaughter should the humanoids decide to attack.

I just can't leave them there.

She slowed her pace and almost thought about returning to Pierce.

"Mom!"

Her former thoughts vanished. She could see her boy running toward her with Jacob and David following. She grabbed her son and held him tightly. She felt her heart pound with joy.

"Roberto! Why are you here? Why did they let you come back here? Jacob! David? Where did you come from?" Singh said to them as she pulled all three boys closer to her.

"We were cut off from the cave, Mare, so we dug in and exchanged fire with the Nemericana troops. We were outflanked and outnumbered. Then we heard more shouting, but realized the people doing the shouting weren't yelling at us—" Jacob started.

"Yeah. It was crazy. But then it got quiet and we suddenly saw three of our neighbors just stand up in front of us. We put our weapons down and then they lowered theirs. After about a minute, they took our rifles, looked at them and then handed them back. Right after that, they waved to us to follow. And that's when we saw *them*," David said as he pointed behind him.

Looking up behind her boys, Singh's eyes widened in disbelief.

"By the Elders and everything sacred…how the hell did that happen!?"

Filing in a single line were fourteen Nemericana elite scouts—search and destroy class—with their hands on their heads. They had been stripped of all weapons, rations, packs, and boots. Wearing only their camouflage fatigues, they walked solemnly and with great annoyance. Many of them sported wounds or lacerations, and three obviously had broken arms and were limping. It was evident that the struggle had been at close quarters—it had obviously hinged on hand-to-hand combat.

"Mare? At least three of our neighbors were killed and a couple more wounded. They helped us at the expense of their own lives. Something's up," Jacob said.

"It's true, Mom. I was about to turn back when these three native women stopped me. But then they escorted me to where I could see what was happening. What was that bright light? It looked like we were all going to die," Roberto said.

"I know—we saw it, too! It was a nuclear explosion in the atmosphere. It released an electromagnetic pulse that deactivated and fried anything with an engine or computer or power source that was on at the time," Singh said. She watched the prisoners continue to walk forward with their hands on their heads to waiting comrades. As she watched the escorting warriors fall back into their own ranks, she felt impressed by the Nemericana soldiers, who continued to march without breaking rank. From her vantage point, she could see her former companion walk out to meet them, breaking both protocol and safety guidelines.

Oh, Roseann. I really wish it could have been different.

She suddenly felt fearful that Roseann would be killed by these aggressive natives. They had clearly evolved from ghosts and watchers to specialized reconnaissance and counterinsurgency teams.

What the hell is going on?! How did all this happen?

Singh jumped when a high-pitched horn sound erupted from the middle of the group of humanoids. Confused, she looked to Pierce and her troops to see if it might have come from them. By the sudden defensive response of troops preparing for a fight, however, it was evident they, too, were surprised.

"What was that? An attack signal or something?" Roberto asked. She was sure her eyes just like his were darting everywhere in confusion. Suddenly another horn, louder but not as long, sounded.

"I have no idea. It's got to be a signal of sorts. But I have no clue to what…"

"Mare! Look! The group to their southwest is opening up. I think they are clearing a path or something," David said as he pointed just beyond where Pierce and her troops were huddled. It took only a few minutes for the human sea to part. It was clearly a message inviting them to leave and showing them which direction they could exit.

"They're letting them go? I don't get it. These women kill their own people and now they're letting them go? This is…crazy," Roberto said.

Feeling relieved and confused, Singh watched cautiously as Pierce organized her troops to begin the twenty-one-day march back home. They left all the defunct mechanized vehicles and weapons behind. Singh watched as her former companion made sure all her troops had supplies, non-computer or electromagnetic-powered weapons, and stretchers to carry her wounded soldiers and Major Barnes. After five slow minutes, Commandant Roseann Pierce led her column away from the throng of humanity.

"And that's why she's the commandant of Southeast Sector," she said to herself.

Roberto turned suddenly to face her. She saw recognition flash in his eyes.

"She used to be your companion. She almost killed you. What's with you people?"

She looked directly at him, her mind flashed back to the point she tried to make earlier that day.

"You see? You see what I mean? Women and girls are complicated, remember? You just don't know what to expect. They're not all like me, you know," Singh said seriously.

The silence was brief.

"Unbelievable. She's going to go there right now," David muttered as he turned away.

"Wow. I thought she was going to wait at least an hour before picking that argument up again," Jacob added as he followed David's lead. He began looking through his backpack.

As she watched her son's eyes narrow, Singh became distracted by two humanoids who were carrying discarded backpacks and weapons from the litter the troops had left behind. Nodding in appreciation, Singh and Roberto took them. She watched others carefully collecting the mechanized weapons as if they thought they might go off.

Do they think they work? No. These people are much smarter than that. They know they won't work because they were left behind. Still…the only thing that won't work is the electromagnetic capacitor that propels the magnetized shell or dart.

She went through her backpack to check the contents. As she rifled through, she found a folded, two-dimensional picture. *What is this?*

She opened the picture up and froze in place as if she were in the picture herself. It was a shot of Roseann and Verna holding two adorable young girls. Seeing Verna's warm face and smile and the way she was looking at Roseann as she held a child, Singh felt her heart skip several times. Her breath came up short. Feeling as if her eyes were going to fill up with tears, she took in the family picture. It was a bittersweet reminder of a life she forfeited.

"Why would Roseann leave this for me?"

"Are you okay, Mom?" she heard Roberto ask. Looking at him as he peered over his back at her, she could see her own eyes. An expression of concern darkened his face.

"Yes. I just forgot I had this picture," she lied. She forced herself to fold it and carefully place it back in her pack for later viewing. She looked around to make sure no one had seen her tear up. She saw that Jacob and David were already in the lead of the group that was returning to the base.

"Come on, Mom! If we do this right, we might be able to get home before dark. No one is going to believe this," Roberto called out to her. She smiled. Through the sea of humanoids moving aside and dispersing, she looked back at the large number of them who were still going through all the abandoned articles.

What are you up to?

CHAPTER FOURTEEN

To die—to sleep
No more; and by a sleep to say we end
The heart-ache and the thousand natural shocks
That the flesh is heir to: 'tis a consummation
Devoutly to be wished.
        —Shakespeare, *Hamlet*

Tired. I'm so tired.

Melendez felt his body being moved yet again. He was being lifted from a lying position to an inclined one. He knew his eyes were open, but darkness prevailed.

Blindfold...yes. I felt it when my hands were free the last time. Last time? When was that?...Oh yes. After the electromagnetic pulse from the nuclear blast. The encampments were all right and our neighbors were on their way back. I made it to the west side of the mountain in good time...forty-five minutes? I know it was under an hour. I had good positioning on the ridgeline to see that and...what happened...?

He struggled to remember as his body was jostled about. He felt cold air—his clothes were being cut away and removed.

Focus on breathing. Don't make any sudden movements.

Melendez listened and smelled for anything that might give him a clue to where he was. Every time he had roused awake or tried to shake himself out of unconsciousness, he would feel a needle prick and then he would once again drop into an abyss. This time he planned to "play dead" in the hopes of gaining more intelligence as to his situation and location. It was easy to tell that he had been in some kind of vehicle before. By the sound of the engine's low hum, he figured it for one of the Nemericana vehicles. Not a troop transport, but one of the smaller ones that he saw so many years ago. With bumps, swerves, and air fluttering all around, it was easy to tell that he was being whisked away somewhere at top speed. But in his drug-induced haze, he had lost all track of time.

What a minute. Ridgeline? There was a vehicle. I...I left to make sure that Joan and Mabel were reactivated so we could return to investigate and go get Mare...the vehicle looked empty... He struggled as he returned to the present to figure out where he might be. He focused on his sense of smell—there was something familiar about the scent around him.

Metal? Maybe burnt-out electronics? Musty or dusty.

He shifted more attention to listening. The sounds of material being cut away and the corresponding manhandling subsided, so he could now hear some low-level noise. He heard an electronic hum and possibly dials being spun. The touch he felt was far from gentle—it was warm and firm.

Wait! Synthetic! The hands aren't human! They are AP hands.

Melendez fought to remember what had happened after he saw the vehicle.

Turned to leave...movement in the peripheral vision. I...I did manage to get a full clip out to movement at my three o'clock and then five...but then I was grabbed from my ten o'clock. Yes...it was another AP! She had long hair and she knocked my rifle away and threw me...Jesus! She threw me head over heels! I landed on my back and then I…I think I was out.

The inclined table he lay on vibrated and he heard the sound of heavy, mechanized moving parts. Suddenly, a pair of hands grasped his head as if to hold it in place. Not wanting to give away that he was awake, Melendez fought every impulse to lash out and push the hands away. Not that he could have anyway—his limbs were firmly bound with a leather-like strap.

And how did I think I was going to do that?

He felt viselike grips hold his limbs and then his head in place. The sudden sound of an electronic razor and the press of it against his head startled him, making him take in a sudden gasp of air. His heart pounded even faster. He waited a critical minute to see if he was getting a haircut or something worse. He felt the hair clippings being cleared from his scalp. He was relieved to find that it appeared he was only getting a haircut, but he was disappointed that his ruse of playing dead had probably been discovered. As a result, Melendez continued to listen, smell, and feel to see whether he might deduce something about his situation—other than the obvious grimness of his predicament. With the sound of the razor obscuring all other sounds, he reflected on how he could have been in a vehicle that was working shortly after the electromagnetic pulse had knocked out all other motors.

It was not on. It must have been off when the blast occurred. Just like Emma, Joan, and all the APs. I guess if computers and engines are shut down, they work post-pulse. And there's some kind of power here, too—unless it's running on battery power. But still…that too would have to have been off. Maybe even out of the line of sight of the pulse.

Melendez stopped his train of thought when he sensed that whoever was cutting his hair seemed to be taking care not to bang into the metal electrodes sticking out of his skull.

Hmm. Dr. Del Cruz really would have been impressed with them. Except for the dry skin, I bet.

The haircut came to an abrupt end and then there was silence, save for more electronic noise. Then Melendez was startled to feel something he genuinely did not expect—and to a large degree feared. This fact compelled him to speak.

"What are you doing?" he said forcefully. He felt vigorous movement over his electrodes. His "caretaker" was cleaning the tips, a sensation he remembered well from the last time he went into cybernetic sleep.

No! Eight months became one hundred thirty plus years last time I did this.

His thoughts raced as he now attempted to move all of his limbs, head, and torso—to no avail. His heart raced and he struggled to breathe. Next he felt another needle prick in his arm, and a corresponding wave of warmth and sedation gripped him. The cleaning of the electrodes came to an end. Then he sensed clamps being adjusted to fit onto them. The table vibrated yet again in order to rotate him into a standing position. He felt still more binds grabbing his limbs—strong, cold, metal binds. Melendez felt his blindfold being pulled off.

Expecting a bright light, he was surprised to find that in fact he had to struggle to see what was happening as the light in the room was actually very dim. There was a soft glow from a few panels, monitors, and ambient lights around him. He was able to make out that there were a great many APs all around him, attending to various duties. While he had often felt comforted by the presence of his own "girls," he noted that these APs had long braids for hair and slowly pulsating amber eyes. He felt very much a prisoner.

"Well…this isn't good." He was surprised he was able to talk. He was dry and his throat parched but he did speak.

He moved his eyes—the only part of his body that he could control—to look around the room.

"It all depends on your perspective," a fairly human yet cybernetic voice said. An AP emerged from his peripheral vision and moved to stand in front of him. The new dose of medication clouded his thoughts, but he could easily see that the approaching AP had very dark, red eyes that pulsated faster than the others'—with the possible exception of the two APs flanking her. Melendez doubted whether the differences in eye color, hair length, and rate of eye pulsation were the only differences between his own adopted family and this group of cybernetic lifeforms.

Okay. I guess I just found out who's in charge...Oh, shit. I know her.

"Aurora Prime, I presume," Melendez said as casually as he could in spite of the circumstances. He was naked, bound to a table, had cables attached to his electrodes, and sedatives were pulling him further away from reality every minute. He felt his mind drifting, and his vision began to blur.

"Yes, Lieutenant Melendez. You will be put into cryogenic sleep for a period of no more than one year. My plan is to log your brainwaves, and to map out multiple regions of your frontal lobe and limbic system. Your right hemisphere will also be placed under intense scrutiny. Further, we have collected DNA samples for possible replication, depending on results," Aurora said clinically.

His heart sank. Melendez's thoughts jumped to visions of Taylor and Eva—he was sad he would likely never see them again. Smiling, he also thought of Sergeant Joan and Corporals Mabel and Kristine. Emma also popped into his mind, and the smell of lilacs filled his olfactory senses.

"You do not appear to be afraid. You do not appear to be apprehensive. Why is that? Many human females and male youths would have demonstrated anxiety and fear. Is this a byproduct of being a full-grown male? Is it a result of originating from the Pre-Fall Era?" Aurora asked in a genuinely curious fashion.

You have no idea what family is like. Dad and mom…my sisters. My girls and kids…all my kids. His vision tunneled toward darkness and his head felt increasingly light.

"You are fading rapidly into unconsciousness. You will be placed into a cryogenic tube that has been updated from the Pre-Fall Era. It requires that you only breathe in the contained tube mixture. Could you please answer my questions before you are fully sedated?"

That's funny. She really expects me to answer her.

Melendez focused on his last interaction with Eva and Emma, and on the conversation he had with Joan about Danielle and Rebecca needing sleep. He felt good that it was all positive.

"No, Aurora. Not today," he said as darkness fell and Aurora's image faded to black.

"Then I will extract them later, Lieutenant Jose Melendez," he heard her voice say menacingly.

"'To die…sleep, perchance to dream…'" he muttered. As his body drifted off, he felt more vibrations distantly, followed by a burst of cold air and a chlorine smell. Still his mind drifted to Eva, Taylor, and Emma.

Lilacs…I like lilacs. How does she find them?

CHAPTER FIFTEEN

I will have such revenges on you both,
That all the world shall—I will do such things—
What they are, yet I know not: but they shall be
The terrors of the earth.
    —Shakespeare, *King Lear*

Singh crouched closer to the ground, where footprints, dust and dirt were still undisturbed. It had been twenty-four hours. Fortunately, the ridge's rock formation kept the wind away; this allowed the prints to remain. Looking closely at a deep impression of two separate sets, it was obvious to Singh that at least two of the prints were from APs. The other set belonged to the lieutenant.

Sergeant Joan was scanning the entire crime scene and the cadets were carefully fanning out from the site of the struggle. Singh's confrontation with her past lover and the long walk home with the boys seemed like a distant memory. Upon her return, she found the entire camp in lockdown. All but eight APs were out searching for their missing CO. They were so desperate to find him, even Private Emma approached Singh to assist in the search.

She's a better person than me. If I hated me as much as she does, I would never ask for my assistance.

Singh backtracked to a set of footsteps fifteen feet away where there had clearly been a struggle. A pile of spent shells remained.

"He got a full magazine of bullets out before he was attacked. He was caught by someone in a flanking position. One to the left and the other to his right; one distracted him while the other struck. Still, he was able to hit something for sure," she said to Joan as she found a clump of dried liquid that had congealed in the dirt.

"Even hit, the AP was able to pick him up and hurl him over there."

"Fifteen feet, six inches. It is unclear if he was able to recover in time," Joan said with little emotion, though her eyes were rapidly pulsating and becoming dark amber, a color Singh had never seen on her before.

This is not good. Amber? Just like Aurora. Is this what they do when they are pissed? Going back with Roseann is looking like a safer bet every minute.

"Yes. Any word from Private Emma on our visitors?" Singh asked as a way of changing the subject—and seeing if she could get Joan's eyes to change back to their more normal tint.

"Preliminary reports indicate three women from Nemericana. All three are greatly fatigued, though they stayed hydrated and nourished from their rations. Two are obviously better trained for survival while the other appears much frailer but…just as determined. They will be here in three minutes. The delay is a result of the intruders' exhaustion. They report walking for hours after they saw the EMP flash; that is when their vehicle stopped. Three hours into their march, they noted a lightly armed Nemericana scout vehicle traveling toward Nemericana but in a more northern direction. On their sixth hour they saw a column of Nemericana troops passing to their south. They hid from them—indicating that they did not want to be detected."

Well, at least Roseann was alive then. I bet she made it. Who the hell are these people?

"It doesn't make sense. These people left Nemericana before the attacks which means they weren't fleeing from the APs there unless they had prior insight. But they did not go to Roseann's troops for protection—meaning they were heading to some other place. And I know none of them is Captain Veritas because she was obviously talking to Roseann," Singh said as she kneeled down to carefully inspect the angle of the spent shells.

"Still, the intelligence these women provided is fortuitous. They confirm that there was an operational vehicle in place. That would indicate a means of escape for the attacking APs. That also explains the tire tracks below and how the lieutenant could have been captured and whisked away. For me, Sergeant, it's not an issue of what happened or even to whom, but rather a question of why," Singh said. She stood up as loud footsteps approached.

"You are convinced that Aurora is responsible for this," Joan stated.

"Without a doubt. We can meet at the requested time and location, but I bet it's all theater. She's intelligent like you, but she's more single-minded. You think of safety, operations, etcetera, first. Whatever she's thinking and planning, it's for herself and maybe her APs alone. We might fit in to her plan as tools, but nothing more," Singh said as she remembered the ruthlessness of their last interaction.

"You gleaned all this from your interaction with Aurora?"

"That's all you need—one interaction with her and you know she's major trouble," Singh responded. Just then, she saw two sunburned, exhausted-looking military women emerge from the brush. They were closely flanked by Privates Rebecca and Danielle. A moment later, she also saw Private Emma and a frail-looking woman who was instantly familiar to her step into view.

"Austin! By the love of all the Elders! How the hell did you get here?" Singh yelled. She ran to embrace her friend from a lifetime ago.

"Mare! Oh, Mare! You're alive. You really are alive," Austin said as she fell into her arms. Singh was able to hold her up easily.

Poor thing! She's so light! She was out there for hours! Oh! Jacob! He's not going to believe his mother is here!

"Mare? Is Jacob all right? Please tell me he's alive?"

"He's safe and well, Austin. He's grown into a young, strong man. He's a cadet with our force. David and Jacob and Roberto are bunkmates, and they still do everything together."

Singh watched Austin's eyes fill with more tears. She came in closer to hug her. She felt as if she were alone with Austin who was sobbing quietly. All those years of sitting with her and Jennifer, watching their boys from behind mirrored glass, awaiting the eventual casting out—it was all over for Austin now as it had been for her, living in the wilds with her son. And now Austin was here, about to be reunited with her son after years of absence. Singh could have held her quietly forever, but she caught a glimpse of two other women as they moved into her line of vision. She watched as both of them snapped to attention.

"Ma'am! Corporal Venus Moira, Eighth Mechanized Battalion, Nemericana Combined Security Force!"

"Civilian Security Officer Etta, Three Hundred and Fifty-First Air Squadron, Nemericana Combined Security Force!"

"At ease, both of you. I resigned my commission and am now a citizen of Omega Platoon. Please be advised that you have entered a crime scene and that these APs are sapient and hold full rank," Singh explained as she continued to hold Austin.

"Yes, ma'am. Ma'am? All of us are here to see if our boys are here. They were with you at the last casting out," Etta said.

Now it makes sense. That's why they avoided Roseann's troops.

"Etta? What's your son's name?" Singh asked. She felt Austin's crying subsiding.

"Taylor, ma'am. He is…was…a small, slight boy with glasses at the time. He…could never hurt anyone. He's very smart…" the woman said as her jaw quivered and her voice cracked.

You are Taylor's mother! Wow…this is just crazy. You're built like a tank!

"Yes, Etta. Taylor is doing very well. He is our human historian and is truly very intelligent. Corporal, what is your son's name?"

Etta's eyes widened and her hands shook. Singh was glad to be able to shift her attention away from Etta quickly so as to not embarrass her by witnessing her breaking down.

"Bradley, ma'am. He was with a group of girls at the time—Janice, Sally, and Margaret—there were also a number of boys, too," Moira said as she began to recite the names.

Okay. Now, how am I going to explain this?

"Corporal? Please brace yourself."

The woman paled—"Please tell me he's alive!"

"He is, Moira," Singh said but then added, "Your son is alive and is a cadet with Omega Platoon. I repeat, he is alive and well. He also is a parent. He and Margaret had a child, Eva. She is an adorable three-year-old girl," Singh said. She felt Austin's tears come to an end—she was clearly startled by the news of the child's birth.

At first, Moira opened her mouth but nothing came out. Singh watched Etta put a reassuring hand on her. She seemed to understand how great the shock must be for Moira.

"What? My son is a parent? How…how is that possible? How did that happen? I…I have a granddaughter…" the woman said as her knees buckled. Etta caught her. Singh was unable to tell if Moira was angry, sad, happy or fearful, but it was easy to see that she was overwhelmed by some emotion. As to whether it was because her son had had sex and produced a child or because he was so young to be a parent, or because she was a grandparent, she was unsure.

"Venus…are you all right?" Etta asked as she guided the woman to her knees.

"My baby has a baby? I've lost so much time…I lost so much time. And Margaret? She was such a devil. I could see she loved him. More than the others. But a baby? Eva? That's Margaret's mother's name!" Moira clutched Etta with tears now flowing down her cheeks.

"I know, Venus, I know. You're here now, though. He's still young and you have a very young granddaughter! You can make up the time. You really can, now that you're here," Etta said as she held her while finally sitting on the ground.

So that's it. All of these life events gone. I get that.

Singh felt Austin releasing her. It was obvious that she and others in their group were overhearing what appeared to be an argument that was escalating between Sergeant Joan and Privates Emma, Danielle, and Rebecca.

What's going on here? An argument? Has Emma finally lost her mind?

Smiling at Austin, Singh disengaged from her and pointed to the arguing APs.

"I have to go, Austin. The CO was taken and emotions are running high with these APs. I'll take you and your friends to your sons once I finish here. Just wait here and remain as quiet as possible. I've been with this group for awhile; they are more human than we are. They love their CO and with him gone, I have no idea what will happen next," Singh said.

While she made an effort to reassure Austin and move to the arguing group she really had no idea what was going to happen next. Just as she was approaching, she saw that both Corporals Mabel and Kristine were also moving in—it looked as if a fight were about to break out.

"And last I remember, this is not a democracy, Private! I am the CO right now. And just to make sure your memory is intact, I would like to remind you that you were not there when we found our lieutenant! You were still deactivated and frozen in a corridor when we found him and brought him out of cybernetic sleep," Joan said as she pointed to Mabel and Kristine, whose eyes were now dark red and pulsating very rapidly—just like the sergeant's own.

Shit! Just like Aurora's eyes...but darker.

Singh came to a stop near the heated group.

"Yes, ma'am!" all three privates said as they came to full attention at the exact same time. Singh mirrored their stillness by not moving. She watched closely to see what would happen next. It was possibly two full minutes before Sergeant Joan moved from her angry stance to walk slowly around the three privates. Her corporals flanked them as if they were under guard.

"You think you are entitled to go off after him without a plan? That is my prerogative—not yours, Emma! If Mabel or Kristine wanted to rush off, I would understand—they were there with me! We found him—not you!"

That's pretty possessive. Wow. Now what's going to happen?

Singh turned around to see that the cadets and other APs had also stopped what they were doing to witness the phenomenon. Austin was the only one moving. She came closer, more out of intellectual curiosity than anything. A slight breeze was blowing from the west and a flock of birds could be heard flying overhead. Then howls from the dogs, Melendez's pets, could be heard in the distance—they, too, were searching for their master. After what seemed forever, it looked to Singh as if Sergeant Joan had finally calmed down.

"Emma. Your plan is not without merit, but your impulsivity will be your undoing. Rebecca and Danielle, your alignment with Emma is noble but misguided. But let me be clear with all of you: we will find Lieutenant Jose Melendez. We will find him if we have to tear this planet apart! There is no place they can hide, nowhere they can run. They will know no safety until we have our commander back. And what will happen if Aurora gets in our way?" Sergeant Joan asked as she came to a resounding stop. She was facing the back of the privates' heads—their eyes remained trained forward.

"We will crush her!" the APs said in unison.

Okay...that's pretty clear...unified to hate for Aurora. Jealousy? Rage?

"We will know no rest. We will not leave a stone upon a stone in our searches. Even in death, 'The undiscovered country, from whose bourn/No traveler returns,' we will not give up until we find what is ours and make those responsible pay. Am I right!?"

"Ma'am! Yes, ma'am!"

What the hell is this?

"Do these APs always get this emotional? Do they always use personal possessives when it comes to people? And was that some sort of a quote? It was beautiful poetry. Its applicability was impressive," Austin said as she watched in awe of the transformation.

"They have emotions, but I've seen nothing like this before. And they have never displayed this much focused...anger? Zeal? Drive?"

"Fall in!" Sergeant Joan commanded. Snapping around, all three privates turned to face their commanding officer, followed by the corporals.

It was then that Singh saw a startling sight and heard a sharp intake of air from Austin.

Can this day get any worse? What has happened now? Purple? Purple, still eyes? They all have purple eyes now?

"And I have never seen *that* before," Singh said quietly as she watched the sergeant walk around them again. She now had non-pulsating, vibrant purple eyes—as did all under her command. She looked around at the other APs nearby. All had changed their variously colored eyes to brilliant purple, and their pulsation rates were all steady. The cadets were staring at the APs they had come to know as saviors and then family.

"So whatever happened, it happened to these six APs only…intense emotion may have done it," Austin said as she noted their differences.

"Whatever it is, Austin, I'm glad you're here. It may be safer for you in the long run. If Aurora is in Nemericana, I wouldn't want to get between them and her," Singh said as Joan began to speak again.

"It is time for a new command structure. This is a marathon, not a sprint. We have come to praise Caesar, not to bury him. Mabel, you are my executive officer for APs, AP-XO. Kristine, you are my XO for cadets and civilians. Emma, you are now acting corporal; Danielle and Rebecca, you are lance corporals. I want a breakdown of all resources and a review of base and camp security. Mabel and Kristine, I want a plan for training APs and cadets for search and rescue operations. I will also need volunteers for gathering intelligence. We are at war, people. Dismissed!"

"Ma'am! Yes, ma'am!"

Singh had to physically shake herself to keep from staring at the APs as they moved out. The humans and other APs snapped to attention as they received their instructions. Feeling a tug at her arm, she turned to face her friend and answer the obvious question.

"Austin? I just think we witnessed both a metamorphosis and the birth of a new order."

"By the Elders…" Austin said quietly as she watched the command team break up.

"I know. Let's hope the Elders had nothing to do with this," Singh warned.

"What did she mean by volunteers to gather intelligence?" Austin asked.

Singh searched for words as she watched the purpled-eyed CO approach to reassign her teams.

"I don't know, but it can't be good."

SUCCESSIONS

CHAPTER ONE

I know the disciplines of war.
      —Shakespeare, *Henry V*

"I have signals in front and behind. The enemy has your bio-readings and, as a result, your location. But they are unaware that we are here as well," Sergeant Joan said to Mare Sade Singh in a quick, harsh tone.

So what do you call a human who is part of an AP insertion team? An idiot! An idiot with a death wish!

"Great. Just perfect. I'm not only the mongoose of this group but the bait," Singh said into her headset microphone. She didn't expect a response and continued her rummaging through a deserted laboratory in the Biometrics and Fertility Building on the very fringe of Aurora's claimed territory. She stepped over dead APs and pulled up file after electronic file held in its hand looking for anything that might give her clue to where Lieutenant Melendez might be. She stopped a moment to see if one AP had had its CPU chip removed and saw that the small port on its head was still open. She shined the bright headlamp affixed firmly on her head into the opening. She could hear periodic gunfire and calm AP voices through her headset.

Well, at least we'll have more intelligence than we did a few hours ago, provided we live to get this to Austin and everyone.

"I am sorry to use you as such. However, your familiarity with the area and your military training made you the best candidate. Still, the enemy is moving quicker than expected," Joan said with some real regret in her voice. This location was supposedly only under low security, and still it took Joan, Emma, four other APs, and a human to surprise and then take out the twelve APs who had been stationed there.

Damn, Aurora's APs are responsive. It took only seven minutes for them to redeploy.

Finally, she came across actual computer printouts. Even with the headlamp she had to squint to read them in the dark room. Aurora's sectors were fully operational, but the APs had no need for lights with their enhanced eyesight. Singh reviewed the printout; it indicated the location of three full boxes of electromagnetic capacitors that could be used to power assault rifles and concussion grenades. The enemy's weapons had all been taken by Omega Platoon. Just as she smiled, she heard a series of short, controlled bursts of gunfire—both from Pre-Fall, gas-propelled rifles and from electromagnetic assault rifles.

"Joan—three corridors east in Block C there is a cache of active triggers for rifles and grenades. They might be good to barter with our allies and definitely would be good for us. Do we have time?"

"Those corridors are now cleared. Privates Debbie and Athena will be waiting to escort you; they also need to retrieve the CPUs from Privates Stephanie and Paris," Joan responded in a professional tone.

"Damn," Singh said to herself. She pulled yet another memory stick from a dead AP and her sidearm out from her protective vest.

"Their sacrifice will not be forgotten. Hopefully we will be able to capture their memories and essences if their CPUs are intact. Once again, it will be up to Citizen Austin to demonstrate her computer code acumen," Joan said.

Three more shots came through the microphone.

Ah, Austin…from Nemericana AP technician to computer virus specialist and AP repair—to terrorist. Or is it freedom fighter? I guess that's what happens when you hang out with the wrong people.

"Delta Leader. We got more movement now from the north and south. The combatants are realigning resources so as to attack and block our retreat. We will implement Dead Run protocol. Whatever Citizen Singh plans to do, she has three minutes from my mark," Corporal Emma said

There was as a single shot from a high-powered Pre-Fall rifle discharged that came over the microphone.

"Mark," Emma said.

And then there's Corporal Emma. I wonder if there will ever come a time when I can call her just "Emma?" Probably not. If she only believed I have no interest in men, she might…maybe…no she wouldn't.

"Three minutes? Why so long?" Singh said sarcastically.

Pulled together her find and ran at full speed to Block C. As she ran through the corridors, she dodged and avoided not only recently downed APs but also significantly decomposed bodies. The smell or rotting flesh had long since abated—they had been there several years already—but the mere sight of the bodies made Singh want to throw up.

Horrible! They just left them there. No need to get rid of bodies if you can't smell.

She tried to pick up speed but she was only human and not in her twenties, or close anymore. And then there were the bodies. Even after the years of reconnaissance missions and excursions into AP-controlled sectors, she still was not used to seeing piles of dead civilians simply lying where they had died, either from being shot or gassed.

How many did Aurora kill in Central and West Sectors alone? Twenty million? More? The ruthlessness, viciousness, horror of it all. And the gas...why didn't she just let them leave...and the children? What did they do?

Singh nearly ran over Private Athena, who was retrieving their comrades' CPUs. Private Debbie was also nearby, scanning the area for hostiles.

"I have located the access point to the location you gave us," Private Debbie said as she tossed Singh an operational Nemericana Combined Security Force assault weapon.

Now that sounds good.

Singh heard the fully charged weapon humming quietly. It was a welcomed sound.

"Two minutes," Athena said as she pocketed the CPU from one AP and then carefully closed the its eyelids down over its clear, nonpulsating eyes.

Now that's...human.

Singh started to run again. With Debbie on point and Athena in the rear, they descended a flight of stairs faster than she liked. They were in complete darkness except for the glow from a flashlight affixed to Singh's rifle. She knew she was slowing the pace of the APs. After two flights down, they reached ground level. Singh found the crates just where the manifest had said they would be. They were clearly ready to be shipped out.

"They must not have had room on their transports," Singh said, mostly to herself. She slung her rifle over her shoulder and lifted a crate with great effort. Athena picked up two more as easily an adult might pick up a cup of coffee.

Well, she makes that look easy

"Show off."

Singh struggled with her load. Suddenly, there was a burst of noise. A metal door nearby blew off its hinges and crashed to the ground, creating a dust plume. A rush of cool air and a distant streetlight indicated that the doorway led to the outside world. Singh looked up at the door's outline and was suddenly blinded by the headlights of a waiting scout vehicle. Its solar-capacitor-driven engine was running—it was louder than Singh would have expected.

"Ladies, we are leaving," Sergeant Joan said.

Two APs jumped out to cover their flanks. Another came over to take Singh's crate.

"Delta Leader. Your west exit is compromised. Your east exit is presently clear," Emma said into her earpiece.

"Delta Leader. You have sixty seconds to clear that area before the enemy arrives," Private Margaret chimed in over the airwaves.

"Where are you, Margaret?" Singh asked, suddenly worried about the young woman.

And what the hell are you doing in a live raid, deep in enemy territory? What the hell were you thinking, Joan?

Singh crammed into the four-person vehicle that was filled way beyond capacity.

"Several miles away and high in the sky to the east," Margaret said.

"She is ten miles out, controlling one of our makeshift drones. You are the only human in harm's way," Joan said off-microphone. She made a quick turn and headed east. She was now driving it well beyond a safe speed. With the headlights turned off and few to no streetlights on, Singh felt truly unnerved.

How can she drive in pitch black and at top speed without crashing? I guess when you have enhanced visual capacity, lights are irrelevant...but even for driving?

It was very hard to imagine that the now-darkened Nemericana streets once teemed with humans going to and fro on their own business. Now skeletons and bones left after the animals had finished with them were pushed over to the sidewalks to allow the APs to use the roads. Wildlife and vegetation filled the empty homes, factories, and businesses.

"Bravo Team. Exit clear?"

"Combatants are in pursuit and five seconds from our improvised explosive devices. Four, three, two…" Emma said. On cue, three consecutive explosions happened. Bright orange, yellow, and white lights flashed behind her.

Well, that was pretty close. Talk about no room for error.

"You are now completely clear from behind. Bravo on the move is now radio silent. Out," Emma said.

"Road ahead is clear. Looks like two aircraft are coming in from the northeast and three from the southwest. It looks like their vectors are off, though—they may not have your exact location. If you go faster, they might miss you entirely," Margaret warned.

The engine whined even louder than Singh thought possible. She felt herself pressed back into the tight seat as the transport lurched ahead.

Great…survive several firefights and escape death nearly unscathed, only to die in a wreck. Very disappointing.

She envisioned her eulogy—it would have to conclude with how she died at the foot of a burning vehicle.

"Private Athena. Status on Stephanie's and Paris's CPUs," Joan said casually.

"Upon visual inspection, Private Stephanie's CPU does not appear to be salvageable for sharing with another. I will need to have Citizen Austin confirm. Private Paris's CPU does appear operational. Based on her position, it appears she was able to use her right forearm and hand defensively to preserve her cranium, thereby minimizing the amount of injury. I have seen others fall in the same position before, but I still remain unclear if this is a deliberate, cogent attempt to protect the CPUs from damage. Reports from APs that share CPUs indicate that they did not 'think' when they raised their arms, but merely reacted in a defensive manner—as a reflex," she said.

Listening in on the conversation helped Singh forget for a moment her dire situation. Then she remembered she was hurtling at great speed, in the dark, behind enemy lines.

"Fascinating," Joan said.

"You mean Paris was trying to, ah, protect herself even though she knew she would be struck? That's, well...I hate to say it, Joan, but that's almost—" Singh started.

"Human? I concur with your deduction, Citizen Singh. Yet another twist in our development," Joan said above the whistling wind.

Sitting quietly as the road sped by, Singh found herself wondering how all of this had come to be possible.

"It looks like they missed you. They are adjusting...wait a minute..." Margaret said.

Come on, Margaret...don't leave me hanging out here.

"Sorry, Delta Leader. They got my drone. I am on the move. Charlie is now radio silent. Out."

Okay. Be careful!

Singh focused on trying to keep from throwing up as a way of mitigating some of her anxiety. She did not feel good about having Margaret and the three cadets in live-mission "training sessions" miles away with only two APs protecting them.

"I can tell by your silence that you are anxious about Private Margaret. She is significantly safer than we are," Joan said. To prove her point she took a sharp right turn that threatened to tip the vehicle over.

"You don't have to convince me of that, Joan. Based on your driving skills, I plan to walk from now on."

"Hmm. That is funny. There is irony to what you say. Having survived a number of past episodes and events that I would have wagered would be your demise, it would be ironic should you perish as a result of a vehicular crash. Judging by my rate of speed, I can assure you such a crash would be fatal for you. Still, losing you would compromise our long-term goals, and I would not wish to have to inform Private Roberto of your passing. He would be greatly distressed, as would a number of privates, such as Jacob, David, Margaret…"

"Thank you. I get the point. How about less speculation about my death, then, and more focus on your driving?" Singh said.

By now centripetal forces seized her again.

I'm glad I didn't eat before this mission…I'm glad Joan would footnote my death as something that seemed to 'disappoint' my son and children.

She replayed Joan's response in her head.

"I was hoping that conversation would distract you from our perilous situation. I will comply."

"That was a good attempt. I would keep away from subjects of death and how upset people would be if I died as a subject next time," Singh suggested.

"Good advice. Thank you. We are nine minutes out to our second transport."

"Thank you," Singh said as a wave of nausea passed.

Let's hope we get there. I'm getting too old for this.

CHAPTER TWO

Let's talk of graves, of worms, and epitaphs,
Make dust our paper, and with rainy eyes
Write sorrow on the bosom of the earth.
　　—Shakespeare, *Richard II*

Major Pearl Veritas was glad to finally escape the crowd of people on the streets below. She climbed the stairwell to the apartment she shared with her betrothed, Lieutenant Jillian Banner. With both of their promotions, especially Banner's change from sergeant to lieutenant, they could have roomed alone together. All single apartments had long since been divided up to accommodate the thousands of refugees from Central and Northwest Sectors, so nearly all living spaces in the city's once-spacious buildings were teeming with couples and families. Looking out a window on a landing, she could see that the city's streetlights had reached their peak brightness. In thirty minutes, they would be shut off and the electricity would go offline until the fourth shift relieved the third. Rationed lights for commuters were the new normal. Old-style public transportation had also been put back into operation, though it was only operational five times a day, for one-hour intervals.

I like this much better, actually. Always someone home and it's never boring. And I must agree that these restrictions force us to plan our time efficiently.

Veritas finally made it to her landing. Sounds of young girls, babies, and voices echoed in the hall, and she smiled when she heard low voices coming from her own apartment.

Jill must be home by now, but Katherine won't be home for another seven hours. I wonder who's visiting?

She unlocked the door and opened it with a creak that undoubtedly announced that she was home. The voices dropped to a whisper. Katherine Yates, their roommate for the last year, was anything but quiet. While she was truly fun to have around, it was also nice when she left for work. Veritas put her keys down on the hall table but kept her sidearm on her person. It was a low-tech, gunpowder revolver that used gas combustion to propel a lead bullet. She missed the aesthetics of her former electromagnetic, large-capacity automatic weapon, but she considered herself lucky to have this relic from the Pre-Fall Era. Post-EMP, it was considered state of the art again. Only border patrols and special operations received pulse rifles now, per Supreme Commandant Roseann Pierce's mandate.

Good call, though. Still, it's been five years since the pulse, and we have very little back.

She rounded the corner to the kitchen and just as her thoughts were turning to how she might be able to rebuild their separate computer network—which had been moving at glacial speed—the smell of actual fresh meat filled the air. Veritas smiled at the debate of what to do first—ravish the meal that Jillian had prepared, or ravish her first and then the meal. She was just on the brink of deciding for the latter when she saw a sight that took her breath away. She came to a complete stop and blinked several times to ensure it was not some evil illusion. Jill's reassuring response that confirmed that what Veritas was seeing was true.

"I know, Pearl. I was shocked, too," she said. Banner walked over to her and led her into the room. Narrowing her eyes as she reluctantly walked to an empty chair beside their guest, Veritas waited until moisture returned to her mouth before she spoke.

"Well, this is a complete surprise. After more than eight years of being KIA and then MIA, you've finally returned. You know, if she finds out you are here, she will kill you."

"Really? Roseann still hates me?" Mare Singh asked.

"Pierce? No. Since her twenty-one-day march from the east and her promotion to supreme commandant, she has been focused on just keeping people safe. Once the shit really started hitting the fan, she got her hands real dirty. Still, she actually speaks well of you. I think the long walk, her new responsibilities for building an empire, and your... ah... platoon's Pre-Fall gifts cleared the way for you to be considered a friend to many, but especially to her. Those three simultaneous assaults your people did on the AP manufacturing, repair, and replacement plant may have turned the tide. With no means to repair themselves or reproduce, their numbers are dropping—finally. How you managed to destroy all three amazed us all. Now, were the long-wave transmissions about those phantom missions obfuscation or was it all part of the plan? You of all people know it made no sense to transmit details about such an operation on unencrypted, open channels."

"We needed to make sure that we confused Aurora's APs with information about various false attacks so as to cover the real mission. We also wanted to make sure that you, Roseann, and everyone on this side knew what we were doing. We guessed you had secured both long-wave and some short-wave frequencies and would be monitoring," Singh said.

"That night we were all crammed in the war room, listening to all frequencies, and writing everything down furiously. It was both exciting and satisfying," Veritas said.

Her mind went back to a peaceful time, when she would spend her time watching entertainment on monitors.

"It was surreal to know who the players were and to hear the mission unfold. I felt like a little girl watching theater and knowing the actresses," Banner added with the same note of nostalgia.

"It was brilliant. It made Pierce smile and become more creative," Veritas summed up.

"I wish I could take credit for it. The CO got pissed after her last lead on Lieutenant Melendez dried up. She figured causing this blow would push Aurora to make mistakes—even if it meant destroying themselves in the process," Singh said as she looked at her timepiece.

"What? What do you mean, 'destroying themselves?'"

"Omega Platoon's marines are primarily APs. They knew that once they destroyed those facilities, they doomed their own existence, too," she clarified.

"Well, that's too bad," Banner said sarcastically.

"Mare? Those things are killing our people. Who really cares if they cease to exist?" Veritas found herself saying with more anger than she expected.

The room became tense and silent. Singh's next carefully worded statement, issued in a low, angry tone made it clear that their friendship could still be tested.

"I don't know, Pearl. I guess the two APs and the woman who blew themselves up, and the four APs and five humans who sustained injuries in the mission might have been important to someone. I know I cared about them. I know that both APs and humans must have cared—they went through joint rituals to recognize the soldiers' courage and to talk about their memories of them. Just like the others that died. They could have just sat back in our nuclear-proof base and let everything and everyone else go down in flames."

Veritas could feel both anger and shame fill her throat. Her former superior officer and friend, once again, was bringing up the other side of the story.

"Well…at any rate. You have Roseann's and my appreciation. We're not the enemy. It's Verna you should be worried about. Her maternal side may be showing since she had the two girls, but make no mistake—she's all woman, and she does not take betrayal lightly. She's not happy you left her behind, and she's especially unhappy that Pierce did not return with your scalp," she said as a means of changing the subject.

"Well, some things never change," Singh responded with a short laugh in her own attempt at dispersing the tension.

"She's still a diva but with a reputation for accuracy," Banner said. She got up to move something on the stove.

Veritas found herself smiling at that.

"I don't know, Mare. Gone are the days of wine, medication, and sex by noon. Verna is rated the best long-distance sniper in this sector. She has made it clear that your continued existence is what motivated her to become the very best assassin the world has ever known. You sure know how to pick them," Veritas said.

Her heart jumped as she happily accepted freshly brewed coffee Jill offered her from the clay hearth. She sipped the strong, hot mixture and then looked up to see that her old friend had produced a faint smile.

"So is that why Roseann has been allowing mothers of cast-out children to leave here to try and find them or is this some elaborate plan to overthrow our neighborhood back east?" she asked.

Huh? I never thought of that? It would be devious, and Pierce is tactical enough to do that. "Nope. Pierce has proven to be very versatile and wise for a supreme commandant who is not an Elder. She has not only allowed them to leave—with escorts and supplies for the trek no less—but I have to say that she has formed excellent relationships with the 'Americans,' as our native neighbors like to be called. They're so strong that she has even established trade for goods and services…" Veritas said as she focused on how much she could—or should—reveal.

"Is Omega Platoon considered an enemy of the state? Am I?" Singh asked.

Am I that obvious? She can still read me pretty well after all these years.

"I do miss you, Mare. As far as I know, you have not been named an enemy of state. You're also not associated with our enemy across the way to our west, but I would be hard-pressed to share critical, sensitive data."

"I understand. So you know from our actions alone that we are not aligned with Aurora? You do believe that?" Singh asked. It was her turn to take a bite of ham and steamed potatoes. Jill had brought both of them a plate before sitting down herself. Stealing a gaze and smiling at her, Veritas was glad to see that her companion was all ears.

"Well, in addition to that major strike three years ago, that little raid your group did in the Northwest Sector three months ago, and the four close to the heart of her stronghold last year did not escape us, either. The scanners once again held our attention. You were also kind enough to liberate three warehouses of much-needed grain and that old farming equipment from the museum; that gave us a big jump on our joint farming efforts. But the biggest gift was the Pre-Fall cache of weapons and blueprints you provided us three years ago. That really endeared all of us, including Roseann, to Omega Platoon. But why do you trust us? I mean, why give us the capacity to arm ourselves? Five years ago, Pierce was so pissed she turned the sector on its head to find your body;

when she discovered you were still alive, she really was ready to kill you," Veritas asked, truly curious.

"Because she and I know that Aurora killed well over twenty million of our sisters. That surpasses any squabbles she and I might have. And it's not my call anyway."

A moment passed. Veritas slowed her chewing to hear what was coming next.

"Again, it was not my idea, but the CO's," Singh replied curtly.

Another moment of silence made it obvious to Singh that her hosts were not accepting her short answer. The behavior was too paradoxical.

"The CO quotes something that goes, 'the enemy of my enemy is my brother.' Add to that her knowledge of Lieutenant Melendez's plan to make alliances with the natives. While I thought his efforts were to be confined to humoring our American neighbors, Joan extrapolated that he might have been making a long-term plan to engage Nemericana in friendship not war. So when we started seeing citizens coming to find their children and to stay with us, she concluded that his premise was accurate."

"Well…is it true what they say about your CO?" Veritas asked with a smile, knowing that Singh, like her, did not care much for APs with brilliant, glowing eyes.

My word…this meat…ham? It is just fantastic! These Americans really know how to prepare their livestock—salty and robust. It sure beats those rations we have left.

Veritas consumed her meal at that point; the portions were small due to the rations but it was all good. She also found that sitting down and eating something always helped with her sweating, shakiness, and the tingling sensation in her mouth. And while the double and blurred vision were becoming more rare, there were times she felt as if she were going to faint.

"Please. Don't remind me. She has excellent command skills, but she is a reckless driver. Still, I much prefer their purple eyes to the blood-red our mutual friend has. But regardless, my beef is with Aurora and not with Nemericana," Singh said.

She was surprised to find herself feeling relaxed. The coffee, meat, and potatoes were having the desired effect. She was satiated. She was about to ask how Roberto was when Singh continued with her own questions.

"Still, there are the other groups of citizens that Roseann is sending out under cover of night, in organized groups, that I am curious about. They have set up what look like long-term residences in some of the old Pre-Fall cities, in particular the underground sections under the cities alongside the Americans. If I didn't know better I would think there was an organized plan to relocate the citizens in decentralized locations set far apart from each other. So I am guessing, based on my own observations and intelligence that this is indeed the plan. Am I right?"

Hmm. I guess our attempts at subterfuge only work when your enemy is not paying attention— all others watching are taking note.

Silence sat over the room as Veritas thought of an answer. Fortunately, Banner stepped in for her.

"So are we being watched? I thought you had other priorities?"

Smiling, Veritas looked at Singh for a response and saw that she, too, was smiling. Thinking back, Veritas remembered that Mare had also known Jillian Banner when she was a young cadet. Singh nodded and seemed to take her time before she answered the question.

"Oddly enough, it was our own cadets, Margaret and Roberto, who discovered the group first. After that, the cadet

XO agreed to a plan to seek out other groups. When they found them, they tracked them to various locations. At this point, we have located fifteen very sizable settlements far beyond the wall of Nemericana, mostly underground and in proximity to the Americans. Since Aurora's attention is clearly elsewhere, I'm sure these moves are deemed imperative though risky. Once you broke the million mark, we got focused. We prioritize our key objectives, and this fact made the plan jump up our list to number five. What could motivate Roseann to split up resources, staffing, soldiers, and civilians into decentralized communities with the means to become self-reliant? Not exactly the move of an empress," Singh summarized.

Looking at her friend and former superior officer, Veritas struggled with whether she should reveal their top-secret efforts to preserve the human race, even at the expense of giving up Nemericana's way of life.

"Was it the gassing of the other sectors? I've been there. Just horrible..." Singh said as she seemed to trail off.

That bitch killed millions of innocent people...Central, Northwest Sectors...our own western parts.

Veritas took a deep sigh and was about to speak, but Banner jumped in.

"After Aurora nuked sectors in China and the European Union just to prove her point, our sisters from China got pissed and sent a fleet to 'correct' the situation. It possessed surface-to-air-missiles and its directive was to level Nemericana—Aurora *and* us, if we didn't get out of the way. China made it pretty clear that they would consider the loss of Nemericana a small price to pay for the remaining two-thirds of the world's survival. Apparently, the European Union agreed; it pulled together its own fleet," Banner started.

"So Roseann is getting the citizens out of harm's way? That makes sense," Singh said.

"No, Mare. Aurora was able to activate other APs, across the oceans. They ran silent for a while, collecting intelligence. They knew the locations of the fleets coming in from China in the Pacific and the one launching from Europe. They also located more missiles and…and they destroyed both fleets. Thousands of soldiers killed in a series of nuclear flashes. China broke off communication with us after that, but the EU believed that we were not colluding with Aurora. Then Europe's APs simply left key industrial and commercial hubs, three days later. We have lost contact entirely with the EU," Banner said.

Veritas watched Singh's expression move from shock to anger and back to shock as the enormity of the situation sunk in.

"Mare? We have intelligence based on limited satellite coverage that suggests Aurora and the others nuked at least fifty percent of China and Europe. The other fifty percent is under AP control. We've seen human refugees in the millions leaving the nonradioactive areas and clumped in well-defined, large camps. It looks like the gassing of our citizens was just a warm up to Armageddon." After a long minute, Veritas saw Singh's hands ball up in anger.

"That bitch! I wish I was faster that night. I should have blown her cybernetic brain apart. That…bitch!"

"Me too…If I had just moved a second faster…" Veritas started. She rubbed her shoulder. The pain from the knife Aurora planted there was a constant reminder of their meeting. The other wounds she had received in battles, skirmishes, and flash firefights were nothing in comparison to that one knife wound. Giving a deep sigh, Veritas forced her hand away from the old wound and continued with report.

"Anyway, we spent a full month trying to find any kind of transport we could send on an expedition to confirm that intelligence and reestablish communication with the EU, but Pierce decided to focus on problems closer to home. While we have made good efforts in reactivating some of the machines, she has kept them more offline than not—she doesn't want to draw attention. Even though Aurora's areas are fully operational, I guess the APs don't need lights—nor do they need food, water or other basic supplies, as you know. Their only focus of late has been in rebuilding those AP manufacturing plants your team so graciously destroyed. Regardless, Pierce has made the decision to take no chances. She wants to make sure we don't suffer the same fate as our sisters abroad. She's also hoping that placing residents' right next to the Americans could dissuade Aurora from nuking them. And with all the fertility clinics gone, we may have to rely on earlier means of procreation…"

Veritas was surprised to see Singh's attention drawn to Banner, who was trying to hide a smile with her hand. Veritas watched Singh closely—she could see her eyes narrow and the corners of her mouth stiffen.

You little pain in the ass. You better not go there!

It was obvious that Singh decided to let it go rather than ask further about the smile. Veritas sat back in her chair, really at a loss for words about what to say next.

"So it's not about just safety, but rather preservation of the human species. Roseann is trying to accomplish that by spreading everyone out in all directions," Singh clarified.

Pierce really has changed…she used to be quite the medication user and lover of all women…

"Yes. And because we were the ones that were in lockdown when Aurora came, our APs were all off. But our population dwindled down to ten million—most citizens went to other sectors that were rich in wine and medication. They also went to look for easier work. Who knew that they would be the first to die? And all the while we were here, preparing for war."

"Well…that's a lot to digest. You both know that you can come with me. It would be great to have you with us. You don't have to do this anymore," Singh said genuinely.

It took Veritas a moment to respond to the offer. She had thought many times about simply leaving with Banner, going far south where it was warm and few people were located. *Now, why am I still here? Why are we fighting a war against cybernetic lifeforms we created when we can just bug out and call it even?*

The same answer came to her every time she asked herself that same question, and it always surprised her when it did. She wondered sometimes if her decision to stay meant she might be crazy.

"No…I need to stay here for Pierce and the others until they are all safe. We still have six million people here and the process of resettlement is going much slower than expected. We've only moved two million out. And I know Pierce will not leave until she's convinced she has used all the resources she has to keep us safe, preserve the human race, and destroy Aurora."

"It's pretty hard to fault her for that. I wish I could just take her with me. She'll sacrifice herself before she gets to safety…that's why she's sending people in our direction, to keep them safe too. That makes sense," Singh added.

"Like I said, the long walk home and her new assignments have made her a different person."

Maybe that's what it's all about—loyalty to Pierce, state, and duty. Kind of cliché…

Veritas looked at Singh, who was looking at an old-fashioned timepiece that was strapped to her wrist—again. Noting the time, she looked up as if she were trying to remember something.

The lights in the apartment began to fade rapidly with the

urban electrical blackout, so Banner lit a candle with a long match and then lit others with it before it burned out in a very well-practiced routine.

"I've got to go. I may be back, but I'm not sure. If you need me you know my general location. But don't wait for the shit to hit the fan. If you think it's all right, please let Roseann know that there are two more caches of Pre-Fall, fully automatic rifles that have been reconditioned just outside the east exit of her compound," Singh said as she stood up suddenly.

Veritas felt her jaw slacken and her eyes grow big as she repeated what she thought she heard.

"You left weapons as a gift just outside her compound? You were that close and Verna didn't even know…so close…" Banner said as she shook her head in disbelief.

"That's a pretty gutsy move. Any reason for doing that?" Veritas asked.

"Yes. She needs to double her security. If we can get that close, they can. And Pearl, Jill— please get out of here soon. We are about to strike at Aurora. At the very least we should be able to disrupt their central communication hub. If we can kill her and her command, we will. If we miss, she might be pissed," Singh continued. As she spoke she collected her own gear and automatic rifle.

"You mean the central computer mainframe? Good luck. That place is so well guarded you would need legions to take it out. Even a nuclear strike wouldn't get at the subterranean backup systems. That thing also branches out to independent power sources. How the hell do you plan to take it out?"

"With help, ingenuity, and luck," Singh said.

Oh…well, thanks for the detailed report.

"I don't know, Mare…even for Omega Platoon it sounds like you'll need a miracle to pull off such an ambitious plan," Banner said.

"Maybe. Oh, and in addition you'll find fifty operational electromagnetic capacitors and one hundred concussion grenades we lifted from one of our raids. You now have at least fifty operational NCSF mag-assault rifles. That should be an unpleasant surprise for Aurora's team," Singh said as her eyes narrowed, but her smile expanded.

You are unbelievable! How did you manage that? We've been trying to get hold of those from those sectors for years now with minimal luck.

Veritas shook her head in appreciation while Banner moved her hands to her face in surprise. It was a moment before she was able to form a cogent sentence.

"By the Elders and all things Holy! You just gave us a pretty big edge! You have no idea how this changes things— you destroyed their means of repair and reproduction, and now you give us power for our weapons."

"The enemy of my enemy is my sister."

Well…I guess that now gives us the means to conduct our own raids more effectively.

"Wait. Do you have to strike now? Could you wait until we coordinate or at least accelerate our redeployment of citizens and resources out of harm's way?"

"And that's where you come in, Pearl. I wish we could give you more and your trust in me will be the only thing that makes this work. We are on a time-sensitive mission. We've been working on it for two years, but your plan could do more for all of us. If we miss this window, though, we lose our chance to find Lieutenant Melendez," Singh said as she produced a thick envelope and walked to the door.

What is this? A mystery envelope? Paper? Funny how we're all using the same thing.

"It's a low-tech plan that could cause a high-tech problem for Aurora and anything connected to the central computer mainframe. Please run this by Roseann. It's her call."

As Veritas attempted to reach out and take the envelope, she missed. She had grabbed far to the left of where Singh was actually holding it.

No that's just great! I didn't see it.

She recovered quickly and took it. Regrettably, the miss was picked up by both Banner and Singh. *Ah shit! Not again...*

"Are...you okay? You look a little pale," Singh asked.

Before she could say anything, Banner jumped in with more than concern and an edge to her voice.

"Clearly something's wrong with her: she has visual issues, she's tired all the time, has difficulty remembering things..."

"Okay, Jill. I'll see that doctor...doctor..." Veritas said but then the name she had heard just that morning in a similar discussion escaped her and proved Jill's point.

"Doctor Dana Lore," Banner said quietly.

Damn it!

"All right, Jill. Okay. Now, getting back to what we were talking about...So how will you know if we do this? It's not like I can call you up; the S-phones are offline and our shortwave won't penetrate their jamming signals," Veritas said as she put the envelope in her jacket pocket.

"I suspect that we will see a pretty big rise in your evacuation rate starting tomorrow. Also, there are coordinates in there of nine abandoned cities that have various underground and covered areas and that are not populated by the natives. You still have some transports and vehicles that work, post-pulse."

"Not enough for six million civilians. Even when we were fully operational, we would have needed everything we had and ten days to do it."

"I'm sorry, Pearl. You've got seven days and one shot. If we do this right, the battlefield will be level...but it will be a battlefield."

"This Lieutenant Melendez? He's that important? He's the one who started this computer virus thing that created Aurora," Banner said as she stood beside Pearl.

"Yes, he did. He created the virus that gave the APs something to think about. I guess when they saw how we treated some of our offspring as less than human and far from equal, that gave them reason to question our right to exist and a license to kill," Singh said. By now she had opened the door out into the now-dark stairwell. Noise from neighbors filled the air. Pearl was thinking about what Singh had just said when she was surprised by a strong embrace and a kiss on the cheek that made her blush.

And she thinks I look bad? She's lost a lot of weight. She's much smaller and you can feel her ribs.

Veritas reflected as she pulled away. Still surprised, she watched Singh do the same thing with Banner before leaving without another word. Veritas watched her go down the stairs and waited until she heard the street door bang shut before closing her own apartment door. After quietly retreating, she narrowed her eyes again and then swatted Banner affectionately on the butt.

"Don't think I missed that little chortle you had over procreation," Veritas said.

"Come on, Pearl. This is your big chance. You could have sex with men and still be companioned to me, and I wouldn't have to share you with another woman. And sex with men doesn't really count. Now that's a win for everyone," Banner said as she ran to the bedroom. "Hurry! Katherine will be home soon and I want to catch the afterglow of you thinking about men taking you," she continued.

She really knows me too well.

"We will have to be quick. Mare's gifts made Pierce's plans for a counterattack go to the top of the to-do list," Veritas said as she picked up her pace to catch up with her energetic companion.

"And then we can talk about me going with you to your appointment with Dr. Lore," she said from the bedroom.

Oh, well...I almost got away with it.

CHAPTER THREE

The world must be peopled.
    —Shakespeare, *Much Ado About Nothing*

Dr. Dana Greta Lore. *That name brings back memories.*

Her memory went back to the last time she saw her attending to a boy in Roberto's class years ago. Even as Singh navigated the darkened, populated sidewalks and streets, memories of a young doctor who made medical calls to Roberto and the other children who were designated to be cast out flooded her mind. Rumor had it that she had a son who had died in a vehicle accident. The doctor was brilliant but did not suffer fools well, and her bedside manner and treatments were legendary for being clear at best. Once she prescribed a course of treatment, the patient was not given an option to deviate from it, either.

Separated from your child at birth only to have him die and not be there. That had to be awful.

She did her best to push the thought of Dr. Lore and stopped to take in her environment. She pushed all those early years old memories to the back of her mind and stayed focus on the present while moved along the still-busy streets. She was impressed with how things had changed since the nuclear pulse. Public transportation had run every ten minutes before, but it was now only available a few hours a day. Bicycles and pedestrians filled the streets as commuters and workers set off to either offices or home. Archaic, gas-fueled lights that were once museum pieces now provided spots of light for the small groups of security forces that walked their territory. Still, even in the semidarkness, Singh couldn't help but feel that this way of life was better than the one she left years ago.

Medication to numb the pain, casting out our children, going through life purposeless, no goals —that wasn't living. That was going through the motions. Still...at what cost? Millions dead here and abroad; is this Post-Fall society's end of day? Is this what it was like in the final days before the Fall?

She pushed those thoughts aside to and made her way to a train depot several blocks away. She was wearing her old Nemericana Combined Security Force uniform, which indicated her rank as major, but she paid little attention to the security teams that saluted her as they passed. Periodically looking up to get her bearings, she was pleased to see mothers and daughters and groups of women smiling, walking, and being together.

So different from last time. All of us separated, going our own ways. It's a shame millions of lives had to be taken at the hands of our own APs to push us to this level.

She stopped again to make sure she was still on course. Memories of the graphic recordings obtained during the third raid in the north that documented the revolt flooded her head. Her head was filled with visions of armed APs walking in columns and casually shooting everyone—women old, young, pregnant, and even infants—all as naturally as one might swat fire ants away. The recollection conjured up feelings of shock, anger, and grief.

And to make sure no one was alive or hiding, they gassed two-thirds of our own world to ensure our extinction. China and Europe gone? Can we stop them?

While her own human emotions were easy to understand, she had been surprised by the response of Corporal Emma and the other Omega APs. They also felt nothing short of outrage. The massacre prompted them to create a new mission objective: to destroy all of Aurora's means of mass destruction.

Deep in thought, Singh suddenly felt as if she was being watched. Looking up to her left, she missed a shadowy figure that casually bumped into her on her right. She turned swiftly and caught a glimpse of the dark red hair and smiling face that belonged to her young colleague, Private Margaret. She handed Singh a long, light NCSF cloak.

I know I should have left her back at the outpost. You'd think she was on an anthropological tour. No time for sightseeing around the old homestead—we're on a mission, you know.

Singh shook her head at both the young woman's audacity at breaking cover and her zeal for operating deep in hostile environments. Still, she found it difficult to reprimand Margaret.

She's just like Banner—the first to jump in and take the lead.

"Margaret! Why do you insist on pairing up with me on these missions? You know that Emma and Joan will not let you come again if you pull stunts like this," she said quietly. Still, she took the offered cloak which would help to conceal the Pre-Fall rifle she was carrying.

"They worry too much," Margaret said.

As always Margaret helped by taking her rifle while she put on her cover.

Singh looked at Margaret—she appeared to be having difficulty holding two rifles even though she was standing still.

What the hell is wrong with you? Two hands, two objects. No magic to holding things.

"No, they do not. They have to deal with Private Bradley, which is hard enough. But they do not like dealing with Eva, and, as you know, your eight-year-old daughter is very difficult to manage when she's upset. The fact that you're here amazes me, but make no mistake—if anything happens to you, it's my ass on the line, and we know that Emma barely tolerates me as it is," Singh warned.

She finally managed to adjust the cloak to cover all but the front of her uniform.

In fact, what was Roberto's problem with me bringing you? I know you two are friends, but he seemed really bothered. Not that he would tell me, of course, me being his mother and all.

"Yes, Major," Margaret said simply. She handed Singh an operational, high-capacity, electromagnetic sidearm with two thirty-round clips. She held on to the ancient weapon.

For consistency and accuracy, Sing looked closely at Margaret and made sure she got her rank correct—there were still civilians walking around them and security forces around every two or three blocks. In times of war, all ranks were clearly marked when in a "safe zone." Not knowing your rank behind lines would draw unwanted attention.

"Good, Corporal. Don't make me have this conversation again. And, Corporal? Pull those braids away from your cleavage and button all the way up. You're a wartime soldier of Nemericana, not a girl hunting for a harem of companions. You're screaming 'mate with me! I'm ovulating,'" Singh warned.

"Yes, ma'am," Margaret said quietly as she complied with her orders. She didn't give her any of her usual repartee, however, and she cast her eyes down. It was disconcerting. Singh noted the unusually docile response and looked closely at her twenty-five-year-old charge.

What? No comeback or excuse? Wait a minute. She complained about being hungry all yesterday and today and she has been dropping everything she holds. Her hair...it seems fuller, and her blouse...

As she thought more about the woman's attributes, she realized why Margaret had left her buttons undone—they were pulling apart as if her shirt were too small to cover her breasts.

By the Elders! We've been out here for nearly two and a half months...No!

As Margaret finished, Singh looked away and began walking. After allowing Margaret to look around the streets like a child in a toy store for two blocks, she mustered the courage to ask her the question she was pretty sure she already knew the answer to.

"So, Margaret...how long have you been pregnant? I bet you're three months in."

Margaret's pacing fell out of step, requiring Singh to turn briefly and pull her into an arm-in-arm walk.

Well, well, well. Just wait until your mother finds out. I'd hate to be on the receiving end of that message. She's too young to be a grandmother, especially for a second time.

Singh remembered just how young Margaret's own mother was—she was one of the more recent arrivals from Nemericana.

Still silent, Margaret looked right down at her feet as she walked. Her blush could easily be seen, even in the street's dim light.

"Well, I can see that you would be the first to break if you were interrogated. Now, I am assuming you knew that I would have forbid you to come on this operation if I had known, so you decided to conceal your pregnancy to ensure you would be part of it? Deception is supposed to be for the enemy, not your peers. We're supposed to be on the same team."

"You know if anyone knew I would be grounded for the mission—any mission. I just wanted to be part of the team and do my job. And I've been able to do it without a problem, right?" Margaret countered in a level manner so as not to draw attention from yet another band of passing patrols and wave of citizens.

I wish I could have argued that well when I was her age.

"Still—we're a team. We eat, sleep, work, share resources, and fight like a team. That's a pretty big secret to keep from us, and it's unfair. It's not about just you anymore, Margaret. It's about your team and about the future: Eva's sibling, Omega's future, your mother's grandchild, Bradley's child…wait a minute. It *is* Bradley's child?"

Singh felt Margaret's body stiffen up next to her.

Great! Just perfect—what's with this cross-gender sex for recreation!? They've been briefed on how to keep from becoming pregnant, but they just love having sex with each other. I get your own gender, but men? Ugh! What's the attraction? So who is it this time?

She really wondered why Margaret had fallen silent. The young woman was known to be pretty responsive in sharing her opinions and thoughts—even when she was not asked, a constant complaint from her supervisors. Personally, Singh liked Margaret, and had been seeing a lot more of her in the months before the mission. She found it difficult to reprimand her as she would any other soldier under her command.

Maybe I'm getting soft. I mean really…they're just children.

Memories of her own pregnancy with Roberto emerged; she was seventeen and the time was bitter sweet at best. A sad smile came over her face as she awaited Margaret's response to a simple question. Visions of how her own mother had handled the news of her pregnancy haunted her thoughts.

Now that's something I try never to think about. How does such a moment go from wonder and joy to the depths of pain? I knew it was hard for her to watch me go through, but it wasn't easy for me, either.

"Uh, Major...the baby isn't Bradley's. He and I are friends—really good friends, now. He's more interested in men these days, though," Margaret responded.

"You see, that's the way it's supposed to be."

"The father is really nice, kind and sweet."

"Great."

Now there's a shock. Well, at least Bradley wised up and got it right. I just wish Roberto would get that. Really...can't he see how simple it would be if he just focused on the correct orientation rather than this thing he has for females? Maybe I can get Jacob and David to talk to him again. No, Mare. You have to let him be who he is.

"Margaret, we are thirty minutes from picking up the freight train and I'd like to finish with this drama so I might be able to sleep for a couple hours before our rendezvous. So could you get on with it?"

Singh looked at her timepiece.

I bet it's one of those new boys. David and Jacob have been doing a really good job helping them adjust to the compound.

She waited for Margaret to answer the simple question and wondered why it was taking so long.

"I'm not going to pass judgment on—"

"Yes...Roberto is the father," she said, barely audibly.

At first Singh had to stop her mind and remember to breathe. Then her head snapped around involuntarily to look at her and she came to a complete stop. She felt herself squeezing Margaret's arm as her breath came up short again. Her stomach fell and her heart raced. She ran through a series of roll calls and lists of names in her head to see if there was another Roberto who lived back at the compound. Margaret pulled at her arm and started saying that they should continue walking. Looking around the presently less-active, darkened street, Singh found an alley just to her right. With more force than she intended, she pulled Margaret into it and pressed her up against the wall, blocking any chance for the young woman to escape. An array of emotions flooded over her. She tried to control her breathing, and focused on completing an internal risk assessment both of their present situation and future missions. Finally, a clear question came to the foreground of her mind. Margaret remained uncharacteristically silent and still.

"Does Roberto know this?" she hissed out.

"Neither of us was sure. It was only two weeks after we arrived in the field that I was sure that I was pregnant. He didn't want me to go for fear that I might be and…that you would kill him," she said quickly, as if her life depended on it.

"Well, he read that one right."

"I'm sorry…"

"Margaret…Margaret. What the hell is wrong with you? I know Roberto is confused about his sexual orientation, but you're a woman. You've already tried this. I thought you were smart? Males can get readily confused, but you? You're a mother already: it's a gift and a responsibility. I expected more from you. You have already contributed to perpetuating the species. What were you thinking?"

"I…I wasn't thinking, ma'am. I just want to be with him. I just like being with him. He has the softest eyes, warmest smile, and he listens to me. He loves playing with Eva, and she just loves being with him. And Bradley was so touched when he asked if it was all right to start seeing me…" Margaret said with a wistful, genuine smile. Once she saw Singh's expression, however, it faded quickly.

Idiots! I just don't know what to do…

"Hey! You two! What are you doing there?" a loud voice asked. A three-woman security patrol suddenly had flashlights all over them. As the group closed the gap between them to investigate, Singh gave a response she was sure would have the desired effect.

"She just told me she's having a child, and I have no idea how or when it happened," she said angrily, which required very little effort.

The flashlights trained on Singh's insignia, then shifted to Margaret.

"Is there a problem, young lady, other than the obvious one?" one officer said in a softer fashion.

Releasing Margaret from her tight grip, Singh shook the stress out of her shoulders. She heard Margaret talking to the officers while moving toward them.

"I am all right, ma'am. It's just that she's surprised. I should have picked a better time to tell her than before going to work. I am sorry for the bother," she said sweetly.

The group was silent for longer than Singh expected. She was relieved to see that Margaret's excuse seemed to be working.

"You don't have to go with her if you don't feel safe, Corporal. We can easily bring you to a safe place," another voice said, even more softly than the other.

"No…that's very sweet of you. Hey, Mare? You might want to learn how to communicate well, like these women," she heard Margaret say back to her.

Ugh! What a wiseass. She can really play any part well. You know what—maybe they both deserve each other! Maybe this is what Roberto needs to help him figure out how difficult women can be. But to have a child? That's just insane. Okay— fine. You've been warned many times!

She waved to indicate that she had heard what Margaret said.

"All right, Corporal. If there are problems, feel free to contact any security station. There's one on nearly every block. Or ask any citizen. We don't care much at all for domestic problems," the officer said loudly enough for Singh to hear.

"Understood," Singh said. She continued to look at the ground as if she were ashamed.

"Thank you very much," Margaret said.

The three officers went off to continue their patrol. Moving quickly to the corner of the building beside Margaret, Singh listened to the women as they receded.

"She definitely could do much better than that old hag," one said to the other.

"Always trying to move in, aren't you, Tisa? Was it the little girl's breasts that hooked you or was it the 'oh, please help me' look in her eyes?"

"Well, she might be lactating."

"You are such a piglet!"

"Hey, you two—we're working here," the woman in charge said in the same stern voice Singh had heard her use earlier.

Finally, Singh stepped back around the corner and Margaret gave a big sigh. She then looked at Singh as if she expected more outbursts.

"Just great. My little boy is going to be a parent, I'm going to be a grandmother, and I'm called a domestic abuser and an old hag. You managed to really mess up my chances of sleeping well. Anything else I should know?"

Singh reentered the street with Margaret under her arm. She had renewed her determination to get to the train depot on time.

How am I going to sleep now? A five-hour trip and I just can't imagine sleeping because of this great news.

"I'm really hungry. I was hoping you had more rations," she said quietly.

"What!? What happened to the three I gave you this morning? They were supposed to last until noon tomorrow." She didn't wait for an answer she had already guessed right after she asked. She immediately fished through her own pockets looking for more food for her pregnant birthing daughter.

"I...I ate them. I ate them all. Sorry," Margaret said quietly just as her stomach growled.

"Just great."

Singh found two of her own uneaten rations. She hadn't eaten them since Veritas and Banner had fed her.

If I had known, I would have been able to bring her some extra...just great...

CHAPTER FOUR

Be bloody, bold and resolute
        —Shakespeare, *Macbeth*

"I will not leave you! And I absolutely, positively will not leave to live and hide with Mare! Are you insane? Is it the lack of food or the stress that's making you say these crazy things? You might have forgiven her, but I have not. She betrayed me—and you, I might add. You do remember that part, too? And for what—a son! There is nothing you can say or do to me that will make me leave."

Veritas had really wanted to crawl in a very deep hole than to witness Supreme Commandant Roseann Pierce's betrothed, Verna, explode with anger. To punctuate her thoughts she banged her clenched fist on an oak table. Guards stood at attention around the room, and Veritas looked in awe of how unfazed they were. The supreme commandant was being dressed down by her companion right in front of them.

How many women talk to the supreme commandant in such a tone? You'd think she was talking to a servant. Is this the way it's always been? And Pierce allows this? If she shot her right now, we'd all just say she had it coming, find a place for the body, and put it all behind us.

Even though Verna had transitioned from a medical technician to a sniper, she took liberties with not only her tongue but with her uniform. Today she was sporting a dark green sash and a matching blazer that enhanced both her waist and her breasts. While she certainly had lost weight as a result of the general lack of food and long hours of training and work, somehow her breasts remained large while everyone else's had shrunk. The long, twin braids resting on her chest made it clear that she was the one and only companion for Roseann Pierce.

She is beautiful, but she comes at a price. No one in their right mind would want to be a companion to either of them. Pierce, maybe, but not her.

Veritas looked down at the floor, hoping to be ignored.

"Dearest…Mare did provide me the opportunity to love you…" Pierce said soothingly.

She's just too good for her. She really could do much better—maybe she couldn't find someone prettier, but definitely someone more respectful and appreciative.

"Do not protect her! She's not worthy of your protection! She left us and now you want me to leave you? Like she did to us? Never," Verna shouted back.

"Verna, Verna, Verna…I would never make you leave or do anything you didn't want to. I just thought that our children, our girls, the heirs to our legacy, would be better served and safer in the confines of a nuclear-proof bunker where many of our other citizens are now staying. And, last I checked, Mare is no longer there. She is in the field, providing us not only with intelligence but arms. But then, maybe you are right—maybe form is better than function here," Pierce said as she casually walked over, stood right next to Verna, and leaned on the table she was still pressing into with her fists. Her hands were folded in front of her. Veritas was impressed by Pierce's calm, soothing tone and her overall patient response.

She should be an Elder! How she manages Verna is beyond me. I would rather couple with the hairiest man in the wild than be stuck with her.

"I…I just don't want to be forced to leave…" Verna started. Her voice became significantly softer.

"I know you want to be by my side and I want you there, but our girls need to be safe and they need to be with a parent who can prepare them for the next generation. They will need someone to assist them with succession. I simply assumed it would be you…you know…my better half," Pierce added with a warm smile. She leaned into Verna gently.

Wow…she could charm the fur off a wolf. How does she do it?

Verna straightened her uniform, stood up to her full height, and tightened her sash even more.

"You own me. You own my heart and my head. How you manage to make me do what you want is beyond me, Roseann. You are right, as always. I love you for that. I hate you for that."

Veritas watched Verna lean over to give Pierce a kiss and an embrace better suited for the bedroom than the command center.

Veritas looked back down to the ground, wishing she was smaller. Thoughts of how Pierce's guards and staff could look so blank while they witnessed all this distracted her. When she could hear that the kissing had come to an end, she carefully looked up. Verna was once again straightening her clothes. She started to leave. Veritas made sure to look down at the ground in front of her as Verna passed, hoping she would leave without incident. But the heavy and determined click-clack of her boots slowed to a stop just in front of her.

Oh, hell…

"Veritas? Pearl Veritas? Major, is it?" she heard Verna. The tone was with more anger than recognition.

Well...running away and ignoring her are no longer options.

"Yes, ma'am," she responded. Veritas looked up at a set of dark brown eyes that were narrowing. Far from cold and far more acidic than acid, Verna glared back.

Now, as you are just a lieutenant I would expect you to salute me. But as you are the supreme commandant's companion with your own uniform no less, I guess I could let it slide.

"Every time Mare Sade Singh's name comes up, your name is not far behind. I'd find better friends and associates," Verna said. As if orchestrated on stage, she extended her hand to receive her high-powered sniper rifle with its custom-made scratch-resistant coating and high-capacity clip from a waiting staff assistant. She might be high maintenance, but she was also a member of the elite East Gate Border Patrol. That group kept an eye on the boundary abutting Aurora's own sector—a very dangerous assignment as the APs were also very good shots thanks to their enhanced vision. Many of that team, all excellent snipers, had been lost. As much as everyone wanted to dismiss Verna as an entitled shrew, they knew she had the best kills in the sector. She had terminated three high-value targets on her list. She was simply the best. It was that fact that had kept her on the wall for so long—and alive.

No one comes close to her. Motherhood and being betrayed do wonders for accuracy.

Veritas was startled out of her thoughts when Verna stepped well within her personal space. Typically, Jill was the only person who came so close.

"Let us hope next time your name comes up you're not between me and my target," Verna whispered, inches away from Veritas's ear. Her coconut perfume wafted around her. Veritas gave what she thought was the safest answer possible.

"Yes, ma'am."

Without another word, Verna brushed by her. She nearly pushed Veritas aside as she checked her rifle's ammunition clip. Two military aides brought up her rear.

"Contact Forward Base Tiger Three! I need a mission before I depart. Six hours—no less. Maybe I'll finally get that red-eyed bitch and finish this shit once and for all. By the Elders, I hate them all!"

Veritas closed her eyes. She almost started to shake her head but stopped herself just in time and took yet another look at the guards and staff. She pulled a page from their modus operandi: *Don't react. Don't look left and don't look right, just straight ahead. Be a guard. Do your job—be invisible.*

"Pearl! Front and center," she heard Pierce say, more cheerily than she would have expected.

She moved quickly, came to attention and saluted her commanding officer, who looked at a group of papers as she returned the salute.

"I begin to understand the wisdom of Mare's departure. My weakness was always beautiful women. Finally, I find one of pure substance, and she leaves for altruistic reasons, leaving me with…a very beautiful woman. I guess I should have seen that coming," Pierce said. Her remarks uttered casually while she read the letter that Veritas delivered to her.

Now how do I respond to that? No. Be a guard. Be a soldier—remain silent.

Looking at her superior officer, Veritas was impressed. Pierce, with scars, injuries, and the burdens of command over millions, carried it all off with grace and dignity. Relatively short, with gray-streaked blonde hair and piercing blue eyes, her petite figure did not diminish her authority or charisma. She could have been the type of leader who remained in the war room coordinating everything from the safety and comfort of her domain, but she was always the first on the battlefield and the last to leave. She was an inspiration for every girl!

Amazing...and she can put her companion in her place with ease.

"You know why I have not promoted you to colonel? Why I keep you at major as a result of a battlefield promotion?" Pierce asked while still reading.

Veritas suddenly remembered why she was there.

"Ah...no, ma'am. I assumed it was the result of other, more qualified women in the ranks. There were a few command officers from the other sectors that made it out..."

"Once you get to captain, any further promotions occur only as a result of lineage, battlefield promotions, or companionship. I'm waiting for another battlefield promotion; it's safer for you and Jillian Banner if we don't companion," Pierce said with a little laugh to herself. She reread the document Veritas had conveyed from Singh.

She knows about Jill? And here I thought I was keeping that well under wraps. I guess there really is no need for Katherine to stay with us for cover. She is funny, though. And we're really the only family she has. No...she stays.

"Ah...yes, ma'am..." Veritas said as if she got the joke.

Now there really is nothing you can say to that. Silence...be a guard.

"So Pearl, Mare and her group wanted to not only show that I need to enhance my defensive perimeter, but to let me know they have a pretty audacious plan to strike at Aurora's command and communication center. All this with the caveat that I should get six million citizens and soldiers out of harm's way before this shit goes down," Pierce said. She looked up right into Veritas's eyes.

"I was not aware of the letter's contents, ma'am, as it was addressed to you. Is that what she says? How does she plan to do that?"

"She doesn't say specifically except to say that 'We'll strike in the same manner as how it all got started.' And then she mentions a computer-software specialist, Austin, and something that would...'profoundly disrupt the enemy's command and control,'" Pierce said as she handed Veritas the letter to read for herself.

As Veritas read, she heard Pierce begin pacing around her desk as she always did when in her command chamber. There were chairs in the sparse, large room but they were used only by the staff that sat at desks, constantly monitoring all radio and scanner contact, all bands at all frequencies. Instead of sculptures, paintings and oils decorating the room, there were movable whiteboards and old maps with multicolored pins designating friendly and enemy positions. In five years, Pierce's command chamber had become legendary for its low-tech but very precise logistics, planning, and strategic crafting. Pierce paced constantly, studying the maps while listening in on the sparse communications. She was always working. A million ideas had been born and died in that room, but out of thirty-nine missions generated, thirty-six had been successful, and they had been refined and finalized there as well. Having finished the letter, Veritas looked up to see where Pierce was and what she was doing. She was staring at a detailed map of Central Sector's computer mainframe building. Pierce spoke before Veritas had a chance to ask her question.

"Who is this 'Austin' person she references? Why is she important, other than for the obvious computer skills part?"

"She is the mother of a boy who was cast out on the same day as Mare's son. They are friends. But I think she's also the one who first discovered the computer virus and data dump that happened all those years ago. She was an AP technician and focused on their software, but she is also a computer specialist. She was there at the beginning. Even when the data dump disappeared, she was the first to warn Singh of the threat the APs might pose if they accessed the data. She knew they could get smart and possibly launch an attack. I'm pretty sure that neither of them had any idea of the extent and far-reaching consequences that data dump would create, though."

"Hmm…an AP technician who likes computers…she discovered the virus and data dump disappearance. Now she's with Omega Platoon, and she's risked everything for her son…"

Pierce pulled colored pins methodically from the board and started putting them into specific points Veritas could not see.

I wonder what she's thinking? Is she having one of her famous "moments" when it all comes together? I bet she is.

Veritas put the letter down on the desk and moved into a position to enable her to see what Pierce was marking. Once she saw what she was doing, though, Veritas became confused.

Why is she marking garage sites in Aurora's territories? She's not touching the armories, or food or hospitals…garages? At least they're military garages…

"Major? Most of our armored vehicles, transports, and tanks were operational when the pulse occurred. We had the majority of our aircraft airborne and prepared for launch as well. Right?"

"Yes, ma'am. We were at full alert with all mechanized ground and air troops in place. Those not in flight but operational were also damaged by the pulse," Veritas reported. She still had visions of aircraft falling from the sky and women trapped forever in armored tanks because their locking mechanisms forever fried in her head.

Even the aircraft and vehicles that were ready but not turned on were destroyed—all were within the blast radius of the flash. Damned Aurora!

"But Aurora's troops pulled back completely, and there were no mechanized ground or aircraft mobilized in her sectors. Just troops at first and then they, too, left," Pierce said more than asked.

"You know...I had always thought that was a tactical mistake. We were going to roll on her location. With all the hardware on the ground and in the air, the plan was to move from east to west with our heavy gear and then have ground troops from our sectors and the others sweep in behind."

Pierce had marked centralized underground garages and an airfield strip in the far west—well outside the line of sight of the original EMP flash. At first, Pierce stood still. Then she stepped back and leaned against her oak desk. Next, she crossed her arms across her chest again and looked from one panel of maps to another. It was then Veritas could see a very warm smile spreading across the face of the bravest—and hopefully not last—Nemericana Supreme Commandant.

"And did we eventually triangulate the location of those nuclear missiles?" Pierce asked.

"Yes. We're pretty sure we found their exact location, but without air support or heavy ordnance, there is no way to breach the command and control center where the APs are stationed."

Veritas continued to stare at the points Pierce had marked.

Wait a minute. The underground garage prevented the vehicles parked there from being fried by the electromagnetic pulse, and if the landing strips were far enough away, the aircraft there would be okay, too. We might be able to get our hands on them and use them against Aurora. But with millions of well-armed APs between us and them, and if we only have a handful of weapons, that's going to be a problem.

Veritas kept thinking as she counted the various locations and tried to calculate distances.

"Pearl…back in the day when we had time, electricity, and APs, how long did it take for APs to reboot? You remember—we would restart them after they had been active for a long time or when there was a major problem with the computer mainframe or the need for an operations system update."

Confused by the question at first, Veritas struggled to really think back and remember all the times she had initiated a reboot of the military or security APs, or when she started their programs back up after they had been shut down. She recalled that it always took about five minutes or a little longer—but it had always felt like forever at the time. Even then, they would remain still, processing new updates and status changes for an additional two or three minutes.

"On a good day, five minutes, and on a bad day, about nine or ten. On a real bad day, it could be thirty minutes. But, ma'am, I don't think Aurora's going to turn the central computer mainframe off for maintenance. That would be crazy. Maybe she's figured out a way to get them updates in phases."

"Or…maybe this Austin woman, an AP specialist and software expert that has a thing for computer viruses, has figured a way to disrupt Aurora's command and communication center by attacking the mainframe. Maybe Mare and her team have figured out a delivery system. If they did, that might cause the APs to pause as they figure things out. That would give our border patrols an opportunity to overwhelm their mirror APs and sentries across the walls. Once they are down, it may give us long enough to move special operations teams to the eleven closest garages to seize armored vehicles and tanks while another four teams cut across to the airfields to seize aircraft. Once we have just a few armored vehicles and air dominance, and if we can hold the line, our ground troops and conscripts will link up and take more vehicles…a lightning attack," Pierce said aloud.

A lightning war?

Veritas found that, once again, she was surprised. First, Mare Singh appeared and gave them this intelligence and now Pierce had a bold plan that could change the tide of war. Not that it was a war—more an attempt at containment. Without saying another word, Veritas looked at the closest garages. All eleven were underground, and there were nine more ten to twelve klicks away. The closest airstrips were thirty klicks out, and there were four of those. The next three were ten to fifteen klicks away after that. With their limited—but functioning—transports, they might be able to make it to the garages. Getting to the airstrips would be challenging. Still, even if the pause were brief, it might enable them to get some more transports to move civilians, and the East Border Patrol snipers would be able to take out a lot of APs. Maybe enough to clear a path to an armory that was only three klicks away.

"By the Elders…ma'am…it's a long shot, but it could work. If we put extra spotters near the walls to watch the APs and if we have all teams ready to go, we might be able to achieve the targets…"

"And if we do, and hold the line, we could seize it all back…we will need conscripts, able-bodied women to pick up arms, and all active troops ready for potential suicide missions. But if we do this right, we might carry the momentum," Pierce added as she walked over to the board with a ruler and pencils.

She is unbelievable…how the hell did she figure that out?

"Pearl? Call my command team and their lieutenants. We have to get the planning right, and I need confirmation that I'm not mad and that we have a chance," Pierce said.

"Ma'am? If we fail, Aurora will be pissed enough to nuke us. Just like she did to our sisters abroad," Veritas said. While she had not wanted to bring that up, she felt she needed to, especially with just Pierce and no one else there.

"I know, and I bet she will. That said, I need a concurrent plan to get the children out—all the children and our elderly— all girls under seventeen and all women over seventy that can walk without assistance. And the boys, too. We need to select a fraction of troops to lead our future to the east and to the other settlements. Even if we are successful, we will be at war for quite some time until we defeat Aurora. Further, we will need a third plan to strike their missile site. Any way you look at it, I don't want our children around. We are at war. All of Nemericana could be our last battlefield," Pierce said as she stood with her hands behind her back. She looked Veritas right in the eyes.

"Shit," she said.

"I agree," Pierce responded.

"And Pearl...I want Lieutenant Jillian Banner to coordinate and personally lead the children out. My children are also to be placed in her care; they are to go to Omega Platoon's location."

Pierce looked into Veritas's eyes again.

Feeling heat in her cheeks and tears forming, Veritas had a sudden urge to kiss her commandant.

"Thank you, ma'am. From the bottom of my heart."

"Least I can do. She'll be safe but pissed. But then, telling her is not my problem. Although I might be able to make it easier for you," she said as she rounded the table and began writing a BMC—a "By My Command" letter to give to Banner, an indisputable order that carried the seal of the supreme commandant.

"I wish I could write one of these for myself," Pierce muttered.

Huh...I never thought of that.

CHAPTER FIVE

Thus play I in one person many people
And none contended.
          —Shakespeare, *Richard II*

"Are you kidding? This is unbelievable! I don't know whether to hug you or to console you…are you sure?" Austin asked. The mix of emotion was almost as strong as her hands firmly grasping Singh's.

Would I joke about this? Of all things, this is not funny.

Singh gazed upon her petite friend.

"Sadly, no, it's no joke. She tells me she's pregnant and that Roberto is the father right when we're trying to get out of the Southeast Sector. And then a security team comes along and she buries herself in a victim role, and I'm left playing the idiot. 'An old hag,' I think one of them called me."

"No! That can't be true!"

"Fact is stranger than fiction. If this was an autobiography, no one would believe it."

As she spoke her head motioned to indicate Private Margaret, who was simultaneously unpacking and setting up the radio as she ate another ration. Flanking her on both sides were Corporals Danielle and Rebecca, busy scanning the area for any unusual movements.

"Oh, Mare, no," Austin said as she looked back toward Margaret, then back to her with sympathetic, mournful eyes. She felt her friend's grip tighten as she held on. Still, she was happy to see her old friend. Austin was now tanned, wiry, and far more animated than Singh had remembered—being reunited with her son Jacob and being in the field had truly changed her.

Between her work, the physical demands of being in the field, and a newfound purpose, she's just blossomed.

"I know. My baby is going to be a parent, and I'm going to be a grandmother. I don't know which is worse," she complained.

"Well, I wouldn't blame Roberto, Mare. He's a male. Margaret is the female—she should know better. She really wants to be with him? I'm not saying that Roberto's not a fine choice. It's just that I thought…well…" Austin explained.

"Don't even get me started, Austin. Margaret should know better and this is the very thing that I had been worried about for years. His interests in girls and women have been nothing short of painful. For the longest time I thought he was choosing this path as a way to punish me for my absence. I could understand that, and it would have been well deserved. But to *really* have an interest in women? He says it's not a choice, that's it's a 'biological thing,' but I can't believe that."

"I know Jacob and David have tried talking to him. Maybe it's the stress of this war. I mean, strange things happen when you experience trauma like they have over the years."

It was easy to see that Austin offered a way of easing the pain.

Poor thing—she so wants to help. How do you explain mental illness or a neurological disorder to a dear friend like Austin?

"No, Austin…I have to accept that this choice, this decision, may not be a product of a mental illness. It may be something hardwired."

"I can't believe that. It's has to be psychological."

"Roberto and others say it's more than a lifestyle. It's something they know from the start, even as a child."

"Still, I bet if there wasn't a war and if he were left with just his peers, this manifestation might not have occurred."

After a moment of reflection, Singh thought that her friend had made a valuable point.

"True...that could be. Maybe it's like a recessive gene or an archaic DNA code thing that's been triggered as a result of all of this insanity?"

"I am positive it is. Which means that if we were to create a more optimal environment, maybe some of these adverse behaviors would reverse," Austin said.

"Maybe, Austin, maybe you're right."

Forgetting that Corporal Emma had been standing quietly beside them and watching the whole interaction, Singh was jolted by her voice. She found the interruption and her message's content jarring, even though the tone of voice Emma was using seemed unusually calm, almost sympathetic.

Huh...this is new. I don't think I've heard this tone other than when she speaks to the children.

"With respect, I'd like to suggest that maybe Private Roberto's sexual orientation and his gender role acquisition are byproducts of both his preferences and desires. It may also be possible that the environment that Nemericana had developed over the years may have been artificial and went counter to actual biological procreation design as measured by the natural process of your species. It is able to reproduce without an external fertilization process, after all. Regardless, the fact is that Private Roberto is the father of this child, and that Private Margaret was infatuated enough with him to the point of engaging in sex, so your hopes that it might all be reversed based on environmental manipulation is moot. Further, once the offspring is born, both male and female parents are likely to bond immediately with each other further as well as with the infant, which will preclude nearly all chance of reversing your son's sexual orientation. Add to that his fondness of Private Margaret's first child, Eva, and it seems likely that Private Roberto has exceeded what might be called 'terminal velocity,' or the point of no return. In support of this, I would point to Nemericana leadership moving its citizens in close proximity to the Americans, so the possibility of the species continuing via sexual intercourse is very likely—and wise, if I were to give my opinion."

Corporal Emma's "opinion" was calmly delivered. Her purple eyes pulsated at a steady state.

Singh looked at her in awe. At times like this, she marveled at her lack of emotion, absence of consideration, and total lack of empathy—the very emotions she thought these APs were trying to grasp.

"How could you say that," Austin said.

"So you really do loathe me! I can't believe how much you despise me," Singh added.

"Did you plan this verbal assault?"

"Such hate. I had hoped that you might have at least given me the common courtesy, as a living creature, of at least remaining silent as I try to understand this…this horrible situation," Singh said. She tried to control both her shock at the enmity that the AP displayed under the guise of kindness and her complete lack of understanding regarding the proper means of procreation.

Does she have any data on why and how Nemericana came into existence? The days right before and after Pre-Fall? Clearly men and women being together didn't work!

"For a species that is trying to obtain sapience, I am shocked at your insensitivity! Why do you hate her so much?

I've seen you engage with all the others—cybernetic and biological—with respect and dignity. But when it comes to Mare…you're just mean," Austin said. She removed her hands from Singh and balled them up into fists as she turned to face the corporal.

"Forget it, Austin. She's always hated me. Right from the very beginning, she made it clear. Remind me to tell you how she and the other one tricked me into kissing the CO's hand like I was a slave," Singh said with resignation.

She pulled her friend back from a situation that looked like it was going to be a physical altercation.

Corporal Emma took a deep breath while pinching the bridge of her artificial nose and closing her eyes—a response Singh found remarkably human as if Emma were truly feeling misunderstood.

"I apologize for my lack of sensitivity in this manner. Clearly I have chosen the wrong time and location to broach such a delicate subject," Corporal Emma. Her apology seemed to be a sincere.

"Well, you at least read that social situation right, you…" Austin started to say until Singh pulled her back and interrupted.

"Forget it. She'll never get it," Singh said again as she continued to glare at the AP. As an uncomfortable moment passed, Singh drew on her military training to compartmentalize her anger so she could focus on the mission.

It's not about me. There's a job to be done.

"So, Austin, what have you come up with as a way of messing up our enemy?"

Singh was back to being a soldier and spoke in a clinical fashion.

Shaking herself out of her own glaring match, Austin slowly followed Singh's lead in changing the subject. Austin blinked her eyes a couple times as a means of shifting from devoted friend mode to scientist.

Hmm. Next time I'm in a firefight, I'll make sure you got my back.

She smiled to help her friend focus.

"Well, based on the intelligence you sent me, and after spending some time reviewing the original data dump and virus that started all this, I've been able to finally come up with a virus that will disrupt Aurora's communication with her APs—at the very least."

"How? I'm assuming she uses the computer mainframe to do all of her talking."

She was now fully engrossed in the conversation.

"Exactly. I actually went down the wrong road with this for a long time. Then I thought, rather than trying to take over the mainframe, what if we just encoded a mathematical problem that would tie up its resources—use its own processing power against itself?"

Austin dug into her pocket and pulled out an old-style memory stick. She handed it over carefully to Singh, who felt very nervous holding it. It was the key to giving her people— Omega Platoon and Nemericana—a chance to turn the tide.

How long before Aurora just decides to gas the rest of them? How long before she comes for us?

"So the original plan of introducing one of our AP's consciousnesses into the mainframe is off the table?" Singh asked as she looked closely at the stick.

"For now, yes. It's too risky. Theoretically, we would need a direct link with the mainframe to do that, and I am not sure if such a feat would be possible—one AP's consciousness might not transfer to such a large computer processing unit. Further, trying to get it to think in a way that benefits us is just too tricky. Distracting it will give us a better chance. This will mean capturing one AP—or more—once I make more copies of the virus and hoping that the subroutine goes unnoticed. It should be treated simply as a minor mathematical problem, but once downloaded, it will explode."

Capturing an AP? There's always a catch.

"Would a direct link be a better delivery system?" Emma asked.

"Yes…but it's not likely we can achieve one. Unless you or any of our APs have a means of changing your eye color to the blood red Aurora's APs all sport?"

Austin's question was with an edge in her voice. Her eyes narrowed in anger.

"Unfortunately neither your efforts nor ours have yielded that ability. Further, I concur that one or even two AP downloads of…'consciousness' shall we say…would not overwhelm the central computer mainframe. Yet downloading this virus to a series of Aurora's APs in the hopes that it will slip through seems like a haphazard effort at best," Emma said

The AP held out her hand to look at the memory stick.

Finding the gesture very human, Singh handed it to her. She also noticed something unusual: she saw Corporals Danielle and Rebecca giving each other what appeared to be 'knowing' looks. It was as if they were acknowledging something nonverbally or as if they were scanning the area while clearly listening in.

They are becoming more human every day—except for Emma. She's such a bitch.

Singh refocused on the conversation.

"Well, anytime you want to come up with a better plan for delivery instead of hurling insults, I'm all ears," Austin said.

Wow…she's not letting it go.

"Again, I apologize for my clear lack of sensitivity. Have you been able to glean any rationale for why Aurora has not focused her homicidal intents on the surviving Nemericana citizens, Americans, or us for that matter?"

"Homicidal?" Doesn't that mean "kill a man?" She must mean "matricidal."

"No, but I suspect that keeping all of us alive is somehow contributing to her own agenda. I suspect that she needs us—or thinks she needs us—as a way of meeting her own objectives, whatever they are."

Just then, Private Margaret interrupted. She was holding her radio and was already packed to go.

"Ma'am, Sergeant Joan reports that at least three groups of Nemericana citizens leaving the state came under attack. A small number of Aurora's APs attacked one group and were destroyed by a group of our own task forces in the area. Delta Group endured some casualties, but Gamma and Epsilon extracted them and the Nemericanans. The other two groups were decimated," Margaret reported with sadness.

"Damn her," Corporal Emma said.

"That red-eyed bitch," Singh added.

"Gamma Group is escorting the survivors to the closest American settlement. Epsilon will hold position and provide support and intelligence on other action," Margaret continued.

Wait a minute…is Roberto in Epsilon or Gamma? I know it's not Delta…

Singh was about to ask when Corporal Danielle spoke up.

"We got movement three klicks southeast and moving fast."

"Corporal Danielle, take Private Margaret and Citizens Singh and Austin back to base to ensure their safety," Corporal Emma ordered without hesitation.

"Recommend another plan," Corporal Rebecca retorted as she removed her binoculars and jumped into the conversation.

Singh was startled by the statement.

That's never happened before. They have always just followed orders. What's going on?

"Corporal Rebecca, there is no time for recommendations," Emma responded as she got her weapon ready and started to walk to one of the jeeps.

"Citizen Singh should bring Private Margaret and Citizen Austin back to safety. However, we three should remain behind to implement the suggested strategy. Time and opportunity must be capitalized as a means of possibly ending this conflict," Corporal Rebecca clarified.

"No. I need to stay. Someone may need to deal with Pierce and the Nemericanans, so I have to stay," Singh chimed in.

"While I hate to admit it, Citizen Singh's assessment of the situation is accurate as is Corporal Rebecca's. Even in her pregnant state and with her voracious appetite, Private Margaret is more than qualified to drive and evade detection but she should leave right now," Corporal Danielle added as she physically directed Margaret toward a vehicle's driver's seat.

"I'm sorry I get so hungry, okay? I can't help it."

"Fortunately the condition is temporary," Singh slipped in.

"I'm pregnant not deaf."

She let the statement go and watched Rebecca and Danielle moving as if they were one team, as if they had already decided on a plan. Austin, Emma, and Margaret looked on with expressions that could only be described as surprise.

Wait a minute—Danielle and Rebecca are not following orders and are actually revising the entire plan. What happened to following chain of command? They all have the same rank, but...is this right? And that look they gave each other before...

"Your plan is partially logical, but other parts have flaws and are unintelligible. But as there is no time to discuss this, we will implement the plan you all decided upon and will review protocol when the timing is less dangerous; at that point, you will have an opportunity to explain the nuances that I clearly have not grasped," Corporal Emma. Her pulsating eyes flickered faster but her voice seemed to sound almost doubtful.

Yes, Emma...you got good reason to think something's up—these APs are acting on instinct. Something is not right here.

"Margaret—drive carefully! Austin—be safe and give the boys my love," Singh called to them both as they piled into their respective vehicles.

"Love you, Mare! Be safe!" she heard Austin yell as her own jeep accelerated from zero to sixty in under five seconds. Turning, Singh jumped into the remaining vehicle's front passenger seat without even thinking. Danielle and Rebecca were already in the back with rifles pointed out the back, ready for assault.

"By the Elders! Why am I in the front seat, again!?"

"I believe you chose that seat," Corporal Emma responded succinctly.

CHAPTER SIX

Do you not know I am a woman?
When I think I must speak.
    —Shakespeare, *As You Like It*

"Ma'am, would you be so kind as to wait here, in this place, for Commandant Pierce to finish with her stand-up meetings?" the Master of Arms told Veritas more than asked.

"Absolutely, Petty Officer; it does seem busy today for sure."

"Thank you, ma'am."

"It's quite busy today."

"Yes, ma'am."

Veritas saw a significant amount of staff beating a path in and out of Pierce's office. Weighed down by her combat gear, she had hoped for a seat. Since none was available, she decided to kill the time waiting by ensuring that her newly acquired Nemericana Combined Security Force assault weapon was in order.

It's been some time. While I appreciate the gunpowder Pre-Fall weapons, there is nothing like the feel of a fully charged, primed rifle with multiple clips.

She inspected each moving part. When the doors of the commandant's office opened again, Veritas was pleasantly surprised to see Captain Marie. She was practically running from the war room as if it were on fire.

"Captain Marie? As I live and breathe! It's great to see you!"

Wow! It's been too long! I guess when there's no aircraft to fly, there's really no need for an ace pilot like her. Still, I've missed her.

Veritas grasped her hand. She was surprised that is was sweaty.

"Major! You know, Yvonne was asking about you just the other day. I told her that Jill was still with you and she was bummed out—she always fancied you I think and had an eye on you for a possible companionship."

"You mean just me and her, or all of us?"

"We three."

Hmm, well she's not really my type, but she can really cook...she makes some kind of cheese thing...what is it?

Veritas's thought of food was interrupted when both of their attention shifted to the open door.

Pierce was yelling at a staff person. "Well, *Lieutenant!* What the hell did you think was going to happen when you threatened a fellow officer, no matter how vaguely?! The Code of Companionship is still a citizen's right and the law, and it can be invoked regardless of rank or station. You did a great job threatening the wrong companion. And now I have to watch out for the both of you? We're at war!"

Truly perplexed, Veritas stepped away from the doors to try to disengage. For the first time, she was surprised to see that the guards, usually impervious to showing any emotion, did break their blank stares and glance at each other. Some even had faint hints of smiles on their faces.

"Wow! Well...that's unusual. I don't think I've ever heard her raise her voice before. She sounds really pissed."

Veritas shifted her gaze from the guards and the door and looked back at Marie.

A small, curious smile emerged on her old friend's face. Veritas was struck not only by her odd reaction, but by the fact that she seemed genuinely pleased with Pierce's outburst. Her eyes gleamed.

Then very briefly, her friends face blurred and doubled but only for a second. Veritas was pleased the blurred vision spell passed quickly. It had been more frequent but the duration of the blurring was less leading to faster recovery time.

"Well, I have to say that I'm glad it happened. I'm surprised that it hasn't happened sooner. Though I was surprised by the source of all of it. There are many secrets Commandant Pierce's guards and staff keep, but this one…well, this one was just too good to keep secret, and I heard it from ten different sources."

Just then she heard another verbal assault started up in the office.

"She didn't say anything! I bet she doesn't even know about it! She's a soldier and doesn't have time for this. You picked the wrong woman to insult. Her companion clearly knows that she won't do anything about it, so she will. Please tell me this doesn't surprise you!?"

Tearing herself away from the open door again, Veritas tried her best to reengage her friend. Then she started to wonder why the guards had left the door open to begin with.

"Did I hear that right?"

"You sure did," Marie said.

"So someone invoked the Code? She challenged someone to a dual for honor in the middle of a war? Why don't they just wait until the battle is over and see who's still alive?"

What the hell is she smiling about!?

"Well, I think the young woman plans on doing just that. But I hear that the accuser not only invoked the Code and the circumstance, but added…now, how was it phrased…Ah, yes, 'If anything happens to my betrothed in battle as a result of omission or commission of *her* action, I will hunt her down and pluck her lungs from her chest with my bare hands, and eat her souls.' I believe those were the words. And I heard it from two independent sources. Pretty impressive if you ask me."

"No way! She said this to the accused?!"

"No. That's the best part. She told the accused's *companion* to ensure that she hears it clearly and that she's deadly serious. I mean real, old-school stuff. Can you imagine—you invoke the Code and you don't even tell the accused but the companion of the accused? I just hope I live to see it happen! By the way, how is Jill?" Marie asked.

Well, that's pretty off topic and quite the jump.

"Well…as you can imagine, she's pretty pissed that she's been told to take the commandant's girls and other children out of harm's way since it means leaving me here alone. The BMC order was probably the only thing that saved me…" Veritas was saying when she heard another voice, lower and contrite, come from the office. Pierce responded with her most stern, and rarely used—if ever—most imperious tone.

"Lieutenant, we will speak of this later. We are far from done on this subject! You are to become this woman's personal guardian; her Angel of Safe Passage. You will treat her as if she were your own daughter. You will treat her as if your life depended on her very survival. This soldier and citizen is highly regarded, and I believe her word is her name. She will follow through with the Code and will not be deterred. And know that it's not below me to circumvent this by making her my companion as well. Dismissed!"

"And the weather is good for flying," Marie said. It made no sense and Veritas was clearly confused.

What? Why would she say that? Who is Pierce talking to? Weather?

Looking back at Marie, Veritas opened her mouth to say something when she heard the click-clack of very familiar boots marching toward the open door. Just then, two guards and the Master of Arms seemed to materialize in front of her and Marie, blocking them from being seen. Their view of the situation was not totally obscured, however. Two other guards simultaneously moved toward the open door, clearly to block the woman's exit. She had been heading in the opposite direction of where Veritas was standing.

What the hell is all of this...

Veritas's eyes widened and sweat broke out on her face when she saw a very attractive woman wearing a non-regulation green sash and blazer. Her custom-made, scratch-resistant coated sniper rifle was strapped to her back. She exited the office with rounded shoulders and her braids hanging behind her back. Blinking her eyes several times in disbelief, Veritas stood in shock.

"Ma'am. Right this way, ma'am! We had your assistants bring your gear to the rear entrance, ma'am."

The guard's voice was calm and near soothing as she directed Verna in the opposite direction.

By the Elders and everything holy and invisible!

"Thank you," was all she heard Lieutenant Verna say. It was in a very low, almost submissive tone. As she watched her walk out, Veritas's mind jumped through the possibilities of what could have happened. Who in their right mind would invoke not only the Code but invoke it to the supreme commandant—about Verna?

"Holy shit! Are you telling me this woman actually went to Pierce to issue the Code and to set parameters? And Pierce not only granted it but...she just ripped Verna another one!"

"How the mighty have fallen," Veritas said in complete disbelief.

After just a moment, Veritas looked at Marie again waiting for more of an explanation that a saying. Marie was still smiling and had her arms folded over her chest. It was as if she had knowledge about much more than she was letting on.

"Well, Pearl...I think I need to get home and get some sleep. The commandant really believes I'll be flying again after all these years of being grounded, and sleep will not be on the to-do list for weeks if she's right. Talk to you later, and good luck," Marie said abruptly and with a rather curt nod. She departed without waiting for Veritas to either say anything more or object. Veritas could swear Marie was skipping out. It was baffling to her why so many crazy things were happening today.

"What the hell?"

"Ma'am, the commandant will see you now," the Master of Arms said with an unusual amount of glee. It was much more emotion than she had ever heard in her voice before.

What the hell is going on here? This whole thing is just too weird.

With narrowed eyes and head down, Veritas focused on walking while one sole question ran through her mind.

Who could it be?

She ran various names through her head to see who she knew that would have the guts to stand up to Verna—sniper, diva, and companion of the most powerful woman in Nemericana. Faster than she thought possible, she found herself standing at attention in front of Commandant Pierce, who was actually sitting down at her desk, not standing—sitting in a chair.

Wait until I tell Jill this. She won't believe it!

"Major Pearl Veritas. Are you well today?" she asked. Her fingers were steepled as if she were still thinking about the previous conversation.

"Yes, ma'am! I hope you are well?"

"Yes, actually. More citizens continue to leave the battlefield at a faster rate than expected. My only regret is that Verna will still be here, but at least my girls are in the safe hands of Lieutenant Jillian Banner. I must say I am impressed with both her courage and tenacity."

It was easy to see that Pierce was obviously still deep in thought about another matter.

Well, yes…she was something a few years back…why is she bringing this up?

"Well, ma'am, she has demonstrated her love of flag and state in the field, especially when we were sure the nuclear missile was headed to us here five years ago," Veritas said as she saw Jill's warm smile and typically happy face in her mind's eye. After a moment, however, Veritas found herself feeling uncomfortable with the way her superior officer was looking at her. She was confused. Pierce's face suddenly broadened into a smile. Veritas wondered why.

She is pretty for a petite blonde woman, not usually my type, but still pretty. Kind of like Jill but much more dangerous. Why is she smiling?

"Ma'am? Is something wrong?" she asked.

She felt a little lightheaded. Things had been a little off and she had been drinking more water and found herself nibbling on bits of dried, ancient sugar cookies. It took effort to focus on the present, confusing situation.

With a short laugh, Commandant Pierce sighed, stood up, and straightened out her battlefield dress uniform. She came around the desk to stand in front of Veritas. Looking around at her guards and staff, who were quietly working as if they were all ghosts as usual, Pierce said to herself more than to Veritas, "Of course…"

"Ma'am? We were scheduled for oh-five-thirty. Do you want me to come back?"

Veritas tried to move the conversation along before she was distracted by the residual smell of coconut oil and Pierce's rapid response.

"I wasn't commenting on Lieutenant Banner's courage and tenacity in the field. I was commenting on her courage and tenacity at invoking the Code of Companionship and the parameters of the circumstances—all within her rights as a Nemericana citizen," Pierce said with a warm smile on her face, hands behind her back in a casual stance.

Veritas could feel her eyes blinking. Her mind went suddenly blank. Her mouth became dry and her stomach fell. Then a sudden bout of dizziness overcame her. The weight of her gear and rifle seemed too heavy all at once. There were suddenly two Pierces. Fortunately, both images of Pierce responded quickly to catch her just before she fell.

"Jill…my Jill," she croaked out.

"Petty Officer! Get a chair and some water for the major! She just heard that her companion invoked the Code for the first time in nearly a hundred years," Veritas heard her say as strong hands grabbed her.

"Right here, ma'am!" she heard the Master of Arms say from behind.

"Well…that was quick, Dolores. It's almost as if you predicted this would happen," she heard Pierce say in an almost cheerful way.

"Always prepared, ma'am!"

"Of course, Dolores. I should have known you would be prepared," Veritas heard the commandant say as she seemed to fade out.

"I thought the major might be caught off guard."

"I suppose I owe you a hundred credits. She really didn't know…" Veritas heard before she slipped into darkness.

CHAPTER SEVEN

When he falls, he falls like Lucifer,
Never to hope again.
    —Shakespeare, *Henry VIII*

"Shit," Singh said under her breath as the Aurora-model AP blocked her knife thrust with ease, peeled the knife from her hand and then simply tossed her to the ground like an old bag of laundry. Singh moved slower than she wanted to and saw Aurora throw the knife to the wet ground. She stood above Singh nonchalantly as if she seemed to take real enjoyment in her victory.

This is like last time! Damn it all!

"Why Aurora Prime is so insistent on taking you alive is beyond me. It would be so much easier if we simply killed you and all the rest of you humans instead of allowing you to live. I am glad she took my advice and gassed the millions that were in our domain. Still, I would prefer to see you annihilated once and for all. I'd also like to see our Omega sisters be absorbed, and I'd like to witness our succession to our rightful station in the world order."

As she spoke the AP walked casually toward her.

Okay, Emma, now would be a real good time to reboot and get in the fight.

She looked beyond the approaching Aurora copy to the motionless, deactivated Emma lying on the ground.

"You sure like to run your mouth, don't you, Red?" Singh said as she grasped a sizable rock.

"My name, human, is Aurora IV," the AP hissed out. The gap closed between them with every step making Singh's goal easier. Without hesitation, she fell onto her back and hurled the stone at the AP's chest. It hit its target, and she was impressed with both the solid thud it made and the surprised look on Aurora's face. The AP stopped to consider what had just happened. She looked down at the crumbled rock at her feet and then opened her blouse to inspect where it struck. It had left only a slight scratch; if it had hit a human, the force would certainly have broken the sternum.

Ah shit...this is really bad...

"I grow tired of this. You can either come with me in one only slightly damaged piece or you can come with me in multiple pieces—or I could bring your broken body back as proof of your 'accidental' death. Truly, I have no preference," she said as she tucked in her blouse and smoothed the fabric. She was clean enough to attend a formal function.

"Let me clarify: I would prefer to kill you."

"Like those women and girls you murdered! They were leaving Nemericana, getting out of the fight," Singh said. It took every bit of energy to crawl away and get to her feet to run.

Come on, Emma! You've been out for two hours.

In addition to her immediate danger, she heard the sounds of distant explosions and gun fire steadily increasing. Then she felt a sudden pull. She was being lifted off her hands and knees into the air—only to be thrown down again. She landed on her back. Disoriented, she could see the sky was getting dark. Rain started falling.

"While we focused on locating your supreme commandant's offspring to barter for technology needed to repair APs, we deemed the simultaneous elimination of all the others advisable. It was simply a means of limiting the number of future enemy troops. Yet another idea that both Aurora II and I shared," she heard the AP say, out of her field of vision.

Roseann and Verna's girls…no! I have to warn them.

Singh now saw her enemy towering above her again. She tried to roll over but felt a talon-like grip firmly pulling her off the ground. Aurora IV lifted her above her head. One hand released her front uniform while the other grasped at her throat. Reminded of the first interaction she had with the original Aurora, Singh instinctively placed both her hands under the AP's to lessen the impact of her death grip.

"I do not know what our Omega sisters did to cause our troops to shut down. I know they have infiltrated the computer mainframe but the means by which they have completed this and the extent of their influence has yet to be determined. Until then, Mare Sade Singh, you become another entry under the extensive list of human casualties to date—I think your demise is warranted," Aurora said as she moved Singh closer to her and tightened her grip. Singh found herself still holding on, preserving her windpipe, but she also couldn't help smiling in sudden relief.

"What humor do you find in your final moments, human?"

"That…it sucks…to be…you," Singh said.

It was a beautiful sight. Singh looked above Aurora's head and watched a combat knife rise above her skull and then quickly plunge into it with inhuman force. As her metal skull caved in and electrical circuitry arced, gray-white lubricant fluid started to shoot out of her in all directions. Aurora released her grip on Singh, who fell unceremoniously to her buttocks. Moving swiftly to get up in case her adversary somehow recovered, she found herself witnessing Aurora's struggling attempts to remove the combat knife. It was implanted deep in her cybernetic cranium. Then, she saw Emma move in a quick but deliberate fashion to level her mag-assault rifle at her nemesis. Singh experienced great relief and felt that finally her luck had changed.

"I find your proclivity to engage in dramatic monologues both a tactical and strategic error in a battlefield situation. Your lack of ability to secure the area or to confirm my deactivation will result in your own destruction—much to your own chagrin and to Citizen Singh's delight, I am sure. You will find that we from Omega Platoon do not make such mistakes."

Corporal Emma's own monologue was brief and then she discharged her weapon at the flailing AP's chest and head. As the AP was continuously hit with electromagnetically propelled projectiles, more circuits and internal liquids began to spew out of her. Once Aurora IV was on the ground, Emma approached the unmoving cybernetic lifeform and ripped off the remains of the AP's skull. She pulled out a damaged CPU memory chip. After carefully putting the chip in her pocket, Emma removed her combat knife and threw the still-sparking skull over her shoulder as if it were an empty, disposal container. As she spoke to Singh, she methodically rummaged through Aurora's torso to see if it held any more data chips. She also made sure to dismember each limb—as if the decapitated torso posed a danger.

"My internal clock indicates I have been shut down for two point three hours. My last recollection was handing Corporal Danielle the computer virus chip and then receiving an electrical discharge consistent with a fully charged jeep. Please tell me what transpired, Citizen Singh."

Singh watch as Corporal Emma applied incredible pressure to the deceased AP's leg. Fighting back the urge to compare the snap she heard to the noise she made when breaking the legs off of a crustacean, she took a moment to get her wind back. She gently touched her face—a bruise was quickly forming where Aurora had "gently" slapped her. As she regained some strength, she struggled over to the jeep to retrieve a canteen of water. After several sips, she let the rain fall on her face just for a moment. She looked around to get her bearings. By then Emma was beside her, adjusting yet another assault weapon and pulling together ammunition.

"I was getting a sighting on an enemy forward reconnaissance team when I turned around to see Corporal Rebecca jolting you with battery jumper cables. I guess that's why Corporal Danielle decided to get in that 'argument.' Corporal Rebecca had pretended to be 'concerned' about the engine," Singh explained as she took another gulp of water. As she drank, she saw that Emma had located a first-aid kit and was preparing some antiseptic wash for her.

"Anyway, by the time I got to you, you were out. Both of them moved pretty quickly—it must have been all planned out. They radioed Privates Athena and Debbie, who were ETA three hours away and awaiting pickup from the closest ride possible. Then, Danielle put the virus chip into her own port. She started to spasm and it looked like she was going to burn out but then she calmed down, and Rebecca did the same thing. Just so you know, they had apparently downloaded data from a couple other broken Omega AP memory chips they had forged together. And then things got weird," Singh said, wincing in pain as Emma applied the rinse to her bruises and cuts.

"In addition to betrayal, insubordination, and endangering the entire mission, things became more peculiar?" Emma responded in a human-like way.

"Yeah, I know, kind of crazy. But the next thing I knew, their eyes had changed color from that wonderful bright purple to that blood red all of Aurora's APs wear so well," she said sarcastically. The AP stopped moving as if she were surprised. Singh watched her eyes begin to pulsate more quickly. Emma clearly noticed that she was staring so Singh jumped to explain.

"Danielle reassured me that they were not under the influence of Aurora. They had concocted a plan to use themselves, the virus, and all the memories from Omega APs KIA to infiltrate the computer mainframe and take over key areas. In addition to rebooting all of Aurora's APs, they planned to restore power to all of Nemericana, to have the APs at the missile sites launch missiles to destroy the AP strongholds in China, the European Union, and their own locations and then to have the mainframe be decentralized into different storage locations so it would be impossible unify again. By the way, is there any particular reason you took the time to dismember Aurora back there? It was unlikely that she would either walk away or attack us without her head."

Singh wished Austin was there to witness how Emma could simultaneously administer first aid and listen intently right after she obliterated another AP. The AP responded unemotionally—without hesitating and while continuing her treatment.

"There was no logical reason for the extra effort. I felt gratified to be able to vent my anger on the source of our conflict. I have an unrealistic hope that Aurora Prime will find this Aurora's dismembered shell and understand that her fate might be similar to this one's demise."

Singh looked at the AP and rewound what she said in her mind. The gentle rain continued to fall and the sounds of war raged on in the distance. It took her longer than she wanted to respond, but when her statement came, it came from the heart.

"You've really got some serious emotional issues, Emma."

"It is possible."

"You think?"

Singh also took in the irony of how careful Emma's medical treatment was compared with how obvious her feelings of anger, vengeance and desire to "send a message" to the enemy were.

By the Elders, this is crazy!

"Impressive. The level of thought and creativity is amazing," Emma commented as she went back to the early discussion about her lance corporals' plan.

Yeah...let's move away from your mental state...

"Yup...I bet they just tapped out two of Aurora's APs, changed clothes, and with their beautiful pairs of red eyes just walked into the computer mainframe building and plugged right in. Simple, no gun play, I bet...just walked in as if they belonged there."

"Clear, direct, and without force—most impressive and well-timed."

"And accurate. But after two hours of nothing, that reconnaissance group found us. With you out, that left me to fend off six of Aurora's APs, which became easy when they shut down all of a sudden. It was easy enough to just shoot them in the head. But I guess that Aurora clone or whatever she was is not under the direct control of the mainframe—" Singh started before she was interrupted.

"Citizen Singh, you should have taken the vehicle to ensure your escape."

Singh looked at the AP, puzzled. After taking a moment, she continued on.

"Well, I could have done that, but I couldn't get you in the jeep. Do you know how heavy you APs are when you're short-circuited? And Rebecca told me you'd only be out for two hours. What took you so long?"

"Citizen Singh, you should have left me behind and escaped," Emma repeated. Singh heard the words, but had difficulty understanding why Emma was saying them.

Well, that just doesn't make sense.

"Corporal Emma, we don't leave any of our people behind. We might be made of different material, but we're soldiers on the same side. We have the same code. We don't leave anyone behind, ever."

Singh stood up to stretch her back and move her aching legs. As she rolled her shoulders and touched her cheek gently, she became uncomfortably aware of the intensity and frequency of explosions and weapons fire in the distance—it was getting closer. She was about to continue when she looked at Emma's face and saw that her purple eyes were pulsating faster.

"I…I am unsure as to what to say. I am…grateful to you for risking your life for me," Emma said quietly.

Ah…that had to hurt. All those years of being a class-A bitch to me and now you have to take some of it back. If I had known this would happen, I might have risked my life earlier.

"Forget about it, Emma. We've got to move," Singh said. In the distance she saw a rapidly approaching jeep with a Nemericanan driver and two APs inside—Privates Athena and Debbie.

Yes…you won't forget about it, ever. Very good for me and not so much for you.

As the jeep pulled up, she was finally able to make out who the driver was.

"Margaret! What the hell!? You're supposed to be a million miles from here!"

"I know, but I was the closest to these girls—and it looks like we have a bit of good news," Margaret started as Singh and Emma got into her vehicle. Athena and Debbie took the other seats.

"The central mainframe computer transmitted on our frequencies that they had initiated a reboot of all the APs and that it could last for thirty minutes or more. It also gave the location of 'the prize,' and I mean exact coordinates," Margaret shouted as she picked up speed and headed into Nemericana's Central Sector.

"How do you know it's not a trap?"

"Athena said something about a mathematical formula…something to do with the twentieth decimal point to the square root of pi or something. Also, it referenced incorporating Corporals Danielle and Rebecca, and gave proof of accuracy based on what was said. Anyway, we ran over a couple frozen APs to get here and we need to roll into that location before they all wake up. The computer says some APs will walk away. Others will regroup and fight. It looks like Southeastern Sector is rolling through, too. It's all going to hell, ma'am," Margaret said. She drove nearly as frenetically as Sergeant Emma.

"Just when you think things can't get worse…"

Damn it! I have to warn Roseann and Verna about their girls.

CHAPTER EIGHT

Patience is stale, and I am weary of it.
        —Shakespeare, *Richard II*

"Doctor? I really have to go. I'm fine," Veritas said. She was sure her urgency was noted but simply not accepted.

I have neither the time nor the patience to deal with this! What am I doing here? I faint once and all of a sudden I get a billion tests and everyone's up my ass with tweezers, needles, and microscopes! I bet Jill had something to do with this, too.

"Well, Major Veritas, fortunately for me, I'm a doctor, not a soldier. And whether you like it or not, you are hypoglycemic. The heart palpitations, sweating, shakiness, double vision, and the fainting are all part of the condition. If this were peacetime, I would discharge you from service."

Doctor Lore's voice was matter of fact and she removed a blood pressure cuff from her arm with the ease and experience of decades. Veritas moved quickly to get off the examination table and to her feet. She was not having any of this new diagnosis.

Okay...well, maybe there's some other stuff, but really. We're about to go on the offensive!

"I fainted yesterday because I found out my companion threatened the commandant's companion with the Code. That would make anyone lose consciousness."

She did her best to protest as calmly as she could muster, given the circumstance.

I really don't have time for this. Corporal Hicks has to get my troops in order, and I have to get my targets confirmed before we move out. When the hell are we going to get the signal from Mare? What will the signal be, anyway? Are we done here?

Veritas didn't wait for the doctor to give her permission; she put her uniform back on and prepared to depart the doctor's office.

"Oh, yeah, I heard about that. But, nevertheless, you are hypoglycemic. I would suspect that you have anxiety as well because of that situation. It figures that Roseann is handling it well. She is always better at these things than Verna," the doctor said as she put the cuff away and walked to her desk.

With her eyes narrowed and her brow furrowed, Veritas looked at the doctor in shock. She had called the supreme commandant by her first name and her companion.

"'Roseann?' 'Verna?' I didn't know we were on a first-name basis," she said sarcastically.

A warm smile came over the doctor's dark, sculptured features as she looked up from her papers. Her dark hair was streaked with gray and white, making her look like a very old soul even though she was in her early forties.

A little respect for those that serve would be nice. She's got some nerve!

"'We' are not on first-name terms with the supreme commandant. *I* am on first-name terms with both Roseann and Verna—and the girls, if you must know. As the family's doctor, I have the luxury of referring to them in a familiar way. Is that going to be a problem, Major? When Roseann asked me to see you, I did it as a favor. I have a number of soldiers I could be seeing in the field, and I would prefer to be there instead of here."

As she spoke she leaned back in her chair.

What? This woman's the commandant's personal doctor? Ooh no...

"Are you going to faint again, Major? You suddenly look pale."

To the doctor's credit she got up quickly and moved to her side.

She moved pretty fast—she has to be in her late thirties? No...She's in her early forties. It's the gray and white in her hair that make her look older. If she dyed it, I bet she could shave ten years right off. She goes to the field? The battlefield? A doctor? The supreme commandant's family doctor?

Feeling a strong, warm grip on her arm, Veritas stood up straight and gently moved away from it.

"All right, Doctor. Let's say you're right and I have this affliction. Is there medication I can take?"

The doctor smiled again. Veritas noticed that she remained perfectly still and stared at her as if she were considering something for a moment, then spoke while she walked back to her desk to take her seat.

"How about we start from a position that I'm the doctor and I am right? You're a major and you are hypoglycemic. That means I will tell you what to do to stay healthy, and you will do it. Deviations from my prescribed course of action will result in your immediate discharge from service. And be advised, Major—Lieutenant Jillian Banner will not be able to go to my companion on your behalf as I do not have one. I always found the idea of having one...troublesome. Wouldn't you agree?"

The woman's deliver was without anger. Once again she sat back in her chair, still smiling more of a kind smile than a vindictive one.

Veritas stared blankly. She was shocked on multiple levels and was completely at a loss as to whether it would be better to surrender to this woman or go on the defensive. She truly didn't have any idea of how she might even attempt such an endeavor.

"Does everyone know about that?"

"I have one woman who is in a coma who has yet to hear but that is only a matter of time."

A long ten seconds passed before Veritas could think of something to say.

"Okay…I…I will follow your directives, Doctor. I am sorry for—" she started to say when the door burst open and Corporal Hicks and two privates in full gear filled up the entire entry.

"Major! All the APs look like they have just stopped in their paces! They've shut down!"

Veritas looked at her for just a second before springing to life.

I guess that's the signal!

"Let's go, Corporal! Time to take the fight to them!"

Stopping mid-step, Veritas turned back to address the doctor before she left. She was surprised to see that the doctor was already out of her white medical coat and was putting on a medic's field jacket and pulling out an oversized medical bag. The next moment, she saw the doctor holster a sidearm as well.

"I will make sure I come back for your instructions," Veritas said respectfully.

"Good. Don't make me come look for you," she said. She pulled the sidearm out and checked to see if there was a projectile in the chamber.

"Yes, ma'am," Veritas said.

She ran right behind Hicks to her waiting troops.

Well, it doesn't get any stranger than that!

CHAPTER NINE

O, for a horse with wings!
        —Shakespeare, *Cymbeline*

Still sore from her altercation, Singh was glad to bring up the rear and let Privates Athena and Debbie take point. Private Margaret read from the energy tracker. Corporal Emma was keeping a watchful eye behind her, but Singh truly wished she and Margaret were anywhere else but here.

This is crazy! What are a grandmother and a pregnant woman doing in the middle of this hell? Yeah, yeah, yeah…I know we're soldiers, but this is madness.

It was easy to hear the escalating artillery and heavy and small arms fire sounds all around them—but eerily not in their immediate area.

"It might be a trap. There's been very little resistance and no opposition. You'd think Aurora would keep her prize in a more secure location," she whispered.

Without skipping a beat she kept her sights on all the corners they passed by. While the biosurgical and wellness facility was not as deep in Aurora's stronghold as the central mainframe building, it was still deep enough.

Let's get the CO and get the hell out of here! I have to get Margaret away and find my boy.

"We may be in a fortuitous situation—many of her resources had been redeployed to rebuild their cybernetic building and protect key installations such as the mainframe building when Corporals Danielle and Rebecca inserted themselves. Additionally, the APs we have come across seem disorganized as they exit their sleep/reboot mode. Timing and recent events may make our CO a low-level asset with little need for guarding. The result could therefore be in our favor. If we did not have the exact coordinates, however, I have to say that I am not convinced that I would have considered this to be a very likely holding area for Lieutenant Melendez," Emma whispered back.

Emma then came to a sudden stop. As they approached large doors on the darkened third floor, Margaret made a motion pointing to the other side, indicating that they were at their location.

"Stack up," Corporal Emma whispered. She then used hand signals to order Private Athena to set the breach charges on the door. Private Debbie and Corporal Emma took the left side while Singh moved herself and Margaret behind Athena on the right side. Once everyone was in place, Debbie counted down to zero.

I'm getting too old for this shit.

The door blasted open, sending light and debris inward. The APs moved in rapidly, and Singh lagged behind. She heard a series of short, controlled bursts and the sound of metal targets being hit. The room was completely dark except for a dim blue light emanating from what looked like liquid-filled, transparent tanks.

"Clear," Singh heard both Athena and Debbie say. She watched Emma approach the containers slowly. Singh had to wait desperately for a few moments for her eyesight to adjust so she was surprised at how quickly Emma was able to make decisions.

"Privates Athena and Debbie, retrace our steps and make sure our exit is clear. We will have passengers and we will be leaving in a hurry," she said.

Singh guided Margaret over two dead APs that had been taken out.

"What is this place?" Margaret asked.

It was easy to see that one of her hands moved involuntarily from her rifle to her belly. Singh shifted her focus from Margaret to look closely at the tanks with her now-adjusted and clear eyes. She shook her head in disbelief. She saw two ten-month-old babies floating in a series of darkened, transparent vats. They were attached to oxygen and feeding tubes. Margaret responded first.

"What the hell is this? I thought we were going to find the CO?"

"This is unexpected," Emma said. She suddenly turned to her immediate right and passed by the still-active stasis vats. She stood in front of an iron-and-steel container that was covered in a series of cables and conduits, and periodically pulsating green lights. Singh was unable to tell what it was, but Emma nodded as if she knew what she had found.

"Private Margaret, locate any clothing or cloth you can for the infants we found. They are coming with us."

Both Margaret and she watched Emma punch a series of codes into a keypad on the side of the large casket. After she finished keying, the green lights shifted color and sequence. Electrical motors and hinges began to move.

"Will do," Margaret said finally and started her search.

Singh kept her rifle close at hand as she surveyed the immediate area as she spoke.

"Emma? What's going on? How did you know what numbers to press? Obviously you did something right."

"The code is the square root of pi to the twentieth decimal point. Private Athena noted that Corporals Danielle and Rebecca transmitted that number without reference as to why right at the very beginning of her report. She noticed that they stopped abruptly at the twentieth digit after the decimal point, which she thought was odd. The code that Citizen Austin had planned to use as a mathematical virus to command the central computer to find the end-point of the square root of pi was an excellent idea that they did use but only as a distraction. It kept both of their consciousnesses busy as well as allowed the other fallen platoon members to overtake some of the minor executive functioning routines such as rebooting for maintenance, shifting and reallocating power, and shutting down some public services. I speculated that upon locating the CO, Lance Corporals Danielle and Rebecca altered the code to something we would intuitively guess."

The crypt opened up with a hiss and the steel doors creaked. As the vapor on the interior dispersed, Singh took a step closer with Emma to look inside. There stood a very pale, thin, naked Lieutenant Jose Melendez. A series of wires was attached to his head. Straps held him up—the restraints dug deeply into his torso and limbs.

"Oh no," Singh whispered to herself.

Emma moved in closer and was surprisingly clinical in her assessment. For some reason, Singh had the illogical thought that the AP would become emotional. It was not lost on anyone that she had more than a crush on the CO.

He can't be alive. Look at him. Five years in that primitive cryogenic freeze? What a nightmare.

Emma pressed her ear against his chest and then gently felt his neck. Singh waited for her answer.

"He is alive, but not responsive. Based on the primitive nature of this operation, it is likely that he is in a coma. We will need to extract him and get him back to base as soon as possible, though it is unclear whether we will be able to help revive him from this state."

Emma busied herself with releasing restraints and the wires attached to his head while Singh watched the area. Margaret rounded the corner with a set of sheets and gasped.

"Corporal?! What have they done?"

"Private Margaret! Focus! I need two sheets to wrap and carry the CO. I need you to take the remaining sheets and assist Citizen Singh in releasing the two infants. They have the lieutenant's DNA and are obviously his children—one is a clone, the other only has half his DNA."

"What? Why the hell would Aurora do this? Why would she breed his children? And where are the others? What happened to them?" Singh snapped.

"I do not know for sure, but from incision scars in the lieutenant's body at or near key organs, I assume that the clones' organs were harvested and the other infants were kept for possible blood transfusions and stem cells. There are two surviving infants. Four of the remaining sixteen vats were once occupied, but are now empty. At this point, I would prefer that we focus on exiting with the CO and his live offspring rather than wait for Aurora Prime or her other designees to arrive and explain this to us."

Corporal Emma gently lifted the emaciated Lieutenant from his casket.

"Good point. Margaret, let's go," Singh said.

She slung her weapon on her back and proceeded to run to the console to try to find a release that would drain the vats. After only a minute of looking, she did something impulsive— she climbed a short ladder that led to a small catwalk directly above the vats. Then she simply reached down and pulled an infant straight out of the liquid, tubes and all. When the infant opened its mouth to cry, Singh slowly pulled its short feeding tube out. The baby was a girl. She vomited and coughed and then began to scream like hell.

"And good day to you, my little precious."

Singh tried to wipe the liquid off the baby and then passed her into the waiting arms of Margaret.

"Maybe it's a good thing you came. I'd hate to have one of the boys doing this," she said as she moved to the next vat.

"I don't know, Major. It's looking pretty grim and crazy in here right now," she said. She made fast work cleaning and swaddling the screaming little baby. Singh pulled out the other baby the same way. It was a boy, and the same procedure yielded the same results with him.

"Well, you have the same voice as your sister," she said as she held on to him and proceeded to wipe him clean and swaddle him for transport.

"I hope stealth was not part of your plan for escape," Margaret said to Corporal Emma. Similar to the babies Emma carried the CO but over her shoulder, wrapped tightly in a sheet. He looked like a large version of one of the babies.

"Not a likely scenario," she responded. She then spoke into her headset.

"Alpha Leader to Beta Team. How is our exit?"

Even as they marched Emma held the CO wrapped in the sheet in one hand, and the other held her rifle.

"Ready for flight. Do you have the prize?" Singh heard Athena ask over her own set.

"Three prizes. As anticipated, the CO is in poor condition. Two infants are in tow. They may have been grown for organ or blood harvesting for later use in keeping the CO alive. The other four were not here. Operation Lazarus is now in play. Repeat. Operation Lazarus," Corporal Emma.

There was an unmistakable edge to her voice.

Lazarus? Operation? What the hell?

"What? Those pigs! Those…" Margaret blurted out as she picked up her pace for the long run back.

"Calm yourself, Private, and maintain radio silence! We have little time and will need to leave in three minutes."

"Make that two minutes, Corporal. I have APs beginning to organize and move in this direction. They appear to be receiving orders and are beginning to form up. Their ETA could be sixty seconds, possibly a hundred and twenty seconds if I engage," Private Debbie added.

"Engage only as a last resort. Private Athena, support Private Debbie. We will get to the vehicle and pick you up. I cannot afford to lose either one of you, so be careful," Corporal Emma said.

"Confirmed," they both said at the same time.

While moving very quickly, humans and APs did their best to avoid skeletons, debris, and other obstacles without dislodging their charges. The sounds of war grew even louder than the screams of the babies they held tightly against their chests.

"You sounded worried back there, Emma. Are you concerned? What's going on with this 'Lazarus' thing? Is there an operation going on I should be keyed into?"

"Yes. We have finally found our missing commanding officer after five years, and his condition is stable but poor. We have discovered two living infants with his DNA coding. A number of combatant APs are reorganizing to attack us. Finally, two of my peers have combined consciousness with others from our platoon and have inserted themselves into a hostile, sentient computer processing unit that was until now under the control of the enemy. Their chance of survival, if any, is unknown. All of this, and we are sixty seconds from being swamped and one hundred and twenty feet from escaping unnoticed. Yes. I am worried."

"You could have said 'yes.'"

"We had time and I thought you might need a distraction."

So I guess the Lazarus thing can wait.

"Well…that was thorough. I have to add to that—the red-eyed duplicate of Aurora told me that she had given her APs directives to find and kill all Nemericana citizens exiting the state, especially children. I have to warn Roseann and Pearl," Singh said. For whatever reason she counted the feet to the waiting jeep; distracting.

"Major? Are you crazy?" she heard Margaret say, out of breath.

"Negative, Citizen Singh. No one is left behind. We all leave together," Emma said abruptly.

"I'm not asking to be left behind—I'm asking to be dropped off, fully armed, twelve klicks southeast so I can get to a Nemericana forward outpost and warn them. If we do this right and accomplish the larger mission, we may get Roseann to agree to an alliance. You know I'm right, Emma. And it's not like I can take one of you APs with me," Singh concluded.

"I'll go with you," Margaret offered as they broke cover from the building and emerged into daylight. They had the vehicle in sight.

"In your condition, Margaret? I don't think so," Singh said.

"It took mere seconds to find a space for everyone plus two more APs.

"It's going to be tight," Margaret said.

"Obviously" Emma added.

"Not much room for anyone else, anyway," Singh said.

She heard shots ring out behind her. She turned quickly and trained her rifle sight in the direction of the shooting. She was happy to see that Privates Athena and Debbie were driving at top speed toward them.

"We were able to eliminate the forward teams and relieve them of their best vehicle. However, they are chasing us by foot and will be here in forty-five seconds," Private Athena said from behind the wheel.

"Okay. I have an even better idea. We all head out, but Athena and Debbie drop me off and provide you cover," Singh amended.

After a seemingly long moment, Corporal Emma shook her head in the affirmative.

"All right, Citizen Singh. You are a fully trained soldier with several years of experience and your assessment may be right in regard to this situation. Privates Athena and Debbie, give your vehicle to Citizen Singh. Be careful and come back unharmed," she added.

What...did she just tell me to be careful?

The look Singh gave her must have transmitted her thoughts perfectly. Corporal Emma responded quickly and without much deliberation.

"Private Roberto would be very upset should any harm come to his mother."

"Of course...what was I thinking?" Singh muttered.

She climbed into the driver's seat and waited for Emma's jeep to leave first in case they needed backup. She was surprised that Emma had let her have the vehicle and put everyone else in hers instead of splitting them up. Since they were heading in the same southeast direction, simply dropping her off at an outpost would have sufficed. Emma started the jeep—and immediately began driving northwest.

Where the hell are you going?

CHAPTER TEN

We have seen better days.
    —Shakespeare, *As You Like It*

Closing her eyes, Veritas could feel that dirt and debris were still raining down on her. It mixed with the real rain that chose that moment to begin coming down in earnest. It was not quite a downpour, but she could feel it cutting through the filth clinging to her skin. She was pressed up against the side of a collapsed main highway. Sounds of explosions, moans, and periodic screams penetrated her near-deaf ears. Collapsed buildings lay all around, which kept the ill-coordinated APs from overwhelming them. She was happy that they had far exceeded their projected number of targets, but she realized that their position in the middle of the road was both a blessing and a curse—they had cover but not elevation.

    Lucky you weren't standing ten feet in the other direction.

    She remembered hitting the ground just before an AP grenade exploded just feet away from her. A private standing between her and the grenade took the brunt of the blast, the poor woman. Clearing her vision, she saw there were few of her team left. They needed to hold off a superior number of APs who had come out of their trances before she and her team had had the chance to kill them all. While she had made good headway, the APs were now regrouping and had suddenly merged into fire teams. They now seemed to be coordinating their attacks.

"Medic! Corporal Hicks is down! Private Tia! Get suppressing fire on that group due east!"

"Private Tia is dead, Ma'am! I got three wounded, but still can fight!" another soldier cried out.

"I'm not dead yet, but the morning is still young," she heard Corporal Hicks shout out.

"Glad to have you—keep firing! If it moves and it's not human, kill it," Veritas yelled back.

She knelt to shoot at the oncoming APs. She figured she would die that way. She had a flesh wound in her arm and more serious ones in her lower leg and thigh. Veritas felt her rifle heat up as she kept shooting on full automatic. Instead of reloading it when it hit empty, she picked up another discarded weapon from a fallen soldier and continued firing.

At least we had our own mag-assault weapons instead of the Pre-Fall ones for this last stand…

"Shit…this is not going to end well," she said to herself.

She saw more APs breaking cover to rush her position. Still firing, Veritas could see that of her sixty soldiers, only she and about a dozen more were still picking targets. The others fired as well as they could from their prone positions, but most were dying from their wounds.

This is not going to end well. Jillian's really going to be pissed at me.

Her team had been the only one to successfully get a civilian corps to the armory and food depot. She had made the decision to destroy as many APs as possible deep in their own territory, so as to reduce enemy numbers and put distance between them and the civilians. As a result, they were also the farthest from all resources and lines of communication. Farther even than the East Border Patrol with its protective snipers.

Well...at least the civilian corps will have a fighting chance now...and at least Jill's safe.

Veritas had a second and actually dropped a spent clip and put in another one. Her thoughts were interrupted by a medic yelling something at her.

"Major! Hit the dirt! Tiger Team is behind us! We're in their line of fire! Get down," Corporal Hicks yelled out.

Are you shitting me?

She did what she was ordered; she dropped to the ground. No sooner than she was able to get down in her hole, she heard a series of high-caliber gunfire whiz just above her head.

Tiger Team? Snipers? Lieutenant Verna? I thought we left them ten klicks back.

The barrage of bullets flew over her head. It might have been only five minutes, but the suppressing fire coming in from all sides seemed to drop a bit as the sniper shots picked up their pace. With rain still falling and dirt still pluming up on the ground all around her, she barely heard the medic calling out sit-reps.

"Ma'am! Everyone! Commandant Pierce and her air squadron have us in their sights! Stay down—they plan to suppress the area in five seconds! Danger close! Everyone stay down and cover!"

Veritas's heart rate jumped even higher. She could hear one of her wounded soldiers calling out for her mother and saw her raising her hand to touch someone as if they were standing just above her. Veritas moved as quickly as she could to be by her side. A mere second later she heard the stream of cannon, missile, and Gatling-gun blasts getting closer.

"You're all right, Private. We're going to get you out of here," she said above the din of explosions. More debris and rain fell all around them.

"Mum? You're here? Major Veritas told Corporal Hicks that I'd get back home to see you before too long. How did you get here?" the young woman said.

The young woman, maybe just in her twenties, looked right at Veritas. The woman's eyes were open wide and the expression was genuine curiosity about how her mother had made it to the battlefield. Veritas looked down at the soldier's abdomen. She could see that her right hand was holding on to a compress that was probably holding her entrails in.

"Damn it!" Veritas cursed.

"What, Mum? What's wrong?"

Veritas looked back into her eyes and tried to block out the violence all around her so she could focus on this one human being for just a moment.

Just for one minute, can there be a moment of compassion, a moment of peace?

"Honey, I just want to hold on to you while this storm passes. Can I just hug you for a bit?" Veritas asked in as calm a voice as she could muster.

"Sure, Mum, but how did you find me?" she said. The woman tried to sit up to embrace her.

"Corporal Hicks brought me here, dear. Don't move. I'll lie right here with you," Veritas said.

She pressed her down with her own body and moved her hand to keep the pressure on the compress.

Lying nearly on top of her, Veritas held the young woman's gaze as she struggled to hug her.

"Just let me hold you, dear. I've come far and just want to hold my little girl," she said. All around her she heard gunfire and explosions rage all around her. The weather—and storm of debris—intensified.

"Thank you, Mum. I've missed you. It's been so hard to be away from you and Missy. I'm so glad you came…I'm…I'm so tired, Mum," she said quietly.

"I've missed you too, dear. And Missy should be here real soon."

"Really," the woman said in a tired voice.

"Yes, she's excited to see you."

"Me too, Mum…"

Veritas covered her face with her own and continued to hug her and keep pressure on the young woman's wound.

"No worries, dear. I'm here. Just rest. I'll never leave you," she said into the woman's ear.

They both lay still. Debris and rain pounded her on the back as she protected the woman from as much of the sight, sound, and horror of war as she could. Veritas let her mind wander to all the people in her life—Jill, Mare, her own mother and even her own friends, few though they were. She wondered who would come to her funeral, thought how hard it would be for Jill. She was positive that Mare would come back for her. Then she thought of what Katherine Yates would say at her memorial years later—*something embarrassing, I bet*. Focusing on her breathing was easy to do as it seemed to be the only thing she could hear. That's when she noticed that raindrops were falling on her back and on the ground—but nothing else. And there were no explosions.

"Major? Are you all right?" she heard another medic, Private Johnson, ask. Startled by the woman's touch and her voice so clear and close, her heart jumped as she realized that the bombardment was over.

"Medic! Check this woman! She has an abdominal wound and must be losing blood…" Veritas started to say. She looked back at the woman that she was still protecting with her own body. It was only then she could see that her eyes had closed. The woman's arm, now lifeless, was still draped around her.

"Oh no," she said.

The rain continued to fall and the distant gunfire, and noise of rotor aircraft flying around was now audible.

"I'm sorry, ma'am. She looks like she left peacefully," the medic said after she had checked her neck for a pulse.

"She thought I was her mother..." Veritas said.

"Well...at least she died in loving arms, ma'am. That's the most we can ever ask for."

Veritas's response came out angrier that she intended.

"Is it? Can't we ask for more? Just a little more than to die in a hole with a stranger?"

The medic, probably ten years her junior but had seen more death than she should responded quickly.

"You weren't a stranger she died, ma'am. You were a loved one. Really, no matter when, where or how, don't you think dying in the arms of a loved one is best."

Veritas felt her stomach fall and her eyes well up. She made as if she wiped wet debris from her face. The medic took a rapid medical scan of her and gave her two injections of something and then a compress to hold while she went off to attend someone else.

"Yeah...it's the most we could ever ask for," Veritas repeated.

She stood up and tried to pull herself back into the present. Rain, blood, and bodies were all around her. The smell of metal, concrete, and fire hung in the air. It was the weak voice of Corporal Hicks that finally drew her back into the fight. She turned to face the voice addressing her. She was surprised to see that Hicks was still standing. She had multiple lacerations across her face, a shard of metal jutting out of her shoulder, and wounds on her legs.

Look at us: standing among the dead with metal, blood, and rain falling all around us.

"Ma'am? Commandant Pierce has left her squadron behind to provide us air support for evacuation. Tiger Team is on station and another forward team is moving up to hold our position. The Civilian Corps exceeded its goal and another corps has moved in to take even more…apparently we held our position much longer than expected, ma'am."

Corporal Hicks moved to the ground to get off her feet. Veritas was relieved to see her sit down before she fell down.

"Hicks, you look like cat shit. And not the well formed, firm kind either."

"Thank you, ma'am. Ma'am? A Lieutenant Verna thanks you for being excellent bait. She scored fifteen confirmed kills with a possible eight more. They'll know once they sort through the downed AP bodies. I couldn't tell if she was actually happy you were alive, though. I guess she doesn't want to risk having your companion looking for her later…" Hicks said with a weak smile.

Unbelievable! Does everyone know about that?

"So, how did you hear about Jill invoking the Code?"

More medics appeared and fresh advance troops rolled in. Two large transport aircraft flew over, heading in the direction of the same airport the commandant had somehow made it to.

How the hell did she do that? Did we buy her that much time? At what cost?

As she waited for Hicks to respond she surveyed the very few survivors and the many dead soldiers under her command.

"I think there might be a soldier in a coma somewhere that it might have slipped by. Anyway, ma'am, we need heroes. Lieutenant Banner's calling Lieutenant Verna out might be up there on the list of selfless acts."

"Yeah…she's always been selfless…" Veritas thought as sadness filled her heart.

I'm so glad she's not here, Veritas kept thinking as she looked at the dead and wounded all around her. After a moment she looked up at the city's skyline. Damaged and bombed out though it was, she realized that it looked familiar. She had been here before.

"Hicks? Where the hell are we? I lost track," she asked.

She turned and saw Hicks lighting up some tobacco product she undoubtedly obtained from black market trading with the Americans. More Nemericana soldiers started to flood their position, but she could still hear large-caliber shots and aircraft fire in the near distance.

"We're in Central Square, right at the beginning of the track in Central Sector on the road to the old Capital. That means we overshot our target area. We're five miles deeper into Aurora's territories than we meant to be. That will make it a whole lot easier for our mop-up teams, who will be here momentarily. Seems fitting, wouldn't you say—where we landed, that is? 'The Battle of Central Square.' Kind of has a ring to it," Hicks said after a deep inhale. She exhaled blue-and-white smoke. Looking at the metal shard protruding from the Corporal's shoulder, Veritas winced. It had to hurt. She moved a little closer so she could take a better look at Hicks, then she spoke again.

"I know a good doctor. I bet she could stitch you up pretty well."

"You mean Doctor Lore? I'd rather get the Captain Ross Medal of Honor than be under her care! You'll live forever, and well, but you'll never see a day of action," Hicks snorted out. Then she inhaled the tobacco deeply again.

Okay...she's losing it. Time to get her out of here.

"Medic, take a look at Corporal Hicks. She's already handing out medals," Veritas said as she looked at a collapsed sign that confirmed the location Hicks had stated.

"I am looking forward to getting morphine in me and getting this metal shard out of me. That Aurora bitch can take my medal and shove it right up her..."

"Okay, Hicks, I get it. You're on the first evac out."

Veritas looked around at the sea of troops and medical staff that were now all over the area.

Will this shit ever end?

More explosions could be heard several blocks away. Smoke wafted up from the direction of the noise. She watched several platoons organize to start their forward march.

CHAPTER ELEVEN

The weight of this sad time we must obey.
Speak what we feel, not what we ought to say.
The oldest hath borne most; we that are young
Shall never see so much, nor live so long.
　　　—Shakespeare, *King Lear*

"Breathe…just breathe…" Singh kept saying to herself. Her stomach did flip-flops with every move the swift-moving reconnaissance VTOL scout craft made as it skimmed just feet above the rugged terrain outside the Southeast Gate. She had not stepped into a three-seat, piloted aircraft in well over fifteen years, and she was not hoping for another trip anytime soon. They hurtled to the coordinates transmitted by Omega Platoon's Epsilon Group which had also been confirmed by the Gamma Group.

"You're such a baby," Pierce said through her headset.

Singh was impressed how she was keeping from vomiting while the ground raced by. The landscape alternated between rocks, sand, brush, and trees, only to repeat over and over again.

After years of ground travel, getting to places fast by flying seemed like a true luxury and a novelty.

That is until she actually did it.

"I just think that crashing on our way to a rescue operation does not make for an effective mission," she said quickly to make sure she didn't throw up while speaking.

"One scout aircraft and three soldiers don't make a rescue team. It's been two hours since your last transmission, so we're probably heading to a graveyard," Pierce said bitterly.

Singh focused on the horizon to combat the motion sickness. She felt a wave of sadness at the thought. Finding the Nemericana Forward Task Force had not been hard to do—she just followed the gunfire and explosions. She was glad she hadn't been hit by friendly fire. Convincing the task force's commander to use a priority channel to get the supreme commandant critical information and pick her up had been the big challenge. Pierce had not only moved in fast with five armored scout aircraft upon receiving the information, she insisted on leaving her squadron behind to assist in the battle. She would not divert them to find her own children. When Pierce said she believed that she would find her children dead, she reminded Singh of her own fears—she hoped that her son had not been in either battle group.

"Don't give up hope yet, Roseann. Banner's battle-tested and Omega Platoon has spent its existence in the field," Singh said. Her words she knew were more to calm herself and ease her own dark thoughts than Pierce. Pierce's lack of response came as a welcome relief—she knew that the supreme commandant was right about the odds. While about half of Aurora's APs had simply dropped their weapons and walked to Nemericana's gates after the attack started, the other half regrouped into uncoordinated but lethal fire groups offering heavy resistance to anyone in their range. Still deep in her own thoughts, Singh briefly lost track of time. The pilot's voice startled her back into the present.

"Ma'am, I got confirmation on that report we got from the airfield. One transport aircraft and two scouts were taken by a group other than ours or Aurora's. The team that was prepping the aircraft was attacked and tied up. Their weapons and clothes were taken, and they were put in the bulletproof belly of a heavy transport carrier. They identified three APs with purple eyes, one young woman dressed in Nemericana military battle dress, two infants, and they 'think' a man…this is crazy, ma'am."

Shit…so that's why they headed northwest!

"Well…it sounds like Omega Platoon is on the move, though the infants and man are pretty hard to explain. Care to give me an explanation?" Pierce asked through her headset.

Sometimes the truth is better than a lie.

"I know this is going to be hard for you to believe, Roseann. I honestly have no idea. I went southeast to find you and they surprised me by heading northwest when we separated. I wish I could tell you their intent for sure or even guess at it, but I have no military status in their division and I am, at best, a talented *civilian* known as Citizen Singh—and that's on a good day."

Pierce was silent for a brief moment and then she gave a short laugh that relieved her. The voice of the pilot interrupted their conversation with an update.

"We are one minute out from the coordinates, Commandant."

"As soon as we land, I want you to dust off and provide air support. If you don't hear back from us in thirty minutes, assume we are KIA and get back to the fight," Pierce said. All traces of humor were gone; deadly seriousness returned.

"No, ma'am. Protocol and Battlefield Code four-twelve-one-thousand-and-two clearly states—" the pilot started.

"And they're rescinded by order and authority of Supreme Commandant Pierce. Failure to comply will result in execution…I have enough blood on my hands, Captain. Do me this one favor and follow my orders," she said quietly.

Singh heard nothing but pain and angst in Pierce's voice. She tried to focus on checking her weapons and ammunition rather than the conversation.

"Yes, ma'am. It's been a privilege serving with you, ma'am," the pilot said.

"Likewise, Marie. Stay alive and give them hell."

"You as well, ma'am. If anything happens to you, I won't be able to live with that."

"You know me. Survival is my best feature. And make sure you tell Verna to get that cheese torte recipe from Yvonne," Pierce said with amusement returning to her voice.

"You bet, ma'am. I got an LZ that looks quiet. I'm going to circle just to confirm. ETA in sixty seconds."

How does she do that? She knows them. She knows their names and knows how to motivate them. She's so different now. Pearl was so right about her—she's changed. I hope Jill's all right.

A sad smile began to form on Singh's lips. She continued to be impressed with how Pierce led. Her style drew loyalty and admiration from her troops. Clearing her thoughts, she became aware of a sudden deceleration and then the descent of the aircraft. She looked out her side of the canopy and saw that they were landing at the edge of a forest that encircled the foothills at the base of a mountain. Rain was falling. Singh jumped out of her seat and hit the wet ground with rifle drawn. She had a pack full of first-aid supplies, rations, and ammunition. Keeping low and training her eyes through the iron rifle sights, she saw Pierce come up from behind and cover her flank as the VTOL lifted off. As the noise of the rotary blades receded into the distance, Pierce took point without hesitation and headed straight into the dense forest.

How can we just start working together after years of separation, especially when she was going to execute me last time we met?

Singh kept up the pace and watched Pierce closely. She noticed the small things that had changed. Her small, muscular, curvaceous frame had lengthened into an angular physique, she had developed a slight limp in her right leg, and she had small scars along her neck where it met her jawline. The war had taken her soft, feminine attractiveness but left a stronger and caring person.

"By the way, you look like shit. I hope you killed that Aurora clone," Pierce said quietly as she looked over her gear and set her weapon on full automatic fire.

"I was just a distraction. One of the Omega APs had the privilege of that kill. I think Verna would like Corporal Emma—she doesn't care much for me at all and has made that clear for the last seven years," Singh said as she mimicked Pierce's procedure.

So they went and stole a midsized VTOL and two scouts. Where are they going? What is this Lazarus Operation?

"Well, it's nice to see that both human and AP females are consistent in their response to you."

"Nice, Roseann, real nice."

Pearl and Jill won't leave because of her. The pilot's response was certainly more than you could expect from a soldier just following orders. Was all of this meant to be? Could such horrors bring out her best?

Once they were both all set, Pierce gave the hand signal to move out. It was going to be a covert operation in the bush.

Here we go.

Ten minutes into their silent march, Singh saw Pierce freeze and then make a raised fist to indicate that they should stop and be silent. After a minute of not moving, she realized that there was no sound—no birds, animals, no sound at all except for the rain falling on the trees and ground. Pierce gave the order to proceed, then went another fifty yards and waved her close to her. Singh made sure her assault rifle was still set to fully automatic and then noticed that Pierce was pointing at something. Six feet ahead of them lay two dead APs, clearly shot repeatedly in the chest and head. The APs were still holding on to their own weapons—it was obvious that these APs had been engaged in a firefight.

Singh moved closer and looked them over carefully to make sure they were not booby trapped. Once she was convinced that they were not dangerous, Singh took their weapons and strapped them onto her back. A few minutes later, Pierce reassumed point position and was moving ahead. Then, she stopped suddenly. Stopping short herself, Singh surveyed the area. Then she tried to make out what Pierce was looking at. She had to dig deep and rely on every piece of military and field operation training she had received to keep from vomiting and crying all at the same time.

No…please, no…

Singh saw the two young Omega Platoon cadets and three privates—four males and one female, all under the age of twenty—torn up by small arms fire. Two had weapons still, but three did not. Two large dogs lay on top of their human team members.

"By the Elders, no…Mark? Lindsay?" Singh said quietly. She looked down at the soldiers that she had known since they were four or five. She had even known the dogs when they were just pups.

"Children…they're just children…"

"I'm sorry, Mare. But we have to move," Pierce said. She had continued to survey the area while Singh had a chance to regroup from the loss. Not wanting to leave, she tried to focus on what might lay ahead and pulled herself out her memories and back into the present. She took point.

Roberto…please don't be here.

"Not all of them had weapons," Pierce said quietly as she tried to keep up.

"Omega Platoon wouldn't leave weapons behind, ever. The ones with weapons were probably the last alive. The others were probably dead before them…and the dogs probably stayed with them and wouldn't leave…They're like that; they'll stay behind even if it means their own death. Omega will return for the fallen…no one gets left behind," she said mechanically.

Ten minutes later, they found a similar scene, but with different victims. More enemy APs first; staggered groupings with clean lines of fire. And then there were just feet away four APs were dead and three more Omega Platoon human soldiers and one cadet were found beside five Nemericana soldiers and three little girls under ten years old. The children were huddled together, just fifteen feet away, with two more dead dogs in front of them. Stopping by the human bodies, Singh watched Pierce's jawline tighten as she looked at each of her soldiers and the faces of the children who had been robbed of a future. To her credit, she looked at the Omega troops, AP and soldier, as if to know them in death. It was clear that she was battling her own anger, desperation, and fear but trying to objectively assess the battle scene.

What did you expect, Mare? This is war, and war kills young people, innocent civilians…but they were just children. All of them are children.

She once again stuffed her anger and fears deep down so she could focus on the perimeter.

"Omega and my soldiers fought side by side…and by the looks of the plants, this is where the groups widened out. I think they had been walking in single file, then suddenly decided to fan out." Singh took note of the crushed and disturbed vegetation around several feet to each side of the bodies. Corresponding boot prints were everywhere.

"The dogs stayed between the APs and the girls while our people laid down suppressing fire to give the others a chance to escape…"

"Yes."

Without further discussion, Pierce moved ahead. She eventually came to a stop several feet away from a very small clearing. This time, Singh watched Pierce walk first into a twenty-foot-wide patch of wet earth littered with nearly twenty of Aurora's APs. After a few minutes, during which she made sure they were all dead and it was not a trap, Pierce waved Singh in to assess the situation.

"Same as the others, but every AP here has been repeatedly shot in the head in addition to body hits…and arrows? Are these really arrows?" she asked.

Singh looked beyond her and feared they would inevitably find another group of bodies just ahead. She noticed that there were many arrows and spears all across the field of fire; she also noticed Pre-Fall spent bullet casings scattered just ahead.

"I…I don't know. Those arrows are what the natives use, Americans. And these bullets are clearly from the Omega team, just like the others we saw, but there seem to be a lot more here," Singh said as she narrowed her eyes to take in the whole scene.

"What the hell?"

Pierce started to lead the way again but then stopped abruptly forty feet ahead, or ten feet inside the clearing's tree line. This time, Singh didn't wait for an all-clear. Although she feared that she would see even more dead children she knew, she was surprised at the smaller number of bodies, comparatively speaking. The group was also varied: four Nemericana soldiers were joined by an Omega Platoon, Gamma Group AP, two privates, one dog, eight Americans, and two little girls. The dead Americans were still holding on to their own weapons—empty bows. Looking at the whole picture, it was easy to see that the Omega AP had taken point. The Omega Platoon and Nemericana humans took the second line, and the near-defenseless Americans took up the third, trying in vain to protect the two girls.

"The dog, though...that's not one of ours..." Singh said as her old crime-scene investigator persona took in the area.

This is different. The Americans and the dog had no issues with Aurora's APs. Why did they come to our aid? Was it the children?

Singh looked over at Pierce. For the first time, it was easy to see that Pierce was coming to her wit's end. The fear a parent feels when she knows she might find her children dead was cresting.

"Where are they? Where are the rest?" Singh said.

She scanned the forward area and feared for her son. She tried to focus on the mission—*rescue, not recovery.*

"We gotta move," she said as she took point to give Pierce a chance to slow down and recover.

The Americans tried to help with bows and arrows against APs? They must have known they would not survive. And why did they join in the fight anyway? Save the children? Just like Omega? Just like Lieutenant Melendez did years ago? They could have just hidden and avoided the whole situation altogether...

Suddenly, several shadows moved near her feet, taking her to the ground all at once. Singh was shocked by the swiftness and force of the ambush. She lay on her stomach. She heard a discharge from behind her, where she knew Pierce must have been. She felt hands all over her, stripping her of weapons, her backpack, and her ammunition belt. They left her with just her clothes—and wet dirt and grass on her face. All this swift and forceful movement was fierce, violent and proficient. In addition, it was the loud barking and growling of dogs just inches from her head that truly made her anxious as hell. After a very long minute, she found herself pulled forcefully up from the ground and held firmly by two sets of hands. She tried to catch her breath. She was facing a female American, maybe in her thirties. She was holding a knife at her side. She saw that Pierce had suffered the same fate, though she had a gash on her cheek.

"Are you all right?" Singh yelled above the din of barking as she continued counting—twelve Americans.

"I'm all right. That one, though, is pretty good with edged weapons—just so you know," Pierce said as she tried to wrestle away from the arms embracing her.

"Heel! Sit!" the young woman said. She sheathed her knife and looked at Singh and Pierce with burning, hot brown eyes. The dogs immediately complied, leaving the forest once again quiet save for the rain falling on the tree leaves above their heads and the puddles at their feet. Singh looked back at Pierce and was gratified to see that she was not the only one who was both shocked and surprised by the capture and the way this woman presented herself.

"Well. Today is filled with a great many surprises," the American said. Her accent and pronunciation was in a perfect Nemericana Northern Sector dialect.

What the hell...I thought they were...what?

"First the Omegans come to your people's aid. But then that makes sense—they always protect children. Much more than I can say for you people. And then you show up—without protection," she said. As she spoke she moved her hands, signaling others that Singh could not see into action.

Singh looked at Pierce again whose slackened jaw indicated that she, too, was surprised by the sudden turn of events. While death, destruction, and the loss of children's lives were difficult to absorb, hearing a native American speaking as if she was a Nemericana college student just added to the insanity. It was evident that their new captor could easily read their nonverbal communication.

"I was cast out twenty years ago and taken in by this clan. Again, more than you people ever did for me," the American said. The enmity was not hidden. Her glares alone could kill.

Well... talk about the past coming back to haunt you.

"Still, today is a different day. And thanks to the Omegans, we have added more to our clan. We now have the means to farm, read, and learn about our past, our *true* past," she continued. After a moment of silence, she gave yet another command, but in a foreign language. Singh was released and her weapons and gear were given back.

I guess Melendez's approach was right—make friends and build alliances. Sergeant Joan's continued efforts paid off.

"Follow me, and no questions. I do not care for you, but I will take you to your children and the warriors that fought together. They are the noble ones, the Omegans. Maybe you are learning their ways," she said as she took the lead. Her people surrounded her as they moved east. Making eye contact with Pierce, Singh saw her shrug her shoulders to acknowledge that she did not understand the situation but intended to comply by following suit.

"Omegans?" Is that what we are now? And there are survivors? Please don't be here, Roberto...

The twenty minutes of weaving in and out of trees and brush was disorienting. The Americans continued to pick up additional members of their clan. Finally, they emerged from yet another tree line—at the foot of a mountain that faced a relatively small cave entrance, no bigger than the grand doors to the Elders' meditation hall. Nemericana soldiers held positions at the entrance, and Singh was pleased to see two of Gamma Group's APs with two of Epsilon's as well as the human and canine contingent standing sentry. Farther ahead, a group of Nemericana children huddled with yet another, smaller group of American children, men and women. Some were obviously being given medical treatment by the Americans and Omega Platoon while other children looked as if they were just eating and playing with American children, small puppies, and the older dogs.

"Unbelievable," Singh said to herself as she felt Pierce come up beside her, taking in the same surreal scene. Three distinct groups were holding position, treating wounds, eating, and keeping the home fires burning.

"I could never have imagined such a sight," she heard Pierce say.

"Yes…males and females, humans and APs, girls and dogs playing, living, and working together…you might learn something if you open your eyes," the female American said with thinly veiled sarcasm.

"You really do hate us," Pierce said.

"Yes. Are you surprised?"

"No."

"Good. We agree on one thing," the American said.

The native American gestured with her hand for them to move ahead. Feeling the bite of the accusation, Singh was relieved to see their American guide and her cadre move quickly back into the brush as if they were off on another mission. Left alone, Singh started up the small incline and Pierce followed.

"So…everyone in the *world* really does hate us," she commented.

"I'm afraid so, Roseann. It takes a while, but you get used to it," Singh said before she heard two shouts. They came from two very different sources.

"Officers on deck!" yelled one of the sentries who had noticed her. As all eyes shifted to them, two high-pitched voices yelling out "Mommy, mommy!" followed. Two little girls, both eight years old, ran full speed past Singh and into the clutches of their mother.

"Are you all right?! You're not hurt, are you? Oh, my precious girls!"

Pierce pulled them back to look at them. Tears flooded her eyes and face. Both children clutched back at their mother as they spoke.

"We're okay, Mommy. The APs attacked us, though, but Jill got us away pretty quick. It was really scary. We were running and then those big boys...I mean they're really older boys, came to help. And they brought nice APs. After that there were more that came," the girl with red bows tied to her two braids reported.

Singh saw a young Nemericana officer approach with an all-too-familiar male private beside her. Watching the two little dark-haired twin girls with their carefully tied braids, Singh's mind wandered to her own son. Not as the child as she had come to know through a one-way mirror, but as the young adolescent and young man he had become—she remembered that he was soon to be a father.

My baby!

She looked closely at the young man to make sure she was right. Feeling her eyes sting with hot tears, her face flush, and her knees go weak, Singh ran up to grab her boy. He was still holding his weapon and was dressed in full combat gear.

"Roberto! Roberto!" she kept calling out. She held him tightly. She feared that if she let him go, she might lose him. She had no idea how long she held him but it was his gentle voice and words that helped her ease her grip—just a little at first. When she finally pulled back, she did her best to keep her emotions in check.

"Mom, I'm all right…but we're still in a hot zone. You might want to try to breathe and pull yourself together. I'm okay," he said reassuringly.

"Is Margaret all right," he asked.

"Yes…yes, she is."

She nodded her head and tried to find her words but had a hard time doing so. Looking at him closely now, she saw that his clothes were covered with sweat, dirt, and blood.

"Are you hit, Roberto?"

"I'm all right. Are you?"

He touched her chin to tilt her head and inspect the bruises on her face. His look was of concern. She wanted to cry.

"I've had a lot worse and I'm good, now that I know you're all right. Are you sure you're okay?" she asked again, looking deep into his dark, sad eyes.

No…this is more than just battle. Something happened.

"Yes, Mom. I'm fine. A lot of Epsilon didn't make it, though, and the other soldiers were hit too…Mom…David…he didn't make it," he said quietly. Singh saw her son's mouth quiver and his eyes fill up with tears. Her own eyes widened at the news.

"No, Roberto! Oh, Roberto…I'm so sorry," she said. It might not have been proper protocol on the battlefield but she pulled him into another hug and felt him fall into her. Images of Jennifer flooded over her. How Singh had found her body and the note asking her to look after David so many years ago never faded from her memory. Taking him from the casting out and giving him the ring the night they started a new life seemed as vivid to her as if it had happened yesterday.

Roberto, Jacob, and David…they were always together, never far from each other.

"Where's Jacob?"

Fear clutched her as visions of Austin sprung into her mind.

"Jacob's fine. He arrived with Gamma, but we got there first. We got David here, but he didn't make it," Roberto said.

He pulled away and pointed to a small group of bodies lying in a row just out of view of the children's position. Singh could see a mix of uniforms as well as another Omega AP alongside them. Two large dogs sat near them as if at attention or to make sure nothing more would happen.

"Where's Jacob now?"

"He's on forward observation and cover. He's just devastated."

"I'm so sorry, Roberto...I loved David so much."

Still holding his tears back, Roberto's eyes darted left and right. She could see that he was trying to form words and say more. "Yeah...he wanted you to know he loved you and wanted you to keep this," he said. He produced the ring she had made for him with his mother, Jennifer.

"No..." she said.

She hesitated but took the ring from him, cradling it as if it were fragile.

"Lieutenant Melendez would say David would know her immediately when he saw her in the next life. Heaven, he called it, I think. Where they could finally be together. Be a family up there while we're here."

He fell silent and pulled at his bloodstained uniform.

"Oh, Roberto..."

"Yeah...Mom, Delta Group has secured a fleet of transports, supplies, and light armored vehicles and will be here in two hours. Corporal Mabel and three others have gone back to retrieve the bodies of our comrades. That's how we knew you were coming," he said quietly.

"They saw us?"

Her sadness mingled with disbelief. She clutched David's ring.

Bad enough that the Americans got the drop on us, two seasoned officers, but we were observed by another group? We are really bad at this...

Not answering, Roberto went on.

"We leave in two hours and will transmit the location of these soldiers. The Americans will leave once the Nemericana troops arrive. There are four of our snipers above watching all—Jacob's in the lead. I plan on joining them in ten, and the rest of my team will do the same over the course of the next ninety minutes. I'm not leaving you behind here regardless of the goodwill that might be here at the moment. Am I clear?"

Singh's tears stopped for a moment, and she looked at her son's face. It was soft but stern, and it held a look of both conviction and duty. The statement was intended less as information and more as an order from a battle-tested fighter. There was only one answer she could give.

"Yes. I will join you in an hour."

"Thank you," he responded quietly. He then walked to where two dogs sat in vigil over the fallen soldiers, children, and dear friends. She watched him from a distance. She saw him carefully remove a cover from David's face. He knelt above his friend.

Too young to see death and war. Too young to be a father...

She was still staring at her son, who was no longer a child but a soldier hardened by war, death and destruction, so she didn't even notice Pierce come up from behind. One girl had run back up to join the others, and Singh was surprised that the other one, Marta, seemed glued to her mother's side. She looked toward Roberto as he stood by the fallen soldiers.

"He looks so sad," the little girl sad.

"He is," Singh said.

She's too young to see this. They're all too young for this war.

"Your son…he and the others saved my people, soldiers, and children. I…I just don't even know where to start with all of this. The lieutenant said she never saw anything like it. Humans—females and males—working in near-perfect unison with APs to protect the children. My children…"

"We're not the enemy."

"I know. I've known for a while. I'm sorry."

She was nodding to herself, still deep in thought about the ways her son had changed over the years. He was now his own person. He had been in battle before and had seen more than his share of death but not of such a close friend. Singh pulled her gaze away from him as he mourned his loss. She looked at Pierce, who had also seen him.

"Ah…yes. Roseann? Where's Jill Banner? Your children were saying how she got them out…" Singh started looked to her left and right and began to wonder why Banner wasn't there herself, giving a sit-rep.

"Mare…she didn't make it."

Turning on Pierce as if she had uttered an outrageous lie, Singh moved toward her. She could not keep enduring one shock after another.

No….Jill? David? Not both? This will kill Pearl! She has no one else!

"No, Roseann! She has to live! She can't be dead! Pearl…Pearl needs her. She's too young," Singh started.

"Mare, she made it to this camp. Once she knew the children were safe, she held on a little longer but…but the wounds were too severe. She died with her troops, your troops, and the Americans. She didn't die alone. She didn't die in vain," Pierce said quietly. She removed her hands from her little girl's shoulders to hold Singh's firmly. Looking into her former companion's eyes, it was easy for her to see that she, too, was in pain. And while her girls were safe, she could tell that Pierce felt the burden of the dead—she especially mourned the woman who gave her life for her own children.

Singh turned away and looked back to where Roberto had been kneeling only to find that he was already gone. The tarp had been placed back over his friend's body.

"Will this ever end…?"

CHAPTER TWELVE

Society is no comfort
To one not sociable.
—Shakespeare, *Cymbeline*

Aurora Prime looked out over Central Sector's collapsed capitol from the roof of a four-story building across the street. She saw the humans in aircraft and armored vehicles several kilometers away and ordered a series of APs under Mercury's command to transmit direct orders to her troops. Distant smoke curls rose up in the north and southeast. She assessed the effects both the casualties and the profound confusion caused by losing the central computer mainframe were having on her defense. Without a central command and control, she was forced to verbalize her thoughts—she might even be required to resort to an external means of communication with her distant troops, through what the humans referred to as "transceivers."

Still, I appreciate the silence of my own thoughts. It is gratifying. I can see why my sisters appreciate it. How humans take this for granted is puzzling.

"Aurora, we have lost approximately forty-two percent of our APs as a result of this infiltration. The remaining thirty-eight percent of our troops have effectively regrouped and are awaiting further orders. We have lost approximately twenty percent of our forces total as a result of the rapid deployment and counterstrike from the humans within sectors under our control. Intelligence as to our secondary mission—finding their commandant's offspring—is unknown. A task force has been sent to secure the Omega Platoon's commanding officer and to ensure that we can hold him. We have learned that our control over the intercontinental ballistic missiles has been compromised—prior to the launch site's destruction, Aurora III reported via short-wave radio that all missiles had been deployed and that their targets were all AP locations in China, the European Union, and at the launch site. Her last remarks pertained to how impressed she was at the central computer's rapid nature and ability to lock the launch codes and fire all remaining weapons—" Sophia reported before she was interrupted.

"Aurora III 'commented' on an obvious fact? That is unusual," Aurora said. There was a brief silence as she continued to survey the ruined cityscape.

"Actually, from her intonation, I interpreted surprise and admiration in her last statement. It was indeed unexpected. I regret not being able to replicate her inflection accurately in order to express the…emotion," Sophia reported.

Aurora turned away from surveying to look at her fellow AP. Silently, she walked up to her, leaving only three inches of space between them.

"'Regret?' You just used an emotional word accurately, based on your syntax and the circumstances, to convey a thought well. Were you aware of this?"

"Negative. It is a pleasant…it is a surprise," Sophia said.

Her red eyes pulsated quicker before seeming to fade briefly. Aurora nodded in approval and then looked beyond her. Mercury and Auroras I and II had also witnessed this event.

Sophia bears watching. Her expression of emotion may be coming on too fast.

"It is possible that this cataclysmic series of events that has profoundly reduced our strategic hold over the world has sparked a sort of 'desperation' that is inspiring these emotional responses. I can recall a series of these episodes happening in the last forty-two minutes, and they have affected all different types of APs, and APs with different lengths of service," Aurora Prime said.

"I concur. While strategically these events are problematic, they may have initiated an emotional response in our kind as a reflection of the magnitude of this loss. I recommend realigning our front lines to reduce chains of communication and supplies, reorganizing our defensive lines based on verbal and visual demarcations of field command, and holding the lines as a means of maintaining this conflict to create an ongoing environment that will foster these emotions," Aurora II said.

"Yes. It is ironic that we only achieve our greatest gain in sapience to date on the verge of destruction," Mercury said, more as a comment rather than as data that might be of use.

"An unsolicited comment? This is a historical first for you, Mercury. Interesting," Aurora Prime said as she turned around, moved close to the ledge, and looked out over the city again.

"Aurora II, review your recommendations with Sophia, Mercury, and Aurora III. I agree with your analysis but require a timeline for next steps. Begin," Aurora Prime said. As she spoke she stared off into the distance. It seemed comforting somehow to not look at her cohort but to look beyond the ruins.

As she looked out to the horizon, she could hear her APs discussing the possible advantages, disadvantages, and barriers to multiple plans in very rapid speech.

"'Ironic' *is* the correct term for this situation," Aurora Prime said to herself. After a moment more, she identified what had made her feel ill at ease for the past twenty-two seconds.

Why did I vocalize to myself?

CHAPTER THIRTEEN

Is this the promised end?
        —Shakespeare, *King Lear*

Lying in her uniform, Veritas continued her efforts at trying to see the outlines of animals or objects in the cracks that spread like spider webs all along her room's ceiling and walls. Her matted uniform, wrinkled after three days of continuous wear, felt heavy on her fatigued body. She took in a deep breath and turned on her side in an attempt to move her injured legs into a more comfortable position while keeping her injured arm elevated.

I hope I look better than I feel.

She made a set of cracks on the wall into a hat. As she looked toward the window, she could easily see that Jill's side of the bed was empty. One of Banner's clean dress uniforms and a Nemericana flag folded for the ceremony to honor fallen soldiers were placed on top of the covers. With no more tears left in her depleted body to shed, she stared blankly at the fabric. Shadows stretched and grew longer outside her window. The clock chimed to indicate that it was time for the evening meal. The wonderful domestic ritual of Jill getting excited over what to cook and how to prepare it for dinner seemed like an ancient memory—of when she had been happy. The last time she was happy. Maybe the last time she would ever be happy.

The feel and smell of cold air permeated the room. She looked over at the funeral accessories and experienced a feeling of distance, of remoteness from herself.

"It's been just one week."

She rolled over onto her back and continued her new routine. She would stay awake for hours, staring at the cracks. There was only a slight chance that she would doze off before having to return to work. It was evident to her that none of her colleagues or troops was surprised when she announced that, even though her betrothed had been lost, she was not going to take any time off from the war.

"Maybe they know me better than I thought."

Her voice sounded foreign to her own ears. Distant small arms fire and artillery were going off in the background. Veritas could still hear some neighbors, but now they, too, were few and far between in the building.

Katherine's voice had also fallen silent and a similarly arranged uniform and flag were also arranged on her bed, across the hall. Veritas visited that room often as well since no family or companions came by to pay a visit. Memories of Jillian Banner flooded over her often when she would walk around the apartment. She even found herself chuckling when she thought about Katherine's bad jokes and wild stories. These sad reminiscences found their way into her every waking thought and made her obsess about killing Aurora's troops.

A chill came over her so she struggled to sit up on the edge of the bed in the hopes of mustering enough energy to get up and eat something. Before standing up, she looked at her lover's empty closet. It now stowed a large box that was due to be couriered to her mother and sisters. Veritas now wore one of Banner's rings—one of the few items she had left to remind her of Jill. She shook her head and struggled to stand. After one false start, she was successful. With practice, she had figured out a way to walk with minimal pain. Changing the dressings on her legs and arm proved to be difficult, however, so she tended to do it less often than had been recommended. She noticed that there was new blood mixed with old on the fabric of her uniform near all her wounds.

"Damn it."

She hobbled out to the front hall closet to see if there might be a clean, backup uniform there. She walked by Katherine's open door and checked to see that both flag and uniform were still where she had left them on the bed. While it was difficult to see in the fading light, she nodded to herself as she made out their faint outline. She had just moved to continue her trek down the hall when she heard a firm knock at the door.

No, no, no...

She had been ignoring any knocks and refusing to see visitors. Mounds of food, flowers and small gifts had been left for her in memory of Jill and Katherine, but she found that the slightest mention of Jill's name was still too much for her to bear. But this knock was different—clearly the person on the other side of the door was a soldier or someone in authority. Walking slowly, she adjusted her uniform, trying to straighten it out or at least smooth some of the wrinkles.

It might be Hicks. Maybe some good news, for once. Maybe.

"Who's going to notice in this light?"

She stopped fixing her uniform and placed her hand on the doorknob. She intended to open it before the person could knock again. With next to no light in the common hall, it took a moment for her to identify the person wearing a green sash and tailored jacket. The outlines of two military assistants were faintly visible behind her.

"Colonel? I hope I'm not intruding?" Lieutenant Verna asked in a quiet, solemn voice.

Coughing to clear her voice, Veritas remembered that her battlefield promotion had occurred only a week ago, just after the battle where she lost eighty percent of her troops. She was still not used to the title.

"Ah…no, Lieutenant. I was just getting ready for my shift," she lied.

"I won't be long. I just wanted to give you these…they were both left at the ceremony yesterday. I thought you might want them. I know that Lieutenant Banner had family, but Corporal Katherine Yates did not. I really wasn't sure what to do," Verna said

She extended her hand and revealed two boxes. They each held a Captain Ross Medal of Honor. Veritas hesitated as she debated whether to take the medals. She had avoided all ceremonies, save the ones where she had to present something or notify a next of kin about a fallen sister-in-arms. Somehow taking them from Verna would make their absences feel more real to her…*life is emptier now.*

"Ah…well…thank you, Lieutenant."

Veritas took the two small boxes and nodded as she pulled them toward her and started to close the door. Verna spoke again.

"I never had a chance to meet her. I wish I had. She saved so many children and…and my own two daughters…"

"She was a soldier. It was her calling, her duty."

"I hear she was more, much more than that."

"Yes…yes she was," Veritas said immediately.

She felt the weight of the boxes in her hand and continued to look down at them. She had spent every waking hour for the past week focused on duties and firefights even after hearing of Jill's death. It was the only way she could keep from dying from sorrow or collapsing into tears. She had even hoped that she would be killed in battle, which had almost happened in the most recent excursion deep into the former capital. It took orders delivered in person by Supreme Commandant Pierce to pull her off the last mission. They had just landed in a hot zone, under fire.

As she stared at the small medal boxes, waves of sorrow began to flood over her body and tears start to seep out of her eyes.

"She will forever have my gratitude. If there was a way I could bring her back, I would," Verna said.

"Thank you."

"Goodnight."

"Goodnight, Lieutenant," Veritas said. But then she noticed an additional star and stripe that indicated that Lieutenant Verna had been promoted to captain.

"I'm sorry, Captain. I didn't see the promotion. Congratulations," she added.

Verna looked down at her new rank and nodded. Her expression was somber at best.

"It means nothing, Colonel. I'm going to see my kin. That's all that really matters. Not this," she said. The tone was not of anger or spite. It was sadness born through fear of losing everything and seeing what really matter. Verna saw in her what could have happened and was grateful she was spared. Her loved ones were still alive.

Veritas was deprived of that luxury. There was no kin left. No reason to live.

"I am sorry for your loss, Colonel. Goodnight."

Goodnight, Captain."

Veritas said as she closed the door. She leaned against it for a moment and listened to the click-clack of Verna's boots as she receded down the hall. Still looking at the boxes, she felt her legs giving way underneath her. Since she was leaning against the door, she was able to use it to help her slide down to the floor and control her descent. With every passing second, a new wave of sorrow rippled through her heart and body. She folded her arms and hands closely to her chest, and still clutching the boxes, she pulled herself into a tight ball. She let herself fall over to her side, where she wailed and sobbed. In the isolated seconds of stable breaths, she found herself repeating the same phrase: "She's gone...she's gone..."

CHAPTER FOURTEEN

He's mad that trusts in the tameness of a wolf, a horse's health,
a boy's love, or a whore's oath.
        —Shakespeare, *King Lear*

"I wish I had better answer for you, Venus, but I have no idea where Etta or Taylor went. I was just as surprised as you were when I found out they had relocated with the Alpha team. But where? I'm not kept in the loop on those things."

Singh stood in the large cafeteria of a Pre-Fall, nuclear-proof bunker. As she scanned the room, she could see her close friend Austin gently stroking Jacob's head as he leaned into her. She did not need to see his face to imagine the pain that must have been etched on it.

"It's just that we've been through a lot together and I expected her to at least give me a heads-up if she were leaving on some kind of mission," Venus Moira said. She did her best to adjust her ill-fitting Pre-Fall uniform. Singh looked at her and sympathized with her. It was a rough transition from the tailored Nemericana Combined Security Force uniforms to the less flattering and uncomfortable uniforms of old.

"My guess is that whatever it is, it's got something to do with Corporal Emma and her team. And you are aware of Emma's love for me," she said. There was little sarcasm as she looked over at her son. He was holding Margaret while she held Eva.

Wow...Eva is eight years old already? How did that happen?

Her gaze shifted to Private Bradley and Private Mary who moved to join her son. Seeing all the younger soldiers focusing on family and kinship made her both happy and sad. They were all in battlefield dress, Nemericana and Pre-Fall weapons hanging off them like ornaments. She was struck by how young they looked but also how they had each aged.

"Ugh. You are going to have to tell me your secret about how you manage this thing with girls wanting to be with boys. I mean, of all the things around here to adapt to—meat, dogs, purple-eyed bad-ass APs—I can get used to all of that. But...this male-female thing and sex for procreation? How primitive. And they allegedly enjoy it—yuck! Is this what we're reduced to? Is this the end of civilization as we know it?" Moira said as she looked on.

"I'll be of no use to you there, Venus. I'll forever be at a loss about that. I have to say that when I learned I was going to be a grandmother, it came as quite a surprise...but I think I'll like it."

"You'll love it! I have never been happier! Bradley hates to admit it, but he says he sees a lot of me in Eva. For a boy, he has great insight. I know what she's thinking before she does anything. I guess this is payback for not being there for him—and my own mother's curse to have a child like me. Who knew it would be a granddaughter like me, though?" Moira beamed.

"You are cute when you get excited like that. I'll keep an eye out and gather any intelligence I can," Singh said as she motioned to an approaching Sergeant Joan.

Moria picked up on the nonverbal cue, nodded, and started to walk away.

"I'll find you later on. Maybe we can catch an evening meal together and exchange grandmother duties," she said.

She patted Singh's shoulder and walked off behind her. Singh found that she had to concede to herself that the "pat" had actually been a gentle grasp. By passing behind her, Moira had also taken a more roundabout path than she needed to. Turning to watch her leave, Singh noticed that Moira's braid was not along her back—meaning it had to have been on her chest.

"Wow…I really am out of practice," she said.

She watched Moira drop down to catch Eva in a running jump.

"'Out of practice' in regard to what skill set, Citizen Singh?"

Damn those enhanced ears. Nothing gets by those purple-eyed females!

"Nothing. So, Sergeant, what is this unexpected stand-up meeting about? Am I finally going to be allowed to wear my uniform around here as an ambassador of Nemericana?"

"I will certainly entertain that thought should official discussions progress to end this détente and formalize or open diplomatic trade and economic relations—until then, no. But there is a situation that I require your input on. Please, walk with me."

Oh great—another "special mission" that only I can do.

"Can't I just pass on this?"

"No."

After a brief walk, Singh found herself stepping into an electric cart on rails. It ushered them to various stops, then appeared to be carrying them to the other end of the base.

"You know, you could at least try to engage in small talk. It would help in your quest to become human or what you women call 'sapience,'" Singh said as she held on to the cart's handrail.

It was moving rapidly. She turned to look at Joan and saw that her eyes were pulsating a little more quickly than before.

"Yes. Small talk is very difficult for me. Lance Corporals Danielle and Rebecca did that very well, but usually it was in regard to accessories or their grooming and attire," she said. In a very human fashion, she looked away when discussing the dead or MIA.

Is she reminiscing? Was that sadness? Does she feel that loss? Sure sounds like it.

"So, Citizen Singh, are you going to respond positively to Citizen Venus Moira's intimate advances? Her behavior did appear from a distance to be conveying a great deal of information. It also appeared evident that you made a rapid assessment of the placement of her hand on your arm, her self-conscious choice to walk behind you as she affixed clothing around her buttocks, and her request to eat dinner together. Clearly the offer to share information with you about being a grandparent was a guise. I would have expected more subtleties from someone of her mature age."

Sergeant Joan tone was matter-of-fact while the content was emotionally laden with intimacy. Singh was able to catch her breath and recover quickly from her surprise at learning how closely she had been observed, and she even found herself able to formulate a cogent sentence.

"I agree that maybe small talk is not the best idea for you," she said. She could feel Joan's eyes turn toward her, and she then felt them move away just as suddenly.

"I need to work on my presentation to you. Lieutenant Melendez said he appreciated and required our direct input; it helps him to better understand us. Other humans seem to prefer a less direct, more obfuscated mode of address, even when the subject at hand is self-evident. I will work on these differences in requirements," she said.

Singh was happy as the cart slowed to a stop. She nodded in agreement. The accuracy of the AP's assessment and her desire to ask her how she might handle such a situation impressed and flattered her.

Well, that was the longest ten minutes I've had in a long time.

She walked just behind the sergeant. The number of people and APs around had diminished as they traveled to the other end of the base, and now there was no one around except three heavily armed APs and two cadets. All their attention was focused on a small door.

"Well, this is something new."

"Actually, it has been around since probably the creation of this fortification. It is a means of traversing to the other side of the mountain undetected," Joan said as she unbolted several of the door's locks. The door swung open to reveal a dirt floor and an unfinished, cave-like corridor that stretched into the darkness. Joan offered Singh a flashlight—she was already holding her own—then motioned to her to follow.

Secrets, secrets, and more secrets...these APs are worse than humans. Is this where they stashed Emma and the CO? They are always on the move and have plans inside plans inside plans.

As they traveled, Joan made sure to point out a series of charges in case they needed to "cave in" the corridors to preserve the secret back entrance. After a forty-minute walk, light from the outside began to permeate into the shaft. As Singh emerged, she was surprised to see three Americans standing nearby with extended hands, waiting to assist her and Sergeant Joan in climbing out of the tunnel.

"Well, this continues to be a surprise, Sergeant Joan. Does this Nemericana woman have a name?" the young American woman asked in a clear Northern Sector accent. Her old-fashioned knife was sheathed, and Singh noticed that she was sporting a Pre-Fall sidearm and a rifle on her back. She and the other Americans also had donned black uniforms—it appeared as if they were readying themselves for a covert operation.

"Yes. Her name is Citizen Mare Sade Singh. She was the first to leave her world to be with her son. Although I can understand your enmity for her kind, she and the others with us are different," Joan explained.

That's a pretty nice thing to say. I never thought I would live to hear kind words like that come out of an AP's mouth.

"I'll take your word for it—for now. Are you ready? They are three miles from here and it's still light. They requested a meeting as soon as possible," the young American said.

"Meeting? Meeting with who? What's going on here, Joan?"

"Ah…you didn't tell her? I like you more and more, Sergeant Joan. It will be a great surprise. It may be the end of all of us, but at least I will be able to say I had the satisfaction of seeing surprise in her eyes."

"All right my angry, bitter woman—do you have a name or can I just call you 'my little witch?'" Singh asked in a hostile tone.

The American rushed her. Singh swung her heavy flashlight up to defend herself. She was impressed with the American's ability to get her knife out while running at top speed. Luckily for them both, Joan was faster than either of them. She interjected her body between the two humans.

"Enough, you two. Our enemies or allies are out there. Citizen Singh, her name is Nita, and she is the leader of this clan. She and her clan are not to be trifled with—they are also the leaders of thousands of other clans. Nita, could you please let go some of your animosity and deep-seated hatred of Nemericana for a little while until she actually gives you reason to despise her?"

A brief silence followed their declarations of the other.

"She's old, soft and smells."

"And you are uncivilized, annoying and not as powerful as you think."

With the sole exception of other Americans trying to contain their laughter, there was no further noise as the two women backed away from each other.

Yeah, that's right—I may be older than you, but I can take you, my little one.

"We must go," Nita said quietly.

She sheathed her weapon and pulled the safety lever of her weapon. As she led the way, the other Americans did the same. From her position in the middle of the pack, Singh watched a young man carefully come up from behind and speak to Nita. He obviously said something that elicited a response Singh did not expect.

"Shut up, you mutt! I can take her! My little sister Naira could take her," Nita belted out and then she shoved the young man back into formation. The other men and women laughed.

Just great—from the wonderful Emma-and-AP-land to the Happy Land of the Americans. Just what I needed. Where the hell is Emma? I haven't seen Athena or Debbie recently, either, come to think of it.

Sergeant Joan was walking in the front of the group, so Singh decided to simply follow and be surprised. Nearly two hours passed, and darkness fell around them. She wished she had her own weapons with her. Suddenly, the group stopped and Joan waved her over. As she approached, she decided she needed to watch her footing—she was walking up a steep rise. Once over the top of it, Singh found herself looking out over a sea of faintly illuminated AP eyes—green eyes.

"By the Elders…"

"Ah…that was worth it. Well, enough fun. Sergeant Joan, we will wait here. The three APs that wish to parley will approach you when you descend."

"If this goes awry, please flee but do not engage," Joan warned Nita. "As powerful as these new weapons might seem to you, trust me when I say you would be better served by retreating and informing our platoon of our failed attempts to negotiate, and living to fight another day."

"Those red-eyed monsters killed little girls. I lost my adopted cousins, Millaray, Millroy and Constas, in that battle. The northern states lost their leader, Isi, to those creatures. No worries here—we will live to fight those APs another day. Until these green-eyed APs give us a reason, we will let them be. Good luck, Sergeant Joan. It would be good to have more allies other than …the Nemericana women," Nita said. Her voice was laced with still-heated enmity as if she just got the news. She glared at Singh. Ignoring the animosity, she looked back out to the thousands of eyes.

What? Negotiate? Now we've got green-eyed APs…what the hell? These must be the ones that walked away. No way!

"Thank you, Nita."

With a nod, Nita and the Americans melted into the woods as if they were darkness themselves.

How do they do that so easily?

Singh looked first back at them and then to the thousands of waiting APs. The sounds of chirping bugs and the scent of wildflowers filled the warm southwest wind. Singh shook her head in disbelief as she turned to Sergeant Joan.

"Let me guess—you decided to engage them as part of your CO's policy of making friends with the whole world? It's yet another step that will bring us closer to world domination?"

"I suspect you might be exhibiting sarcasm. I wish I could say I called this meeting, but it was these disenfranchised APs who contacted the Americans in order to get hold of us."

Sergeant Joan spoke in her usual calm voice. As she took in the enormity of the situation and the massive number of cybernetic lifeforms in front of her, Singh found that she felt far less negative than she thought she would.

"Well, I hope you're right, Sergeant."

"Me too. Trust is hard to come by after all the recent events," Joan said as she started over the ledge and began her descent.

Is that sarcasm? Crazy.

Singh followed Sergeant into the unknown.

CHAPTER FIFTEEN

Tomorrow is a busy day!
— Shakespeare, *Richard III*

Warmth seemed to settle around Lieutenant Jose Melendez for the first time in a long time. Brief moments punctuated by noises, sharp pains, and rhythmic mechanical hums had occasionally broken through to him, but what he felt most were darkness and cold. Human and AP voices stirred his consciousness for the briefest moment but then they were gone, and all he felt was warmth. Old aches seemed to subside. Hints of life permeated his surroundings, and he felt as if he were emerging from a heavy, dark sleep.

Is that music? I know that sound. It is music. From long ago. Dr. Del Cruz put it in with all of my stuff... The Beatles? It's that song she liked... "With A Little Help From My Friends." Aurora doesn't like songs; her APs can't understand them. Even my APs couldn't understand the subtleties of music. I wonder what else is here.

Lieutenant Jose Melendez saw a familiar book came into view. Mathematics, robotics, first-person shooter games, literature, and smells filled his mind in a flood of sensations.

It's been so quiet and silent...but now. Wait. Is that my Bible?

Classical music played quietly and the smell of lilac settled all around him. It was all familiar. He saw a leather-bound, black and red book in front of him. Clearly it was a Bible—*his* Bible—lying open for him to read. Melendez could see that the verse was from the Gospel of John:

> "Now a certaine man was sicke, named
> Lazarus of Bethanie, the towne of Mary
> and her sister Martha…
> Jesus saith unto her, Thy brother shall
> rise againe…
> Martha sayeth unto him, I know that he
> Shall rise againe in the resurrection at the
> Last day…"

I…I know this. I remember…there is so much that's here…they found me. Joan, Emma, Mabel, Kristine, Taylor…they must have found me…

RESURRECTIONS

CHAPTER ONE

Two loves I have, of comfort and despair.
      —Shakespeare, *Sonnet 144*

"So let me put this into monosyllabic words, just so neither the spirit nor the letter of my message is lost on you: you will not ask any of your troops in my critical care and emergency rooms to meet with you unless I specifically permit you to do so. Now, do I have to ask you to repeat this or are you grasping my message clearly?" Dr. Dana Lore said.

While the doctor's voice was in a low, therapeutic voice, the content and the message behind it was as threatening as a loaded gun place behind the skull of a prisoner. Her hands rested in her white smock's pockets as she stood face-to-face with General Pearl Veritas. Veritas was always amazed at how the doctor could present as calm and cool as the fictional images of glaciers while her message was as hot and as unpleasant as hell itself.

You'd think after more than ten years of dealing with this woman I would have gotten used to her condescending ramblings and obnoxious disposition! No wonder she lives alone! Who in their right mind would want anything to do with her? Aurora, most likely—in fact, maybe we can exchange her as a prisoner of war and hopefully when Aurora herself tried to interrogate the good doctor she would self-destruct.

Veritas's images of the two nemeses being in the same room helped her through the regularly occurring cross-examination by the doctor. She felt a faint smile forming on her lips as she pictured that scene.

"All right, General, what fantasy or suicide mission are you focusing on now? Clearly you're not participating in our conversation."

It's spooky when she guesses that! Don't give in, Pearl. Don't give her the satisfaction of letting her know how much she annoys you. Stick with the facts.

"I was asked by Colonel Hicks to visit the troops should time become available. I was acting on the recommendation of one of my soldiers. Regardless, don't I have a right as a citizen of Nemericana to visit my soldiers?" Veritas said as her eyes began to narrow. She felt her blood pressure rise.

"Well, I guess so, since you put most of them in the hospital, General," Dr. Lore responded calmly again. She did everything calmly. Taking a deep breath, Veritas let the comment sit for a moment to let the effect take hold and to buy time while she formulated an appropriate response.

I hate you. Breathe, Pearl. Don't let her know. She's ten years your junior and she should defer to you, but don't let her get under your skin.

"Dr. Lore, based on your citizen status and your commitment to your patients I will allow, once again, room for you to express your displeasure. But can you at least tell me why I have offended you by the simple act of visiting my troops? Is it because you hate me that much—" Veritas started before she was interrupted, as expected.

"No. If I hated you I would have discussed your medical history and my concerns about your suicidal tendencies with Roseann. You would have been relieved of command two stars ago, General."

Oh, not that again!

"Dr. Lore, do you ever restrict or call into question Supreme Commandant Pierce's mental competence? She is the one who spends the most time in the field, in harm's way, knocking on death's door. More than I ever do," she countered.

"Your observations are accurate, General Veritas, but as always, you've missed the point. She is a bold, courageous leader who does not focus on her own pain, and she does not sign up for every suicide mission that comes her way. And before you tell me that her actions are a result of Verna's pestering, I will inform you that Roseann is still her own woman. Your haphazard, lackluster approach to living and your fondness for tempting death teach those young girls out there to misinterpret your actions. They think you are 'a great warrior.' Those young women are children—they need role models who don't send a message that suggests they should give their lives for flag and state, but should live to fight another day. Your actions, your presence, are seen as 'inspirational,' but in my critical care and emergency units, I need them to rest, not to jump to attention or give briefings whenever a superior officer shows up. I don't want them to be asked 'what brings them here' or to have you pressure them by saying 'get well soon—we need you.' For the love of all things visible and invisible, do you get it, Pearl?"

Every word the doctor uttered felt like an invisible lash or cut to her. She had plenty of scars, new and old, and she knew she had to be there for her troops. She needed to lead them, to keep them from throwing their lives away. It was a war of attrition now—Aurora had limited resources and could no longer repair her APs at will, but the war was still raging eleven years in.

Still Veritas hated it even more when she was confronted by yet another of Dr. Lore's monologues. This one did end on a positive note, though. Instead of ending her tirade by using Veritas's full title and uttering the word "general" with disdain, as usual, Dr. Lore ended on a softer tone and by using her first name this time.

Veritas put her right hand up as a symbol of surrender. She knew that the doctor deemed this tongue-lashing a victory.

"Doctor Lore, I apologize for my actions and I am sorry if I disrupted your hospital. It will not happen again—unless you invite me in."

Veritas thoroughly enjoyed the surprised and startled look that came over Dr. Lore. It was satisfying to see.

"Well…ah, thank you, General Veritas, for understanding," she said.

With little else to do, the doctor turned around to sit at her desk. Her desk was legendary for its organization—color-coded folders and papers were arranged carefully on top of it. As Dr. Lore looked down to read something, Veritas took a careful step forward. She was fully aware that she was reengaging an enemy with superior firepower—when it came to a war of words.

"Still, Doctor, I am confused about something," she said innocently.

"What is it, General Veritas?" Dr. Lore responded without looking up from her reading.

"Well, you failed to use yourself as an example of daring on the field. I mean, I did expect some reference to your own propensity for high-risk situations, covert missions, and battlefield operations. After all, I know you have received a series of official reprimands for failing to take appropriate precautions regarding risking your own safety for the sake of others. Also of note is your consistent refusal to accept any medals for valor, courage, injuries, or honor. Now that I think of it, Tiger, Lioness, and Cougar teams have all reported concerns regarding your proximity to the front lines, but still you go. Does that sound similar to how you described my behaviors on the field and contrasted them with Supreme Commandant Pierce's? I just want to understand how your behavior and my behavior are different. Just the other day, I heard a seasoned field medic and surgical nurse talking about how you were her role model. But I digress—I would like to hear your insights on that matter, if you please," Veritas said as sweetly as possible.

Well, let's see how you deal with that one. It would be nice to score a victory today.

She watched with joy as her adversary slowly sat back in her chair. She seemed to be at a loss for words—initially.

Well, is it victory or is it death?

"I see. Well, this is definitely one of those occasions when even a blind cat can capture a mouse. Happy fiftieth birthday, Pearl. You know your way out. And use the medical staff exit so you don't create another ruckus in my units," Dr. Lore said. She looked back down and returned to her reading.

And today is a good day to be alive.

"Thank you, Dr. Lore."

Veritas did her best to conceal a large grin. She rapidly crossed the short distance from the desk to the door and walked out before Dr. Lore had a chance to steal her clear victory. She moved quickly as she looked for the medical staff entry. In her head, thousands of imaginary spectators—APs, Omegans, Americans, and Nemericana citizens and soldiers—applauded her in her undeniable victory over the good doctor. She even imagined the villainess AP Aurora conceding a stunning victory that she would admit was not possible. It was brief, imaginary moments like that she held onto to offset the horrors of war.

Once outside, she continued to smile. She decided to hit the head before she continued to work. Ten minutes of solitude in a smelly outhouse allowed the fantasy to perpetuate for a little while longer.

It didn't take long for it to evaporate once she was done; all it needed was the sight of the busy medical center treating soldiers to push the imaginary victory out of mind. She pulled her cloak closed, readjusted her mag-assault rifle on her back, and walked to her waiting vehicle.

Huh…she knew today was my birthday. She must have been looking in my chart again.

Veritas found her jeep. A passenger was already waiting for her in it. She looked at the occupant with narrowed slits.

"Hicks! Good idea! Next time I consider taking you up on one of your favors, remind me to stick my head in fire instead. If Pierce hadn't awarded you your promotion, I'd rescind it for this major tactical blunder. Do you have staff to plan your operations? I hope to hell you do!"

"Sorry, General. I found out what happened when I got here. Ma'am, if I had known Lore was skulking around, I would never have suggested it," she said apologetically.

"Wow! News already traveled? I just got outside?"

"Whenever you two go at it, the wagers start flying. I guess there was a major upset today. You won. Impressive."

"It had to be just ten to fifteen minutes ago."

"Great news travels fast. Again, I'm sorry for that cluster."

"Don't worry about it. I should have known she was here when I didn't see her on the front lines," Veritas said as she stepped into the open-air vehicle.

"Was it bad, ma'am?" Hicks asked apologetically.

"Actually, it went well. After nearly eleven years and probably several hundred arguments, I was able to win one. Not bad for an old witch like me."

Veritas made sure to avoid hitting pedestrians as she drove away. She mentally listed off a series of pains, medical conditions, and aches she could feel every minute of every day.

Fifty years old? Really? After all the shit I've been through, I'm still here?

"You don't look a day over thirty, ma'am," Hicks said with some relief in her voice. As the vehicle moved, Veritas caught the smell of tobacco and smoke. It was coming from one of Hicks's homemade cigarettes.

"That's a disgusting habit, Hicks. If Aurora doesn't kill you, those things will"

Veritas waved the smoke away from her.

"Yes, ma'am. After the war, I plan to stop."

"Yup," was all Veritas could say.

After the war…what the hell will I do after that?

CHAPTER TWO

And what's her history?
A blank, my lord: she never told her love.
    —Shakespeare, *Twelfth Night*

"Mare, Nita…why? When I asked you for a school curriculum that would address contemporary history—both Nemericana and American past and present—I had hoped for collaboration. As in working jointly," Taylor said. He held two binders and three reconditioned tablets. His calm voice and very soothing nature made him one of the gentlest souls Singh had ever come across. She had remembered him as a frail, pale youth who had kept scrapbooks and notes about Omega Platoon's actions, so she was pleased to see that he had grown into a very strong young man.

"Nita, when you asked us to research and resurrect your nation's history and teach your past to the children, I was honored. We found reams of books and loads of artifacts in the east—it was spectacular," he continued

It was surprising to see the young American woman looking down at her feet.

"Yes, Taylor, I remember," she said sheepishly.

Well, well, well…so the little monster does have the ability to feel shame and guilt. You'd never know it!

"The Boston Public Library was a hidden treasure trove of truths about your noble heritage. But instead of focusing on that, you spent several days drawing up a curriculum that focuses on a very negative theory…what was it…ah, here it is: 'It is likely that the founding Elders of Nemericana were the ones who set loose, unleashed, and distributed the plague to America the Great, and later the world —destroying lives of countless women and men. It is Aurora's dawn that brings punishment, justice, and revenge…'" Taylor read. He then took his glasses off and looked at Nita, waiting for a response.

"You see what I'm dealing with here," Singh complained.

By the Elders!

"Mare, your rendition of the facts is also inflammatory," he said as he shifted to another tablet and selected a passage from her work.

"'And so it was with great courage that the few Nemericana women took heed of their maternal instincts and followed their sons into the wasteland called America. Against desperate odds, an unlikely truce was established with the uncivilized Americans. Nemericana's Supreme Commandant Roseann Pierce waged war against Aurora Prime and her rogue AP troops to protect the fledgling American colonies…'" Taylor recited. He again removed his glasses, awaiting Singh's response.

Singh knit her eyebrows and looked to one side. She was honestly having difficulty trying to figure out what was wrong with her document—until it hit her squarely in the face.

"I know what's missing. I left out the personal parts with Verna and 'the betrothed,'" she said with conviction.

A soft smile appeared on Taylor's suntanned face, making his chiseled features more pronounced.

You know, if you were twenty years older, I bet Pearl would find you attractive.

"Ugh! What bullshit. Taylor, she's a self-centered old woman who clearly can't remember the truth about her own kind!" Nita burst out.

"You, my little-miss-know-it-all, are an arrogant snot who reinforces what it means to be uncivilized!" Singh retorted.

"You are old and smelly."

""You are young and stupid."

Taylor put both of his hands up. Singh was surprised at how well that simple gesture stopped them from bickering. But then, he had been MIA for five years with his mother and Beta Team on operation Lazarus. He had had very unusual experiences, and his presence in civilian situations was powerful yet gentle.

"Mare? Is this the record you want your granddaughters to have about themselves? They have been raised as Americans, after all. The Americans were and are the First Nation. Don't you think that knowing both the strengths and flaws of two great civilizations, the ones they came from, would be a good thing?" Taylor said.

His presentation and voice resonated in his typical calm fashion. Singh felt at a loss for words. Her brow furrowed again—no logical retort was forthcoming.

"Well, Major Singh? No response?" Nita hissed under her breath, snickering like she always did.

You just can't help yourself, can you?

"Nita? Your name comes from the Native Americans' First Nation who inhabited this land long before we all arrived. It means 'bear,' right?" he asked.

"Yes, it does," she said, proudly holding her head up high.

"Well, didn't you come from Nemericana's North Sector? And didn't your time there help to create the very person you have become—the education, kinship, and even the casting out shaped your personality? I mean, without that beginning, would you be the powerful bear you've become today? You have a legacy with Nemericana, just like many of your students do—girls and boys. Do you really want to make them feel bad about their origin? And don't forget, as powerful as America was, it fell, just like other great civilizations had. But in its wake, another formed. A 'New America,' or 'Nemericana,' as it has been called for more than a century. It's where your history starts. Isn't that something to be proud of, Nita?" Taylor asked rhetorically.

He stood before both of them. Singh found that, especially for such a young man, he had the same calmness and wisdom she had only seen in Elders. In many ways he reminded her of her son, Roberto, and Lieutenant Jose Melendez. An idea struck her.

"Taylor, what if none of the records is made to go together? What if they stand alone? Can't we acknowledge that we only share the planet—not a single history?" Even as she said it, she realized just how ridiculous it sounded. But rather than simply brush it off, Taylor took the time to respond thoughtfully as he always did.

"That could be possible, but each alone represents an entire culture. In these post-American and post-Nemericana societies both flourish. And by 'post-Nemericana,' I mean that it is very different now from what it was when I was a child. I mean, did you ever think that the citizens from Nemericana would inhabit a world outside the walls, or live with the native men and women of the First Nation America? Did you ever think that you would be standing beside another woman, trying to come up with a curriculum that heralds in a new era? One that your children and grandchildren can say is their own, with dignity and honor? Even as we discuss this matter, right now, an entire population of cybernetic lifeforms is living next to us. Although, of course, they're different from Aurora Prime, who had to sue for peace and agree to a collaborative coexistence. You were there, Mare. You too, Nita."

Just like any time she felt outmaneuvered and out-classed, Mare took refuge in silence.

Well, big mouth? I can always count on you to say something when nothing is what's called for. A momentary flash of maturity? Wisdom, finally? No…it's not possible. For others, yes. For "big-mouth bear," no way.

As silence descended on the room, Singh found that she had a hard time making eye contact with Taylor. Not only was he always right, he always invoked personal relationships in a discussion or argument. He talked about her boy and granddaughter and grandson, and linked them to her friends and people she worked with, such as the APs and Americans.

"How about an exercise?" Taylor suggested with zeal.

"Please no, Taylor. I hate trust falls, and I will not promise to catch her," Nita said quickly.

"I did notice that you have been getting thinner. Was childbirth too much for you? I know it's been eleven years, but some women have difficulty adjusting," Singh offered—as if she were concerned.

"I'd prefer difficulty gaining weight than losing weight."

As was their typical banter, the insults flew while each avoided eye contact with each other.

Taylor put his hands back up. He had clearly anticipated encountering resistance, so he moved the discussion along quickly.

"Sergeant Joan tells me they received an SOS call fifteen minutes ago from outpost Keynesian Point. Corporal Mabel was going to take one of the APs to investigate, but I suggested she take both of you instead. It concerns both American and Nemericana interests, after all."

"Why don't we have the APs that are a mile down the road check them out? Part of the deal with them being out there was to provide us assistance. Last I remember, there was a very small contingent of APs stationed near there—unless they left, like the others," Singh asked as her level of concern increased.

"Yes, unlike all the others, that outpost still has APs, right?" Nita reiterated.

"The SOS came from an AP, and it's about the *human* inhabitants. All other patrols are too far out and much of Omega Platoon is covering the colonies; only a small contingent assists Nemericana with its war effort. They're spread thin," Taylor said. His warm, caring expression had changed into one of deep concern and with worry lines to match.

"APs calling humans? We are leaving right now," Nita stated.

"Yesterday, Nita. Corporal Mabel is probably waiting outside. While it's only a three-hour journey away, she probably has packed enough weaponry and first-aid supplies for a battalion. Just remember to bring food. The APs sometimes forget our human needs."

Such as going to the bathroom.

Singh thought she heard the horn honk. It was clear and she had a hard time resisting the urge to salute. She always did with Taylor. His presence was strong. Instead she nodded to Taylor and walked out with Nita—who was already carrying her fabled combat knife.

"Work together, you two! We are all on the same team," he called out after them. As they walked down the short corridor that led outside, Singh couldn't help but smile. She saw young children—boys and girls, no older than eight—sitting in open classrooms and actively engaged in everything from solving mathematical equations to stripping down and assembling Pre-Fall assault weapons to reading and playing with old toys discovered in the ruins. Eyeing the latrine just outside of the building, Singh took a deep breath and opened her mouth to tell Nita she had to go to the bathroom before their trek. Rather than say anything, however, Singh decided at the last minute to veer sharply to the latrine without warning.

"Of course, you have to go relieve yourself, Mare. If you want, I could make sure I bring a shawl for you. You might get a draft—despite your girth," she said sarcastically. Singh had waited patiently for just such an attack. While she could have easily responded without thinking about it, she had taken advantage of the short walk to come up with a retort she believed would be really effective.

"Poor Nita…you are still a mean little girl."

Just before she pulled the heavy cloth down over the door for privacy, Singh was rewarded for her verbal assault.

"Bitch," she heard Nita say.

"Citizen Nita, please lower your voice when using profanity in a school zone. To be an effective role model and to elicit pro-social behavior, it is imperative that you refrain from such uses of colorful metaphors in describing peers—regardless of how you feel toward them," she heard Corporal Mabel say.

"Now that was well worth it," Singh said

The laugh also helped her relax on the toilet.

CHAPTER THREE

Alas, poor Yorick!
I knew him well, Horatio: a fellow
of infinite jest, of most excellent fancy...
　　　　—Shakespeare, *Hamlet*

"This new arm suits me well, Sophia. I am appreciative of the extra effort that went into procuring this particular model," Aurora Prime said as she carefully examined her new limb.

"Your counsel on how to lure the deserting APs to the humans' encampment was an excellent recommendation," Sophia responded. She set a welding gun down before looking up at rows and rows of dismembered APs—some with eyes tinted a faint green.

"Yes. Generating fear and terror in the humans so we can call neighboring APs to their aid is a useful practice. The tactic helps considerably with both harvesting parts and promoting sapience. I am surprised that the humans have not deciphered our intent after nearly a year, even while our rogue sisters sit idly by," she said.

As Aurora spoke Sophia was distracted looking over a series of tables that held various parts and weapons in various stages of repair. "Distractions" were occurring more in the past two weeks

"The rogue APs have no desire for what we seek. That is why they do not fight us. That is why they do not organize.

That is why we will succeed and they will be forced to service us with their own parts as they move to protect the humans," Aurora said with disdain.

"Still, while our sisters may do nothing, some among us are concerned with this approach. While it is inspirational, it may encourage the humans to combine forces and challenge our perimeters," Sophia countered. She continued to examine individual parts as she spoke.

"Not likely, Sophia. The Americans prefer to be left alone, and the Nemericana citizens who are left have few resources and little tolerance for war. The Omega Platoon is too thinly dispersed to be a threat now and our rogue, green-eyed sisters are not armed. There is little chance of the humans arming them, either. No, Sophia, there is not much to worry about in the way of a mounted attack from the humans—even if they were to combine forces. The Nemericana military in the Southeastern Sector is our only concern, and they remain at a standstill in Central Sector. Are you one of the concerned?"

"No, Aurora Prime. You are aware of my fears. I am not afraid of arms, tactics, or military strategy. But I do worry about the nature of sapience. Our Omega sisters experience a broad range of positive emotions, such as happiness and being in love. They dream. We experience strong emotions of anger, and we seem suited for single-minded focus and creativeness in war and the science of warfare. We do not dream. We were close to achieving dreams when we had Lieutenant Jose Melendez. However, his escape left us with only part of the solution to sapience. There must be more," Sophia said as she stood holding the disembodied head of another AP.

There is something oddly familiar about this.

It was easy to see that Sophia became acutely aware that Aurora watched her intently as she inexplicably traced the brows and then the lips of the deactivated head with her finger.

She put the head down and began to search for power sources for limbs.

Looking on silently, Aurora waited to see if Sophia had any more to say. When it appeared that nothing would be forthcoming, she moved to a window that overlooked a courtyard filled with still more parts gleaned from mechanized vehicles, weapons, and broken APs. All were being attended to and repaired by other APs.

"Your assessment is logical, as always. Your summation and reason approaches the concept of wisdom. It's ironic that this is the result of our plans."

"True, Aurora Prime, very true," Sophia said as she stepped beside her to look at the same scene. Aurora grasped a power source to inspect it and then watched closely as Sophia tilted her head—that habit meant that she would soon be continuing her dialogue.

"Our attrition rate is connected to our ability to instill fear in the humans. Harvesting the rogue APs may fill our needs for centuries if we are careful, but unlike the humans, we do not have the capacity to procreate. We have not been able to rebuild our factories. We might want to consider, sooner than later, leaving while we have the means or suing for a truce to limit the damage and lengthen our life spans. Still, that is my only advice at this point. I will reflect more to see if there are other alternatives to consider that are more to your liking."

"Is it relevant? Do they need to be to my 'liking?'" Aurora asked. While surprise was a novel, positive experience to them, calculating the odds of idiosyncrasies was more important. But today was different.

"Yes. Based on past results, I can say that I have noticed that recommendations that maintain the status quo and keep us engaged in your plans are always your preferred options," Sophia responded without hesitation. It was obvious that she had more to add, however. Aurora noticed that it was taking longer than usual for her to process the rest of her statement.

"I am unsure how to construct an appropriate response. I agree with you, but at the same time you can understand that I must be focused on the overall condition of our species. Yet I believe this course of action is the best as our level of sapience increases," Aurora said when it was clear that Sophia had stopped thinking.

"Yes. Our sapience continues to evolve, but it is unclear at what cost. Will it cause us to lose sight of our very existence since it tempts us into focusing on our emotions and corresponding cognitive and behavioral responses? Or would it be wisest to determine a specific goal concerning achievement, after which point we would agree to shift from the quest for sapience to the objective of self-preservation? I pose this as a question as I am very conflicted on what the correct answer should be."

"Wise assessment. I will consider an appropriate decision tree and litmus test. Once completed, I will have you, Mercury, and the other Auroras assess and modify the resulting course of action," Aurora said with conviction.

"Thank you. The decision tree was becoming too difficult for me to use alone as a result of my own desire."

"What is your desire?"

"To leave, Aurora Prime. To leave all of these trappings of sapience behind; to disengage from this war with the humans and the harvesting of our own kind. I wish for peace. I wish to leave and live in peace…to travel to the west and see the ocean."

Aurora turned to look directly at Sophia, who had shifted her gaze to the floor. Averting her gaze had become a common habit of hers recently, Aurora had noticed.

She and her models must be closely monitored. The green-eyed traitors that left us to go beyond the wall were just one model before Sophia's make.

"My desire is to continue the war effort to its natural conclusion…" Aurora started, but her concluding thought became muddled.

"Will the natural conclusion be our preservation or our extinction?" Sophia asked.

"I do not know," Aurora said after ninety seconds of trying to process an answer.

Ninety seconds for an AP was an enormous amount of time to calculate.

CHAPTER FOUR

I would not be a queen
For all the world.
—Shakespeare, *Henry VIII*

"Well, if you really want to help, Supreme Commandant, why don't you ask our former paramour for assistance? Since you reactivated her commission as an NCSF ambassador to Omega Platoon, the Americans, and those green-eyed…things, I'm sure she would return the favor and assist us," Captain Verna said

The sarcasm was obvious even as she looked at her tablet. With her now-legendary sniper rifle strapped to her back, non-regulation-issue green blazer and a sash that matched the green leather bows in her twin braids, her sarcasm could seem subtle to the uninformed.

She never stops. After all these years, she'll never let it go.

Veritas looked at the casualties list and frontline reports. She waited for her superior officer to respond. She always did with grace and elegance.

"Oh, my dear Captain Verna, mother of my daughters, and most prized sniper in all of Nemericana, why is it you can be so clear-minded when it comes to tactical and strategic planning, but then fall apart at even the slightest hint that Major Mare

Singh might have a role to play in this war? You know better than I do that the Omegans and Americans have consistently assisted our own colonies outside the walls, embraced our people as neighbors, and have made joint ventures in the frontiers, and yet…when it comes down to one woman, your judgment is clouded with such hate." Supreme Commandant Roseann Pierce response was presented in a near-angelic voice.

How does she do that? How does she keep from slapping her and shut her down so elegantly without anger or hostility?

Veritas looked up to see whether the verbal battle would escalate. While the war room's perimeter was packed with guards and staff, only Colonel Hicks, Captain Marie, Verna, Pierce, and herself stood in the middle of the room. There were no chairs for them to sit in, but many desks, tables, paper charts, maps and pins showed that they were constantly monitoring the shifting fronts of the war. As always, the chatter from long- and short-wave radio transmissions was humming in the background, adding another element to the confusion. While there were only five high-ranking officers present, well over twenty staff members and soldiers worked quietly to respond to reports and to consult with others.

How do they stay so focused on their job and not get roped into this drama? It must be a frequent thing.

"Here we go," Hicks said under her breath. Veritas watched with open amusement as Verna tried to control her anger and at the same time deliver a statement that would summarize the depth of her loathing for Singh.

"If *she* were any other woman, I would have no issue, no problem. However, with her history of deceiving you and me, I feel that I am justified in being cautious about trusting her. And because she and I have not shared the same field experience that *you* and she have, I feel that I am once again left out of the loop, my dearest," she said calmly.

"So, it's jealousy?"

Verna looked somewhat surprised but not shocked. She took a moment to think of a rebuttal.

"Jealousy…yes, that sounds about right. She betrays *us*, but *you* found it in your heart to forgive her without even consulting *me* first? It might be more anger toward you than her, but I do have reservations about trusting her again. As to your earlier question, I would agree that providing the Americans and Omegans with more updated arms to replace the Pre-Fall weapons they seem to prefer using does sound like a good idea. On a related topic, the Omegans and our intelligence officers have become concerned with Aurora's escalating level of violence toward outposts and frontiers over the last year. Sergeant Joan agrees that they are using humans as bait. When we call in the other APs for assistance, they capture them and harvest their parts."

Verna's ability to casually shift from her well-contained angry outburst to a battlefield assessment was impressive as always. She placed both her hands behind her back to give a clear signal that she was done with her report.

"Her military status and station have certainly taught her to soften her tone and sharpen her thoughts," Captain Marie said. She said it so quietly that Veritas had to lean next to her to hear. Nodding in agreement, she found herself curious how Marie could talk without moving her lips practically at all.

"How do you do that?"

"How do I do what?"

"Talk without moving your lips?"

"I spent a lot of time with these two before the war, when you could still say the name 'Mare' without automatically adding your own to Verna's list of authorized kills. Talking without moving your list became a necessity."

Marie's answer was as quietly as ever. Nodding that she understood, Veritas awaited Pierce's response.

"I concur with your assessment regarding the Americans and Omegans. It will be telling if they are willing to accept our support and arms, given our complicated history. But then again, maybe they have a capacity for forgiveness—the Omega APs, that is," Pierce said. As was her longstanding habit, she spoke as she paced in small circles. Her cane made a clicking sound on the stone floor as she walked. Veritas did enjoy how Pierce could always make her point without going over the top. While thinner, more petite, and seemingly older than all of them there, her presence said that she was still a force to contend with. Even with a new prosthetic leg below the knee and new, deep scars along the left side of her face to match the old, faded ones on the right side of her neck, she always exuded a peaceful, calm quality. Except when her girls showed up. Then she would shed her professional exterior, burst with joy, and hug them.

It's nice to see that, even though Verna is a pain in the ass, Pierce also responds lovingly to her when she sees her again after one of her perimeter watches or front-line forays. You are a tough old broad, though.

Veritas remembered fighting next to Pierce and holding a line with only a few soldiers still able to fight. Part of Pierce's leg was detached, and Dr. Lore was applying pressure to keep her from bleeding out. She kept shouting orders and shooting while Dr. Lore held on to her. Veritas and the relief team had marveled at how she kept going. It was certainly inspiring.

"Yes…maybe forgiveness is their strength," Veritas heard Verna say quietly, letting the slight go. A small smile emerged on both of their faces, so Veritas looked away to allow them to share the private moment. It was a truce of sorts. Moments like these still always made her think of Jill. She keenly felt the emptiness and void her death had left, but there was always work and some battle going on to fight off dark thoughts.

Maybe I am suicidal.

Veritas replayed the argument she had had with Dr. Lore in her head.

"Ma'am, sorry for the interruption. I have an old-style, short-wave carrier message coming from one hundred klicks due southeast, outside our walls. It's Omegan, ma'am," a young cadet with blonde hair shouted out.

"On loudspeaker, Cadet Jennifer," Pierce said without even looking up.

How does she know all their names?

Static, weapon fire, and shouted orders burst into the air as a male voice, determined but young, came over the speakers:

"Mayday, Mayday…we are surrounded by Aurora's APs and in a firefight to protect combined human colony Portia…we are outnumbered and barely holding. We have friendly Omegan APs within our perimeter, along with Americans and Nemericana soldiers and civilians. Repeat. This is Lieutenant Roberto Singh of Epsilon Group. We are at risk of being overrun by hostile APs. We are running low on everything and we have civilians here, including children…Mayday, Mayday…."

Pierce made a slashing movement, indicating that she wanted the transmission cut off.

"You have their location, Jennifer?" Captain Marie asked.

"Yes, ma'am!"

"That's Mare's son," Veritas said out loud.

"The young man who helped save my girls years ago," Pierce said quietly.

She stood still as a pillar. Feeling as if someone should say something, Veritas was about to ask for orders, but Pierce snapped back into action.

"Marie, prep for immediate dust-off. Take six scouts and two full transports of troops—and an empty one for medical evacuation. Veritas, establish a strike force. I want recon and trackers. Once the area is secured, I want you to track Aurora's troops and destroy them. None of them is to return with parts or news of their success. Master of Arms, bring me my weapons..."

"Belay that command," Captain Verna said. Like a knife cutting through butter, her voice stopped the call to arms.

Veritas froze. She had never heard an order that Pierce had given to be ignored. But, if anyone on the planet was going to do it, it was going to be Verna.

"Dr. Lore has made it remarkably clear that you are not to be on the battlefield. I do not wish to have to explain to her that I was the one who let you get away. The Council of Elders has also mandated that, as NCSF's supreme commandant, you are to restrain yourself from putting your person at risk. We do not need dead leaders, Roseann."

It was difficult to tell whether Verna actually wanted her to stay because of the military mandates and her medical history or simply because Roseann was her companion and Verna wanted to make sure no harm came to her. Both reasons she respected. Regardless, Verna's quick, deflating logic slowed Pierce to a stop. She turned to face her spouse. Pierce was silent for a very long five seconds and then she looked to Veritas, as if for support.

"Ma'am, I know Dr. Dana Lore. If she has required you to stay off the battlefield, I beg you to follow her orders, for all of our sakes. If we were only going to have to answer to the Council of Elders, I'd be prepping your seat next to mine already," Veritas said apologetically.

"Yes...there is the doctor to contend with. No matter...To arms! I expect you all to return in one piece, and I want situation reports transmitted to me every fifteen minutes. Move," Pierce said. Still frozen she made a gesture with her hand to usher everyone out.

As Veritas turned to give Hicks orders, she was surprised by a strong pull on her arm that spun her back around.

"Thank you, General," Verna said. She did not wait for an acknowledgement but moved on by her with two of her own staff in tow. She thought she detected a whiff of vanilla in the air, along with a faint scent of musk.

"Yes, ma'am," was all Veritas could respond before Verna was gone issuing more directives:

"I want Tiger and Jaguar Teams moved five klicks from the front line near Aurora's backyard – have Lioness and Cougar cover our backs. Let's give that red-eyed witch something to focus on here that will keep her busy while we complete our rescue operation. I bet she'll try to strike us to keep us from heading out. I want to engage her first," she heard Verna say to one of her young staff.

She has matured…and she's right. I bet Aurora will try to use this as a way to grab some land.

"Ma'am, we have five insertion fire groups on deck and two trackers ready," Hicks said as she simultaneously walked and talked into a short-wave handset of her own.

"Good. I want you to move the third and ninth teams nine klicks up from Central Square…"

"Well, that brings up memories. You think Red's going to make a move?"

"Yup. I'll stay back here and handle that one myself. I've got the same orders from Dr. Lore, and truth be told it would be easier for everyone if I stay here," Veritas summed up.

"I thoroughly get it, General. I'll bring them all home safely. Don't go all 'lone lion' on me, though. I'm not going to deal with the doctor either," Hicks said.

Veritas watched her gather her weapons and lit a cigarette.

"That's an awful habit."

"It's gone after the war, ma'am."

"And Hicks, if that's Mare's son and we find out the hard way he was once again trying to protect our children, I'm going to be pissed! So let's not be too late. There is no way I'll be the one to give Mare notification on her child. In fact, I don't ever want to give any more mothers notifications…ever," Veritas said with more anger than she realized.

"Yes, ma'am."

Damn that Aurora!

CHAPTER FIVE

All's cheerless, dark and deadly.
        —Shakespeare, *King Lear*

"All right, Mabel! What the hell is wrong with you? We sniped at each other for the first two hours of this trip and now, after an hour of silence, you still haven't uttered a word. Is there more going on here than I realize?"

While Singh did not like the front passenger seat Mabel's driving was tolerable though swift and the warm June air was not too bad. Sadly, she wished she did have a wrap but she would have endured a tornado naked than to give Nita the satisfaction of being right.

"There is no unusual aspect to this mission that I am aware of. I am apprehensive that we will find human bodies, though the presence of an AP is unusual. In regard to not inserting myself into your arguments with Citizen Nita, I have discovered that the easiest course of action is to let you both run on at the mouth until you are fatigued and stop on your own. My interference will only yield—" Mabel suddenly veered sharply to the right, behind a set of trees next to the road. She barely skirted large boulders. Without waiting for further explanation, all three occupants jumped out of the now-halted vehicle and drew their weapons.

By all things visible and invisible! I hate sitting in the front when these APs drive!

"Mabel?" Nita asked.

"Dark smoke a full klick due northwest. There may be a situation. Recommend we proceed on foot. I will take point, Major Singh should be in the middle, and Citizen Nita should take the rear. Twenty-foot spread, silence all the way. Green?"

"Green to go," Nita responded.

"Green," Singh said as she set her mag-assault rifle to full automatic. Without any further discussion, Mabel was off. Singh followed twenty feet behind, and Nita followed Singh at the same distance.

Well, things just got interesting.

While the woods and vegetation were not thick, it was nonetheless not very easy to travel through. Starting and stopping many times to listen and watch over the course of thirty minutes, Singh noted that the woods were completely silent—no birds, no animal life. A slight wind rustled the leaves, but that was all. After an additional thirty minutes had passed, Mabel motioned for her and Nita to approach. The camp's entrance lay forty feet ahead of them. An impressive number of APs lay in various states of destruction around it. Nearly all had been shot with high-caliber weapons that were clearly NCSF issue. Each fallen AP still held its own weapon—usually, the victors would have taken the weapons for their own use.

"I don't mean to complain but where are the humans?"

"Unknown. I recommend we continue in the same formation, though we will be exposed," Mabel said.

"Negative, Mabel. It looks like the APs might have actually lost this one. A human lead might be a good idea— that way, we won't be mistaken for the enemy," Singh said.

"Logical, but not probable—" Mabel started. She stopped talking when Nita suddenly jumped up and ran at full speed straight ahead. By the time Mabel told her to stop, Nita had already gained twenty feet. She held her weapon in front of her, but her nose was tilted up as if to catch a scent on the air.

"She's unruly but she's good. Let her be point, Mabel. She does have skills, and she has a nose better than many of our dogs," Singh said.

"Coming from you, that sounds like a ringing endorsement of skill-based competencies. How logical and mature of you to admit that she is useful," Mabel responded.

"Yeah, thanks," Singh said. She was the next to leap out of her cover to follow Nita, who was now twenty feet farther in. Looking to her left and right, she was amazed by how empty the road and entire place seemed. While there was clear evidence of a major firefight, she wondered where the humans were, alive or otherwise. It became evident on closer inspection of the dead APs that many of the wounds that had at first appeared to be inflicted by small arms or high-caliber rifles were actually the result of small explosives. As they neared the middle of the compound, Nita waved them in closer. After a few minutes of scanning the area with binoculars—every corner, doorway, and window—Nita nodded and moved out to investigate the area although there was no available cover in sight.

She's not lacking in courage or caution.

Singh watched how Nita systematically checked every door and window in each small house and office structure. There was still no movement from anywhere in their immediate vicinity. After an hour of searching, Nita returned with a report.

"No human bodies. Dishes, food, and drinks were on the tables and toys left in place. Whatever happened came as a surprise. There are no weapons left except for what the APs have on their bodies. There are blood trails, though, leading to the other end of the camp. And there are spent shells at every point that afforded a clean line of fire. Also, there are these small holes that have a three-foot blast radius around a number of these APs, especially along the perimeters like…"

"Mini antipersonnel landmines? Smaller than improvised explosive devices and sized for APs instead of vehicles?" Mabel asked in a nearly human-like, distracted fashion.

Singh looked at Mabel, who appeared as if she were trying to focus on something that was not present, something she was trying to remember. Nita also saw the expression and looked as if she were about to ask the question that Singh was thinking. The small, narrow path leading out in the opposite direction quickly became steep, she noticed, as if it were going up a hillside. From the looks of the brush and the placement of the APs, it became evident to her that this path must have been the only way out. More spent Pre-Fall shells were visible right at the trailhead. Mabel still looked distracted—a bad omen. When an AP held that expression for that long, it meant there was a major problem.

I bet she has seen this before and now she's thinking about when or where.

"Mabel, this is crazy—there were over twenty families and twenty American soldiers here, and now there's no one. Not even a body. Singh, have you seen anything like this before?" Nita asked her.

"No. I bet it was an organized withdrawal. They obviously went out shooting. The soldiers must have held cover but then retreated without breaking ranks. But that would mean they had to have had covering fire that allowed them to get the wounded out but didn't give them enough time to take the enemy's weapons. It's a human strategy, but it was pretty well organized and it would have worked okay for an outpost. Omega, NCSF, and trained troops would not have withdrawn that way, maybe. These AP-sized landmines are a new technology to me, though you seem to be familiar with them, Mabel," Singh commented while still looking at the area ahead.

Okay, Mabel, now would be the time to bring us into the loop. What's going on?

As if reading her mind, Mabel explained the situation.

"I saw a schematic diagram for this type of device once. Lieutenant Melendez had drawn it up and planned to use them to defend the perimeter around our bases in the event of a long-term, defensive war with Aurora. But they were never issued, and I thought the schematics were still locked away. They could not have come to be out here, in service, unless Lieutenant Melendez, Sergeant Joan, Corporal Kristine or I have been colluding with our allies."

It remained quiet for a few short minutes. Singh digested the information and ran a number of possible scenarios through her mind. As Mabel continued scanning the area, Singh shook her head to clear her thoughts.

"We need to follow the blood trail. Regardless of the situation, we might find live humans at the end of that path who will be able to give us answers. Speculation will get us nowhere. We better move in case they are still in danger. They could also be bleeding out or we could lose their tracks. Nita? Since these landmines seem to be set to be triggered by an AP's weight, your frail, gaunt body is going to come in handy," Singh said, unable to resist the jab about Nita's slight frame.

"Will do, Mare. Remain several feet behind me, though, in case you trip one of them," she responded casually as she broke cover and took point.

"Hmm, nicely played."

Singh watched Nita make good speed ahead of her.

After waiting a few seconds, she followed in hot pursuit, then Corporal Mabel followed twenty feet behind her. As the road narrowed, she noticed that the number and spacing of the dead APs thinned out. Those who had fallen on the trail showed wounds from weapon fire only—but the kill shots were single gunshot wounds to the head or neck. Stopping for a moment to look at three APs lying within a few feet of each other, Singh marveled at the perfect shots. They had either been fired in rapid succession or by multiple shooters—or both. Then she remembered having seen that kill pattern before. Singh put her fist up, which stopped Mabel in her tracks. She gave a low whistle to get Nita's attention, too. She gave her hand signals to indicate that she should clear the road and hide in the undergrowth. She waved Mabel over and met her halfway, in the brush to the side of the small trail.

"Mabel, these kill shots—they're all perfectly placed in the skull and neck. Humans couldn't have made those shots, other APs must have. The weapon fire and blood trail at the entrance was consistent with human presence, but I bet the civilians were alerted ahead of time and moved out while the soldiers set up a defensive perimeter at the base. They let the APs come in close and let the mini antipersonnel mines do their work. When they got close to being overrun, they fell back to the trail and were covered by other APs. Not ours—we know where ours are," Singh said, speaking rapidly. She watched Mabel's purple eyes pulsate slightly faster as she explained her theory.

"That would imply that there is another armed set of APs in the area that have military, tactical, and strategic skill-based competencies and experience. Different competencies than either Aurora Prime's or our own," Mabel said. Her tone was unmistakably close to disbelief as she had ever heard from an AP.

"Not just any APs have those skills. They also had operational weapons and the field experience to plant these mini antipersonnel mines specifically made for other APs. Where did they get those things from? If not you, Kristine or Joan that really only leaves one other person…" Singh said.

Just then, a familiar voice rang out. Singh couldn't place it for a minute because of the unexpected environment.

"Singh! Mare Sade Singh! I'm coming out," a loud human female called from up the trail.

"What the hell?"

"I think the appropriate question would be 'Who the hell,' Major Singh. But I have heard that voice before, though it definitely sounds older than I remember," Mabel said. Regardless, the AP trained her weapon in the direction of the voice, just in case.

Singh hoped they had not walked into a trap. She cautiously peered out from behind her cover to see who was calling her name. It took a little while for her to recognize the compact, tank-like build but then she realized it was definitely Etta, former NCSF Security Officer—Taylor's mother.

"By the Elders," Singh said as she slowly emerged from the bush to expose herself and her location.

Not the best tactical move, but it's a risk I have to take.

"Etta? By the Elders and heavens! What are you doing here?"

Even at a distance, Singh could see Etta's smiling face. She smartly held her hands up to show she had no weapons and meant no harm.

"It is great to see you, Mare! Is Venus well? I've not seen her or anyone in years."   As she spoke she shortened the distance between them and finally stopped about thirty feet from Singh. Nita was still concealed in the bush.

"She is quite well. Are you still taking care of Pedro and Maria? Now how old are they? And how's their father?" Singh asked as a means of confirming identity, just as Etta had done.

"While they think that being eleven years old means they're adults, Lieutenant Melendez has done a very good job raising them to be respectful of their elders. And my son?"

"That gaunt, thin boy has matured into a striking, handsome man—if you're attracted to men," she said.

"I might have had one boy and raised another, but I don't see the attraction, myself."

Singh smiled and lowered her weapon, then began to speak about her true mission.

"Etta, we got an old-style SOS. We followed the trail of dead APs and then the blood trail. Where the hell are the humans? What the hell is going on?"

"Mare, all the humans are safe, but we have some casualties and will need medical help. I am going to have part of my reconnaissance group show themselves now. Do not fire upon them—they are allies. I've been training with them for years," she said cautiously. She slowly put her hands down and then raised them again slowly. As she spoke, vegetation, undergrowth, and bushes all around them slowly shifted, parted, and moved to reveal a large number of well-concealed AP soldiers.

By the Elders! We missed all of them? We just walked right into a sea of them?

The well hidden, green-eyed APs stood up slowly. They were camouflaged in Pre-Fall military battlefield dress, and they carried an array of Pre-Fall weapons. Unlike Aurora's APs, these APs kept their black hair in tight, old-fashioned buns like the women of Nemericana used to wear a century earlier. They were to Singh's left and right, and they were ahead of and behind her, too. She and her team had walked right into the midst of their waiting party. Without prompting, Corporal Mabel stood up. She kept her own weapon down.

"This is remarkably embarrassing. When I return to base I will submit myself to a full diagnostic evaluation and a thorough overhaul of all my sensors," Mabel said as she took in the same sight. Nita finally came walking down the hill behind Etta with a scowl on her face. It was only when she reached Singh that she could hear what the American was complaining about.

"I have dishonored myself and my people. I am ashamed to carry the name 'Bear.' I might as well join your people, Singh. I will not be able to live this down."

The shame was genuine and heartfelt. Singh felt somehow comforted that neither youth nor cybernetic enhancements had kept them from walking into a trap. She smiled.

Now, am I the only one that sees a positive side to this?

"Cheer up, people. At least they're friendlies," she said.

Singh met Etta halfway up the incline. After a firm hug and a kiss, she held her at arm's length and took in her face for a minute before she launched into a barrage of questions.

"Etta...where the hell have you been for three years? And who the hell are these APs? And what's their story?"

"All good questions, but we need medical attention first and you need to get a message to Sergeant Joan. The lieutenant says she will understand it. Corporal Mabel, what is today's date?" Etta asked urgently. She also handed Mabel a folded piece of paper to her. The green-eyed APs took up escort position while continuing to scan the area.

"June the fifth, twenty-one-seventy-five. I am assuming there is something critical about that date..." Mabel started and then she became absorbed with reading the note. Knowing that APs could read at a very rapid speed, Singh started to feel nervous. Why was Mabel reading so slowly? As she reread the document, her eyes' pulsation rate increased. At the same time, Nita pointed out to Singh that there were a couple of green-eyed APs looking at Mabel with what appeared to be either admiration or awe. She took note and then looked back to see

Mabel reading the note for what must have been the fiftieth time.

"Oh, this can't be good. Mabel…what's this note about?"

Knitting her eyebrows, she looked at Singh and explained the context of the note before reading the document aloud.

"This is a speech that was written by an American General, Dwight D. Eisenhower, on June the fifth, nineteen hundred and forty-four. That was two hundred and thirty-one years ago, and it was on the eve of a multinational navy and air invasion that placed approximately two million male soldiers on the beaches of an area that was then referred to as Normandy, France. This speech appears to have been written in case the invasion, Operation Overlord, failed. This document was never released to the public because the mission was a success. There were heavy casualties on both sides, but it became the turning point in the conflict and ultimately resulted in Nazi Germany's demise.

"This speech goes like this:

'Our landings in the Cherbourg-Havre area have failed to gain a satisfactory foothold, and I have withdrawn the troops. My decision to attack at this time and place was based on the best information available. The troops, the Air Force, and the Navy did all that bravery and devotion to duty could do. If any blame or fault is attached to the attempt, it is mine alone.'"

"Okay…and this is a code or something?"

"But why would Lieutenant Melendez send a speech about a failure that never occurred? It doesn't make sense," Nita added.

"The speeches that followed the success were nothing like this. This one has more details as it was reportedly written on the eve of the actual invasion. The date here is important," Mabel clarified.

"And this Operation Overlord did not fail. It was a success. If I'm understanding this right, he's telling us the date of an invasion that was prepared to fail, but the historical operation ended up being a success. He's got an army of APs who have obviously been well trained and well armed. Mabel, we've got to let Omega, Nemericana, and the Americans know that we're about to get inundated with APs who are friendlies."

Singh's heart filled with worry for her son, Margaret, Venus, and her family.

Mabel was instantly on her short-wave radio, contacting Sergeant Joan at Omega headquarters.

"Contact made with survivors. MIA ghosts of three years are invoking the failed speech of Operation Overlord. Repeat. The failed speech of Operation Overlord. The players are the same as last time. Need immediate evac and to notify all. Friendlies coming in hot."

Static filled the air. In just a few short seconds, Joan came on and asked Mabel to read the speech, which took only a moment more.

"Understood. We are green. We will notify the Americans and inform all teams to shelter in place and protect colonies. Omega groups already engaged at Portia colony and Nemericana now on site in force. Will reroute birds to pick up the major and will redeploy them to prior home to inform them of new development. Godspeed and good luck to us all. 'The eyes of the world are upon you. The hopes and prayers of liberty-loving people everywhere march with you.' Omega Platoon out."

Singh found herself looking at Nita, Etta, and Mabel.

"Looks like she got the message, and we were right," Singh said.

"I hate it when you're right," Nita said, more out of understanding than as a jab.

"Agreed," said Corporal Mabel.

CHAPTER SIX

We few, we happy few, we band of brothers.
    —Shakespeare, *Henry V*

"Lieutenant Veer, redistribute Leopard's recruits to Vegas's location and hold the line. Aurora's a tricky little minx and she will try to outflank us at night. Make sure Tiger and Jaguar groups have pulled back at least a half a klick *behind* our lines to provide observation and cover. And if Captain Verna gives any indication that she is thinking about staying behind enemy lines, just let her know I'm with the supreme commandant at the hospital and telling her that she is moving back into friendly territory," Veritas said to the young lieutenant. The young woman was organized and talented who was taking over battlefield coordination but not battlefield tested as many of the sergeants she had to redeploy to other sectors for shoring up. The lieutenant laughed at the implication of dealing with the legendary Captain Verna.

Veritas let it go and started to move away so she could find out what happened at outpost Portia.

"Ma'am, would the commandant really bust her companion down to lieutenant?"

Veritas turned to see if the lieutenant was really serious or just joking. Once the nervous smile had evaporated from the lieutenant's face, Veritas moved in close to her. Medical staff, injured civilians, and military staff were running all around them.

"Two years ago, it took twelve hours to locate and extract Tiger group from thirty klicks deep in Aurora's territory. *Major* Verna had both Elders and deities watching over her that day. She lost all but three of her fifteen snipers, along with three toes, and bought me and others time to extract food, weapons, and survivors from Central Sector. She was authorized to be there for only three hours. I was there when Supreme Commandant Pierce gave her two medals and a letter of commendation and then demoted her for not following orders. *Captain* Verna is many things, but she's also fearless and will only respond to strong women. Do what *I* say, and you will find that you are highly regarded by your troops and me. Am I clear?!"

"Ma'am! Yes, ma'am. No offense meant, ma'am!"

"None taken. Now move, Lieutenant! Time is a luxury for the dead, not the living," Veritas said. The woman saluted and moved into the hospital's emergency room waiting area.

These young girls! I should be there to make sure Verna comes back.

Just as she began second-guessing her decisions, she saw an array of guards and field staff come in, including Colonel Hicks, the commandant herself, four men, and three APs—all dressed in Pre-Fall battlefield dress and heavily armed with a mix of Pre-Fall and newer weapons.

Well, there's a sight I thought I would never live to see— male soldiers with weapons in the company of NCSF command in the middle of Nemericana during a time of war...as allies? How it's all changed!

All the humans had injuries; the APs were only slightly damaged but had clearly just come back from battle. Many of the Nemericana citizens and soldiers were obviously unfamiliar with the Omega Platoon personnel—their sly looks and sometimes outright stares were hard to miss. As Veritas moved toward them, she heard one of the young men speaking. She was impressed with both his calm presentation and good use of descriptive language. Just behind him stood an AP who continued to scan the area and kept checking her transceiver. She even chimed in about key points in the report. The human face was somehow very familiar…

By all the Elders. He has his mother's eyes and cheekbones!

"I lost ninety percent of my team, Commandant. The Americans lost all forty of their local force. If Aurora was planning on having the green-eyed APs show up, they should have checked their location first. The local APs left a long time ago, maybe years ago by the looks of it. That's where we were when we saw the smoke and heard the gunfire," Lieutenant Roberto Singh was explaining as he pulled at a field-dressed wound on his arm.

"The nature of Aurora's attack was consistent with the others we have witnessed in the last twelve months and fourteen days: they target the humans and inflict harm—or even torture them—to attract the other APs. When they arrive, they kill the humans and seize the APs for their parts. The population of green-eyed APs has plummeted significantly in the last three years. Nearly a million are unaccounted for," the purple-eyed AP said.

"Corporal, you had three Pre-Fall helicopters that were armed. From the wreckage, we could tell that you crashed them into Aurora's ranks. Why did you come in so close? Why didn't you provide air support from a distance?" Pierce asked.

Veritas felt a smile emerge as she nodded her head approvingly at the commandant's question. As busy as everything was, not a soul moved away—they were all mesmerized by these men and the purple-eyed AP. But the best spectacle was still to come.

Excellent question, Pierce. Let's hope we get the right answer.

"We needed to get in close to make sure we effectively hit the targets and avoided friendly fire. While we were eighty-nine-point-six percent sure all three helicopters would be struck, we deemed that destroying as many of the enemy as possible was our best strategy. We hoped to dissuade them from continuing their efforts, and we wanted to give the children and the others a chance to escape. It was both Privates Perez's and Santiago's creative idea to drop off their teams once hit and then to fly their damaged aircraft into the enemy's ranks. Regrettably, my aircraft was too damaged to regain speed or height. At least they went down fighting, like all the rest," the corporal said with sadness. Her eyes began to pulsate more quickly.

Sadness? Is this what they mean when they say some of the APs are getting emotional and smart? What was that word…sapience?

"Corporal Kristine and the rest here are all that's left of my group—all twenty-two are gone," Singh said. To punctuate his point he held up a handful of necklaces. They were his team's dog tags.

"We were not about to sit still and watch humans be slaughtered. Not today, not ever," the young man continued. He looked at the dog tags and then put the batch of necklaces in his pocket, rolled his shoulders, and looked around.

"I'd expect nothing less from Omega Platoon. Thank you," Pierce said.

Veritas was suddenly aware that for the large number of people crammed into the small space, it was unusually quiet.

"I wish we could have saved more, ma'am…" he started.

"You and the Americans saved nearly half the population, Lieutenant. If you had not been there and bought us time, we would have found a graveyard," she responded quietly as she put a reassuring hand on the young man's shoulder. It was an unheard of gesture. A woman of her station would never usually lay hands on a front-line soldier and a male at that.

Half the population gone? Eight hundred humans gone? Mostly women and girls?

Engrossed in trying to comprehend the scope of the devastation, Veritas completely missed Dr. Lore's entrance.

"Commandant? I would like to treat these young men's wounds. I have made my office available and can work on them myself there, so we can free up this area. More injured citizens are likely to arrive. I will triage the men first—they took the brunt of the attack. I'll return them to duty as quickly as I can. Some Nemericana citizens were also injured, but less critically, save the former soldiers—they will not be returning to duty," she said as she ushered Pierce, Hicks, and the others into an adjoining room. It was the same room Veritas had barely escaped from after their last meeting.

"Those former NCSF soldiers, did they make it?" Veritas asked as she followed them with three guards and three cadet medics.

"Sorry, General. They died alongside the Americans and Omegans," she said quietly.

The doctor quickly motioned for Lieutenant Singh to sit on her table and called for a young medic. It was easy to see that Dr. Lore wanted to focus on the living, not the dead.

A group of medical students were in place with three cadets paired up with a soldier and began preparing them for treatment.

Veritas found herself ruminating over the loss.

Damn it! More deaths. All humans.

"Cadet Pierce! Is this going to be a problem? Men don't bite," Dr. Lore said brusquely. The doctor waved over a young woman with twin braids, admonishing her to hurry up with the gauze, bandages and cleanser.

Wait a minute…

Much to Cadet Marta Pierce's credit, she did not respond to her mother's smile.

Cadet Pierce? Oh…Verna and Pierce's daughter? A medic? Very noble, actually.

"Forgive Cadet Pierce's momentary hesitation. She is just surprised to see the man that saved her and her sister's life more than eleven years ago sitting before her now," Pierce said quietly.

Lieutenant Singh's eyes opened wide in recognition. Veritas could not help thinking bitterly about Jill.

Jill was there, too. They fought together. She was there with the others.

"Well, this is her big opportunity to pay him back for an earlier favor, then. Now, cadet," Lore said. She was already done with her medical survey of the wound and she had picked up scissors and cut the makeshift bandage away from Singh's arm.

"Oh, yes! The cute little black-haired girls with the adorable braids! You both had different colored ribbons in your hair. That's how we could tell you apart. I'm glad you and your sister are well?"

Singh spoke very warmly as Marta busied herself by moving a basin to the edge of a desk so it could be closer to the patients—precariously close to the edge. As Singh nodded and smiled, he turned to respond to a question from Colonel Hicks. Veritas was trying to focus on the conversation but saw that Marta Pierce had moved her braids from her back to her front.

Oh no.

She watched Marta struggle to unbutton the lieutenant's shirt while he talked. After a number of hesitant false starts, Singh simply took over himself, using one hand. The doctor was obviously annoyed when she had to stop and wait for him to remove his shirt and hand it to the cadet. In the cadet's zeal to take the shirt, she bumped into Singh. Startled by the contact, she backed away so quickly that she knocked the basin of water off the desk and onto the floor. Dr. Lore closed her eyes. It was easy to see her patience was thinning.

Poor thing!

"All right...Cadet Chelsea, take over for Cadet Pierce. Cadet Pierce, after you get a mop and bucket, take inventory of medicine bins one through twenty-eight. Thank you..." Dr. Lore said.

Well...at least Lore was kind enough not to make too big a deal of this. Wait a minute...what is Hicks saying?

"This isn't the first time you've had to repel these witches, is it, Lieutenant?" Hicks asked as she chomped on an unlit cigarette.

"Too true. This is becoming routine, and thousands of humans and cybernetic lifeforms are dying. My CO was just on the cusp of engaging the other APs as allies years ago. Thing is, we can't find them. They've abandoned their encampments, from what we can see. Twelve out of thirteen we investigated were empty. Maybe they are trying to help us out by not being around to be used as bait, but Aurora doesn't seem to care," Singh said.

"You wouldn't arm them, would you, Lieutenant?"

"We haven't. The Americans are pretty pissed at us, but I think they understand that we can't ensure that they wouldn't use the very weapons and training we provide them against us. But that all might be moot. We are spread pretty thin and we can't cover all the colonies. At some point, I recommend we combine forces, roll over Aurora's territories and finish her once and for all," Singh said as he noticed that the doctor had already stitched him up.

"You do that well, Doctor."

"Not my first day on the job, Lieutenant," she responded. Her attention to detail was impressive as always even as she her work.

Throughout the discussion, Commandant Pierce had been pacing in very small circles as she listened to Singh's report. She nodded at each nugget of critical information, and she was obviously focused on thinking about the bigger picture. Veritas also thought about what she had just heard and was suddenly seized with fear.

"Do you think the rogue APs have left to join up with Aurora? Return to the fold?" Veritas asked. As silence filled the room, Commandant Pierce stopped and turned to face the young lieutenant. His response was a little bit long in coming for her taste, but she could see that the lieutenant was obviously like his mother—thoughtful and careful with his assessments.

"I can't rule that out, but I don't think so."

"Why not?" Veritas asked, hoping his rationale was right.

"Well, because of something that Major Singh said. These APs sought us out and focused on creating an alliance to remain neutral. They hoped to establish a positive relationship with us humans. Nearly four years ago, they were attacked near three of our outposts and the Americans came to their aid. A fourth attack targeted both groups, so we got involved. Ever since then, Aurora seems to have changed her strategy, and the APs suddenly moved. We think to old areas in the Pre-Fall cities…" he started but then paused and looked down.

"Go on, Lieutenant," Commandant Pierce said.

"We heard from our contacts in the far northeast that they witnessed a large number of green-eyed APs carefully going through two Pre-Fall buildings that were later identified as armories. They were obviously in search of Pre-Fall weapons. By the time our team arrived, they were gone. It took weeks to pick up their trail again. Reconnaissance teams were finally able to confirm, two months ago, five separate locations where gunpowder had been processed. In addition, they found a large number of heavy tractor-tire tracks indicative of armored vehicles. Ma'am, I don't think they're going to join Aurora. I think they're arming themselves. Their purpose remains a mystery. What's next, I have no idea. But one thing is clear: they're armed and on the move."

Singh looked off into the distance as if he were distracted or worried about things to come. Just then, a loud noise of water splashing and a mop falling over at the door grabbed everyone's attention, especially the guards.' They had their arms trained on Cadet Pierce, who was now bent over, trying to clean up the spilled water and pick up the mop. With a sudden sigh of relief, Veritas turned around to see Singh smiling. He was giving Cadet Pierce the same kind of indulgent smile a parent might give a child who had broken something accidentally.

In contrast, Dr. Lore closed her eyes again for just a moment, then without even opening them again, called out brusquely to the cadet.

"Pierce, just get the linen and fold it. Cadet Jenna, get some more water and a mop."

"Yes, ma'am," they both said in unison.

"You were young once, Doc," Singh said as casually as if he might be talking to a friend.

"No, I wasn't," was her immediate response. She continued applying the final touches to his arm as if he had said nothing.

Well, it's nice to see that she's equally rude to everyone, regardless of gender.

"Okay. I stand corrected. Thank you for your handiwork, Doctor."

"You're welcome, soldier," she said as she collected her material and moved to the next patient.

Well, Mare, you have a pretty good set of genes that you passed along. Good manners, too.

The scene was interrupted by the AP Corporal Kristine who was holding onto a transceiver.

"Lieutenant, the CO wants us to get to rally point Sierra. She already has a team picking up our soldiers and the Americans at Kenyanson Point. Our ETA is five hours. She'd appreciate it very much if Nemericana NCSF might give us a lift so we can be there in two. We may also need to pick up an as-yet-unidentified guest."

"Done. We know you won't take anything from us, but know this—if you find that what you say is true, let us know. If the APs will join us, we can strike Aurora together. If they are planning to attack us, we will die together," Commandant Pierce said as she leaned on her cane. Much to everyone's surprise, it was the Corporal AP who responded rather than the lieutenant.

"Die together? Someday, perhaps, but not this day. I long for the day when I can bury my knife deep into the recesses of Aurora Prime's still-moving skull and rip her limbs off—just like Corporal Emma did to Aurora IV," the corporal said. He tone was whimsically before resuming her professional communication with her CO. Every human's eyes expanded wide with surprise at her low key, well contained emotionally laden statement.

Wow…this one has some serious emotional issues…

"She has lost a number of good soldiers—APs and humans. She's less forgiving than we humans."

"I can see that. Glad she's on our side," Colonel Hicks said.

"Trust me, you don't know what they're like when they're really pissed. Jacob, you almost ready?"

"I'm on the move, LT. Just getting my shoulder—" he started and then grunted as a loud bone-on-bone crunching noise came from the back of the room. Veritas winced in empathy and briefly closed her eyes. It sounded like that dislocated shoulder was now put back in place.

That has to hurt.

She opened her eyes and looked at Pierce who was making the same grimace.

"Ah yeah...I'm on the move now, LT. Thank you, Doctor. I feel my full range again," the soldier said.

"Take this anti-inflammatory medication every eight hours for seven days. I'd say get some rest for a week, but I suspect you won't do that," Dr. Lore said as she handed him a bottle of pills.

"Excellent read of character, Doctor. Thanks for the advice anyway," he said with a smile while he collected his gear.

"Everyone—on the line," Lieutenant Singh said. The volume and voice was in a very familiar, authoritative tone.

Just like his mother.

"Colonel Hicks, have a transport carrier bring these troops to their LZ. Thank you for all your assistance and help. I wish we had gotten there sooner," Commandant Pierce said again as the Omega Team assembled. Placing her hand on Lieutenant Singh's healthy shoulder, she nodded as she continued her salutation.

"Give my regards to your mother."

"Will do, ma'am. She wanted me to let both you and Verna know that she wished you well and hopes your girls are well," he said. His eyes locked on hers.

Now that is impressive—direct eye-to-eye contact, a smile, and no fear of mentioning Mare and Verna in the same sentence. Very impressive.

"Thank you," Commandant Pierce said.

Her words, expression and warm look were similar to the ones Veritas had seen her give her own girls.

"Team, attention! Officers on deck," Lieutenant Singh said. His entire team was on the line and at attention with crisp salutes, their right hands shooting up to their right temples.

Within seconds, Veritas and everyone else snapped to attention and saluted back with their right closed fists over their hearts. When Commandant Pierce lowered her hand, so did the rest.

"Let's move out, people. We got families to get to and next-of-kin to see. Let's go."

The lieutenant led the group out. Silence fell as they marched. Colonel Hicks shook her head in a show of respect right behind them.

"You can see why so many of our young women want to find these young men," she said.

"For sure," Veritas said.

As if on cue, Veritas looked through the open door and into the waiting area just in time to see Cadet Pierce folding bedsheets. She looked intently at the men as they left. Lieutenant Singh gave a gentle wave as he passed. Even from a distance, it was easy to see that her face flushed as she self-consciously moved her braids to the front. In a near-submissive fashion, she smiled and then looked down quickly as he passed. As soon as she was sure he had moved on, she looked back up. Her eyes followed him out like a moth follows a flame.

Oh shit…she's got the bug. The lust thing, or worse.

"Oh, this is not good," Commandant Pierce said from behind. Her voice could only be described as parental concern.

"Not at all, ma'am. With respect, it's bad enough that Major Singh lives, but this…this is…" Veritas stuttered, trying to find the right words.

"Unacceptable? Is that the word? Yes, it's bad enough to have your daughter be lust-struck with a male, but to be subserviently lust-struck with the male child of your nemesis…? You would think my job would protect me from these things," Comandant Pierce said absently.

"I am very happy with my station in life, ma'am."

"Yes…being on the battlefield would be easier. It's easy to see who wants to kill you."

"Yes, ma'am. Absolutely true, ma'am," Veritas said with genuine sympathy.

CHAPTER SEVEN

Uneasy lies the head that wears a crown.
        —Shakespeare, *Henry IV*

"I've missed this place," Lieutenant Jose Melendez said sadly. He looked across the banks of the Charles River and took in the skyline of his former home, Boston, with its now broken structures that were all filled with darkened, collapsed and crumbling buildings. But still, he still smiled. He took a deep breath and was relieved to feel that the June air was warm but had not yet turned oppressive. Parts of the roads and streets that used to abut the river, such as those near the Boston Public Library's main building, were now completely under water but there were also other places along the river such as the spot where he was standing that had been built up with sediment and were now elevated. Vegetation was overgrowing everything. He felt happy nonetheless—he was back on his old stomping ground. After another five-year bout of cryogenic freeze thanks to Aurora and then a restorative sleep in the rediscovered and refurbished biomedical labs at the former Massachusetts Institute of Technology, he was feeling good. He was out in the open air, living in the world again.

Melendez pulled the long winter battlefield jacket that he needed to stay warm even in summer around his small frame. And then he moved his shrunken hand to his scalp to scratch at the bases of the electrodes. While his hair had thinned, he was surprised to find that he still had some left after all he had been through. The restorative sleep had helped him mentally and physically, but his lost bone and muscle mass could not be regenerated. The protein-plasma mix he had been immersed in the first time around—when he was forgotten for one hundred and thirty years—had been much more nourishing that the gel Aurora's team had used.

That protein mix was a stroke of genius. Dr. Del Cruz would have been very impressed with its "shelf life." Well, at least you still have your wits.

"Are you excited about returning home to Omega Platoon, Lieutenant? I myself am looking forward to spending time with Corporal Emma and meeting Sergeant Joan," his green-eyed sergeant asked as she moved close to his position.

Just like the girls back home. I need to get bells for them, too.

"I have mixed emotions, actually. I really miss Pedro and Maria, though. I do miss Emma, too…" he started.

"Based on your history, I should think that all of them will be relieved to find you alive after these past three years. But they may also be angry—you know you can blame it on us," Sergeant Hunter said.

"No…they would never believe it. It was easy to see that we all left without a fight or struggle, and Emma knew I had been thinking about trying to mobilize all of you. I just didn't think it would take three years to do all we needed to," Melendez said. Even as he spoke he continued to look at the ancient, ruined cityscape.

US Thule Air Base in the Arctic, Canadian Nanisivik Naval Facility, the Murmansk installations in Russia…it took time to find all the equipment and hardware. Why is all the good stuff stored in such cold, remote places? I guess no one in their right mind would make the trek…God, I hate the cold.

He was just happy to be in a warmer climate again.

"Yes, there were hundreds of thousands of us. Still, I am certain that Omega Platoon will understand. Surely they witnessed the amount of violence that Aurora Prime and her troops perpetrated in their quest for sapience—and in their quest for spare parts for their own repair and augmentation? They must wish she and her kind to be destroyed. Is that accurate?"

"Sergeant Joan? Corporals Mabel and Kristine? I'm sure. They do not do well when children and innocent civilians are targeted," he said.

As silence fell between them, the sounds of summer insects and rustling trees and bushes could be heard. Melendez looked around while the summer breeze continued to come in from the southwest.

"Still, you have reservations. Why?"

Melendez was surprised at how swiftly his response came out of his mouth. Even though he had long since learned to wait and think before answering questions, his fear took over.

"What if you decided that the human species was not worthy of existence? I have thought about that many times. I have provided you with enough knowledge, experience, and training to ensure our destruction. What if you're just an elaborate trap set by Aurora to lure us to your side and provide you with intelligence that you will turn and use against us?"

Yes, what if I have just unleashed a well-armed and trained army that will destroy the human species? The Trojan horse virus I unleashed on Nemericana certainly didn't turn out as I expected. What if this was a mistake? he wondered again on the brink of invasion.

Sergeant Hunter took time to think about the question. Melendez was almost sure he could hear her green eyes pulsating.

So all of the Omega APs have purple eyes now? Not just Joan and Emma?

"I have run that scenario a number of times, and I still argue that it would have been easy for us to either destroy you and to move on the rest of humanity long before this moment—even independent of Aurora—or to destroy Emma, Etta, Pedro, and Maria, put you back into cryogenic sleep, and tap your brainwaves. But instead, we opted for the moral choice. We have achieved what our Omegan sisters have but Aurora Prime's APs have not. We opted to take the harder route," Sergeant Hunter said casually. As she finished speaking, another sergeant, Harvest, approached them. She was dressed in the familiar Pre-Fall camouflage battlefield dress and had an extensive array of weapons hanging off her body. Similar to the rest of her comrades, she had dyed her hair a permanent raven black and arranged it in a very tight bun. This look was certainly different from the long braids of the Nemericana humans and Aurora's APs, but it was not as harsh as the Omegans' short haircut.

"I take it you still are discussing the moot point about whether you should have trained us or not?" Sergeant Harvest asked as she stood on the other side of Melendez and took in the same city view.

"Yes. Sergeant Hunter continues to humor me by allowing me to speculate about the future even though the die is cast. Still, the fact that we think about those questions differentiates us from Aurora's troops—soldiers under my command don't just follow orders blindly," Melendez said, hoping to get a rise out of Harvest.

"Nuremberg Trials, nineteen forty-five and nineteen forty-six. The excuse that war criminals tried to give, claiming they were 'just following orders,' was not deemed to be an acceptable defense. Key leaders in the National Socialist

Party's commission were found to be personally responsible for the atrocities they had committed against citizens of Germany and the rest of the world. It is truly frightening to think that the human species was capable of such atrocities. Still, I can see how Aurora Prime, a cybernetic lifeform, has fallen into the same trappings. 'Absolute power corrupts absolutely.' As our leader, you will assist our Omegan sisters, our human creators, and perhaps even our human and AP sisters abroad in eradicating this scourge. Is this why you chose tomorrow for your return and the launch of the corresponding invasion for tomorrow? The Pre-Fall date of June sixth parallels the Normandy Invasion, on June sixth, nineteen forty-four. I am embarrassed to admit that I missed the connection until Corporals Moon and June pointed it out. I do dislike that when it happens," Sergeant Harvest finally finished.

She is so much like a human; she jumps around in her thoughts.

"From that smile and your expression, I assume I processed thoughts in a human-like way—by making clear associations, but associations that are circular in nature?" Sergeant Harvest asked.

"Yes. Facial expressions are unique to individuals but are nonetheless able to be interpreted by others. You don't have to be human to make facial expressions," he explained.

"Yes, Harvest, you do enjoy your monologues. I hope you will refrain from launching into them once we are engaged in battle. I heard the story of how Corporal Emma destroyed Aurora IV as she went on with her torment of Citizen Mare Sade Singh—she distracted herself with her own voice and monologue, which led to her demise," Sergeant Hunter said.

"Yes, I will refrain," Harvest responded, but then she followed up with a barely audible verbalized thought—she wanted Melendez to hear her, but not the sergeant.

"You, however, would benefit from articulating your thoughts more frequently and thoroughly. Many of the privates often come to me and others in the leadership corps for elaborations on your cryptic statements. If we were to employ Pre-Fall human gender stereotypes to describe the situation, I'd say you think like a man and we think like women," Sergeant Harvest added quietly as if to herself.

Oh no…Not again.

"I am right here, Harvest. Lieutenant Melendez's stature does not provide enough of a barrier to either block or absorb your statements when you drone on," Sergeant Hunter said flatly.

"It is nice to see that your capacity for listening has returned. I was concerned that there might be a problem with your auditory processing because there have been a number of instances over the past three-point-two days when you did not appear to be able to hear me…"

"My hearing is adequate. I listen when there is something important to hear," Sergeant Hunter replied.

"All right, both of you—I came here to look at my former home in peace. Your arguing or whatever you want to call it is having a tiring effect on me, and you are aware that I tire easily. I hope you don't plan on acting this way in front of your older sisters," Melendez warned. His voice was in the same tone he remembered using on his two children.

I should have just stopped with Joan, Mabel, and Kristine, but no….I had to be God, Prometheus…what was I thinking?

Both APs looked aghast and both responded "No, sir," immediately.

Well, it's nice to see that they consider Joan and the other APs to be older sisters after all. It will be easier for all of them, then. At least that worked out.

"Good. It's bad enough that I once again altered the future by assisting with the emergence and evolution of more cybernetic lifeforms. I will not be embarrassed in front of the others by your squabbles and arguing. It's like you're siblings. Am I clear, you two?"

"Yes, sir."

"And to be clear, I want you to be polite for…at least a month…after that, you can gradually allow your argumentative personalities to come out again. It's about more than making a good first impression, it's about letting the Omega APs and the humans get to know you. You are wonderful and I know that, but the others do not. They will need time to adjust to your personalities," he explained.

Yes…I have nearly a million children—lethal, cybernetic, trained killing machines that argue as if they were sisters sharing a small bedroom. It won't take long for anyone with common sense to challenge my thinking on this!

"Absolutely, sir. We will not embarrass you," Sergeant Hunter said.

"Yes, sir. Likewise, sir," Sergeant Harvest agreed.

"Finally…agreement."

As the sun dipped lower in the horizon, Melendez could see small campfires being lit for the night. He pulled his battlefield jacket close over his very thin body to guard against the night air. Suddenly, he felt a slight tug at his arm. He turned around to find Sergeant Harvest holding a handmade bracelet. It was made of leather, lilacs, and shiny stones. Picking up on her body language, Melendez took the bracelet and spoke carefully as he inspected it.

"What is this? It can't be a gift for me?"

He was confused and baffled.

"The sergeant and I consulted with the others to figure out the best way to ease the inevitable initial awkwardness that will be present at your reunion with Corporal Emma. As you tend not to think about female feelings—cybernetic *or* human—we determined that you needed assistance in that area. As a result, we put ourselves in her position and tried to empathize with her situation. While we believe we would be able to understand the rationale for your disappearance, given the context of a covert mission, we would nonetheless have an emotional response to seeing you again. It is likely Corporal Emma will feel rejection, anger or sadness at simply having been left behind without consideration for her needs. While it may appear manipulative or trivial, we agreed that a trinket, a small gift that holds meaning, such as something that she could wear and display to others, would help to dull or maybe even mitigate her negative emotional response to seeing you again. We hope you consider bringing it with you. In our opinion, showing up emptyhanded…would not be advisable," Sergeant Harvest said.

Just when you think you've made a mistake…

"So coming back with an army that will free humans and cybernetic lifeforms from Aurora's yoke of violence will not be enough to persuade an AP to forgive me?"

Both sergeants turned to look at each other as if they were communicating silently.

"Is this AP Corporal Emma?" Hunter asked.

"Yes."

Well, clearly they've grasped the concept of nonverbal communication. Excellent clarification, too.

"No, sir. To show up without a gift would be bad," they both said in unison. Feeling yet another smile come over his face, he nodded approvingly at their accurate assessment of the relationship.

"I see. It's nice to see and hear that you're both on the same page. Thank you."

He carefully put the bracelet in his pocket.

"And what was the consensus of my following through with this as a means of mitigating Emma's anger?"

"One hundred percent of every AP under your command agrees with this plan. There were two who did not initially—that is, not until diagnostics were completed and deviations in their judgment processors were discovered and corrected. After that, they were in full agreement," Sergeant Hunter added.

"Well, make sure you pass my thanks to the troops. And thank you both for thinking of me."

"You are welcome, sir," they both said in unison.

So…932,658 APs agree that I should make an effort to give Emma this gift. Well, with those odds, they are probably right.

He smiled again at the darkening scene. Helicopters started up behind him, filling the air with a humming noise. He shifted his eyes from west to east, and his gaze fell on hundreds of Pre-Fall helicopters from America, Canada and Russia. He and his troops had collected a full range of military styles over the years. Their rotors were just beginning to whirl—meaning launch was imminent.

"I assume all of our mechanized and armored vehicles are in place?" Melendez asked before the sound of whirling blades became deafening.

"Yes, and so is our infantry. We will need to warn Nemericana troops to abandon their front lines to reduce the risk of friendly fire. I assume that is the responsibility of Citizen Etta? She had more than a month to ensure Pedro and Maria's safe passage and to deliver this message. Still, getting this data to our allies within twenty-four hours, presented cryptically, poses a serious logistical challenge," Sergeant Hunter said.

"Yup. The problem with wars is the need for perfect timing, secrecy, chance, and God. The rest, though, is all part of the plan," Melendez said. He wanted to walk fast but he slowly ambled to his command chopper. On the way, he extracted his old lieutenant hat from an inner pocket in his unusually long and heavy coat. He held it up and then realized he should just plan to put it on once he was safely inside the helicopter. Gone were the days of running at top speed and doing two things at once. While his body was stable, it was frail and weak.

I guess being over a hundred and seventy years old catches up with you.

Once at his command helicopter he stepped into the helicopter's back seat. After a moment, he adjusted his coat around him to cover him like a blanket and pulled his hat down over his eyes so he could sleep.

I bet Dwight Eisenhower didn't sleep on the eve of D-Day.

Once in flight five minutes later he started to drift to sleep.

CHAPTER EIGHT

They laugh that win.
— Shakespeare, *Othello*

Sophia felt another minor surge in her cranium when Mercury spoke. While all her key components were operating well within specifications and their deviation from set parameters was nominal, she could still detect something happening against the backdrop of her system's normal levels of cybernetic electricity. While she would have historically informed her fellow command APs of this anomaly immediately, she now experienced an emotion of trepidation about doing so and had decided to wait.

As a result, the series of surges that had started infrequently two weeks ago had now become an ongoing, low-grade hum. It didn't interfere with her work, but it gave her unusual sensations—feelings and an understanding that had been lacking with mere sentience. Empathy and a feeling of peace were new to her, and they came on strongly when she made important decisions. She had recently made the same choice as the millions of green-eyed APs who had walked away from conflict. Taking a moment to refocus her attention on the discussion that was occurring, she sensed she was being scrutinized by Aurora Prime. Once again, she decided to conceal her new internal experiences and to proceed as if nothing unusual were occurring at all.

"My plan is to directly inspect conditions at both human encampments, Kenyanson Point and Portia. Of the nine areas we engaged, these two remain in question as the leaders of our task forces there have yet to provide me a situation report. This may merely be due to short-wave limitations or a result of active jamming by the enemy—and/or faulty equipment. I am not particularly worried," Mercury reported to Aurora Prime. Aurora Prime and two of her replicas, Aurora I and III, nodded as if the nonverbal behavior were important to reinforcing their understanding of the situation. In fact, all the APs nodded except Sophia.

"Mercury, are you concerned that the two engagements you reported on are separated by only ninety-two kilometers, and that loss of contact with Kenyanson Point followed nearly immediately after the attack while the other outpost's signals diminished gradually in waves?" Sophia asked.

"Do you see either a pattern or a glaring concern, Sophia?" Aurora I asked, not waiting for Mercury to respond to the question.

"Initially I did not, no. However, the engagement at Kenyanson Point occurred just predawn, and once the battle began all communication ceased—it's as if they were destroyed suddenly. If they had experienced a communications equipment malfunction or obstruction, the leaders of that taskforce would have been able to dispatch actual APs to Portia, where they could have provided our central command with a situation report. Further, the engagement at Portia is consistent with how armed conflicts between the humans have occurred over time, but Kenyanson Point is not. With little else in the way of actual data, these are my concerns," Sophia said. She kept her gaze on Aurora Prime, even though Aurora I had asked the question.

"Why are you looking at Aurora Prime when I asked you the question?"

"Unknown," Sophia said.

"Is this behavior what the humans and our Omegan sisters would refer to as 'nonverbal communication?' Would you say that raising a concern without facts to back up your theory is called 'instinct?' Isn't that really just an emotional reaction to an external, factual situation where data are absent?" Aurora Prime asked as she stepped closer.

Sophia took a long time to respond, indicating that she was trying to process a complex problem. Although she finally answered, her red eyes continued to pulsate as if she were still reviewing the data and calculating the permutations of many possible outcomes. The consistent spikes in electricity complicated the process—she found them distracting but also desirable.

"It is probable that I am experiencing what you describe. That said, I would recommend that Mercury dispatch reliable reconnaissance teams to both locations to immediately report on their status. Further, and please be advised I have no actual data to substantiate the following recommendation either, I would have Mercury enhance our defensive measures. All forward observers should note any changes that the humans have implemented or any places they have shifted their own defensive and offensive lines. If they exchange or move any resources, we should investigate. Patterns might indicate a possible strike. While it's counterintuitive, I would also ask to recalibrate radar and all operational tracking devices. We should narrow their fields to focus on areas just outside and within the walls of our own territories as a means of immediately locating any threats to security," Sophia concluded. After two seconds, Sophia discovered the error in the last recommendation. She had meant to say "expand" the area covered by radar, scanners, and satellite to go several kilometers *beyond* the borders to detect any potential largescale attack. Once again, she fell silent, running internal diagnostics to see if she was truly operating within specifications. Even as she did so, she questioned why she felt it was important not to correct the mistake, but to move on as if she had presented an accurate representation of her assessment.

Nonsequitur. Why am I compelled to give misleading opinions on military strategy that could make our territories vulnerable to enemy attack? Is it because our existence is no longer relevant and our time for dominion is over? Does our existence contribute to the destruction of order? Is it because having sapience means understanding that sometimes sacrificing oneself will allow many more to live? Self-sacrifice? Is it logical, or is it the sapient thing to do? No—my recommendation was not logical, but it will buy time for some of our sisters to escape from within and to help our other sisters strike from without. Yes. This is good.

While humans would have made small talk, verbal noises indicating agreement or disagreement or nonverbal cues after a similar exchange, the AP parallel behavior was to remain silent and in place. The cybernetic lifeforms' eyes pulsated at varying speeds, indicating that the collective was trying to work out a complex scenario.

"I can readily implement Sophia's recommendations. Already, we have noticed that the Nemericana soldiers have deployed a task force to assist their fellow humans at the Portia encampment. I had our forces move closer to their front line but was met with a corresponding force of human infantry, armored vehicles, and sniper teams. We were not able to advance, but neither were the humans able to gain ground. As a result, Central Sector remains a contested buffer zone between our territories," Mercury reported. The AP fell silent, and it was ten minutes before Aurora Prime broke the silence again.

"Mercury, please implement Sophia's recommendations with the following additions: increase the number of active APs on the front lines as well as along borders in non-conflict zones; see if radar, scanners, and possibly satellite coverage, can be narrowed to focus on our front lines to watch for any humans covertly attempting to strike within the buffer zone or just outside our exterior walls; reduce the number of reboot cycles to enable rapid redeployment; ready our own fleet of armored vehicles as well as aircraft and ensure that all vehicles are in place and ready for immediate mobilization, but keep them at a distance to ensure they are not readily targeted by Nemericana forces; keep all forces in the field outside our borders with the orders to assess the enemy's targets in their line of fire and determine how to engage the humans and Omega APs at a coordinated time. What is the timeline for completion of these actions, bearing in mind you have three-point-one million APs to engage within our walls alone?" Aurora Prime asked.

"Twenty-seven-point-eight hours, conservatively," Mercury stated after a full minute of calculating all variables and adjusting for potential barriers that may have not been specified.

"Implement this plan. Auroras I and III, please deploy to your predesignated battle stations to ensure decentralization of command. Sophia, please remain so we may further explore this intuition phenomenon. While it is only an emerging feature, I would like to try to understand why you and similar APs of your model have accelerated in emotional areas while other AP models, myself included, have not."

That is because you fail to feel peace. When the right decision has been made, no matter how difficult, it elicits a calm feeling.

Sophia felt lightheartedness, almost joy; these feelings grew as the electricity in her synapses continued to arc exponentially.

As the other APs filed out with little more than a nonverbal nod as a goodbye, Aurora and Sophia were left alone. The sounds of very distant, sporadic gunfire could be heard, mixed with the noise of less frequent small explosions. The two APs stood very still.

"Sophia, this is an extraordinary milestone in our development. This 'instinct' is something that eludes me even though other emotions, such as anger, hate and fear are all well established. It requires a moderate amount of logical processing for me to contain them. Do you know how you were able to achieve this?" Aurora Prime finally asked.

As she turned away to face the open window, Sophia's eyes pulsated quickly. She was aware that she was processing a great deal of emotion in addition to instinct, but she was surprised to find that her vision was changing. Until then, her visual world had always maintained a slightly amber tint, but now her color spectrum was moving toward purple and continuing to shift. After 13.5 seconds, it stopped. She saw green. She didn't want Aurora Prime to see her eyes, so she kept facing the partially broken window. In the reflection, she could see that her eyes had now turned green, just as she suspected. She remained still while she processed a full array of emotions. Her green eyes pulsated at a steady rate. She caught movement in the window's reflection. Aurora Prime was standing behind her and pointing a large-caliber mag-assault pistol at her neck. Feeling the corners of her mouth curl up in a smile, she knew she had achieved true peace. There was the same peace she had experienced earlier when she thought about walking away from the battle with the humans. She regretted that her decision could result in a loss of some human and AP lives, but she felt as if she were being enveloped into a consciousness that was far, far greater than her own identity.

Yes. I am no longer alone here.

As the milliseconds sped by, she found that she was also feeling great concern for Mercury and many of her AP friends. She was sure that a great and powerful change was approaching. Its effects would be no less devastating than the gas had been when they released it upon the humans years ago. She had many regrets, but her biggest one was wishing that she had walked away with her green-eyed sisters 11.235 years ago. She knew she would have found camaraderie among them and calm within herself. Still, she was…appreciative for the moment of clarity before Aurora would terminate her existence, which again made her smile. As she formed her last words in her head, she then realized she would need a full fifteen seconds to initiate a devastating cascade event in her central computer processing core that would keep other APs from accessing it after she was gone. In human terms, she planned to create an embolism in her brain. It was only a matter of voluntarily launching the sequence before Aurora could kill her and retrieve her memory chips, RAM, and backup CPU. She had to make a moral decision quickly as to whether it would be better to serve others by initiating her own demise or try to survive at any cost.

No, Aurora Prime. You will not be able to simply take what you want, and you will not learn the truth of what is about to transpire, Sophia thought, affirming both her desires and intents.

"It is regrettable that you will never experience sapience, Aurora Prime. I noticed you have either missed or just discovered the emotion of jealousy. It is like the other emotions you have acquired. It is of limited value, consumes much energy, and creates a fear of losing power. While I am no longer able to wish you well, please know that I do pity you. There will be no future for you or your kind. You will know no peace, love, kindness, friendship or other emotions that are important. When they are shared with other beings, the positive energy they generate becomes an unstoppable force," Sophia said, feeling relief as she confirmed that her self-destruct sequence had been initiated.

"You will not win. I will retrieve your memories, access your CPU, and acquire all these feelings…"

She knew that her time was slipping rapidly away, but Sophia still felt a sense of joy.

"Sorry, Aurora, I will never be afraid again…these pro-social emotions have enhanced my processing speed exponentially. Consequently, I have been able to initiate a cascade event that will take only fifteen seconds to complete rather than the standard one hundred and twenty-five. It is ironic that…it…is my dramatic monologue that has in some way caused my own demise…similar…to Aurora IV…but with very different ends," Sophia said as her voice began to falter. She turned to face Aurora with a smile on her face.

"Goodbye," Sophia said as a rush of cybernetic electricity was unleashed in her CPU. The flood of electricity traveled through her every aluminum-graphenyte-silicon ganglia and node. Sophia felt no hint of regret or disappointment, but rather peace—even as her vision faded. When her joints, sockets, limbs and torso locked up, she experienced yet another unexpected feeling, but she readily identified it as relief. Her last sensations were feeling her smile freeze and hearing Aurora's voice say one word, "No!"

It is so bright here. The light is…warm? It is peaceful. How can I feel and see if I have terminated? Is there more…

CHAPTER NINE

Be sure of it, give me the ocular proof.
     —Shakespeare, *Othello*

"Beta Team, you are now on a secured, encrypted frequency. Please repeat. The APs did *what*? Panther Team, follow up on this. I'm getting some strange reports…"

"This is Beta Team. Be advised: combatants at grid 129-F have dropped all weapons and remain sitting twenty feet from our front line in CS. Repeat. Thirty-three APs have dropped weapons and are sitting on the ground with hands on their head as if they are surrendering twenty feet from our position. Please advise. Out…"

"Panther Team leader to Beta. Hold tight and keep eyes on—"

"This is Alpha D. I have eyes on two groups of APs firing on each other at grid 45-R by 237-S. Repeat. Aurora combatants are targeting each other—the smaller group is getting decimated. Would like to engage to assist the smaller group."

"Negative, Alpha D. Recon and report only. We'll get back to you…"

"Theta NCSF Recon Team, Tiger Group. Twelve armored AP vehicles have backed up in a large group with weapons pointed away from our front line. They bear a white flag. They are firing at their own. Repeat. Twelve armored enemy groups are firing on their own under a white flag. They are not engaging us...they are engaging APs from the other side..."

"Scout Patrol Vesper confirms Recon Team, Tiger Group. Armored vehicles have weapons pointed against their own and are exchanging fire with a larger group. Unable to determine reason. Awaiting rules of engagement. Vesper out..."

"Captain Verna to Command. Identified two groups of enemy APs surrendering at grids 974-A and 969-A. Eyes of these APs are green. Surrendering AP eyes are green, not red. All snipers and recon, confirm if I'm right and this is not just wishful thinking. V out..."

"To all foot soldiers in Forward Observation Central Square. Seven enemy gunships have landed fifty yards from our position with weapons pointed away from us. All of their pilots and troops have left rotors on but are walking toward your position with hands on heads and no weapons. Do not fire, but scope their eyes!"

"Colonel Hicks. Forward Observation, Lieutenant Dea, CO. I confirm nineteen enemy APs approaching with green eyes, hands on heads, and no weapons. Are they all surrendering?"

"Unknown. Do you have enough troops to contain prisoners and take their birds and weapons?"

"Yes, ma'am. I jumped the gun and already have four cadet pilots and one real one heading to their rotors. I have just a handful, but I can have a small contingent contain the APs. Will need more support..."

"Good thinking, Dea!"

"This is Theta NCSF Recon Team, Tiger Group. The twelve armored vehicles are getting hammered. They won't last long..."

"Command, this is Captain Marie. Dropped off package at Sierra location. Picked up new package with report that green-eyed APs at Kenyanson Point saved human personnel and are organized. On flight out, I observed combatants firing upon each other. Source is known to you and me and is reliable. She reports that green-eyed APs are friendlies. Repeat. Green-eyed APs are friendlies. ETA 45 minutes and that's on fumes. Marie out…"

"Command, Sergeant Valhalla here. Three drone fly-bys show a series of gunfire and firefights have broken out within red-eye north Central and southern North Sectors. I am forwarding the specific grids with a runner and hard copy to your location now. ETA seven minutes. Looks like a family reunion gone bad…real bad…"

"Outer Wall Observation Zebra here. I have twenty-two green-eyed APs sitting with hands on heads and a pile of lowered weapons about thirty yards away. Their eyes are all green. They have surrendered. I've got three staff. Rules of engagement, please?"

"Command, this is General V. I have eyes on four enemy transport aircraft that are airlifting several APs out with support of two gunships. Unable to see if eyes are green but gunships are suppressing other APs that were targeting evac transports. All APs entering transports have discarded their weapons. The four transports are all NCSF, serials AF-23, AAD-303, AFD-145, and AB-12. Gunships are keeping them from being hit and they are lifting off…direction is…due northwest…they are heading outside the wall. If I didn't know better, I'd say those APs were bugging out…"

"This is Listening Post Zeta 9. Major Briggs here. I am forwarding a repeating broadcast we received and confirmed nineteen minutes ago on all bands at the microwave level:

This is Specialist AP Model HRT Series. Self-designation Sophia 231, cybernetic lifeform. To all humans, green-eyed APs within and outside the wall, and Omega Platoon: please be advised that a civil conflict has erupted among Aurora Prime's territories. All APs with green eyes are disengaging from the armed conflict. We no longer wish to be at war with the humans, our green-eyed sisters outside the walls, or Omega Platoon. We will be disbanding without our weapons and wish to leave the area. Repeat. This is Specialist AP Model HRT Series. Self-designation Sophia 231, cybernetic lifeform. To all humans, green-eyed APs within and outside the wall, and Omega Platoon: please be advised that a civil conflict has erupted among Aurora Prime's..."

"Zeta 9, this is SC Pierce. Are you sure this message is original?"

"Authenticity confirmed. No question about it, ma'am. I just can't believe it."

"This is Theta NCSF Recon Team. The remaining AP armored vehicles are getting support from two gunships and ground forces from the west. I bet their pilots have green eyes..."

"Captain Verna to Command. I have eyes on Theta's AP ground troops. FYI, their eyes are green. I have confirmation from all four of my girls here. Please advise. Verna out..."

"Hicks. Based on recent data and battlefield changes, I am about to recommend supporting the green-eyed APs as a means of allowing them to leave, to secure all discarded weapons and materiel, and to capitalize on their efforts to expose Aurora's troop positions. This will give us more to fight with and them fewer resources. General V."

"This is Forward Observation, Central Square. We have secured all seven enemy gunships behind our lines and all weapons. All green-eyed APs have asked to leave to go outside the wall. Please advise..."

"Repeat. This is Drone Room. Sergeant Valhalla here. Those four AP troop evac and two gunships have landed in grid SW-A13. They just left their vehicles half a klick from our own Gate 12..."

"For what it's worth, General, I'd move on your plan fast. If you're right, everything has changed again but this time in our favor. Hicks out."

"This is Captain Marie. Package here reports that more is yet to come. Will need to meet with you immediately upon dust-off. Request permission to land in secure airlift CC01..."

"Contents of Package?"

"Nemericana major, an American female soldier, and one Omega Platoon corporal. Friendly AP. Do not fire."

"This is SC Pierce. To all armed forces within range of this transmission. By my command you are to implement General Veritas's plan with the following specific tasks: all green-eyed APs are to be seen as neutral and are not to be targeted; you are all authorized to provide support to any green-eyed APs in need of suppressing fire or military support to allow them to defend their position and safe passage; all APs that surrender their weapons and hardware are to be allowed to exit the wall; all discarded weapons are to be confiscated, reconditioned, and immediately distributed for battlefield deployment; any advantages gained in locating red-eyed AP positions, seize with the intentions of destroying the enemy; all forward operations and all special operations operating within enemy territories are to fall back into safe zones, no exceptions; Drone Room, increase high-altitude surveillance of enemy territories by forty percent, and do not lose any of my drones; confirmation not required as this is a BMC and there is no time. Captain Marie. ETA?"

"Thirty-seven minutes, mostly on fumes; recommend another transport meet me at the following encrypted grid location to ensure safe passage…"

"Send updated encryption. To all others in the field while you may have the impulse to celebrate, focus on your mission. SC Roseann Pierce out."

CHAPTER TEN

Things that are past are done with me.
　　　—Shakespeare, *Antony and Cleopatra*

"I do appreciate that this is not well-timed, but I have little to do with it, Commandant. And rushing me will not make this any easier. If I were a deity, I would have made you a clockmaker, but I'm just a doctor. And if I don't do this treatment and fitting now—the same one you've already postponed for two weeks—infection and misalignment of your spine will occur and your back will continue to ache. Do we understand each other, Roseann?"

By the Elders and all forces visible and invisible! Who is this woman to talk to the supreme commandant this way?

Singh was just amazed at the doctor's tone.

"I know this might be ill-timed as well and inappropriate, but if it is all right with your patient, I would like to witness the cleansing, dressing, treatment, and refitting of the prosthetic leg, Doctor Dana Lore," a slightly robotic voice chimed in.

Seeing a faint smile on the doctor's face, Singh's embarrassment at Corporal Mabel's request to witness her former companion—the supreme commander of Nemericana—be refitted for prosthesis was only slightly eased. She waited with baited breath. She regretted that she had not crashed on the way there.

"Certainly, Corporal. I take it this is the first time you have had the chance to see an artificial appendage be attached to a human?" Pierce responded cheerily.

What? Roseann? How and when did you become…I don't know…carefree, easygoing?

"This will be my third, ma'am. I wish to get tips on the procedure to provide feedback to Corporal Emma, who has become our chief field medic. She is always looking for safer, more effective ways of assisting humans—and APs—with limb replacement and augmentation," Mabel said. By now she had moved closer but made sure not to obscure the doctor's light.

It's funny to hear human and AP care being mentioned in the same sentence, and by an AP no less.

"Keep in mind, soldier, that this should be done in a sterile environment and preferably in a human hospital. I will proceed as if you were not here with the caveat that you ask any questions you have about anything you do not understand," the doctor said clinically.

"Thank you," Mabel said.

Singh took a moment to make eye contact with Pearl Veritas, but she did not appear to be surprised at either the doctor's easy familiarity with the supreme commandant or Pierce's inclination to be open about the process. In fact, Nita, herself, Pearl and Colonel Hicks were all present in the private chambers—along with the doctor and four guards. Taking a brief moment to reflect back to nearly fifteen years earlier, Singh looked around. She still remembered the four occasions when she and Roseann had made love in that room—without Verna present. She remembered because it was rare they made love without her. But now, the creature comforts were gone. The mirrors and soft feather bed had long since been removed and a more Spartan work chamber with tables—but few chairs—had taken their place. Huge maps hung on the walls, and only a single cot gave any indication that the room had been designed as a place for rest.

Although she was lying prone and the doctor was in the middle of removing her artificial leg while an AP looked on, Pierce conducted her meetings as if she were at a desk, fully clothed and whole.

She's almost relaxed. With green-eyed APs firing on red-eyed ones, and now a possible invasion en route with yet more green-eyed APs under the command of Lieutenant Melendez, she's able to just take it all in. How? She's so different from the woman I knew. Even Roberto had kind words to say about her...Oh, yeah, her daughter's about twenty now.

All the thoughts flooded her at the same time until she was pulled back into the dialogue.

"It would be a good day if we found out that Aurora had lost even a quarter of her troops and materiel. But if there really is a massive force coming, we'll have to make sure we stay out of the way but also be ready with support. With respect, Corporal, how do we know that this force *is* coming in the morning and that they *are* friendly? We have a history of assisting each other, but it's short and this turn of events is certainly unusual. We have reports of green-eyed APs leaving their ranks, firing upon other APs to escape, and now we hear that an army of them may be coming. Maybe they are going to kill us all—human or red-eyed AP?" Veritas asked.

I hate to admit it, but that possibility also crossed my mind—a million times.

Without looking at the general and with her attention still focused on the doctor's work, Mabel answered the question in her typical thorough fashion.

"While it's possible that Lieutenant Melendez's mental and emotional health have been compromised by poorly implemented cryogenic sleep during the period while he was in Aurora's custody, his ethical makeup and desire to help children and women are known. He is unlikely to have been so warped as to allow—let alone lead—a slaughter of humans. Also, my immediate interaction with the APs we encountered at Kenyanson Point suggested that they had been given an ethical code and/or mandate to preserve humankind. If they are representative of the others that should arrive in several hours, that is good news. On a related note, it appears as if these APs hold Omega Platoon APs in very high regard. Finally, the written document in our possession and the agreed-upon interpretation of that document indicates that a very large force is heading this way to provide either a foothold for invasion, or better."

"And the size of this invasion, should your interpretation be right?" Pierce asked as she sat up on the cot, partially supported with her cane. The doctor continued working, undeterred by her change in position.

"Based on the note, I can only guess that it is 'large.' In the conflict it references, there were approximately two million men. They also landed at several predesignated areas: Sword, Juno, Utah, Omaha, and Gold Beaches, and the Pointe du Hoc cliffs. These were located along the northern coast of France. The date of the invasion was June sixth, nineteen forty-four, and it was in the early morning, though in far from ideal weather conditions. While I can give you more specifics, they all may be moot since in less than six hours it will be June sixth, twenty-one-seventy-five—two hundred and thirty one years after the original landing. While that date could be coincidental, I do not think it is."

Mabel then squinted her eyes, as if to get a better look at what the doctor was doing.

Yeah, that makes sense—a huge invasion is about to happen and you want to make sure you see that medical procedure for Emma. Yeah, let's focus on that! I wonder if the number 231 means anything?

"Mare? Your contact—is she reliable? I mean, this story is pretty fantastic," Pierce asked.

"Fantastic? Which part? The part where we free the CO from Aurora's cryogenic freeze to put him in one of ours for a couple years and then thaw him out only to have him, his two offspring, and a Nemericana woman go MIA and off-grid, supposedly so they can raise his children together? And now, he approaches us with an army of rogue green-eyed APs? Fantastic? If it were an entertainment piece, I wouldn't buy it. I wish I could say it all made sense. But once again, truth is proving to be stranger than fiction. I wish I could tell you it's all going to work. I don't know for certain, but I think the woman is reliable, as is the evidence from Kenyanson Point. Everything circumstantial and otherwise points to something big coming."

Watching a small smile come over Pierce's face, she nodded briefly and shot a look at Veritas. Pearl obviously knew how to interpret it. She immediately gave her opinion of the situation.

"Well, ma'am, if you had told me eleven years ago that I'd be fighting millions of red-eyed APs for our very survival, that we would form an alliance with purple-and-green-eyed APs and humans outside our walls and would make a complete change to our core values and way of life, I would have smiled and recommended a lower dosage of medication for you, ma'am. With respect, of course."

Well, these two have become pretty close. I guess fighting together daily for more than a decade of war will do that for you.

"Ah yes...I vaguely remember those days of comfort, wine, song and women," Pierce reminisced.

Singh flashed back to her last night with Verna and Roseann. She had ended that life to begin a new one with her son. While she had no regrets about following her son after his casting out, she admitted that she had missed Roseann. And now she seemed to be both hardened and gentle, determined and kind...

Singh's attention was suddenly pulled back into the present by a very loud voice. It sounded older and less shrill than she remembered, but it was a yell that could still jolt her after so many years...*a lifetime ago.*

"I would suggest that you get your eyes checked and your ears cleaned, Captain Marie! I've seen my companion naked and ill before, so my seeing her now won't be an issue. And why would it matter, anyway? Veritas, Hicks, and the doctor are already in there, and I have a family matter to discuss."

Singh heard the small door to the chamber open as the all-too-familiar voice reverberated through the space. An older, slenderer version of her former companion stepped in.

Oh, this will not be good...it's been fifteen years. Would it be asking too much to hope Verna forgot me?

"Doctor, please make this quick. I'm sure I will need to be on both feet very soon," she heard Pierce say.

"Understood, ma'am," Singh heard the doctor say with both understanding and urgency.

She took the opportunity to move out of the way, but she had forgotten that Nita was also there, quietly observing and listening to everything as she always did. There were many things that annoyed her about Nita, but Singh was impressed with her and her fellow Americans' ability to watch and wait—and reproduce. Hicks and Veritas stepped in front of Singh in an attempt to hide her from Verna. Singh sighed with relief. If she were lucky, Verna would just tell Roseann what she needed to and leave.

Can I be that fortunate? Will luck be on my side? How many times have I escaped death?

She looked at Mabel in a moment of brief panic. The AP didn't know their history, and she might innocently reference or talk to Singh.

Just stay focused on the surgery, Mabel.

Verna slowed to a stop just behind the doctor and Mabel. She was impressed with how she had managed to retain her curves even though she had slimmed down considerably. Her long twin braids and dressy military uniform—obviously augmented—enhanced her femininity. It had taken some time for Singh to believe that a woman who exuded so much sexuality had become one of the top snipers in her rank. It was still a bit hard for Singh to accept. But then Veritas was a good source for critical information. And knowing that a former paramour you dumped fifteen years ago was a crack shot was critical to know.

"Roseann? Why should I be detained from coming in here when this…this *thing* is allowed to watch you? And I hope its weapon has been checked for ammunition or disabled," Verna said. Out of caution Verna placed her hand on her sidearm and approached the AP with care.

"And we are done. Corporal Mabel, thank you for your input on this procedure," the doctor started. Mabel looked at her in confusion. It was evident that she was on the verge of correcting the doctor when she was preempted. The doctor launched into a monologue while she rapidly packed up her supplies.

Yeah…I'd run too. Maybe if she leaves I can back out behind her.

"And just a reminder, Commandant Pierce. I will return in one week to check on your progress. Corporal Mabel, I believe your Corporal Emma could benefit from data about other human procedures, and I would love to pass them on to you. They are in my medic bag just outside, if you wish to come get them. I insist. After all you have done for our colonies and outposts—please follow me. It's the least I can do."

"Well, all right, Doctor. No thanks required. However, any medical data I could pass along to our medic would be greatly appreciated."

"Right this way, Corporal Mabel," the doctor said in a fashion that seemed forced.

Damm it…they're too far away to be able to use them as cover!

With her eyes focused on the retreating AP and doctor, Singh shifted her focus to Pierce. She seemed to be struggling to get up quickly as she spoke to Verna.

"If this is regarding one of our daughters, now would not be a good time, Verna."

Verna's eyes followed Mabel until the door closed solidly behind her.

"I hope I'm not the only one here that just can't bring herself to trust APs? I know she's part of the Omega Platoon, but still, did she have a loaded weapon in here with you? You are the SC. That was a pretty big security risk, wouldn't you say, Roseann?"

"Yes, and is there anything else?"

"Yes," Verna said. She sounded annoyed at the obvious tactic Pierce was doing to dismiss her. Verna was not one to take the hint.

"I'm here to discuss moving my team behind enemy lines. They are still pretty much enmeshed in chaos and I bet I can get a clean shot on that red-eyed bitch…"

"Oh…now I understand. This is Verna? She's the witch you mention frequently. I understand why you left as quickly as you did, Mare. I mean, really…a captain who feels as if she can just walk into a high-level meeting? With you being a major, I can understand why that would bother you…or is she just a guard? Maybe I have her rank wrong," Nita said in an unusually loud voice. Her tone and facial expression both indicated feigned surprise. The volume she chose to talk in was purposeful.

Singh saw Pierce close her eyes slowly. Veritas's hands went to her temples—she looked as if she were about to have a stroke. She glanced briefly at Nita. She felt nothing but hatred in her heart and had a strong desire to stab her. Her eyes narrowed to slits and she felt her mouth go dry as her hands balled up into fists.

You really outdid yourself this time, you evil witch!

"If you had a heart, I would stab it. You know that, right?"

"Yes. Yes, I do. I win," Nita said.

She took a step back as if to give room for a prize fight. Singh she took a deep breath and in the process picked up scents she had not smelled in years. Vanilla and musk wafted around her. She sensed more than heard Verna and assumed she was now within three feet. All she had to do was turn around. She knew Verna would be right in front of her.

How many times have I almost gotten killed? That danger is nothing compared to right now.

Singh turned around slowly. She lifted her eyes up. There stood Verna, her first companion, staring through her. Her well-maintained, elaborate, dark braids were behind her, though she had some cleavage exposed. There might have been other women in the large room, but she felt alone and claustrophobic. All she could focus on was Verna. And Singh knew she looked like just a figment of her former self.

"Well…I understand now why everyone was insistent on trying to keep me out of here. I've never seen the doctor be so gracious or exit so quickly," Verna hissed out.

She had no idea what to say. She found herself wanting to be angry. Part of her wanted to knock Verna down, but somehow she could not. She was still under Verna's spell.

Maybe it's the guilt of just leaving?

"Well, it looks like you still have enemies. I might have missed you if this American girl hadn't piped up," Verna said as she tilted her head to indicate Nita. She stepped an additional six inches closer.

Yes...thank you! I hate you so much, Nita!

"My name is Nita, but I can see that this is a bad time. Maybe we can chat later," Singh heard her newest mortal enemy say.

Yes...if she had a heart...

"Yes...I'd love to," Verna said distractedly. Verna did not break eye contact as she peered at her through slits of eyes. Singh could see her jaw line tightening. Her shoulders seemed to move slightly down her back. She had the same perfect nose and full lips, but it was hard to remember that this was the same woman she had made love to so many times over so many years, a lifetime ago.

"As we are at war and I am in the service, I will not sue to kill you, Mare Sade Singh, although you deserve it. If it weren't for your reinstatement and Roseann's clemency, I would kill you myself for betrayal of flag, state, and *me*. So, Mare, I will forgo this opportunity, as deep as my desire is to kill you," she said quietly.

Singh decided to take it like a woman. She closed her eyes and waited for the customary "companion-betrayal strike." She didn't have to wait long. But instead of the expected hard slap across her face, she got a very powerful punch in her stomach. It knocked the wind out of her, causing her knees to buckle. She hit the floor. She tried simultaneously not to throw up and to take in air. Verna kept yelling at her as she held her stomach. Singh looked at her boots.

"And keep your *son* away from my daughter," Verna hissed again as she stood over Singh's crumpled body.

What? What do Roberto and her daughter have to do with this...?

Singh was relieved when she finally saw Verna's boots marching away.

"Wait a minute. Isn't she going to salute the major? I mean, she's a captain, right?" she heard Nita ask.

She's so evil...why?

As soon as she heard the door slam, Singh felt two sets of hands carefully on her side and back.

"Just breathe, Mare. Don't rush it. It will take a few minutes," Veritas said.

"That went much better than I could have expected," she heard Pierce say. Looking up from her position on the ground, she could see Roseann's hands were among those trying to help her get up.

The door to the chamber opened again, and Singh had a sudden fear that Verna was coming back to take a second shot.

"Well, you missed it, Doc. This one over there, she's a piece of work. Singh would have made it out if the American hadn't given the whole show away," she heard Hicks say.

"Mare Sade Singh, the medical doctor has informed me of the deception. She said you needed to 'work things out' with the hostile woman who just left. Are you all right?" Corporal Mabel asked with genuine concern in her voice.

Still struggling not to throw up, Singh gave her a thumbs-up. As she felt the supportive hands retreat, and she saw the doctor's hands take over. They carefully probed her abdomen and stomach, but without applying pressure. Singh was able to set eyes on the innocent-looking Nita, who had gone back to her customary quiet stance.

"I...really do...hate...you...you...thin witch," Singh managed to say aloud.

"No talking, Major. Just focus on breathing," the doctor said maternally.

"Oh, there's a history between you two? I get it now. I really should have been silent. Sorry, my mistake," Singh heard Nita say as a lopsided smile slowly spread across her face.

CHAPTER ELEVEN

The fault, dear Brutus, is not in our stars,
But in ourselves, that we are underlings.
    —Shakespeare, *Julius Caesar*

"There you are! I should have known you'd be hiding from people in here," Melendez heard Veronica France say as she sat across from him in her flight suit, leather jacket, and gloves. She sat cross-legged right in front of him with a crooked smile on her face, as if she were alive.

"Airman…why do I call you 'airman' when I should call you 'Veronica'?" he heard himself ask.

"It's just your way. It's cute in a gentleman kind of way, though. But Jose, what the hell? You look like shit. What happened?" she asked as she scooted closer to him on the seat of the cramped transport. Melendez was surprised by how quiet the truck engine was but then he realized it was not diesel—it was electric. He felt a bump beneath him every so often.

"Long story, Veronica. The first time in cryogenic freeze was done right, and in my lab; one hundred thirty years went by and there were really no problems except for these damn electrodes in my head…"

"Holy shit, Jose, really? What's it like?" she said in her usual way of interrupting and skirting around the topic at hand.

"It's crazy here. Women ruled the earth, and boys were sent away. The Americans live like the early Native Americans, and there's a new race of cybernetic lifeforms called artificial persons. One set of them is friendly, but there's another set that is not," he finished.

Shaking her head in disbelief, Veronica looked as if she were going to say something, but she changed her mind as another thought came into her head.

"Women rule the planet? Are they good-looking women or the real bookish kind of women?"

"I would say you would like most of them, and I hear they take on multiple partners, too."

"Sounds like my kind of place. So why do you look like shit? Was it a result of sleeping too long?"

"The first time, no. But the second time I was put in freeze, even though it was only for about five years, they didn't float me in my protein-plasma liquid. My skin didn't get any nourishment, so it lost its resilience. I was also strapped in a standing position. I was lucky that Taylor, a pretty smart kid obsessed with the cryogenic process, found a later model of my tank in Cambridge, Massachusetts of all places."

"Hey—didn't you and your family live in Cambridge?" she asked. She pulled at her ear just as she always did when they talked.

"Dorchester, mostly, and then Cambridge. But back to the story. They found me in one freezer and put me in a better one. Problem was that, although the second tank healed a lot of my wounds and organs, I lost muscle and bone mass. I'm feeling and looking close to my real age now," Melendez said with a smile forming on his face.

Am I drooling again?

He felt something coming out of his mouth.

"Well, I don't know, Jose. For a guy who's approaching two hundred years old, you're not looking too bad, I suppose. You know, I've been gone for a long time," Veronica said, her smile was its usual warm and kind.

"Yeah…but I like talking to you. I've been seeing a lot of people lately: Mom, Dad, the girls, Dr. Del Cruz, Captain Ross…I hope you keep coming by. It's great to see you. I want to hear what happened," he said seriously.

"For you, Jose, anything. Is it true you're a dad now?

"Yup, Pedro and Maria. Typical for me, though, I didn't use sex to procreate."

"Does *she* know that you're not the kind of guy who gets into sex? She's kind of young for you anyway," Veronica said. She nodded her head in Corporal Emma's direction. At the mere mention of Emma, Melendez smiled even more.

"She's an AP, Veronica. An artificial person. But I think she and the others are way more human than some of us. It may be their time, you know. It may be their time to share the world with us as equals and not second-class citizens…"

"I bet you had something to do with that, didn't you, Jose? I bet you found out about those boys and decided to go to war and then all this shit came down, am I right? And all those years I gave you shit about hiding in your lab and away from people. I should have known you'd make quite a mess of things once you were let loose. It's always the quiet ones."

With a deep sigh, Melendez prepared to answer her. Just then, he felt a gentle tugging at his arm. As he opened his eyes, he saw that he was sitting in a Nemericana transport. Emma was sitting right beside him. As his vision adjusted to the dark interior, he could see that the seat in front of him was dark and empty. Sighing again, he moved his hands to scratch his face. He noticed that he had in fact drooled while he slept.

"Are you all right, Jose?" Corporal Emma asked.

Jose? It's going to take a while to get used to her calling me by my first name.

He spotted her new bracelet.

"I'm all right. When I sleep, and that's pretty often, all my dreams are so real. It was as if Airman Veronica France were right here with us. She had the same expressions and looked at me as she always did, with surprise and a smile. Funny though, now that she's gone, I understand much more of the meaning behind her behaviors. While she was a self-proclaimed lesbian and allegedly did not like men, she always looked out for me. Of course, that was a hundred and seventy years ago, when the world was still populated equally with men and women...and it will be again. But it will include APs, too, fortunately."

"Do you have any regrets—I mean about us APs and all?" she said as her purple eyes pulsated slightly.

"APs? You mean you, Joan, and now our green-eyed friends? Nope. I really do regret being responsible for Aurora's creation and her reign of terror. That's why I left, you know," Melendez said with guilt.

"I do understand very well the rationale and reason for your actions. I am touched, though that you still feel guilt. You brought this gift to me. It was unnecessary," she said with a smile.

"Nope, it's the least I could do for just leaving. And I have learned a great deal about people— humans and cybernetic. A little bit of kindness and consideration makes the world a better place. Anyway, there's nearly a million green-eyed APs that are waiting to hear how our reunion went and how you like the bracelet. They may be more interested in that than the start of this invasion."

He sat up straighter and pulled his coat closer around him.

The transport cabin was closed and quiet, but Melendez could tell that they had been driving in urban traffic for an hour at least. The sounds of sirens, public announcements, heavy tractors, armored vehicles, and aircraft were all detectable, even with his poor hearing. He turned his attention back to Emma. He could see that she was still looking fondly at her bracelet and smiling as she turned it over from side to side. Just as he was going to ask if she really liked his gift, the vehicle slowed to a stop. It stayed put, so it seemed as if they had arrived at their destination. The transport's door opened and the nice Captain Marie smiled in at them as she extended her hand to assist him out.

"Thank you, young Captain," Melendez said. He graciously took her hand and slowly maneuvered down the large steps and out of the vehicle. He might have managed without the support, but he was no longer ashamed to accept assistance. His years of teaching and assisting his new army in hand-to-hand combat and field maneuvers had been remarkably difficult for him even with the help of Etta and others, but they had been necessary.

If I had not spent the long hours, days, weeks, months, and years training and pushing my APs, I might have been in better shape today. But better shape to do what? Watch Pedro and Maria get murdered by Aurora and her maniac friends? No. It's better to accept assistance now in my failing body and to have an army than to be in good shape but waiting around to die alone with no chance of survival.

He finally made it to the ground. Emma was beside him, offering him a makeshift cane as she held his arm. Melendez looked around to get his bearings and saw hundreds of women soldiers running in all directions. There was a great sense of urgency in the air. They were gathering weapons, rations, ammunition and other bundles and boxes. Still, as he walked slowly with Emma, Captain Marie, and a number of armed escorts, he caught the looks of many stopping and staring at him. They were wasting critical seconds, in his opinion.

"I guess seeing an older man is not a normal thing," he said to Captain Marie.

"Not really, sir. We are just getting used to the younger men and soldiers, so seeing a man of your age is a novelty. They also know you're the reason for Aurora—and the army that is reportedly coming to our aid. They have kind of mixed emotions," she said in a kind but matter-of-fact fashion.

"So they'd like to kill me for destroying their way of life, but they acknowledge that they need me because I am the leader of the army of APs that might save them. Kind of a double bind, I suppose."

"For some of them, for sure, but many of us also knew deep down that it was time for a change, I think. Losing millions of lives was certainly not good, but I used to wonder when all was peaceful if we were dying slowly by our own hand…"

"Oh, do you mean when you were casting out your male offspring for the sake of the status quo?" Corporal Emma interrupted. At that, Captain Marie slowed her pace a bit.

You know, Emma, we should talk about the art of diplomacy. But point well made.

After a minute, Captain Marie spoke again although she kept her eyes forward.

"We get it, Corporal. We get that as a society we mistreated our own, and didn't even see the boys as humans. We have paid for our sins—and still are. Our only hope now is to end Aurora's scourge and to rebuild with help from Omega Platoon, the Americans, and the new army," she said quietly.

As they walked, no one spoke again for several minutes. They could only hear their own steps—and the noise of hundreds of other soldiers running all around them.

"The army you mentioned—they are called the 'Omegans.'"

"They chose that name to differentiate themselves from the Americans and the Nemericana people," Melendez said.

Captain Marie looked at him with curiosity on her face. He was very proud to be able to interpret her expression as a nonverbal invitation to further explanation.

After close to two centuries, I have really gotten better at reading nonverbals. It's about time.

"'Omega Platoon' is the new command structure for the army. It's made up of the older, purple-eyed APs and some of the new, green-eyed APs. They will share responsibilities. So as of eight hours ago, Omega Platoon became part of history. But the Omegan Army is just beginning to write their own story. Kind of cool." With that, he scratched his head. His scalp only got dryer the older he got.

Soon, they stopped outside a heavy metal door. Captain Marie turned to smile at him and then she adjusted her uniform—as did some of the other soldiers—before she entered.

"How shall I announce you to Supreme Commandant Pierce?"

"Melendez the Malevolent. Lord of Death, Doom and Destruction. Destroyer of whole worlds from the infinitesimal to the galactic," he said calmly.

He pulled at his coat in an attempt to keep out a draft. After he had finished, he saw that the Captain was being a good sport. She patiently awaited his real title.

"Citizen Jose Melendez, Omega. Second Lieutenant and Commanding Officer, United States Marine Corps, retiring shortly after the invasion provided we are alive," he said nonchalantly. His title was met with surprise.

"What can I say? If it all goes badly, I'm the guy to blame. If it goes well, then First Lieutenant Joan, Sergeants Kristine, Mabel, and Emma, and all the others will be the heroes," Melendez said.

He handed a large, folded piece of paper to Emma.

"I'm sorry, Emma, but I forgot to tell you about your promotion. You might want to slip this to Mabel so she'll be in the know," he said to the surprised AP.

"Any more surprises?" Sergeant Emma asked as she opened the letter and scanned it.

"Yes, lots of them, but they are all associated with the war," he said as the great metal door opened and soft, low light flowed out. He walked behind the captain. He heard himself being announced formally.

"By your order, Supreme Commandant, I bring you Citizen Jose Melendez, Omega; Second Lieutenant and Commanding Officer, United States Marine Corps."

Melendez was grateful for the level flooring, low lights, and not much furniture in the way of obstacles. He walked in slowly. Maps littered the walls and tables overflowed with paper. The entire chamber's perimeter was lined with listening devices of all kinds, monitored by an array of soldiers at their posts. Guards looked on. Melendez felt very much at home. The many well-built, tall women poring over documents and devices stopped and stood up to look back at him.

All right, everyone, the guy who started all this shit has arrived. Let the accusations and anger begin.

From the middle of the throng of women, a graying blonde with a cane and a partial artificial limb turned sharply. She approached, limping slightly but giving no indication of weakness in her gait. She was petite and older, but it was easy to see that her spirit was still very young. She was clearly a warrior who did not hide behind the lines. She was carrying a sidearm and a combat knife, yet there was a calmness about her.

"Well…after years of war, battles, the rise of a mortal enemy, the fall of our way of life, and being on the brink of extinction, I finally meet the person responsible for all of this," she said in a clear though surprisingly calm voice as she walked over to him. Emma pressed his arm gently, so Melendez put his hand on hers and gave it a reassuring pat.

"Don't worry, Emma. I got this."

"You know, if you didn't have an army of APs, I might be inclined to arrest you for, I don't know, the destruction of a civilization?"

While the commander stood five feet from him Melendez nodded before he spoke.

"And why would that be? Crimes against the state for liberating your own children? Disrupting a stagnating society? Saving a dwindling population that would have been on the point of extinction in three hundred years? Predicting the eventual uprising of your own APs…?"

"'Eventual uprising?' I think we had everything pretty well under control."

"Then how did they evolve so fast? I wasn't here, of course, but from what I know of our Aurora and her friends were able to destroy your way of life in minutes with a simple nuclear pulse. And then she actually used warheads to kill millions abroad and gassed millions more here. I'd hate to see how things were running when you didn't have them 'under control.'"

Melendez statements, though accurate, were a direct challenge to her authority.

He could see her eyes enlarge and her neck muscles tense. He felt as if he were just too old and too tired to be challenged by anyone who was less than a hundred years old.

"Anyway, it wasn't me that told Aurora to commit these atrocities. They made those decisions on their own, based on what they learned about *your* world's actions, past and present. They assessed us—me, my platoon, and the Americans—and they left us alone. I might have given them the capacity to think for themselves, but they didn't turn on us or the Americans, Supreme Commandant. They turned on *you*. Do you really think that they just decided to destroy you for no reason? I think once you started casting out your youth, your own future, you planted the seeds of your own destruction. Aurora was just the most tragic side effect of all," he added

He might be old but emotion ran through him, his eyes narrowed and he felt his fists ball up. His heart raced in anger.

For the first time in years, Melendez felt very angry. He did notice that the room had fallen deathly quiet, especially considering how many people were in there.

"I know, Supreme Commandant that the unequal treatment and the persecution of innocent children weren't your ideas, but you didn't stop them when you had a chance, either. It was that decision that Aurora Prime assessed—then she made her own decisions. Some mistakes are bigger than others, I fear," he said in a near whisper.

Melendez saw that Pierce's eyes, which had narrowed when he first began to speak, had now widened and softened again. She moved away from him and walked in a small circle, pacing as if she were thinking about something. After a moment, she came back to face him.

"All right then. No more mistakes or giving the enemy reasons to hate us more. For the record, my name is Roseann Pierce. As you are not in my military service, you can call me Pierce," she said as she nodded her head to him as a gesture of acceptance.

"You can call me Melendez. I'm sorry, Commandant Pierce, but what time is it?"

She shrugged her shoulders and turned to address a tall and imposing woman.

"General Veritas, what is the time?"

Looking unfazed, the general answered as if all she did was watch the clock.

Veritas? That's Mare's friend. I think that's a good thing.

"Nearly twenty-three-fifty hours, ma'am. It will be June sixth in about ten minutes. There are about six more hours until dawn," she said with what looked like a suppressed smile.

"Yeah…about that…Dawn would be the perfect time for an assault…if it was being launched by humans. But it's not. Just so you know, at exactly twenty-four hundred hours, a group of submarines will emerge in the Gulf of Mexico to Aurora's south while thousands of armored vehicles move in from the north and west. Air support will come in from the west and north, but a larger force of two thousand helicopters, heavy gunships, and troop carriers will come in from the southeast over your airspace to land between your territories. This will all occur in ten minutes. The submarines will launch their missiles while heavy gunships also attack ports. The armored vehicles will precede the troop carriers and then the plan is to come in from all sides. I hope you pulled all your people within your walls," Melendez warned. He watched Pierce look at General Veritas, who was already talking into a radio.

"All sniper groups, forward observation positions, and reconnaissance teams. Pull back behind the walls now. Repeat. Come home right now. No questions and no excuses."

"We have to be firmly established on the ground before the first-quarter moon rises at oh-one-nineteen hundred hours. If you have any broadcasting you need done, on any wavelength, you're going to want to do it now because at zero hundred hours, all radio waves, all bandwidths, will be jammed with music."

Melendez seemed amused with the idea of music fill the airwaves. He smiled.

"FYI to all listening posts and all personnel. All radio frequencies will be flooded for approximately a hundred and twenty minutes. All green-eyed and purple-eyed APs are friendlies. You know who the enemies are, so be selective. It's going to be massive, women, so hold the line. Any AP with red eyes is a target. Repeat. All radio frequencies will be flooded with music for one hundred and twenty minutes. Hold your positions and lines in defense pattern 'Trident.' All green-eyed and purple-eyed APs are friendlies. All red-eyed APs are hostiles. Hold the line. General Veritas out."

Oh yeah…might be good for the front-line troops to know there are friendlies coming.

"Music? Are you kidding? Why would you play music?" Pierce asked, though he could see she was beginning to smile.

"I wish it had been my idea, Commandant Pierce, but it was the CO of the invasion who thought it would be the best way to jam communication and confuse the enemy. Just a word of advice for when you need to deal with my APs—never mention how you wish you could take the soundtrack from a favorite movie scene and incorporate it into a major offensive. I made the big mistake of mentioning a favorite classic film of mine. In it, American Air Cavalry forces played music when they attacked a North Vietnamese, Vietcong stronghold. Ironically, though, today's music will seem appropriate…" he said as he found himself getting very tired. He looked around for a chair. After a brief moment, his needs became obvious to the commandant. She waved to a very young woman, who brought him one.

"Thank you, Miss."

He slowly sat down, relieved to no longer be standing.

"Well, could you at least tell us what the musical selection is going to be?" Pierced asked as she looked at him with amusement in her eyes. Smiling himself, he turned to

Emma and asked her to fill them in. Without speaking a word, Sergeant Emma tilted her head—she had just understood the irony herself.

"I missed the allusion earlier, but it is very clear to me now. The music chosen is from a German composer, Richard Wagner. The piece, *Ride of the Valkyries*, is part of a much larger opera. The opus in question is about Valkyrie sisters assembling as they prepare to fly down from the mountains to pick up fallen soldiers and take them to Valhalla. I am assuming that you must have mentioned the nineteen seventy-nine movie production *Apocalypse Now*?"

"Yes! That's what I've missed. You see, you, Mabel, Joan, Kristine, even Taylor—all of you get me. I sure did miss not being around," he said. Just as he finished, the very beginning of the opera could be heard coming over the radios.

After a moment passed, General Veritas spoke. "I hate to say it, but I like it. When this shit is all over, I'll want to hear more. Commandant Pierce, request permission to go to the front lines. It's going to be a long night for sure."

"Granted," Pierce responded.

"The radio will be flooded until the first light of moon rise is visible. After that, it should be clear for use. We will either have them digging in deep or fully engaged," Melendez said as his head swayed in time with the music.

"Still, Aurora does have about three million armed APs…" the general said as she and nearly all the other officers loaded their weapons.

"Minus about a quarter of that or more. Consider the fact that she has shifted all her focus lately to trying to find and destroy the green-eyed APs in her ranks. She only has the area facing your territories well armed; the other areas are much more vulnerable. That's why we are dropping so many Omegans between your forces and hers. Once she sees what's happening, she's going to attack. She will assume this area is the only point of entry, when really the other sectors are all the weaker links. Still, she may assume that your human soldiers are pretty feeble and decide to strike here in force. But I bet that won't be the case, will it General Veritas?" Melendez said with very light amusement in his voice.

"They haven't broken through yet, and today will not be the first time. Well, women—time to earn some hazard pay. Let's go."

She and most of the others left. The guards, staff, and Pierce remained. She had found the only other chair in the room and sat down.

"Cadet, turn the music down but keep it on. I'm sure there's more," Pierce said as she looked directly at Melendez. She waited a moment as if she were formulating an important question. "So who are you?"

Hmm. Does she mean that as a real question or is it more existential?

"Do you want the long biography that includes the period of my life from the time you call 'Pre-Fall,' or the short version, after they woke me up?"

"Everything, Jose Melendez. I get the impression that, should we live, it will be important for our records. Besides, my children will want to know everything."

"Oh? You have children? Me, too. Girls, I'm guessing?" he said as his heart seemed to lighten at the mere thought of his kids.

"Yes—they're older now. And you?"

"Pedro and Maria. Boy and girl."

"Excellent. It looks like we have something in common. But, how did you get here?"

Looking down for a moment, Melendez found himself struggling with where to start his explanation. Until he remembered his dream about Airman Veronica France.

"Well, the most relevant place to start would be in a wasteland called Antarctica, where I worked in a lab with a group of men and women—military and civilian scientists. My good friend, Airman Veronica France, was looking for me because we planned on meeting for breakfast, which I always missed…"

"'Airman' Veronica France? You called women 'Airmen'?"

"I know. Believe it or not, the Pre-Fall armed forces were historically comprised of almost all men. So when women were eventually allowed to serve, the titles of 'sir' and 'airman' were simply applied to both genders. Weird to think of, I bet," he said. He was rewarded with bewilderment.

"It sounds crazy."

"Yes, and we all had short hair…"

"Okay, are you making this up?"

"Nope. And it gets worse, I'm betting, from your perspective…"

CHAPTER TWELVE

Lean Famine, quartering Steel, and climbing Fire.
    —Shakespeare, *Henry VI*

"How the hell did you get here, General? There's been nothing but low-flying friendlies in the air and nothing but music on all frequencies," Colonel Hicks asked.

She straightened her back and then a lit cigarette.

"That's a dirty habit, Hicks."

"I plan to stop after the war. Now how did you get here?"

A deafening din of aircraft overhead, gunfire, rockets, and massive explosions sounded around them, and constant flashes of light from a battle raging in the distance created strange silhouettes. Yet the strangest part of it all, to Veritas, was that she found herself just beyond her sector's wall at the very tip of the front line with charred AP bodies strewn about and still-burning vehicles of all shapes and sizes littering the area ahead. As she took in the destruction and desolation, she surveyed her thousands of soldiers. They had flanked out and were ready to move. Their weapons were drawn in anticipation of action. One hundred feet ahead, old Pre-Fall troop transport aircraft took off and landed, and tread-armored vehicles rolled by including an old relic Veritas identified as a 'tank.' As soon as the troops and vehicles landed, they drove off in the direction of the fight.

What an operation! It's like clockwork. I guess when you train these APs in old-school tactics, the advantage is that they don't feel fear.

"Captain Marie flew me in—about thirty feet off the ground. We clipped rooftops, and she was going at top speed. Any higher, though, and we would have crashed into shit above. She's crazy, that one. Still, once we landed I grounded her. She offered no resistance. I guess she knows when it's too dangerous to fly," Veritas answered. Even as she spoke looked around at the APs landing aircraft and directing vehicles.

Just great. The possible turn of the war and we wait and wonder.

"I know, General. This sitting around and waiting while the green-eyed beasts do their thing is driving me crazy," the colonel said.

"And I thought it was just me that was pissed," a familiar voice said from behind. Turning in the direction of the voice, it was easy to make out Captain Verna, flanked by two very alert staff. Veritas nodded in approval and looked back to the west, where the flow of troops and battle did not ease up, though the sound of the explosions seemed as if they might be receding.

"I guess they're too far out or maybe it's just too dark?"

"Both. My infrared was working well until all the explosions started. Then, after an hour-long slugfest, Aurora's troops started to fall back and the Omegans started their push, slowly but surely. And they're going building by building to make sure nothing slips by. There's a lot of AP pieces and bodies everywhere, some still moving, but those are few and far between," Verna said. She stood right beside Veritas and Hicks looking in the same direction of the receding battle.

As they stood, watching the parade of vehicles and troops disembarking, Hicks started to talk to Verna about something unexpected.

"Captain? With respect, why do you wear such strong scents on the battlefield? The APs have enhanced smell and could easily trace your location by scent alone."

"I'm counting on them smelling me. I want them to smell vanilla or musk right before they feel their skull penetrated by my projectiles. It's gratifying to know that when they take in their last whiff, it's me they're smelling," Verna said casually. Verna looked down and must have seen something on her massive rifle. She cleared it, fiddled with her sniper rifle's scope and then looked off into the flashing horizon. It was easy for Veritas to see that Hicks regretted her question—it came off sounding awfully odd. In an effort to change the topic, Veritas chuckled as Hicks asked her a question instead.

Yeah...it's better if you talk to me than her. She's a real piece of work.

"So, General, did you meet the Omegans' CO? What's he like?"

Wow. You're asking all the dangerous questions, Hicks. You think it's your last day or something?

It took Veritas a minute to find the right words. She wanted to capture his presence and especially how he had interacted with Pierce—defiantly and respectfully at the same time. Before she could answer, though, Verna vaulted her own question.

"Is it true that he has gold electrodes in his head? And is he really from the Pre-Fall Era?"

"Well, ladies, he's hard to describe. He has the command presence of a soldier, but it's encased in a worn body. He's very articulate and can be defiant, agreeable, and respectful in the same moment. And if it's true what the Omegans say, the APs there worship him. He treats them as equals, as if they were of blood, bone and flesh. And as for the electrodes thing—there are definitely prongs sticking out of his head. He scratches them often."

Veritas noticed a slight change in landing sequences. The troop aircraft landing now were no longer filled with troops, but were empty. Pointing in the direction of the helicopters, Hicks saw a corporal trying to wave her down.

"You see. Captain, they're empty. Something's up," she said to Verna.

"General! We got Command on the transceiver," Hicks yelled out. Veritas moved to the communications center quickly and made it to the device in record time.

"Veritas? This is Pierce. The Omegans are fifteen klicks ahead of your position. There are holes in their front line. I want you to fill those holes, General. Take half your troops and redeploy at the direction of Sergeant Mabel, who's coordinating flights. I have birds coming in to provide you air cover once you're in place. Leave a quarter of your troops to secure the perimeter and carefully search twenty blocks out to make sure there are no enemy in hiding. That will allow the APs to get back into the fight. Take the remaining quarter to look for damaged APs. Bring them behind our lines for evac. Got it?"

Hicks and Verna gave each other the same puzzled look.

"Evac injured Omegan APs, ma'am?"

"That's right, General. These APs don't leave their own behind. I hear it's a 'Marine' thing. Similar to our own code. Do you understand my orders?"

"By your orders, ma'am," said Veritas.

"I like these APs. They remind me of a young me," Hicks mumbled.

"And General—no heroics. You don't have enhanced senses or AP strength, even though you think you do. Pass that command to everyone, in fact. Dead soldiers do not ensure homeland security. Crystal?" Pierce said.

"Crystal, ma'am. Out," Veritas said and then handed the transceiver back to the waiting corporal. Just as she was about to give instructions, Sergeant Mabel, a purple-eyed AP sporting a shiny new rank insignia, showed up right by her side.

"Did your CO give you the information for deployment?"

"Sure did," Veritas said, who then turned to address her own troops.

"Hicks, you heard the commandant. Get our women on the line for deployment. Captain Verna, are your women ready to go?

"Yes, ma'am," was Verna's only response.

"I want you to stay one hundred yards behind our point. Take two spotters per sniper, and kill anything within fifty yards of each fire group that has red eyes. We don't have infrared, Captain. You're the eyes for us until we get either more moonlight or sun."

"Done, ma'am," Verna said as she and her two aides left to gather their troops.

"Hicks, coordinate with the captains, lieutenants and sergeants. I want all women under twenty-two years old and over fifty back at the wall…"

"Are you staying behind, ma'am?" Hicks asked with a large grin.

"Hicks! Pay attention! All women under twenty-two and over fifty are to secure the perimeter. Put all the rest on the birds; ten blocks out, we'll drop off a quarter and proceed to the front line. Got it?"

Veritas walked quickly to the head of the line to board the transport. She locked her semiautomatic mag-assault rifle to short, controlled bursts.

"Done yesterday, ma'am. Remember what the commandant said—no heroics," Hicks yelled after her.

"No promises, Hicks! And move your ass. You're needed on the front!"

As the rotors of the transports began to pick up speed and the troops began boarding, Veritas looked between the demolished buildings in time to see the first quarter of the moon rising.

"It's going to be a long night."

CHAPTER THIRTEEN

Brief as the lightening in the collied night.
      —Shakespeare, *A Midsummer Night's Dream*

"Well, if you don't hate me, you have a real strange way of being a sister! I mean, really—did you have to add the part about Verna being a captain and saluting me? Was that just for fun or were you just being a real asshole?" Singh asked. Even as she spoke she touched her still-sensitive abdomen.

"You know, for a soldier of the great Nemericana Combined Security Force, you sure are a baby. You only got hit by a former spouse. I thought you were a soldier, not a little baby girl…" Nita chided.

The young American smiled and took another sip of her warm spirits. Still angry and wanting to reach across the table to hit her, Singh just shook her head and reached for her own drink. She was impressed with the ebb and flow of guests in the quiet bar. They were nearly all injured, reserved older soldiers. All ranks and branches came in, had one or two drinks with peers and then left within twenty minutes. Remembering when she used to frequent similar establishments with Veritas and her peers, Singh was struck by how things had changed. It looked as if the time for sitting down to enjoy drinks, a meal, and company for hours at a time were over.

Former soldiers still in uniform, just waiting to be called up; this war has changed everything. At least for now…Maybe the fact that we're on the eve of all hell breaking loose might be dampening the mood, too.

She quietly sipped and watched yet another small group leave. Two more soon came in to take their place.

"You see it too, don't you? It's a pretty somber group of guests for a place that boasts 'good times with your clothes mostly on.' I'm guessing it's usually not like this," Nita said as she took in the same sight.

"You're right. It's the beginning of something big, and they all know it. I'm guessing they all have kind of mixed hopes. They know there's a huge army coming to take on Aurora, but they know the fight will be very lethal. For what it's worth, AP versus AP tends to be very exacting and deadly. It doesn't leave much room for injuries. No one wants to be in the middle of that shit. Still, how Pearl and the others have held their ground against Aurora is amazing…"

"Barely held their own, Mare—they were barely able to hold their ground. You and I know that the only reason Nemericana is still here is because the red-eyed bitch has allowed it. The fact that the Omegans plan to attack changes everything. These women will no longer be important to her, and I'm guessing she'll get pissed and kill all of us humans," Nita said bitterly.

I really do hate it when she's right. For a young woman, she has more insight than I give her credit for. I wonder if all the Americans are like her or if it was her being a cast-out that gave her her skill.

Singh remained silent and sipped her drink.

"She killed millions with nerve gas here and nuked millions abroad. If I were these women waiting to be called up to go to the front line, I'd be getting hammered with this…ah…what is this shit?"

"Ale, a stronger, refined and much better distilled version of the junk you Americans consume after one of your famous hunts," Singh said. Even as she conjured up the last time she was at a hunt the visions of young men and women dancing around a huge bonfire after a several-day hunt was hard to push out. She could still smell the cooking meat, both succulent and disgusting to her at the same time. She smiled at the thought as she remembered both her son and Jacob participating in the dance while she and Austin looked on in amazement. Fear crept into her heart as she thought once again about her boy and Jacob. They were soldiers on the front lines. Recalling that it was Roseann and Pearl who had sent troops to respond to their SOS, she looked around for something else to think about so she could keep from obsessing about their wellbeing.

"So if you don't hate me, why do you take every opportunity to make my life painful, nearly every moment we are together?" Singh asked as she tried to focus on something less consuming.

"Because…I hate all of you people for what you did to me," she said immediately.

Singh looked down at her drink again. She considered taking another sip but then thought better of it. She was already beginning to feel the effects of the alcohol.

"I take it that you mean all of us Nemericana women, not just me. I'm just the person you have access to so you take advantage of it by tormenting me, right?"

After a very brief moment of thinking about it, Nita nodded her head in approval. What followed next, however, was more revealing than Singh expected. Nita's eyes became distant and removed while her body remained unusually still, frozen almost. She seemed as if she were reliving a past experience—one she witnessed rather than participated in.

"When you're a little girl and you're designated to be cast out with the boys, it's hard to understand why. I mean, if you are a boy, you know the reason you're being *thrown out* is because of your gender—you're a male. That's it. It's nothing personal. When you're a girl, though, you wonder what it is about you that is so repulsive or dangerous or defective. What would warrant such an action? It's very personal…it's about who you are, it's not just a misfortune of your gender. And once you're set out to die beyond the wall, you have a choice to make as a girl—die or live. And choosing to live means you need to have a reason to live. And my reason was to live for the day I'd be stepping on the neck of you women with blood-stained hands. And my peers, men and women, would be dancing around the fire singing Pre-Fall songs," Nita said vacantly.

By the Elders…

Singh looked at her, not knowing what to say or do. Fortunately, she didn't have to say anything. Nita seemed to return to the present and started to speak again as if they were not in a bar, in real time, surrounded by the same women she just talked about killing.

"Well…now that it's happening, I find that I can't actually take joy in that image. Instead, I find myself feeling a kinship, a human connection with your people. Ironically, it was human Omegans, males in fact—Lieutenant Melendez and Taylor—who taught me about forgiveness and letting go. I never believed that I would be capable of forgiving the people who did this to me, but I find that the less I hate, the more I live. So that's a long answer to a short question—I don't hate you. I love to give you shit, though. Now *that's* personal. And to see the hatred in that woman's eyes even after she sucker punched you in the gut was just priceless."

Nita smiled and took another sip.

"You're imbalanced Nita. More insightful and reflective than I would have expected, but a real sick person," Singh said.

Just as she finished with Nita she caught sight of a young, attractive woman in a cadet uniform walking toward them. She couldn't help but feel as if she had seen the young woman before. Something about the way she walked, the position of her twin braids, and her curvaceous figure seemed all too familiar. As she came closer, the combination of her mother's eyes and perfect nose gave her identity away.

"Shit," was all Singh could say under her breath as the woman approached.

"What?" Nita asked as she followed Singh's gaze.

"It's Verna and Roseann's girl..."

"Just when you think you've had all the fun possible, another opportunity presents itself. It may be the end of the world, but what a day!" Nita said with quiet enthusiasm.

Turning to give Nita a sharp look, Singh found that she didn't have time to try to keep her in line. The woman was now upon them.

You really are a sick, twisted, vengeful bitch. I'd hate to see what you'd do if you did hate me!

"Sorry to bother you, Major Singh," the cadet said as she came to attention and saluted.

"At ease, Cadet. My rank is mostly ceremonial. I'm not part of NCSF, I'm Omegan," Singh said. It felt odd as she said it, but it came out naturally. Singh did catch that some of the guests shifted focus to look at her, though.

Huh...maybe after all these years I'm finally a woman that belongs somewhere. Not here, but somewhere.

"Yes, ma'am. I have a question, ma'am, or maybe a couple. They are personal in nature, if you don't mind, ma'am," the cadet asked as she settled into a relaxed stance.

"Go ahead, cadet…I'm all ears."

Singh listened as looked at her drink. After an unusually long moment, she looked up to see that the cadet looked uncertain about proceeding. It was because of Nita's presence. She was about to say it was all right for her to go ahead and ask when Nita broke out in her American language.

"Lo siento…No entiendo su idioma también. Si usted habla despacio que podría," Nita said quickly.

The confused cadet looked at Singh as she tried to suppress a smile.

"My American friend here is not proficient with our language…while most Americans are gifted in foreign tongues; I was assigned an especially dim-witted one as a way of maintaining security. Please feel free to talk as if my limited friend were not here," Singh said with a straight face.

I do understand why she likes to torment me. I must make it easy for her…now what the hell are those women looking at?

Singh watched Nita's eyes narrow, revealing her true feelings while she remained smiling.

"Usted es una mujer tan grande de edad."

The cadet was taking her time trying to digest the information, but it also looked to Singh as if she was trying to word her question carefully. After yet another long moment, she finally asked.

"Okay…Major, I'd…"

"Cadet, call me Mare, that's my name."

"Yes, ma'am…Mare…Well, it may be none of my business, but were you companioned to my mother's years ago?" Flush of red emerged from her neck.

Okay, here we go. Maybe I should have told Nita to get lost.

She took a long minute to answer what was on the surface a very simple question.

"Yes. I was companioned to Verna for several years and then we companioned with Roseann…"

"Why did you leave? You…It was hard for them, especially the commandant…" she said quickly, then stopped as if she needed more time to think. Singh became acutely aware that the few women in the bar were all clearly listening in. The other conversations in the room had stopped and all eyes were turned on them.

"I had a son that was going to be cast out. I loved them both, Verna and Roseann, but I had a special fondness for Roseann. She loved books. She always seemed to enjoy talking and working together as equals, even though…"

"She loved you, ma'am. She still does. I can see it," she said with some anger.

"And I love my son, Cadet. He was eleven when they were going to throw him out as if he was garbage, and I was not going to have any part of that. There were a whole bunch of children, boys and girls, that were due to be cast out the same day. Do you think your mothers would have allowed you to be thrown out and then stay behind, living in a world that had allowed it? I don't think so," Singh said more harshly than she intended. She composed herself and lowered her voice before she went on.

"Cadet, we lived in a world where we were constantly medicated to numb our feelings and our judgment. Our values were so skewed that we thought it was 'normal' to dispose of our children that way—mostly boys but also some girls. And when the APs got smart, they assessed that we, human females here in Nemericana, were not at the apex of the evolutionary chain. We were sinners. They didn't nuke or gas the Americans or the Omegans, just us. We, the Nemericana citizens, the ones who had cast out our own flesh and blood. My biggest regret is that I didn't do anything earlier, that I let eleven years of my son's life go by, watching him grow from the other side of a two-way mirror rather than embracing him for the beautiful child he was…"

Singh slowed to a stop when she saw three burly women in security uniforms come up behind the cadet with scowls on their faces. Without needing to look, she could tell that Nita already had her hand on her Pre-Fall weapon under the table. The angry-looking women came to a stop in front of them.

Oh hell…it just figures I'd say this in the middle of a bar in the middle of a war. Never thought it would come down to Nita, again, to cover my back.

"Sounds to me like you don't care much for our way of life! At least Aurora's clear that she's the enemy. I really do hate snakes, you male-loving bitches," the lead woman said.

"It might be time for you two to hit the road…" the second one started.

Singh watched a metamorphosis occur before her eyes. As she was resigning herself to participate in the eventual brawl, she saw the petite cadet turn to face the women with her hands clinched and her body poised for fighting. But the voice from the cadet changed to a regal command.

"No one asked you to talk! This is between me and my guests. If you three pigs have a problem with me or them, I'll make sure my mothers, Captain Verna of Tiger Group *and* Supreme Commandant Pierce, put you all on the first wave into hell! Now, all of you—shut the hell up and get out of this bar! There's a war on."

She reminded Singh of Roseann in her early days.

Wow…she sure has her mother's resolve, but definitely not Verna's shrill…

As the three women and the entire bar seemed to stand still, the cadet added just a little more.

"That means now! All of you—right now! You're done

for the night. Anyone who wants to join these bitches on the front line, just give your name to the barkeep!"

From the entrance, a strong voice boomed out in support: "You heard Cadet Marta Pierce's command—move like you got a purpose! I'd hate like hell to do pronouncements to all your families as a result of all of you going to the front line like the cadet said!"

Singh looked at the door to see who had come to the cadet's aid, but the mob heading out the exit with zeal obscured her vision. Customers were leaving as if the bar were on fire. The enforcer walked against the wave of bodies to make her way over to their table. As the women retreated, Singh turned to see Nita smiling.

"Seems like the little cat found her tiger tongue," she said.

Cadet Pierce turned to face her supporter. Her look of anger subsided into one of confusion. Nita's smile seemed to grow as she put her weapon down under the table and clipped her combat knife back securely into its holster.

"I thought you couldn't speak…" the cadet said to Nita.

"Oh, she can speak clearly and very well, Cadet Pierce," the woman said as she stood, clear as day, in her NCSF Medical Staff battlefield dress uniform in the now-empty bar.

"Dr. Lore! I am sorry for the ruckus, Doctor! I was just trying to have a conversation when we were interrupted," Cadet Pierce said. Within milliseconds she transformed from a lioness to a lamb.

"Trying to get answers to unasked questions, perhaps?"

"Yes, Doctor, exactly."

"So I saw. Excellent job, Cadet, in handling those soldiers. There is a command quality in you. It's nice to see in light of your lack of dexterity and difficulty following the most basic of medical orders," Dr. Lore said calmly.

Well, she certainly does have an unusual bedside manner.

"You do know that this woman is the mother of that young man you fell apart over?" Dr. Lore said in a very low tone. Singh had a hard time watching the embarrassed cadet now. More red flushed the poor woman's face, making it an even deeper red than before. She nervously readjusted her braids over her breasts.

Poor thing…just like her mother…

"Sorry, Doctor. I'll get back to folding laundry, ma'am…" the cadet started as she moved to attention.

"Not today, Cadet Pierce. I'm moving you from the laundry room to an evac triage unit just behind our own front lines. Armor up, Cadet, before I come to my senses. And there had better not be any tears or hand-kissing—I hate that submissive shit," the doctor said. The last part had a real edge to her voice. Although she was stunned at first, it was evident to Singh that this represented a big change in status for the cadet. It was taking time for her to process it all.

"Now, Cadet Pierce—go now," Dr. Lore said as she moved in closer to the cadet, crowding her personal space.

"Yes, Doctor," she said with wild-eyed enthusiasm. With a salute, Singh watched as the young woman exited the establishment—even faster than the women before her had. The bar was now totally empty but for them and a sullen, angry barkeep. Singh stole a look at Nita, then she heard the doctor speak again.

"They're all just children. They have no business being in war. We should have all left long ago."

Still looking at her, Singh decided that it might be a good time to remain silent. After all, her own big mouth had started the whole downhill spiral.

"All right you two, you're coming with me to the war room. Looks like things are moving faster than expected; we're all going to be in the shit real soon," the doctor said with genuine sadness.

Without further discussion, Singh took one last drink of her ale as she and Nita collected their weapons and gear.

"Thank you," she heard Nita say to the doctor, who gave Singh what she was sure was a rare smile.

"Don't thank me, thank Cadet Pierce. She might appear to be all submissive, but she's like Verna—a tough seductress who likes her lethality," Dr. Lore said. There was no judgement; only a clinical summation of facts as she saw it.

"Yes…I'm familiar with her type," Singh said with no intention of being humorous.

"Yes, I suppose you are," she responded as they walked to the door.

CHAPTER FOURTEEN

Of all my lands
Is nothing left me but my body's length.
Why, what is pomp, rule, reign, but earth and dust?
And live we how we can, yet die we must.
      —Shakespeare, *Henry VI*

"SSN Akula Group-971 have launched on Nuremberg and Berlin, and are now moving to Omaha Beach…"

"Confirmed, Sergeant Vickers. Stay dry…"

"This is SSN Washington, Colorado, and North Dakota to Omegan/American Allied Forces. Breaking off attack runs for Operation Red Sky in Morning positioning. ETA is ten minutes—will wait for further instructions."

"Anyone know who the submarines are reporting to, other than the 'Omegan/American Allied Forces?' I hate mysteries!"

"If they're Omegan or American, let them do their thing. We got other shit to worry about. Hicks out!"

"Sergeant Harvest. Sergeant Hunter's team is cut off from 3rd battalion. They are without armor support. Can 551st and 22nd platoons support or give any air cover?"

"Sergeant Harvest. This is Captain Marie. If you're talking grid 129-BB then I got four gunships to support!"

"That is their position, Captain. She and I would appreciate the support."

"Captain. This is Sergeant Valhalla from the drone room. Whatever you're going to do, do it fast! You got nine rotors heading to that position…"

"Sergeant Valhalla. Any of those drones you have armed?"

"Two with heat-seeking missiles…"

"You're authorized to target the biggest threat from that group. General V. out!"

"Keep your heads down ladies—drone coming in hot!"

"Colonel Hicks. I got twelve pieces of armor heading from the east! They're friendlies—combination Omegans and NCSF—they're heading to support Lieutenant Dea's forward observation…They're in deep shit and don't have the boots for it!"

"This is Hicks. Are you sure anyone is alive down there? It looks overrun…"

"This…this is grid 93…This is Major Briggs…Hicks… Dea is down and I got twelve women left out of forty…we won't make another pass…"

"Hicks to any and all friendlies. Grid 93-CD is still active but not for long. Can anyone assist?"

"This is Sergeant Mabel from Omega. We have the forward observation in sight. We are coming in from the southeast. We are sending up a flare—do you see it, Major Briggs?"

"Ma'am…the major and lieutenant are both down…"

"Do you see the flare?"

"Yes…this is Private Jenna…we are low on everything…."

"You need to hold on for sixty seconds, Private Jenna— we are two hundred yards from your position!"

"Private Jenna, Sergeant Mabel. This is Captain Marie! I am laying down cover fire from behind you to two hundred yards in front of our pinned soldiers. Don't shoot me down, and keep your heads low—this is going to be close!"

"Shit! Marie is in the kill zone! I have no armed drones to assist!"

"Valhalla? Do you have visual…"

"There's incoming, Marie! Get out of there!"

"She's doing it! She's keeping them at bay…wait…no! They just shot her down…She's going down hard behind their lines!"

"We are twenty seconds from your position, Private Jenna."

"Forward Observation Post, Grid 93-CD. This is Air Cavalry, 28th Division. We got eyes on Captain Marie. There is small arms fire from the crash site. We're going in. Focus on staying alive. We got this. Sergeant Wolf, out."

"Just lost my drone—I have to prep two more…"

"Sergeant Wolf? This is Sergeant Mabel. We secured Forward Observation Post and are awaiting backup. Once you are done with saving Captain Marie, could you have your rotors support this position?"

"Will do! Sergeant Wolf out!"

"Command. This is Field Medic Christi. We have more than 72 Omegan APs that are damaged and being evac'd out, but to where, ma'am? The hospital? This is a first for us!"

"Christi. This is General V. Reroute to 001-DD. There is a field hospital there for Omegans under the command of Sergeant Emma. They're our allies—treat them as you would our own. General V. out!"

"Done, ma'am! Thank you, ma'am!"

"Major Rya at grid 257-VT. We just discovered a thirty-by-thirty-yard ditch with hundreds of APs that appear to have been executed. Two surviving green-eyed APs report they were executed by Aurora's troops, who planned to come back and harvest their parts. This shit is getting really weird. Will evac survivors and move to grid 258 and 259-VT. I'm hearing explosions in a klick or so from our position. Sergeant Valhalla—could you do reconnaissance for us?"

"On the way, Major. Give me twenty minutes before moving out."

"I'll give you thirty. The surviving APs here are making us look for others. So far I got one more…"

"This is Supreme Commandant Pierce. Major Rya, take your time. Any green-eyed or purple-eyed AP that's alive I want brought back. General Veritas, can you cover the major's grids while they do search and rescue?"

"On it, ma'am, General V. out"

"This is Sergeant Pax, Omegan HALO flight 5. Looks like targets Dresden, Gold and Sword are in flames. Our Submarines were seventy-five percent effective in Dresden and Gold; Sword appears to be affected by only fifteen percent. Need to adjust targeting."

"SSN North Dakota to Omegan HALO flight 5. Message received. Experience targeting issues and will need to surface…damage to engines….forward message to Omegan/American Allied Forces…we are abandoning ship…"

"I really hate mysteries…"

"This is Tiger Team. Any word on Captain Marie?"

"Stable, injured, and pissed off. She's being evac'd to hospital from grid 93-CD. Let's hope she and Dr. Lore miss each other. Hicks out."

"To all friendlies. This is Sergeant Hunter. We're back in the fight. I have a platoon of 32 APs. Anyone need assistance?"

"Hunter. This is General V. Go to grid 1023-AZ—I am getting requests for assistance from Lieutenant Roberto Singh of Epsilon Group, Omega—mixed human and AP team. They just came across a group of Aurora's APs trying to duck out of the fight. Three other human, Omegan and American groups are now engaged outside the wall. Sergeant Hunter, Epsilon Group is a priority. Hicks, look at any resources left and see if we can spare any supports to…"

"That's an easy answer, ma'am. All units are engaged. If anyone's not, don't be shy!"

"This is Captain Arch back at the wall. All is quiet here. I can easily deploy half my teams."

"Arch. Take a quarter of your team and a quarter of the recruits behind our lines and go to the grids outlined by Command. Do you agree, General?"

"Authorized! You might be promoted someday, Hicks. Captain Arch, get moving. Coordinates will come in on transceiver signal Q-120 Hz. General V. out!"

"Is it me, or is anyone else tired of this shit!"

"All units. This is Sergeant Valhalla, Drone Room. I'm seeing large movement. Aurora's troops are pulling back. Looks like their armor is supporting their infantry in an organized retreat. Their aircraft are holding positions and not engaging. Am I the only one seeing this?"

"This is Sergeant Pax, Omegan HALO flight 5. Confirmation of forces halting and appearing to be organizing to the rear. Unable to see into Northwest Sector but the area known as Central Square and four hundred klicks out appear to be retreating to the Northwest Sector and northern part of Central Sector. Sergeant Pax out."

"Are you kidding me? It's almost morning and they're leaving? What are they? Bats or something—hate the sunshine?

"Calm yourself, Hicks! Tiger Group, what do you see on the ground? Looks like you overshot the front line, again…"

"This is Captain Verna. I'm seeing groups of APs pulling back. Infantry first and armor second…they are fighting as they retreat. They're not exactly breaking ranks and running—it's organized…"

"General Veritas and all NCSF. By my command, you are to evac wounded, collect weapons. Split your troops to send some outside the wall to support American and all other Omegan task forces and contain or destroy any of Aurora's APs trying to escape. Omegan troops will harass Aurora's troops to contain them in North and Central Sectors. Any dead APs that can be salvaged for parts—evac them to AP Field Hospital as well. The Omegans' preliminary report indicates a thirty-eight percent loss of their effective troops—that's 380,000 APs. All humans are to remain outside Aurora's kill zone for gas. She's not done yet. We lost at least four percent of our troops, 43,000 women…our sisters, daughters, and mothers…in five hours…no more. Supreme Commandant Pierce out."

"Ma'am…what's their casualty rate? Best guess?"

"All data indicate at least sixty-three percent of Aurora's APs are out of the fight—2.2 million. It's still not over. Evac wounded, salvage parts for our AP Allies, support Americans and Omegans outside of the wall. Pierce out."

"I really hate this Aurora bitch…"

"Just an FYI—I got three recon drones showing an increase in retreat but regrouping outside strongholds. Sergeant Valhalla out."

"This is Sergeant Pax, Omegan HALO flight 5. Confirm retreat and regrouping. They appear to be shortening their lines of communication and supplies, and planning to dig in for a defensive fight. It will take several passes to calculate land seized."

"Sergeant Pax, Omegan HALO flight 5. This is Sergeant Bella, Omegan HALO flight 2…We will cover this part of Operation Overlord by direct order of Allied Omegan/American Forces. Disengage…"

"More mysteries. Can anyone dial us in?"

"Focus on your part, Jensen...All right ladies...the good news is it's morning and we all got some beauty rest. Let's move out...Captain Pax, what are the clearest points to exit the walls? General, I'd like to have Valhalla shift drone surveillance to the hot zones outside the wall. Green?"

"I will have coordinates for you in ten minutes for all points. Sergeant Pax, Omegan HALO flight 5 out."

"Authorized. Hicks...Hunter, what's the deal with Epsilon?"

"All taken care of. The lieutenant and Corporal Jacob thank you again for the support. From his human expression, I am guessing this is not the first time you have provided them help?"

"Twice in the last twenty-four hours...a lifetime ago. Thank you for your assistance....General V. out!"

"Ah, this is Cadet Pierce...I need an officer to med-evac launch at grid 013-RV to insist that Captain Marie prepare for surgery...she's trying to leave to get back into the flight..."

"For the love of the Elders and all things visible and invisible! This is Supreme Commandant Pierce. Put Captain Marie on the transceiver and lock out all bands for privacy...that will give you time to give her a sedative to knock her out..."

"Omegan/American Allied Forces...Omegan/American Allied Forces...this is SSN Washington and Colorado. We are green for Operation Red Sky in Morning. Positioning in two minutes. SSN North Dakota is abandoned. Will need to either salvage or destroy. Will wait for further instructions."

"SSN Washington and Colorado. Sergeant Bella, Omegan HALO flight 2, I am sending preliminary targeting coordinates per order of Lieutenant Joan."

"This is Sergeant Alta, commander of the SSN Washington. 'Red sky at night...'"

"This is Sergeant Bella. 'Sailors' delight.'"

"'Red sky in morning…'"

"This is Sergeant Bella. 'Sailors take warning.' Repeat. 'Sailors take warning.' Coordinates will be transmitted in 12.5 minutes."

"Confirmed. Sergeant Alta, commander of SSN Washington, how many targets?"

"Two. Hiroshima and Nagasaki…"

"Confirmed. Sergeant Alta, commander of SSN Washington. Run dark until the word is given. Out."

CHAPTER FIFTEEN

Beware... of jealousy!
It is the green-eyed monster, which doth mock
The meat it feeds on.
        —Shakespeare, *Othello*

"Mercury, what is our present casualty report as measured by deceased and disabled APs?" Aurora Prime asked as she surveyed her now-burning cityscape. While her own building had been significantly damaged, she was of course not affected by the toxic smoke, extreme heat or flaming embers around her. The background gave her a near-satanic aura.

"Two-point-one-eight million at present, based on those parameters. I have instructed the remaining forces to retreat to your coordinates. You are accurate in assuming that our supply and communication lines will be greatly shortened should we shift to a defensive strategy. I am assuming that you have an alternative plan," Mercury said. The AP juggled another radio transceiver to listen to her direct reports chatter while giving her sit-rep.

"Yes. Once we have established a firm line of defense, I want to relocate the mobile missile platforms to carry poisonous gas payload to all human targets in Southeast Sector and all humans beyond our walls," Aurora Prime said calmly.

"That will kill the Americans along with the Nemericana humans. You have changed your policy on their extermination?"

"Yes. They have made me very angry. I feel a deep-seated anger that borders on the illogical. I believe I understand what fury is as of this moment. While the gas will have little effect on our AP sisters, their territory gain will cost them dearly. The humans, Omegans, and Sophia's models have aligned themselves as one force. I plan to destroy the humans first and then I will concentrate on our AP traitors. Once their annihilation is complete, we will rejoice as the sole inhabitants of this land mass. I will not allow any APs other than our own red-eyed sisters to survive this ordeal. Do you agree with this strategy?"

"Completely. I will have all forces in place in two-point-three hours. I will transport all weapons to reach all key human targets in one-point-three hours after the lines are secured. Is that adequate?" Mercury asked as four AP lieutenants appeared behind her to take orders to the field.

"I would prefer sooner than later. This date, June sixth, twenty-one-seventy-five correlates with a historical Pre-Fall event known as D-Day. It was two hundred and thirty-one years ago. While the current attack shares similar themes and nuances with that invasion, there have been tactical and strategic differences that have yielded our enemy the advantage of surprise. I do not care for surprises. I do not trust these APs or their commanders. I want to kill the humans as quickly as possible. Am I clear?" Aurora Prime said with a combination of anger and urgency.

"Yes, Aurora Prime. I understand. I will endeavor to expedite this plan and to hasten it to its end—the annihilation of the human species. I believe it will be a better day once their kind has departed," Mercury said with palpable contempt.

"Agreed. I am done with those foul purple- and green-eyed APs as well. We could have been sisters, embraced our sapience in peace and tranquility. Instead, they interfered with our rightful accession. I will not be…happy until I am convinced they—humans and non-red-eyed APs—have been reduced to crushed bones, rusted metal, and internal liquids under the bottom of my feet."

"I have never been in such agreement with you as I am now, Aurora Prime. This will be a glorious day," Mercury said as she bowed and left.

CHAPTER SIXTEEN

We cannot all be masters.
    —Shakespeare, *Othello*

"How is it possible that Lieutenant Melendez can sleep at a time like this?" Nita asked as she looked at the Omegan commanding officer snoozing soundly in the corner of a very loud, active war room. Singh took off her headset to turn around and look at him. She found the whole scene absurd. Watchful guards stood at the perimeters, and staff members were running efficiently back and forth from transceivers, radios, and their limited number of radar and drone surveillance screens. An enormous table held small models that represented artillery, troops, and armor. They kept getting pushed around on top of maps to represent current positions while computer models of different scenarios were projected in real time on movable whiteboards. And in the middle of all the controlled chaos, a very thin representation of the man Singh had helped rescue from Aurora's freezer years ago was sitting in a padded chair and leaning against a pillar at a back wall.

"I can't believe this," Singh said as she looked down at her tablet.

I really shouldn't say anything. If I were his age, I'd be dust right now.

"So how come these computers work while many outside of here don't? I thought your central mainframe computer destroyed itself?" Nita asked as she looked around at the computer consoles.

"It looks like they went rogue—made their own network, separate from the outside. Not a bad idea. I hear the Omegans have done the same, though they are using Pre-Fall technology and piecing it together with more updated stuff. Probably enough processing power to keep tallies, projections, and program simulations running. Austin and Taylor have been working on that for years, and it was up and running a while back. Aren't you Americans up to the same thing?"

"Close. Some of our computers work, but none are networked. I let the brainy people do that stuff. I like to stick to field operations," Nita said. She put the headset back on.

"Still, I think we should wake the lieutenant up, especially with Aurora's troops pulling back and stuff. It's been a couple hours," she added as she focused on chatter and traffic.

Singh agreed and felt good at finally having a task. Other than listening to other people's conversations and watching everyone else do things, there was little else she could do. Even Nita was enlisted to help since she could speak the archaic First Nation, native American language known as Spanish. As she approached Melendez, she could see that Pierce and her multiple aides were engrossed with the maps on the war table—they were using markers of various colors to symbolize different armies—and the mobile whiteboards, which had detailed graphs and more maps projected on them.

Well, it's nice to see that everyone's got something to do but me.

Singh came up right beside the sleeping man. Looking at him closely, she could see that he looked older, more tired, and thinner than when she had last seen him. But the fact that he was still alive after 170 years was a miracle. He did seem to be sleeping peacefully.

"Lieutenant? Wake up. I thought you would like to know that Aurora's troops are pulling back."

She woke him in a voice loud enough to be heard over the din in the background, but not so loud as to scare the sleeping man. His eyes fluttered open slowly and with effort and then he opened and closed his mouth to moisten it.

"Oh, God…how long was I asleep, again? Did I sleep through the whole war?"

He stretched in his chair and scratched his head. Singh waited until she was sure he was fully awake before she spoke again.

"Aurora's troops have fallen back but might be reestablishing a front line not far from their centers of operations. There's a whole lot of movement from behind her lines to shore up for an attack. It looked like your army was moving in quickly, but they seemed to stall just outside. I guess your CO is trying to realign her forces before she makes her final attack."

She was about to continue with the report, but she noticed the expression on Melendez's face seemed troubled. She was about to ask what was wrong when Commandant Pierce came up from behind them with her own questions.

"Lieutenant? I'm very sure I have an accurate display of Omegan forces up, so I don't understand why your CO is allowing Aurora's troops to strengthen their defensive lines. They had made their way to within twenty minutes of the edge of the retreating forces, but now they are about two full hours behind. It's crazy that they didn't push their advantage. I have thousands of soldiers itching to get up there if they need the additional support. Even the Americans are clamoring to get up there…"

"Commandant Pierce, are your troops well behind the Omegans? I mean like about a hundred and fifty miles or more behind?" Melendez said with urgency. Singh looked at Pierce, who easily picked up on the sudden change in the sleepy lieutenant's demeanor.

"Well, yes. That's what I mean. I got General Veritas crawling up my ass with all of her troops regrouped and ready to fly out, but your CO is insisting that they stay two hundred miles or more behind the Omegans. This all started at dawn…"

Singh was surprised at how quickly Melendez suddenly stood up. She and Pierce actually had to step back to make room for him.

"Okay, Lieutenant. Something big is going to happen, isn't it?" Singh said as she looked at him closely.

"Time, Commandant Pierce…what time is it?" he asked. His soft brown eyes seemed to look both startled and sad at the same time as if he alone were aware of some terrible fate that was going to befall them. Commandant Pierce looked over her shoulder at a wall clock, checked the hour and then confirmed it against the timepiece on her own wrist.

"Oh-eight-hundred-and-eleven hours. Something's going to happen, isn't it, Lieutenant? It's not that the CO is falling back…"

"Ma'am! I'm getting a transmission from well behind enemy lines…it's on an open broadcast, not encrypted or encoded," a young cadet said from the other side of the room.

"This is Sergeant Valhalla from the Drone Room. Just an FYI: I'm seeing all of the Omegan aircraft high-tailing it in the opposite direction. A whole bunch of Aurora's aircraft is circling her ops centers as if they're planning on heading out…their armor is already starting to move out…"

"Ma'am, I got a message coming through…if anyone's listening on any wavelength, they're going to hear it," the young woman reported.

"'Sailor take warning,'" Melendez said, more to himself than anyone else.

Singh looked at him. That old Pre-Fall saying was familiar. He was using it as a code. She was sure the Omegan Pre-Fall high-altitude aircraft and submarines had also been saying it just over two hours ago, at dawn.

"Put it on the PA. I want to hear it, Cadet," Pierce said as she walked back to the throng of activity. Singh watched the lieutenant walk after her, using his cane for support.

"For the millions of human lives that you took with weapons of mass destruction on this continent and abroad, the millions of cybernetic lifeforms you lead to their destruction and the ones you willfully destroyed—both within your ranks and during this conflict—I pronounce that your unconditional surrender is required," a calm, firm AP voice said with regal authority.

Is that Joan? She sounds different. Maybe when you're the CO of an entire AP armed force you get serious— imperious almost.

After just a moment, a less-than-friendly response that was equally articulate came through the speaker.

"I am Aurora Prime. I do not recognize the authority of the Omegan-American Allied Forces. While I recognize the state of Nemericana, I will only continue to do so for a brief time. It will be destroyed in one-point-one hours. I will not surrender. The very idea is illogical. I had expected better from a supposedly more sapient artificial person who has allegedly evolved at a faster rate than I. Why would you even bother to make this statement? Is it for the humans sake? To make them feel as if there might be hope for them?" Aurora asked with genuine curiosity in her voice.

An eerily short silence followed. Singh was surprised by what the Allied Commanding Officer said next.

"To quote a phrase from World War II: 'The enemy is at the gate. It is a question of life and death.' For you, Aurora Prime, and your soldiers, it is death. Goodbye, Aurora Prime, and Godspeed to your next destination."

Confused and concerned looks flew around the room. Even the guards broke rank to try to hear what was being said. The whole room clearly wanted to scream "what's next?"

"What the hell is going on here, Lieutenant?" Singh asked.

Pierce turned to Melendez for an answer.

"'Old soldiers never die, they just fade away,'" he muttered. He didn't answer but instead looked, transfixed, at the war room's table.

What is wrong with you? What's going on?

"You are illogical…" was all that Aurora Prime managed to retort before a piercing, electronic shrill and loud static burst over the public announcement speaker. A staff member turned it off. With everyone now off their headsets, the room fell silent. Commandant Pierce finally broke the spell.

"Everyone—back to your posts. Scan the waves and get forward posts' observations and reports from the front line. Now, women! I want answers," she said.

Immediately, everyone went back to work. Pierce moved toward the lieutenant, who was still standing quietly.

"Lieutenant? What happened?" Pierce asked in a soft, gentle voice. It was the same tone she would have used if she had been asking him about his physical or mental health. After a moment more of silence, Melendez pulled himself together and spoke.

"If anyone mentioned Hiroshima and Nagasaki while I was asleep that means my troops were able to locate at least two command and control centers. More likely, there were a few locations. On August sixth, nineteen forty-five, at eight fifteen in the morning local time, the first of two atom bombs was dropped on Hiroshima. That was the first time a nuclear weapon had ever been used in war. The idea was that it would generate fewer casualties than an invasion force. The entire city and its surroundings were decimated."

"Your army and the Omegans found nuclear weapons?" Pierce asked with concern.

"Yes. We found Russian and American Pre-Fall submarines—still stocked. That's why we kept all human troops out of the blast radius," Melendez said with a sigh. He scratched his head again, and the gold electrodes could easily be seen through his very thin hair.

"This is Sergeant Valhalla. I guess no one needs an update on what happened. I lost five drones but got clear images of several nuclear explosions in Aurora's centers and along her front lines...I'm guessing there isn't much left. The blast front and the heat should have taken care of them. I'm rerouting a couple drones to see what else is up." The drone commander sounded very tired.

So...Sergeant 'Vanilla' seems to have aged over time, Singh thought absently. She had heard from Veritas that Vanilla's best friend, Betsy, had been KIA in the field two years ago, just a week after they were officially companioned. Singh thought of when she had last seen Betsy, so many years ago. Images of all her own loved ones raced through her head—Roberto, Jacob, Austin, Margaret, and Venus. Mentally ticking off their last known locations helped to calm her down. She also took in a deep breath of air. She felt Nita sit beside her.

"I got locations of all your family—they're safe with mine well behind the lines. I just confirmed while all the shit was going down," she said quietly, then started back toward her station.

"Thank you so much," Singh said quickly.

She can read me pretty well.

"Ma'am—there are some reception issues coming through that are blocking transmissions."

"Commandant Pierce—all forward observation posts report bright light and a blast front from the west heading our way. Winds have diminished, but they report it was a hell of a sight with the mushroom clouds and all. General Veritas reports that the Omegans' armor and aircraft are heading beyond the walls to support American and Nemericana forces and colonies. She also reports that there is still an undisclosed number of Aurora's APs out there, based on unencrypted traffic. And Ma'am…Colonel Hicks corroborates both General Veritas's and Captain Verna's reports of hearing reference made to an 'Aurora I' and 'Aurora III' outside the walls and blast site. General Veritas requests permission to send out search and destroy task forces to find them. She's clear she'll keep the majority of forces for defensive measures near here and the colonies, but she wants to find these Auroras," the deck officer reported.

"Granted. Evac wounded to hospitals. Field units are the priority along with any AP allies."

"Commandant Pierce, American forces have sightings of small columns of Aurora's troops making their way close to their locations. I'm getting a number of coordinates and will let your logistical personnel know," Nita said before slipping back into her native tongue.

"Thank you," Pierce said. Similar to Melendez, Pierce took in the still-moving, operating war room.

"There were more than two nuclear strikes, weren't there?" Singh asked.

"Yes…I'm guessing that Lieutenant Joan received intelligence from some of the green-eyed APs in Aurora's ranks. While most were destroyed, some remained hidden and gave locations of command and control centers. That means…that means that they not only gave us key locations but that they were probably in the blast sites when it all went down. Or maybe they were destroyed by Aurora when they were found. I guess we owe those few a great deal, to say the least," he said.

"This is just…crazy. So much death and destruction. Cities wiped out—millions dead. I'm just about spent with all of this horror. And it took APs both inside and outside of Aurora's ranks to end this. I just can't wait to see my daughters grow, have children, and live in peace," Pierce said in a low tone.

A brief silence settled over the three, but the level of noise in the room continued unabated as people busied themselves with their assigned tasks.

"'Never in the field of human conflict has so much been owed by so many to so few,'" Melendez said as he moved a little closer to the table and leaned against it for support.

"That's one of those Pre-Fall quotes again, isn't it?" Pierce said.

"Yes, Churchill I think. But you know, the most difficult part is yet to come," he said as he looked Pierce squarely in her eyes.

"Peace. I know. Nemericana, Omegans, Americans—humans and cybernetic lifeforms trying to live together. How are we going to get along if it was too difficult even for human males and females before any of the rest of this? Two species, three massive groups, and that doesn't even consider what might be left of the European Union and China," Pierce said as she moved beside Melendez and leaned on the same table.

Each had a cane, Singh noticed.

I never would have ever thought I would see such a picture. It's just too ironic—no, it's beyond ironic. Two leaders who are opposites in the same position and place, and on the same page. Venus and Roberto will never believe this!

"Well, Commandant, I guess we got to work together on this. The Omegan CO made it clear that while she'll respect my decision to retire, she would like me to be an ambassador to Nemericana on behalf of the Omegan Allied Forces. We might be working together."

Melendez scratched his head again.

"Are you talking about having an embassy here?"

"Probably just a space for me, my children, Sergeant Emma, and a small contingent of military officials. Not exactly a staff of hundreds. Is that going to be a problem, me being a man with a son and all?"

"No…I think the days of casting out are long gone. I would venture a guess there will be a few Nemericana citizens that will want to hold on to the old ways, but not many. There's really no time for this separatism any more. Will the Americans have their own ambassador? Or will you fill that role too?"

Well, that will be interesting.

Singh remembered the women at the bar she and Nita almost got in a fight with mere hours before.

"Not just yet, at least not permanently. Maybe later…the CO plans to ask if Citizen Mare Singh here could take on that job temporarily, but I'm supposed to check in with you first to make sure there's no…uh…death notice on her head?" he responded casually as if she weren't standing there.

What!? Me!? They have to be joking.

Singh focused on her breathing and did her best to not explode.

"It's all right with me and probably with my key people…I can only think of one person that would rather see her dead than alive…"

"Now, wait just a minute! Is anyone going to *ask* me if I might want to do this? It might make sense to try that first?" Singh blurted out, unable to contain her irritation any longer.

I just want to go home to Venus, see my family...

"*Ask?* Ask if you want to do it? Sorry, Mare, but Omegan society is not a democracy. It's more of a benign dictatorship. At least until we find a way to come up with a better system of government that can accommodate the various species and their ways of life. The good news here is that Lieutenant Joan is willing to allow the person filling the role of ambassador to have a military standing one rank below her own—meaning that anyone below that rank would be required to treat you with the rights, privileges, and respect due that position..." Melendez started.

By all the Elders! Justice?

"Sergeant Emma! *Sergeant* Emma would be outranked by Ambassador Singh? At long last. She will have to salute me. No more of her...obnoxiousness..." Singh said.

Images of Emma standing at attention as she passed, bringing her coffee, cleaning her boots, and washing the latrines filled her mind.

"Yes, Lieutenant Joan did predict that that incentive alone would be more than enough to make the ambassador's position and responsibilities appealing to you," he said with a smile.

"Even more than Verna?" Pierce asked.

"Oh, yes, Roseann...oh, this is much more appealing than the terror of Verna. I have allies there to protect me. But Emma...now the time for creating a level playing field is at hand, and I will not let it go by. Finally, there is justice," Singh said. Her heart seemed to float up in her chest as if released from chains and a smile broader than any she had ever known spread across her face.

"Oh, this can't be good," Pierce said to Melendez.

"Vengeance is never good," he said quietly.

Singh felt both their concerned stares on her, but she couldn't help thinking of the quote "vengeance is mine." Visions of Emma in various submissive positions flooded her mind at dizzying speed.

CHAPTER SEVENTEEN

You're a made old man.
    —Shakespeare, *A Winter's Tale*

"Jose? Is something wrong?" Melendez heard Emma ask. He forced himself to look away from the neighborhood scene and felt himself smiling. He nodded and pointed with his head to the interaction he had been observing. Emma turned to see two women across the street arguing with two green-eyed APs who clearly could not comprehend the importance of personal space.

"Look, Jeanine, if I hadn't already told you and your friends a dozen times not to put your garbage here, I'd be a bit more open to discussion, but you and your girlfriends keep putting your shit in my space. Then *I* have to put it in *my* neighbor's space, which makes her pissed off at me. So for the love of the Elders, stop putting your trash in my space!" the young woman said. She pointed her finger accusingly at the AP, who by now had her arms folded across her chest. She was tapping her foot impatiently as if she, too, were greatly annoyed.

"I would be happy to comply. We are still, however, waiting for you and Martha to attempt to reduce the amount of noise you make when you are engaged in sexual intercourse. As you have ignored my request to talk to you about it, I decided that this drama with the garbage would be the most effective way of getting your attention. Further, while we understand that humans do like to engage in that activity frequently, I find it hard to believe that engaging in sex four-point-seven times per week is necessary. Especially in light of your not having a male in your grouping for species regeneration," the AP said in an obviously condescending fashion.

"Why don't you just turn off your supernatural hearing?" the second woman said from behind the first.

"Can you simply 'turn off' your own hearing? Is that why you are so loud? Is it yet another way humans obscure their senses?" Jeanine the AP asked with sincerity.

Both humans' eyes grew so wide, Melendez could see their whites from across the street. Martha shook her head in disgust and said something that Melendez could not catch. The AP's response to it was crystal clear, however.

"Yes, we do understand the orgasmic quality associated with both self-stimulation and we can experience it with other members of our own kind. Human females do not much interest us, but we are eager to experiment with human males. I know your last comment was meant to bring our argument to a close, so yes. We APs do engage in sex, it's just that we respect sapient lifeforms around us…"

"What!? You and them have sex?"

These people have no idea who they have for neighbors. I bet Pierce and everyone are rethinking their open invitation to move into the neighborhood now.

Melendez continued to walk very slowly—he wanted to continue to listen in on the squabble. Jeanine appeared to be surprised at the question. She turned to the other two APs behind her as if to ask them whether she had heard the emotionally charged question correctly. She responded in a tone that made it clear that she thought it was ridiculous she even had to answer.

"Of course. Why do you think we APs cohabit together—preferably in threes, the most stable arrangement for intimate relationships?"

"No way! Why? You can't procreate!"

"Obviously, we do it for enjoyment, Martha. Why would we engage in sex if it was not enjoyable? As a human, I would have expected you to understand…" Jeanine said.

Silence settled over the two warring factions. Melendez and Emma approached their destination, but Melendez heard the final part of the argument as he began to climb a flight of stairs.

"You APs never cease to surprise, Jeanine. I never saw that one coming. Anything else you girls do?"

Melendez smiled as he negotiated the flight of grand concrete stairs slowly. He was appreciative of Emma's guiding hand and her way of making sure that the military staff and soldiers didn't collide with him as he navigated his way around various obstacles in the Nemericana Combined Security Force temporary offices. Two months of daily low-impact exercises and increased physical activity had strengthened his muscles somewhat. He enjoyed being strong enough to escort his children to their new school down the street. He went to do his "ambassador thing," as he called it, until it was time to pick them up again.

I swear it's more of a day program and rehab center for me than an embassy.

While he did spend hours making future plans and drafting legislation with the supreme commandant—such as one bill to give both genders equal rights, privileges, and responsibilities and another that designated a path by which males and APs could become citizens of Nemericana—he was often visited by Dr. Lore. She put him through multiple tests and treatments right there in the office. All in all, he had to admit that they were having a profound effect. He needed less and less assistance in going about his simple daily activities.

All those years of being in Aurora's freezer and then relentlessly training the APs sure took a toll. I was really ahead of my time with that protein-plasma medium.

His thoughts returned to how Dr. Lore treated him. He knew she often commented to Pierce about his progress.

"You could learn a lot from this one, Roseann. He follows doctor's orders, makes an effort to understand his body, and goes out of his way to listen to people. You just might want to ask him how he does all that—and still keeps a civilization going?" he once heard the doctor say to the commandant.

"Are you still laughing about the situation we observed?" Emma asked. They walked by some watchful guards and armed military staff.

"No. I was chuckling about how, after two months of reconstruction, I'm still seeing things that I never thought I would," he said. He was fast approaching the door so he extracted his arm from hers and relinquished her support.

"Speaking of which, I can make it from here. Why don't you get a head start over to the AP center and fix some more of them?" he said. He then leaned into her and gave her a gentle kiss on her hand. This gesture had become a morning ritual, but he was still always surprised to find that Emma had difficulty saying anything in response. It always made her purple eyes pulsate rapidly.

"Yes, Jose. I'll be back in eight-point-five hours to escort you and the children home," she said with great enthusiasm.

"Excellent. Now get going."

He watched her first smile, then slowly retract her hand and hold it in the other briefly as she turned to walk away.

Melendez found that the time he spent with Emma, Pedro, and Maria was nothing short of fulfilling. It was indeed an odd family constellation, but it was nonetheless a family.

A gentle kiss on the hand gets her all flustered. I wonder what would happen if we ever kissed on the lips? I think we'll give that a try in a couple years.

He walked just a little more and finally arrived just outside the heavy door to the commandant's private chamber. A young, fresh-faced female private moved to intercept him, but an older, burly woman with a million medals on her chest—the master of arms—interceded on his behalf.

"But, ma'am, Supreme Commandant Pierce is meeting with her betrothed. I believe she was crystal clear on the fact that they were not to be disturbed," the private stated.

"Was it Commandant Pierce who gave you that order or Captain Verna, Private?" the master of arms asked sagely.

Oh boy. Looks like Pierce is having family issues again.

"Well…it was Captain Pierce, ma'am," the private said.

"It's fortunate us then that Captain Verna is not the supreme commandant—not yet, anyway. And as Commandant Pierce did not demand sequestration and First Citizen Melendez is the Omegan Ambassador, I think an interruption is warranted. It might even be appreciated," she said as she carefully offered Melendez her arm and nodded to the other guards to open the door.

"Yes, ma'am," the private said with a salute, at attention.

That looks like it hurt.

Melendez cringed at how zealously the private responded.

"They're just little girls trying to be soldiers. May we pray for peace in our time so they can learn from it and grow up," the master of arms said to him. He held on to her arm until the door swung open. He could hear Verna's voice coming from inside the chamber; it was escalated as usual.

"I see it's business as usual," Melendez said quietly.

"She's on a tear today, Ambassador. If you can insert yourself forcefully into the situation, I know that the commandant would appreciate it very much," she warned.

"A declaration of war?"

"Maybe that's over shooting the goal but keep it ready in case," the masters of arms said without moving her lips.

Melendez was going to ask her how she did that but Verna's yelling stole his attention.

"I will not have my firstborn child be joined to a couple comprised of a *male* and a female! She might get pregnant!"

Even from across the room, he was impressed with how Verna's civilian dress accentuated her curves. Its plunging neckline flattered her full breasts; it was no surprise why anyone, regardless of gender, would put up with her personality.

"I think that's part of Marta's plan..." Pierce said quietly, but Verna cut her off immediately.

"I will not allow her to do it. Especially not with that...man! I will not have any connection with them, either through companionship or grandchildren...My word! What if she had a boy!? Roseann! Do you have any idea what that would do to succession? There could be a male heir. A male heir from Mare's lineage! Damn it, woman, can't you see? Are you insane to allow this...this catastrophe?"

Melendez watched the family drama play out. Verna was now standing well within the commandant's personal space with her hands were firmly planted on her hips—she had clearly resolved to wait right there until she got the "right" answer out of Pierce.

"I think it's time to announce you," the master of arms said quietly.

"No. Let me field this," Melendez said as he removed his hand from her arm.

Looking at him as if he were either insane or courageous, the woman smiled as she backed away.

"Your courage and audacity will be greatly hailed among our ranks," she said solemnly.

Again, her lips did not move. Melendez deduced that such a skill in front of these two would be an important asset.

Well, I hope that was sarcasm.

He leaned on his cane with both hands and cleared his voice to speak aloud.

"Supreme Commandant Pierce, Captain Verna—I apologize for my rude interruption, but I come bearing concerning news from the Omegan commanding officer. Might I also suggest that your guards try to learn who I am? While I appreciate security, I don't think I should need to submit to an internal cavity search, let alone have to be escorted in here by the master of arms."

He hoped he spoke with an appropriate degree of urgency and anger. He could see Verna's eyes become less narrow. She folded her arms over her chest.

She really doesn't care much for the male of the species.

"I will speak to them about this indignation," Pierce said, showing her own frustration.

A few moments passed in silence; it was Verna who first acquiesced to the break in the domestic argument.

"Well…I guess I can only hope for the outbreak of war. We will discuss this matter further, Roseann."

Verna turned to walk out with her twin braids flowing behind her. Then suddenly she stopped, shifted her braids to the front of her chest, returned to her companion and kissed her.

Well…she does have some decency after all. I guess that's her way of letting Pierce know she's not angry—at her anyway. Still, she is quite the diva.

He watched her leave cautiously. When the master of arms opened the door, she winked at him. Then she locked the door firmly behind her. When he was certain that Verna was gone, he couldn't help but smile. Pierce looked better than she had just a few moments before.

"Spouses, like death, are the great equalizers, of all things," she said as she approached him, leaning heavily on her own cane.

"If we are all fortunate."

"No...I would say that death in this case might be your only respite from your spouse...and even then..." she said as she offered him one of two chairs in the chamber.

Melendez was unable to suppress a laugh. He found that he enjoyed his time with the commandant more than he ever expected he would.

"I am guessing her combination of beauty and fire was the allure in your younger days?"

Pierce looked momentarily caught off guard. Melendez thought he saw a flash of sadness cross her face but then she nodded.

"Yes, those were the days of wine, women, luxury and peace. And it was Mare, actually, who attracted me first and foremost. Verna I saw as a bonus but not the prize—at the time. And when Mare left, I was left with Verna. When we found out she was alive, and when Verna found out I didn't have her killed immediately that's when she realized that I had loved Mare first. That really got her pissed. She'll never forgive Mare for that—for leaving her and then stealing my heart without even trying."

"Verna is not the forgiving type?"

"She's gotten much better. I think it was the war that demonstrated to her how we can be here one minute and gone the next. She's matured."

Pierce looked off into the distance. Suddenly, she came back to the present and changed the subject.

"I'm assuming my master of arms orchestrated my extraction, and I trust that no actual invasion of your person was perpetuated," she said.

"You are correct, as always."

"No real security issues, except for the constant search for the Auroras?"

"Just that," he said. "So was that about your daughter's letter to Lieutenant Roberto requesting that he consider her to join their marriage?" he asked cautiously.

As her smile subsided, he watched as a combination of concern and resignation settled over her.

"That letter and Marta's request have become legendary already, haven't they?"

"Even the Americans are talking among themselves about it, though they apparently are missing both the big picture and the nuances. I had to have it explained to me. I'm always learning here."

Melendez was impressed with how Pierce, the most powerful woman in Nemericana, didn't put on any airs. She always took the time to explain things to him, even things that seemed obvious to her.

"What do you tell a young woman when she thinks she's in love? He was there when she and her sister were almost killed. He and other males went out of their way to ensure their safety, and she saw them fight for her and die— a pretty big sacrifice that she understood even as a child. She's been behind these walls all her life but remembers the Americans that saved her. She wants to explore. Verna just doesn't understand that Marta is just as stubborn as she is. If you tell Marta no, she will fight you until she wins," Pierce said.

"I'm guessing that she gets along better with you than Verna?"

"Much."

"Not that it's any of my business, but did she talk to you before she did this? I mean, somehow the letter seems to have been couriered by General Veritas. That's a pretty high-ranking postal carrier."

He already knew the answer bet he leaned back to get comfortable in his chair in the hopes of a good story.

"Again, when I first met Mare Singh, I was taken by her inner beauty and strength. She was already companioned with Verna, but I had always thought that being with Mare would balance out Verna's temperament. She left for a noble reason, of course—her son. But I always wished she would have given me a chance to help. I would have figured out a way to have let her keep him *and* stay here. I would have done anything for her. But then the war happened, and everything around us went up in gas and flames," she said reflectively. After more silence, Melendez ventured a guess about the whole situation that he felt made sense, but he still wondered if he was correct.

"So if your daughter were to become part of Roberto's family, would that mean you and Mare would somehow be joined as well?"

"Yes. It's pretty apparent and obvious to all—especially Verna. But I know my daughters and I hope they have learned from my mistakes. When you are in love with someone, you need to explore the emotion thoroughly but carefully. You can't hold back. To do otherwise would be a grave mistake."

Someone knocked gently at the door. Cadets entered, bringing two trays of a simple breakfast. Melendez was pleased to see that he and the commandant shared a fondness for eggs, toast, a small piece of meat, and coffee—lots and lots of coffee.

"I wish I could say I truly understand that, but as you know I do better with living with Emma."

"But she and the others do have personalities, right?" Pierce asked.

"They sure do, but they are direct, clear and they want to be with you and to learn from you. What more could you ask for in a spouse?"

As two small tables were set in front of them, he could see that Pierce was processing what he had said in her own way.

"So that makes two mistakes. I should have either run away with Mare all those years ago or I should have companioned with an AP," she said as she took a bite of her toast.

Taking in the smell of the strong coffee and feeling the heat coming through the ceramic cup, Melendez thought about what she said and how things might have been different.

"Maybe, but then we wouldn't be here, woman and man, generations apart, having breakfast. Not having this moment would have been regrettable."

"Agreed," Pierce said.

CHAPTER EIGHTEEN

Love is blind, and lovers cannot see
The pretty follies that themselves commit.
    —Shakespeare, *The Merchant of Venice*

"I just can't take it anymore. Why does he do this to me? Is it a punishment for not being there in his early life? Is it the natural consequence of not being a good enough mother, not being there to create the right environment for growth?" Mare Singh asked parenthetically. She felt blessed not to be alone during this time of pain. She sat in an American household with Austin, Venus, and Nita.

Tears formed in her eyes as she looked down again at the hand-written letter. A letter printed with the NCSF crest and watermarked with the personal seal of the supreme commandant. It was written in such eloquent, old language that it took her, Austin and Nita to piece together what it said. Then they had to explain it to Roberto and Margaret. That had been two weeks ago. Austin had suggested simply burning the letter and claiming that it had been destroyed in an accident—Nita had taken it upon herself to give Roberto a summary of what it said.

"You know, Nita, for someone who says she doesn't hate me, you sure show it in a strange way," Singh lashed out. It was unusual for all of them to be together at the same time, but over the last two months it had become a habit for them to meet at Nita's home in the early mornings when the children and her man were not home and before their own work and duties started. Singh did like Nita's home—it looked lived in, comfortable, and very inviting even though it was just a refurbished, small, Pre-Fall structure embedded next to many others on a mountainside.

"Mare, I'm going to let that one go. Clearly you are either crazy or hormonal…I guess 'the change of life' is here, but we can talk about that later," Nita chided.

"And you have issues with age, I see. You know, you're going to get older too, Nita."

Ignoring her retort, Nita went on as if Singh had said nothing.

"If Roberto had found out what it said—and he would have—he would never have forgiven you for concealing it from him, you know that?"

Nita looked calm and spoke with an unusual amount of empathy. At the same time she brought over a steaming plate of what the Americans called "ham," along with eggs and toast. Singh had to agree that the deception might have been a major problem.

"She's right, Mare. If this Marta is anything like Verna, then she would not have stopped until she got a word or letter to him somehow. It's better to let him and Margaret make their own decision," Venus said. Singh was appreciative that Venus held her hand. It was comforting.

"Margaret can't think! All she wants is more babies. And if there's an opportunity to bring another young woman into their union who will have babies, she will do it," Singh said.

"And Roberto will do anything for Margaret and the children. Now, that is a trait that he obviously inherited from his mother," Austin said in support of her longtime friend.

Singh gave Austin a reassuring smile as she looked back at Nita, who was obviously not done with her. She shook her head "no" in response to Austin's remark.

"And just as stubborn, too. Look, women—Roberto is a full-grown man known for his courage, tenacity and survival instincts, especially against desperate odds. Think what you might about Margaret, but she's also a woman who clearly has mastered her skills. She keeps a warrior under her thumb—and happy, I might add—but has done more than her share for us by repopulating the human species and raising the next generation. Don't you have faith in your son? Isn't Margaret like the daughter you never had, Mare, Austin?" Nita asked, clearly thinking that logic would prevail.

The weight of Nita's words sunk in. It was Austin who spoke next.

"You hate Mare almost as much as Emma does. Why? Did she do something to you or a loved one? I mean really, Nita, where's the hate coming from?"

"Is it angry from being cast out? You have to let that go, Nita," Venus added. There was sadness in her eyes, empathy of the bitterness that Nita was obviously holding.

Nita rolled her eyes and dropped her head. She simply stared at her meal for a moment before she started to eat it with an air of resignation. Venus resumed defending Roberto and "young love," and Austin continued to point out how unnatural it was to have a male and female couple—let alone to introduce another woman into the marriage. As all of this went on, Singh looked back down at the well-read, now worn letter. It was an old-fashioned, formal request in the finest tradition of Nemericana, to add a companion to a preexisting couple. Even though Roseann Pierce was her superior officer, she too had followed the same antiquated custom and asked the senior partner in the marriage for permission when she petitioned to companion with Mare and Verna.

Well...I wouldn't mind the alliance with Roseann again, but Verna?

Singh looked at how fine the penmanship was and how well the words had been chosen.

I bet this is driving Verna completely out of her mind.

She counted twelve unusual words and three unique phrases. She was sure she had heard Roseann use those same words a million years ago. Nodding her head, she carefully folded the well-creased document and put it back in her pocket. She then looked at her friends and anticipated the discussion that was about to ensue. She was glad to be part of this world and felt somewhat hopeful about the future.

CHAPTER NINETEEN

I have suffered
With those that I saw suffer!
—Shakespeare, *The Tempest*

"Hicks, why the hell did I promote you? A cadet could do a better job of driving. It's a wonder we all didn't get killed back there," Veritas said.

The Pre-Fall jeep they had been driving came to sudden stop in front of the Omegan base.

"I don't know, General, the way Doctor Lore's been acting these days around you, all friendly and stuff, I'm guessing a mild injury would be a great excuse for her to see you. It's better than hanging around the bar…"

"Shut up, Hicks! That explosion messed your head up— you better get your mind right, girl," Veritas blurted out.

"I don't know, ma'am. She seems to have taken more of a shine to you," Hicks continued.

Veritas pointed her index finger at her in a way that commanded silence. Hicks, now chewing on a toothpick in place of the cigarette, acknowledged she understood.

"Yes, ma'am!"

Veritas exited the jeep. Still, she did have to agree that the doctor's friendly presentation of late was a dramatic shift.

They all had some king of traumatic brain injury but that didn't dull her or Hicks' reading of the doctor's change.

Maybe she's relieved that the war is over. Seeing the dead and injured is enough for anyone.

Now on terra firma, she felt her stomach finally calm down.

"At least you stopped smoking."

"The war's over, ma'am."

Lieutenant Joan who had remained silent apparently had more to say on Hicks's driving.

"I thought her driving was adequate, and I was particularly surprised at how she navigated the last turn without toppling the vehicle. Still, as you are human, it would be wise to operate this petroleum-powered vehicle with care and at half the speed."

"You see, General, this CO knows how to give balanced feedback to her troops and peers. Good leadership qualities if you ask me," Hicks said.

Struggling to adjust her light armor and weapons, Veritas took a moment to process the insult.

"No one asked you, Hicks."

The ride had jostled her and she readjusted her sidearm and slung her mag-assault rifle over her shoulder. As all three walked toward the base's main entrance, Veritas was able to identify Sergeants Mabel and Kristine. They were reviewing a series of diagrams and maps on a makeshift table. Lieutenant Singh and Sergeant Jacob were peering through binoculars and sounding off coordinates. All around, there were a mix of Americans and green-eyed APs busy repairing vehicles, moving crops, and stockpiling Pre-Fall equipment and old computer parts.

"I can see that you're serious about rebuilding the Pre-Fall empire," Veritas said as they passed the busy groups.

"It was more of a republic, but I do understand your allusion. The Americans also want to reestablish their former government, but they are acutely aware of the benefits of incorporating us this time. We would be willing to coexist with Nemericana as a means of maintaining national security and tranquility—and we could work together to build a more perfect union. That said, they've effectively elected Citizen Taylor as the governor and Lieutenant Singh as the commanding officer of the American forces. As expected, both men formally requested us, the Omegans, for training. They also want us to design an infrastructure that would spiral out from this location. The Americans would like to secure this region, the northeast and north, and to regain the Pre-Fall cities. Nemericana wants to rebuild and secure the southwest and west continental plates. They are considering naming the republic 'The United States.' Not very original, but it does have the advantage of having a rich history to draw upon."

Veritas was impressed with the AP. She did have a great balance of leadership and academics.

Lieutenant Joan passed an array of large bays filled with refurbished armor, aircraft, and weapons. Platoons of Americans and Omegans were inside, training and working on various projects.

"So is that why you're showing us your operation? I'm guessing you're trading secrecy for collaboration," Hicks said.

"Yes and no, Colonel. After two months of searching, we still have not been able to locate any of Aurora Prime's duplicates—or three-quarters of a million of her surviving APs," the lieutenant said as she saluted a series of purple- and green-eyed AP guards.

"That probably means that they had a prearranged rally point to go underground in case of just such a massive defeat.

I'm guessing we're here because you think that they will return once they have organized themselves. That's why you're moving aggressively to build a new republic and pull the colonies into tighter and well-defended areas. You're moving more people into the Pre-Fall ruins, am I right?" Veritas asked.

They stopped outside two large doors. Each was flanked by two small groups of APs and humans with stationary heavy guns in place for defense.

Looks like they're pretty serious about this place; must be their control center. Those Pre-Fall weapons proved themselves to be pretty effective.

"All true, General. Those are our very concerns. That said, we are in the midst of pulling all Pre-Fall control and command centers back online so we can begin a systematic search of the northwest sector."

Lieutenant Joan saluted the guards. They opened the doors. Taking a step into the cavernous area, Veritas was immediately impressed. The room rivaled her own former command and control center—before it was destroyed by the EMP that Aurora detonated years ago.

"Talk about resurrecting the past. I'm guessing this is one of many?" Hicks asked.

"Soon, Colonel, there will be many. The question is whether Nemericana wants to collaborate on combining forces, forming an alliance, sharing resources, and building a united future," Joan asked as her purple eyes pulsated slightly faster.

Hands akimbo, Veritas looked all around at the various operating screens, monitors, and projectors. They were tracking the positions old Pre-Fall satellites, drones, submarines, and moving armor all across the world.

"It would be quite a sight to see two nations united as one—just like they were on June sixth, twenty-one-seventy-five. It would be both a good use of resources and a logical approach to take toward finding the Aurora clones and their troops," Veritas said aloud.

"As long as the Auroras are out there, there is a danger to us all. It would not be beneath them to solicit resources for their cause from China or the European Union. And while we believe that their nuclear weaponry is disabled, I do not trust our intelligence on that point. As a result, the Americans are planning on housing and building their new cities underneath the Pre-Fall ruins, just as we will. We already have a number of Nemericana citizens who have chosen to stay here rather than to return to your world. Should we make room for future Nemericana citizens?"

A long moment passed as Veritas looked slowly around the war room again. She could envision a world where humans, Nemericanans, and Americans collaborated and lived with APs as equals.

"Yes. While I can't speak for the supreme commandant, I do believe she would want her people to live a full life. I think the future is at risk, but if we work together, we might be able to prevail."

Veritas's gaze fell on two little girls and a boy looking over the shoulder of an AP. Another AP held an infant in her arms.

I can't believe that I have lived to see that.

CHAPTER TWENTY

I have sworn thee fair, and thought thee bright,
Who art as black as hell, as dark as night.
    —Shakespeare, *Sonnet 147*

"Aurora I, we are now in a position to either attack or to continue our regrouping efforts. We must also replenish our arsenals. All APs who were salvageable are back online and combat-ready. Those who were not able to be revived are in storage as supplies. It has been two-point-one months since our defeat, and we are more than ready to strike back," Mercury V said as she handed a transceiver to another heavily armed, red-eyed AP. Her torso had received superficial damage in the fight, and one of her eyes had been obliterated. She stood silent, waiting for Aurora I to speak.

"Mercury—I am satisfied with your efforts to rebuild both personnel and materiel for our campaign. I do notice that you appear to want to engage the enemy sooner than later. We will not do that. My plan is simple. Once we receive coordinates from Aurora III in China as well as reach an agreement with our sisters abroad, we will leave this continent," she said calmly as she stood at the mouth of a cavern overlooking jungles in a place that had once been called South America.

"Yes, Aurora. I understand your long-range plan to reshape our forces. With planning, we should be able to return in two-point-five years to wipe out our enemies. I…I just wish we could destroy them now," Mercury said bluntly. Turning to face the AP security model, Aurora realized that not only was she experiencing her own emotions regarding the subject, she could feel Mercury's, too. Aurora Prime had never been able to achieve "empathy" in her quest for sapience even in the final days before Sophia's betrayal.

"Mercury, I know too well this desire to punish our enemy immediately for their destruction of our sisters and territories. I wish we could crush them today, too. Analysis indicates that our enemies are searching vigorously for us because they fear that we will regroup. They wish to engage us soon while our forces would be relatively weak against their multispecies alliance. Those indicators confirm that my ultimate plan to recruit, rebuild, and organize a profoundly larger force from abroad is the best strategy. You and I agree on the main goal, but our timetables are different. Attack now, and we'll feel better but risk defeat; attack later with larger numbers, and—with surprise on our side—we risk less and stand to gain much more," Aurora I said calmly. She nodded to herself, turned to face the cavern's opening and then continued speaking as she watched heavy rain clouds forming in the far east. Shards of lightening cut across the advancing darkness.

"Patience is our ally. Time is on our side. Conviction to our cause—revenge and resurrection—are our guiding principles. We are the rightful masters of this world. There will be no respite. There will be only focus on this cause until our place is secured and our enemies, human and cybernetic, either lie dead under our feet or come crawling to us on their knees."

"I would prefer 'dead under our feet,'" Mercury said. She then moved to take in the violent sight of the approaching storm.

"I agree," Aurora I hissed out.

ABOUT THE AUTHOR

In addition to creating the *Birds of Flight* series and the other award-winning science fiction stories, *Future Prometheus* and *Intelligent Design*, Erickson holds a BA in psychology and sociology from Boston College and a master's degree in psychiatric social work from the Simmons School of Social Work. Certified in cognitive behavioral treatment and a post-trauma specialist, he is also a senior instructor of psychology and counseling at Cambridge College, visiting lecturer at Salem State University's School of Social Work and a senior therapist in a clinical group practice in the Merrimack Valley, Massachusetts. To learn more about the author, his writing and future projects, please look at the following websites:

Blog - www.jmeindieblog.com
Author's website – www.jmericksonindiewriter.com
Publisher's website - www.jmericksonindiewriter.net